DEATHSPAWN

Aubry hit the hall door, bursting out into the hall, firing wildly. His shoulder and the door hit two people on the other side. One went down instantly. The other was smaller. Much smaller. The tiny figure had rebounded like a rubber ball, snapping back to guard and attack faster than anything human could possibly move.

In the instant it took him to adjust to the shock, a foot arced and hit his gun hand with a move that was timed to perfection. His arm went dead.

Aubry was ready for the second kick. But the follow-up never came. His opponent folded into a smaller target, jacknifed. The kick spread out directly, striking Aubry in the ribs.

Aubry rolled, mind numbed with shock. What in the hell was he fighting? All he had felt was *bone* and *movement*. It was the most perfectly executed technique he had ever experienced.

As fast as the kick had been launched, it was retracted twice as swiftly. Aubry's flashing hands found nothing to grasp. He bounded off the wall, managed to get his chin down before a kick intended for his throat smashed into his jaw. Lights exploded behind his eyes.

But this time he caught the leg as it slithered away. He was shocked at its lightness. Was he fighting a woman?

A child?

Tor books by Steven Barnes

The Descent of Anansi (with Larry Niven)
Gorgon Child
The Kundalini Equation

STEVEN BARNES

GORGON CHILD

A TOM DOHERTY ASSOCIATES BOOK
NEW YORK

GORGON CHILD

Copyright © 1989 by Steven Barnes

The song ''Susan A.'' by Leslie Fish, which appears in Chapter 10, is used by arrangement with the composer. Copyright © 1980 by Leslie Fish.

A TOR Book
Published by Tom Doherty Associates, Inc.
49 West 24th Street
New York, N.Y. 10010

Cover art by Royo

ISBN: 0-812-53152-3
CAN. ED.: 0-812-53153-1

First edition: December 1989

Printed in the United States of America

0 9 8 7 6 5 4 3 2 1

All children are by nature children of wrath,
and are in danger of eternal damnation in hell.
    —Jonathan Edwards, *Sermon to Children*

Every child enters the world carrying the message
that God is not yet discouraged of Man.
                    —Rabindranath Tagore

Once upon a time . . .

In a place called Los Angeles, in the year 2022, a professional Nullboxer named Aubry Knight was framed for murder. He was sent to Death Valley Maximum Security Penitentiary, where delicate modifications were made in his personality. There they twisted his mind, sealing away the anger which had always been his most powerful ally.

Finally he escaped. Returning to Los Angeles, Aubry sought vengeance against the man who framed him—Luis Ortega, head of the largest crime syndicate on the West Coast, and Maxine Black, the bait used to trap him.

But while Aubry was imprisoned, Maxine had created a hell of her own, becoming an addict. Desperate, Maxine met an exotic dancer named Promise who took her to a drug rehabilitation clinic. In the clinic, Maxine accidentally discovered that a drug called Cyloxibin could function as the world's first true aphrodisiac, a substance worth billions of dollars. Before she could profit by this knowledge, she was killed by the Ortegas.

Aubry's Nullboxing skills saved Promise from a pair of Ortega killers. Forming an uneasy alliance, they assassinated Luis, and fled to the earthquake-ravaged center of Los Angeles, a terrible slum called The Maze. Here, they met Kevin Warrick and his crew of Scavengers, who were literally strip-mining the shattered buildings.

Their stay with the Scavengers was intense. Both became addicted to Cyloxibin, and fell madly in love. The drug nearly destroyed them, but ultimately saved each from a lonely, meaningless life.

Life might have been good, but the Ortegas came after them, and a pitched battle was fought beneath the streets of L.A., with the secret of the world's most addictive substance as the prize. Many Scavengers died, and Warrick ultimately sacrificed his own life to defeat the Ortegas.

Promise, pregnant with Aubry's child, was kidnapped. To rescue her, Aubry gave the Ortegas a mushroom spore print necessary to produce Cyloxibin, and delivered himself for their vengeance.

They were taken to the island of Terra Buena, for the entire Ortega family to judge them. At the trial, it was revealed that Tomaso Ortega, brother of Luis, actually engineered his brother's assassination, using Aubry as a guided missile. Civil war broke out among the Ortegas.

Aubry and Promise made their escape. Bound, Aubry was forced to fight the enormous, invulnerable Diego Mirabal, a member of the ultramale separatists called NewMen.

Aubry was victorious, but in the battle Promise was wounded, and eventually miscarried. The two of them returned to Los Angeles, savagely ill-used in many ways, but with each other.

And love is love, whether a whim of the heart, or a product of artificially altered brain chemistry . . .

Isn't it?

PROLOGUE

Naked, suspended in clear nutrient solution, Medusa-16 regained consciousness. It was not supposed to happen, but sometimes did. If he kept mind and body quiet, those outside would not know he was awake, would not send darkness to cloud his senses. He, and the other Medusas, were supposed to be healing, and growing. Pads covered his eyes and nose and mouth. Tubes carrying nourishment and oxygen pierced his thin arms and legs, crowded his throat. The steady, low thrum of the maintenance machinery pulsed against his skin.

He could not see, or feel: the fluid which buoyed him was almost precisely skin temperature. But he could taste the salt, and if he concentrated, could hear sounds from the room outside.

"—hundreds. Cyloxibin saw to that. But how many with whole minds? Trainable nervous systems? We're lucky to have eighteen."

The voice was thin, loud. The lab tech—only a human, not even a NewMan. Then a second voice:

"You say number 16 is functional? Even considering male genotype?" The second voice was deeper, a rumble that Medusa-16 recognized instantly. Quint. Warmth flooded 16's body. He fought for control, but the reaction was too strong.

"Yes, sir. Quad-gonadal. Two ovaries, two testes. Minimal surgical reconstruction. The perineum was large enough to accommodate a vagina."

"Both ovaries and testes functioning?"

"Fully."

"It is a miracle. Our miracle. Our time is coming."

There was a jarring beat, as if someone had tapped a finger against the plastic wall of the tank. "Mother's endocrine system was fouled up before the drug ever hit her. Father is a physical freak."

Quint's voice was ruminative. "A 'freak' I'd like to meet."

Medusa-16 burned. *Father!* How could Quint even *mention* that word. *Mother!* Naked loathing flooded him. Abandoned! Betrayed! Cast aside like garbage. Like the hideous thing he was. That all the outer world considered him to be.

Only Quint understood and loved him. Only Quint had saved him, trained him. Prepared him.

The world hated the Medusas? Very well.

Then it would find out what hate truly was.

Mother. Father.

A nervous edge had crept into the human's voice. "We're getting a rise in blood pressure on 16, sir—"

Panicked, knowing what would come next, 16 began to thrash, twisted against the tubing.

"Pulse up and . . . checking EEG he's all the way up in Alpha."

No! No—

16 felt the narcotic tingle, fought to resist it, failed as blackness rose up like a shroud.

Mother. Father.

You hated me. Abandoned me. Tried to destroy me.

I'll find you one day. And then—

CHAPTER ONE

The NewMen

Monday, May 15, 2028

The room's boarded windows shuddered as a barbed tear gas rocket smashed against them. The wood began to burn: gas and smoke curled between the slats and pooled darkly against the ceiling. The room's peeling wallpaper slowly turned a deep, poisonous yellow.

Five men squatted on the floor. They wore ancient, obsolete, gauzy gas masks. The stench of unwashed bodies and unprocessed human waste was gut-wrenchingly strong. There had been no tap water for six days.

One of the men rose. He banged a gloved fist at the smoking window, and cursed impotently. He leaned against the wall, felt the street noise vibrate in his head: strident voices, klaxons, the rumble of machinery, the rush of feet, the whipping hiss of aircars as they hovered overhead like vultures.

"Not long now." His voice was startlingly deep, a bass rumble in the confined space. He stood almost six and a half feet tall, and weighed two hundred and sixty pounds. His musculature was abnormally thick, denser than that of the average bodybuilding athlete. He moved like a machine, as if his limbs needed oil more than exercise. His face was flat and square, his features leanly Native American. His brown hair was a raggedly cut mop that fell almost to his shoulders.

"Miles," one of the others said. He turned. The new speaker was smaller than the others, just an ordinary human. His left arm terminated in a clump of bloodied bandages at the elbow.

"Richard." Miles Bloodeagle knelt by the boy and took his pulse. Richard's skin was pale, his pulse erratic. He was slipping into shock, and there was no more medicine. There was no more time.

"Why don't we just give up?" Richard's voice was syrupy. "Maybe they'll just shuttle us back to Arizona."

Miles shook his great shaggy head slowly. "If that was all, I'd be first into the tube. But this is pure DeLacourte, no matter what label they're hiding behind. He smells blood." The roar from beyond the window was louder now: the Mercs would make their move soon.

A searchlight's oval slid over the window, and the light filtered through the curling mist in yellow wedges.

"Come out. This is your final opportunity. This is not a federal operation. Bounties have been registered. You are hereby warned. Come out—"

No, there was no escape. The Omnivision cameras would record and broadcast their deaths for the entire nation to see. In the end, Miles and the other NewMen wouldn't even be a body count: they'd be a ratings statistic.

"If they take us, we're headed for the camps, and a little diagnosis and 'treatment.' Surprise, surprise: these faggots are precontagious!" Miles sneered. "They'll make sure of that. Count on it."

He held Richard tightly. "We can die in the Hoopa Spider camp, or we can die here. There isn't any other choice."

Miles tousled the boy's fair hair, and left the room.

The building was one of the few spared by the earthquake of '24. It was old, it was unstable, but it was theirs. Its long yellowed hallways were papered in posters and peeling photos. To his right was a sprawling aerial map of the NewMan Nation in Arizona's Monument Valley. Opposite was a poster of a fully armored and armed Gorgon, stun rifle leveled and ready.

Gorgon, the elite antiterrorist unit created and implemented by President Harris himself. The ultimate pride of the NewMen. Even now, in their desperate straits (desperate straights? Miles laughed at the unintentional pun. What were DeLacourte and his lackeys more intimidated by: homosexuality or physical superiority?) the tall, proud figure of a Gorgon in night-black battle garb thrilled him. Miles was faster and stronger than ninety-nine percent of the NewMen but he had cracked muscle and sinew qualifying for Gorgon. Detached duty had brought him here, to Los Angeles. And here he might well die.

A squad of Gorgons would cut through the rabble of Mercs like a bayonet through butter. Of course, that was what DeLacourte was angling for.

In every room he passed, clusters of NewMen held each other, or their human lovers, waiting for the end. Miles choked back his bitterness. Why couldn't DeLacourte just leave them be? Was any prize, even the presidency, worth so much death?

Why . . . ?

The crackle of an Omnivision receiver cut through the low babble. It sounded as if they were pulling in the Merc band, and some perverse instinct drew him inexorably closer.

". . . we have them pinned now, and with the help of God we'll rout this filth before midnight . . ."

Miles watched from the doorway. Six NewMen and two humans were clustered around an ancient television set. It didn't have holo or enhanced tactile, or even stereo. It was just a cheap flatscreen revamped for sale by the Scavengers. It pulled in only two of eight simultaneously broadcast bands.

A Latino woman's flushed, excited face appeared on the screen. Behind her stood a great gray rectangle of a wall, dotted with crosshatched windows. Cracks and fissures grooved the external plaster. The paint peeled away like scales from a dried fish. A bright red "condemned" stripe slashed the front door.

"I'm Marina Batiste, for TriNet. Here, on the corner of Broadway and Twentieth, in that section of Los Angeles known as The Maze, a grim scenario is being played out." She might have used the same tones to say, *And the results of World Steelworker 103 Firerunning championships are—*

And indeed, to her that might have been its only significance. "Here, a splinter group of the homosexual supremist cult known as NewMen has refused to evacuate a three-story warehouse which has been declared unsafe and unsanitary . . ."

"Damn dem," Minotaur grumbled. The mammoth Exotic sat hunched against the wall. No one remembered Minotaur's real name anymore. Grafted horns and cosmetic surgery made his already taurine appearance more pronounced. Minotaur bared his teeth. His jaw was smashed on the right side, skin torn where his own teeth punched through. Another memento from the last attack. A trickle of blood ran from his left ear. His eyes were narrowed, and he trembled.

"Dey know dey could condemn any building in Maze. Dey just hate us."

No one needed to answer him. Minotaur dropped his chin and slipped back into his private fantasy world. Miles brought his attention back to the set as the image changed.

His throat tightened. This was no real-time broadcast. This was a stock clip from one of Sterling DeLacourte's programs. The Prophet was in full swing, in the middle of one of the evangelical tirades that had brought him staggering wealth, and created an army of followers that awaited his pronouncements like dogs groveling for table scraps.

DeLacourte was a whipcord of a man, as slender as a live wire wiggling across a wet street. His hair was iron gray, the shade that suggests virility more than infirmity. His age lurked somewhere in that chasm between forty-five and seventy, the years when exercise, nutrition, and plastic surgery can create the illusion of agelessness.

Even buffered by his hatred, Miles felt the dizzying pull of DeLacourte's charisma. The man was almost preternaturally beautiful, as hypnotic as a deathcap mushroom.

"—if our nation is to regain its greatness, we must rise up and cast out the filth in our midst. Why does disease run rampant in our country? Why has the dollar fallen to its lowest value in a century? Why has Satan sent his most terrible temptation, this last drug which has wrenched so many souls from the righteous path, and twisted so many innocent children in the womb? Why? Because we have turned away from God, and at last He has tired of our lies and faithlessness—''

DeLacourte's image froze, paling, and faded into the background. Killinger, the shock-armored Merc police leader, appeared.

It was all very subtle, very well done. Behind the Merc the frozen figure of DeLacourte, and behind him, doubtless, God Almighty.

"We're not looking for glory," Killinger said. "We're just concerned about their health. It's not safe in there. These perverts just won't listen to reason." He paused, and the hint of a smile was visible behind the Plexiglas faceplate. "We're going to have to call in the crabs."

"Isn't that severe?" the reporter asked. Her pink tongue flickered at her lips, moistening them. "Many injuries and deaths—''

"We did our best. I wash my hands of the whole thing. If they want a fight, they've got it."

There it was, a death sentence pronounced on international Omnivision. The setup had been so damned neat. There was no escape, there would be no surrender. So be it.

The NewMan leader went to Minotaur, and cradled his head. Very soon now. Miles heard the growl of battering rams outside the window. Minotaur tensed, hungry to hurl himself once more into the battle.

The armored vehicles were being pulled into position. The Los Angeles mini-commune was only a test. If it worked here, it would work on NewMen groups across the country. And eventually someone would find a way through the federal treaties protecting the Arizona encampment. Under the guise of confining the dread contagion of Thai-VI, a few thousand ''disease-riddled perverts'' would die. Then DeLacourte's juggernaut would roll on, rooting out new meat.

No tragedy, that. No tears would be shed for them. No one would mourn.

Except perhaps . . .

Possibly Warrick, the mysterious black man, and his crew of Scavengers. The Scavengers mined and rebuilt damaged high-rises in central Los Angeles. Warrick controlled a network of sales, construction, demolition, and salvage outlets from San Diego to Portland, and as far east as Chicago. Warrick had dealt with the NewMen honestly. A man of courage and dignity, Warrick might mourn them.

Miles held Minotaur down, and the enormous Exotic NewMan made a low mewling sound. "Don't mind dying. Just don't want die here. Can feel dem. Why dey hate us so much?"

The wounded Minotaur gradually relaxed. As he did, Miles flared with hatred for the men and women outside. The ones who watched and waited for the end.

Why shouldn't Minotaur want to kill? He had given everything. Had played the straight game, bowed and scraped and mutilated and humiliated himself in a vain attempt to win their approval. And in the end, he would die because he was different. Because he didn't look the way they looked, or love the way they loved.

Dimly, Miles heard a crackling sound, accompanied by the distant sensation of pain in his right hand. He looked down, and winced: without conscious volition, the hand had whipped out and smashed into the plasterboard and plywood. Splinters of wood and pieces of wire ripped at his skin. He didn't give a damn.

He fought to dampen the killing flare as it burst to life in his mind. Too late: it was there now, but it didn't matter anymore. The straights wanted war? Then war they would have.

Miles stalked from the room. His body ached with his efforts to control. This was no time to Berserk. Too many lives were in the balance. His people needed him to remain clear-headed. Cold. Calm.

God, but he wanted to kill. He steadied himself. Perhaps the situation could still resolve peacefully. Perhaps.

The Mercs were not public servants. They were basically bounty hunters, operating in the legal no-man's-land created by America's dozens of bankrupted municipalities.

Unless lethal force was used against them, they had to use "restraint," a word often applied in a manner which would have shocked Mr. Webster.

The crabs. The battering rams. Gas. Fire.

Death.

He ran halfway down the rickety wooden stairway and peered down at the front door. Its frame was almost totally obscured by a hastily rigged jumble of wooden beams, wire, and metal braces.

Six exhausted NewMen clustered at the bottom of the stairs. They had only makeshift weapons: spears and knives, and homemade firebombs. All of it was pitifully inadequate to cope with the threat to come.

The walls and floor rumbled as an armored battering ram backed into position across the street. "Dammit! It's coming down!" he screamed, voice hoarse. "*Fast*, hit your positions!" The NewMen emerged from the hall above, Minotaur ahead of all of them, carrying an axe. His eyes were fever-bright, but his shoulders were slack. There just wasn't much energy left. How could there be? His men, and the few humans who had joined them, were all exhausted and underfed. For four long days they had breathed bad air and drunk nothing but filtered urine.

For perhaps the last time he assumed the role which had once come so easily to him. Throwing back his shoulders and transmuting fear and fatigue into anger, he snarled savagely. Once again, he was Miles Bloodeagle, NewMan, Gorgon, the leader they loved and had followed unto death.

He raced down to the ground floor as the rumbling stopped, and the patchwork wooden door began to buckle. Something sharp and metallic crushed the center, chewing through the barricades. It hissed and whined and spit splinters at them.

"Crabs!"

The first of the Merc 'bots wriggled free, landed, and found its balance on six stubby, gleaming metallic legs. Its video stalk probed, craning for its first victim. Minotaur raced into the fray, screamed as his axe blurred into an arc.

The crab's stun nozzle was even quicker. It spit a capacitor dart, a charged particle which traveled only a hair slower than a bullet. The projectile punched through cloth and skin, lanced into bone. One thousand volts jolted into Minotaur's nervous system. The NewMan's arms and legs splayed wide. His teeth ground tight and splintered. Blood jetted from his mouth as he dropped to the ground. His body thrashed spastically.

With obscene delicacy, the crab walked over the Minotaur. Its eyestalk swiveled for another victim.

With hormonally amplified agility and speed, Miles vaulted down the stairs, snatching a length of pipe from another NewMan on the way. He smashed the pipe into the crab's eyestalk, somersaulting in midair as he did. A barbed capacitor dart missed him by less than an inch. He struck again and dropped to the floor as the crab's thermal scan found him. Its second dart struck the wall an inch above his left ear. Miles whipped the club sideways, crunched into metal again and again. Its oval body armor cracked with a shriek. The crab spit sparks, hissed, and died.

Miles forced his arms under the paralyzed Minotaur's, and dragged him back as a second crab began scrabbling through the hole. And a third. And a fourth.

Even for Miles's huge and desperate strength, the inert Minotaur was a burden. His body still twitched reflexively. Miles panted, cursing venomously as he dragged Minotaur around the corner, deeper into the building. He had to stop and get his breath. The crabs crawled in through the shattered door, probed the air with their slender video stalks. They scampered up the walls as the NewMen fled.

A video eye fixed on him, and the crab's nozzle orifice came up. He dove into a side room. Panic clouded his mind but conditioned reflex made him roll off his shoulder. As he moved, he struggled for thoughts to form. There had to be a way—

Tear gas foamed through the shattered door in a great dark cloud. This was a different mixture from the rocket gas, and his ancient mask filter was useless against it. His chest clinched until his ribs creaked. Every breath felt like inhaling fishhooks. He sagged weakly against the wall as the first crab clacked around the corner.

Its eyestalk found him in the misted air. Miles hissed at it as its ejector homed in on him.

And then . . .

The floor buckled, like a ship's deck peeling back from a ram.

Miles laughed hysterically. Overkill. One thing that he could count on from DeLacourte was overkill.

The floorboards gave way, twisted and groaned as they split. Metallic claws reached through, gripped the wood. The beams shrieked as they were pried away.

What . . . ?

A human form pushed through. A huge man, extraordinarily broad across the shoulders. Gas masked and gloved. For a fleeting instant Miles thought, *Gorgon! They've broken every primary rule and come for us* . . .

Then Miles heard the voice and knew the truth.

"Move it!" The man's words were muffled by the mask. "We don't have much time. Killinger is backing up the gas with another assault. He's not taking any prisoners."

"Warrick?" Miles gasped through the pain.

The masked figure nodded. "Get your wounded down into the carts. *Move!*" The Scavenger leader shifted. His automatic shotgun jerked suddenly, zoning in on the crab. The movement was so smooth and quick that Miles was shocked.

The robot exploded into fragments. Gears, wires, chunks of plastic, and green fluid oozed down the wall in an oily slop.

The hole in the floor widened. Through the haze Miles saw six Scavengers in full body shields. Warrick hurried to Miles and ripped off his mask. *What? I thought—* Miles clawed at him, panicked as the unfiltered gas rushed in. Miles was strong, even for a NewMan. Gas, fatigue, and starvation had weakened him, and the big man batted his hands aside easily.

A second mask was clamped into place, and Miles could breathe—

BREATHE!

—again.

The dark face behind the mask nodded, and helped Miles to his feet. With a movement so fast that Miles could barely track it, Warrick spun into a crouch and fired. Miles turned in time to see another crab's fragments spatter wetly against the wall.

"We can hold them for five minutes. That's it. Get your people OUT!"

Miles took another deep, cleansing breath, clapping the man on the back. There was no option but to trust Warrick to hold the breach.

Five minutes. The NewMen were known to have no weapons. It was all that had kept them alive. The Scavengers were well armed, and the sounds of the weapons would register quickly. The Mercs would reply with deadly force.

Five minutes. Warrick was an optimist.

Miles leapt up the stairs, taking them three at a time. "Quick—everyone who can walk carry someone else. We have ninety seconds. *Move!*"

He saw a slender Scavenger, bundled tight but moving like a dancer, pass out gas filters from a clutch at her belt. It wasn't whole body armor, but it gave the NewMen a fighting chance.

His mind raced, a hundred considerations intermingling at the same moment. How many. Where. How long . . .

And mixed among the survival imperatives was the trace of a memory, bubbling crazily, inappropriately to the surface.

What had he heard? That three years ago the Scavengers had fought a war of their own against horrible odds. Nerve gas had been used against them. Little wonder that they were now prepared for gas attack.

There was no more time for thought as he reached the top of the stairs, and repeated the message: "Out! Everyone—"

But there was no need. Three Scavengers were already there. The wounded were hoisted up on shoulders and stretchers, and hustled toward the stairs. Another explosion tore his footing from beneath him, slammed him

against the wall. Smoke belched up from the lower floor.
Miles fought back to his feet and continued on.

Just two minutes since the floor had ruptured.

Four minutes to go. Not all of the NewMen had received the new gas masks: there simply weren't enough to
go around. Those in obsolete equipment convulsed in the
grip of the gas. Their muscles contracted fiercely, and they
spewed vomit into their faceplates.

What kind of gas was that bastard Killinger using?
Something outlawed by the Geneva Convention, no doubt.
Can't use it to kill enemies of your country. Only against
your own citizens . . .

At first he thought that the top floor was clear. Then he
heard a voice: "Miles . . ."

Shit. Richard.

Forgotten somehow, Richard lay against the wall. Miles
rushed to him, got under him, and hoisted him to his feet.
Richard's stump was oozing, and he looked at Miles with
eyes that were beginning to fog. "No, Miles. Don't worry
. . . about me. Just go."

"To hell with that." He silently completed the response: *You're not dying here. I won't have those damned
crabs climbing over you, picking at you . . .*

Richard wasn't a NewMan, but was a decent-sized human, weighing over a hundred and eighty pounds. Fatigue
burned every muscle in Miles's body. But if he left anyone
behind, *anyone*, he wasn't fit to be their leader.

He paused for a moment and listened to the countdown
timer in his head. Three minutes left.

With a grinding howl a second truck pushed up to the
door. Doors slammed. The sound of quick, purposeful
movement.

To defend without killing was the challenge. If Warrick
and his Scavengers killed any of the Mercs that would be
"murder." A clear license for Killinger. There was no
room for error.

Miles helped Richard down the stairs. His shoulder and
whole body ached. He rested on the second floor, watching the evacuees stream past as Minotaur's voice echoed in
his mind: *Why dey hate us so much?*

"Everyone! Everyone out!" He rested Richard against the wall for a moment, and scanned the rooms. Not one of them, human or NewMan, would remain to be paraded in front of the cameras. None would be shamed, tortured, killed in the observation camps.

His heart thundered, each breath sandpapered his lungs. Staggering, Miles searched the first floor. The rooms were empty.

Somehow, he made it back to Richard. All strength had fled his limbs, and he couldn't get the wounded man up, just couldn't. Perhaps a moment of rest . . .

Richard's blood-rimmed eyes, blinking through the mask, stared up at him. "Save yourself . . ."

Gorgon!

No physical strength remained, but Miles fought down to the dregs of his emotional reserves.

He was halfway down the stairs when the first Mercs burst through the door. Warrick would have to kill now, and that would be the beginning of the end for the Scavengers—

Then Miles saw something that brought a warrior's oath to his lips.

Warrick scooped up the smoldering ruins of a crab and hurled it at the first two Mercs who clambered through the door. The first jerked his machine pistol up to block the hurtling mass of smoking metal. In that moment, the first blocked the second's field of fire. Warrick moved.

He covered the ten meters to the door in three giant strides. At the end of the last stride Warrick launched himself. He twisted like a circus acrobat so that the forward momentum propelled him feetfirst into the first Merc. It was all much too fast to comprehend, let alone avoid. Warrick's booted feet struck the first Merc in the stomach, smashing him backward into the second. Both flew into the door as a third armored head poked through.

Bullets couldn't penetrate that armor. A blow from a human being should have done nothing but stagger an armored Merc back a step. Then balance would be regained, lethal retaliation following a moment later.

Miles distinctly heard the *crack* as armor split under the

impact of the fastest human movement he had ever witnessed. The second Merc's armor wedged into the door, blocking it. The first rolled out of the way and rose, groping for his machine pistol.

Despite the fatigue and fear, fascination nailed Miles where he stood. Somewhere in the flash of that first engagement, Warrick had disarmed the Merc. Where? What?—

Miles ran the sequence back, the battle computer in his mind working automatically. Now he remembered the flash of Warrick's leg as it flickered out, the edge of his heel accelerating to invisibility as it cracked against the back of the gun hand. The gun did not fly from the hand—the movement had been too quick. The Merc's fingers simply opened, numbed by the snap.

Through shock armor? What kind of human being was this?

The Scavenger leader turned and screamed, *"Get OUT!!"*

Miles stood, still frozen as Warrick faced the armored Merc. The Scavenger would die now, torn to bloody pieces. He simply couldn't . . .

Could he?

The Merc swung a huge, armored arm at Warrick, and the Scavenger leader slid back, balanced as delicately as an ice skater. There was no way Warrick could injure a man protected by shock armor. What was he trying to do?

The Merc saw his opening. He twisted, the augmented speed and strength of the armor powered the move. The hips pivoted and the reinforced plastic-shod foot spun up, zoning in at Warrick's midsection.

At the last instant Warrick moved. Not quickly at all. He swayed as if the rest of the universe was moving in slow motion. The Merc's foot slid by him with barely a quarter inch to spare. It struck the wall with the force of a wrecking ball, crushing through plaster and wood. For an instant the Merc stood there, looking like a tilted "Y." Then Warrick kicked the Merc's standing leg from under him. The Merc went down in a split, screaming as the armor's perfect joints accommodated where his body could not. His butt hit the floor, his legs spread as wide as any ballerina's.

Miles winced: every muscle in the Merc's groin had to have been ripped out. The second Merc had almost pulled himself out of the hole. Warrick torqued in with a thunderous spin kick, driving him back into the door.

Miles finally broke the trance and lowered Richard into the floor tunnel. Warrick followed, dragging the gigantic Minotaur.

Scavengers from underneath helped him lower Minotaur down into the dark recesses of the tunnel. Miles could see nothing down there, but he followed. What choice was there?

He slid down a rope ladder, almost turning his ankle on an old subway track. He crouched, taking in the surroundings quickly: an ancient transport tunnel. Six large handcarts were already rolling away along a rusty monotrack.

Warrick landed in the dusty tunnel in perfect balance, and snapped, "Move it out." They moved, Miles too overawed by this man to bow to his own fatigue.

He looked back down the tunnel. "They'll be after us in a second."

Warrick shrugged. "That woman said your building wasn't safe." He pulled a black, teardrop-shaped transmitter out of his pocket and depressed a trigger switch. There was a soft *whumpf* from above. That sound sharpened into a ragged creak, then a groan, as explosive-sheared timbers gave way. A blinding cloud of dust belched down the tunnel after them as the house collapsed.

The cloud dissipated, and Warrick wiped his faceplate. "I'll be damned." He grinned brightly. "They were right."

CHAPTER TWO

The Scavengers

10:17 P.M.

A half-dozen motorized carts slid through the darkness, humming silently along their tracks. Each carried two or three wounded NewMen.

Warrick and Miles remained at the rear, behind the wounded and the advance guard. They listened for the telltale clacking of a crab, watched for the ominous silhouette of an armored Merc.

The only sound was the distant creak of the tracks. The only shapes were the sinuous forms of the cats that haunted the underground. They slid by in the darkness, their eyes glowing, before vanishing into the gloom.

Pushing his exhaustion away, Miles observed the silent Scavenger leader. The man sat quietly, squatting on his haunches. He was fully as large as a NewMan, and, from what Miles had seen, incredibly fast, even by Gorgon standards.

And Warrick's fluidity of movement was . . .

A flush of heat washed through Miles, one he swiftly repressed. "Who are you?"

"We've traded. You know who I am."

"That's not what I mean. Where do you come from?"

Warrick spoke without turning. "What difference does it make?"

Perhaps none.

In spite of the danger, Miles felt incredibly comfortable around this man. They were Warriors together beneath the

earth, with every passing moment widening the margin of
safety for the wounded. He overcame a wave of dizziness.
It was improper for a Gorgon to show weakness before a
normal human. Especially a human who had risked so
much for him.

"Why did you come?"

Warrick said nothing.

"I don't think you came out of obligation. Or because
we have traded together. Not solely."

Still, Warrick did not reply. But he did turn to face
Miles. Fervently, Miles wished that he could see past the
mask, to read his expression more clearly. Warrick reached
into his pocket and retrieved a pair of square foil packages.
"You talk a lot."

He handed one to Miles, and unfastened his own face
mask. Warrick's face was very dark, almost African, unusual for an American. His hair was chopped short, and
came down on his forehead in a slight widow's peak. A
dark, neatly trimmed beard covered much of his face. His
eyes were piercingly dark, black perhaps, or dark brown.
The face was not classically handsome—it was the face of
a warrior, a survivor of countless battles. He peeled foil
away with his teeth and took a deep bite from a concentrated food bar.

Miles peeled the foil away from his own bar and bit in.
His knees weakened as his tastebuds melted into the luxu-
riance of survival chocolate, nuts, and dried fruit.

A whiff of wind puffed down the tunnel toward them,
preceding a dull echo that sounded like the howl of a dying
cat. Warrick's gun barrel cocked a couple of inches.

The Scavenger leader rose from his crouch and motioned with his head, and the two of them continued down
the tunnel. Miles finished the candy bar, grateful for the
flood of energy as his body scrambled to metabolize the
precious nutrients.

Warrick broke into a trot, and the two men ran side by
side. Human and NewMan, together in the tunnels beneath
Los Angeles, moving along the singing track toward a
distant light.

*   *   *

A woman came into Warrick's arms. She touched him lightly on the chest, then pressed herself against him and nuzzled his beard, her throaty laugh enjoying some shared secret. Miles was not attracted to women sexually, but he could admire a healthy body. This woman moved with the grace of a professional athlete. Her fine muscle tone and coordination were obvious. Her face was a graceful oval, features as fine as a chocolate cameo. There was Asian blood in her veins, and perhaps Polynesian as well.

She opened her mouth to speak, then glanced surreptitiously at Miles. "*Warrick,*" she said. "We haven't lost anyone. It's all right."

"Good."

"Only one . . . the one with the bull horns." She whispered the next, but Miles still heard it. "We've seen him before. Remember the nightclub where you met my friend Cecil?"

Warrick thought for a moment, then shook his head.

Miles interrupted them. "Where are my people?"

"This way."

The tunnel suddenly opened into a maze of steel and gleaming tile. Smooth lovely arcs curving away sliced into a multilevel structure that opened like a gigantic hourglass.

Suddenly Miles knew where he was. "The Los Angeles Mall."

The woman grinned. For a moment Miles thought he saw a rainbow of color fluxing through her hair. Trick of the light. Hallucination. "It's all ours," she said happily. "The Scavengers were awarded this territory in the emergency Reclamation Code of '25."

"For rebuilding?"

" 'For enriching the employment potentials of Los Angeles.' That's what the certificate reads. We'll have to sell it off, eventually, but two square blocks of downtown Los Angeles is nothing to sneeze at."

They moved around the edge of a seventh-story balcony, and past what must once have been mall shops. Former clothing stores, Exotic accessory shops, and sex toy and appliance stores rolled past. They had all been restructured for living spaces, teaching spaces, entertainment and meeting halls, food kitchens, and more.

Inquisitive eyes peeked out at them. Young and old, man and woman. Wrinkled, damaged flesh and smooth, beautiful faces. Light and dark skin, bodies of every description. The Scavengers seemed to be caring for most of the unloved and abandoned human debris in the Maze.

And animals. Cats and small mongrel dogs ran through the complex. They seemed to be communally owned, and would stop to receive a pat on the head here, or a scrap of food there. One small black and white mongrel terrier sniffed at Miles's hand, and he scritched it behind the head.

The air was warm, and moist, and smelled distantly of cooking vegetables.

Warrick walked among his people like a benevolent monarch. Here he stopped to listen to a problem, there to tousle a head. One young girl said, "Aubry—" The older man with her placed a finger to her lips and moved on.

Warrick looked back and smiled. "This is it. You're Bloodeagle, aren't you?"

"Yes. Miles Bloodeagle."

"Your people can stay here for a day. Can't protect you any longer than that."

"We have our own resources. You've done more than enough."

As they turned the corner, Miles stopped in surprise. Images of a dozen holo stars stared back at him, dancing in air as they might have in Thousand Oaks or Westwood or any of the other more glamorous and celebrated sections of the city. There were scenes from the latest installment in the *Leviathan* fantasy series, with the space whale attacking yet another flying city. There was the scandalous screen exposé of Guru Amadi Reeshananda, *Profit Without Honor.* The great man stood smiling beatifically, his beard and robe full and fluttering in a nonexistent breeze. His right hand stretched out to the patrons of the theater. His left rested affectionately on the head of the blond woman who knelt in front of him, her arms wrapped around his waist.

Warrick grinned wickedly. "It's our hospital, but I like the holos."

Warrick's companion pretended to grimace. "It appeals to his twisted sense of humor."

Miles followed them into the clinic. The theater had been sectioned off into a maze of booths and smaller rooms. Medics already cared for several of his men. Some sagged dazedly on cots, eyes closed, leaning against the walls like the battle-fatigued soldiers they were.

"What happens if Killinger follows?"

"We can stall them while you get out. Twenty-four hours, Bloodeagle." Warrick's dark eyes glittered. "I've got obligations to these people."

"Absolutely." He held out his hand. "One day, you will need a friend. Anywhere, anytime. I expect it."

Warrick gripped the offered hand. Miles was astonished. Warrick was as strong as he. Miles was not the strongest Gorgon, but to meet an ordinary human being who had such power flowing in his veins was astonishing.

"Miles . . ."

He knew that voice, heard the desperation in it. "Where . . . ?"

Miles wound through a labyrinth of sectioning walls, Warrick following closely. Around a final corner, Miles finally found the Minotaur.

Minotaur could barely breathe. Blood was crusted stickily around his left ear, and his eyes were unfocused. He held out his hand for Miles to clasp. "Not . . . afraid to die, Miles."

Miles blinked hard, trying to clear his eyes. God, *why?*

"I know you're not."

Minotaur managed to turn his head. His eyes focused on Warrick. "I . . . know you."

Warrick took Minotaur's other hand, squeezed it gently. "Maybe you do."

"You . . ." Minotaur sniffed the air. He pulled Warrick down closer to him. His heavy, bovine nose wrinkled as he sniffed. "You brother. I asked you once. You said no. But you are. You brother. Thank you." He gripped at

Warrick with what had to be painful pressure, but the Scavenger leader didn't pull away.

Minotaur closed his eyes, and his chest moved rhythmically.

Silently Warrick's woman had moved up behind him, leaning her cheek against his shoulder. Silent, supportive. Again, her quiet strength impressed Miles. That, and the fluid economy of her movement. For a moment he envied Warrick for winning the love of such a marvelous creature.

Warrick touched her arm softly. "Get some morphine here."

"No," Miles said emphatically. "It is not our way. Let him have his pain."

Warrick made a soft *tch*-ing sound. "If you're sure. If there's anything you need, you can find me. Remember. Just twenty-four hours. Not twenty-four and a half."

"You've done more than enough. Remember, I owe you."

"I remember. Now, get out of here before the violins start playing, will you?"

Warrick and his woman left. Bloodeagle was alone with his people, with the wreckage of bodies and dreams. They did not move him—pain and death he had lived with for far too long. It was something new he felt, something faintly puzzling until he identified it.

Hope.

CHAPTER THREE

McMartin: In My Heart

Tuesday, May 16

The block was burning. Flames and dense, billowing clouds of smoke vomited into the night sky. The few fire trucks that belonged to or would intrude into the wretched ghetto called the Maze merely kept the blaze under control. All efforts concentrated on containment, preventing the spread to neighboring blocks. The building at the corner of Broadway and Twentieth, old even at the turn of the century, was dead now. Broken glass covered the streets like a glittering carpet of hail, crunching and tinkling underfoot. The ground-effect skirts of the aircars blew gusts of powdered glass into the air. Maze dwellers shielded their faces, or fled to cover.

Smoke and chemical fumes belched from the shattered glass windows. Occasionally another pane gave up the ghost: a brief burst of light colored the sky, and fractured crystal rained into the streets below.

The Omnivision remote trucks had packed up most of their equipment. There simply wasn't much that was newsworthy in the Maze. Oh, yes, there were the usual dosages of death and carnage, the usual squalor and human misery. Families who could afford full-spectrum Omnivision service didn't want dead rats and heavy-metal poisoned babies floating over their *duck à l'orange*. It was too depressing, too discouraging and unappetizing. And too damned common. Every net had thousands of hours of digi they would never use. Just no ratings in it anymore.

McMartin's Omnivision module projected its image into the air two meters above the surface of his flotation pool. The pool was ten by fifteen by five meters, covered by an immense emerald plastic environment dome, and eternally warmed to ninety-three degrees Fahrenheit. Tons of glycerin were dissolved in its depths, greatly increasing the water's buoyancy. Drifting there, he watched and felt and listened to the disaster, his eight hundred pounds of tissue supported by the water. A gentle whirlpool action swirled away body wastes. He swam many, many laps in that slimy tank every day, but rarely moved from its depths.

McMartin's bloated fingers roamed over a floating tray of truffles, dithering as if they had noses and palates of their own. They hovered above a particularly fat one, a starburst carved from white chocolate, and popped it into his puffy pink sphincter of a mouth.

"How?" McMartin's characteristically syrupy, cherubic voice was even sweeter than usual. The voice was disorienting, coming as it did from his incredible mass of glistening pink flesh. McMartin used that disorientation as a weapon. "How did they get away? We had the block sewn up. There was no way out. It should have been resolved in one of two ways: a massacre, or encouraging the illegal intervention of the Gorgons, which would have put pressure on President Harris to dissolve the unit. Instead you turned it into a total cock-up."

In a wheelchair at the edge of the pool sat the leader of the Mercs, Marcel Killinger. Killinger wore no makeup now. There were no Omnivision recorders trained upon him. Without the latex and prosthetics his appearance was grotesque. Killinger had no lips, no face, souvenirs of a prematurely ignited firebomb. McMartin wondered how much of the man was still the original equipment.

And now, of course, he was suffering torn ligaments as a result of this raid. He *really* should have been in surgery already. Or at the very least on painkillers.

"We have a report . . ." Killinger rasped. His voice was another souvenir, won in his escape from that long-ago, smoke-filled inferno. "The crab video units were active, and we have a positive identification on the people involved in the rescue.''

Grimacing, he spread out a series of tridee sheets on the table in front of him. As always, so eerily convincing were their illusions of depth that they gave the impression of holes opened in the tabletop. As he spread them out, the identical images appeared in the air above McMartin. ''Definitely Scavengers. And this man''—his finger trembled as it tapped the center picture—''the one they call Warrick, is their leader.''

McMartin's swollen hands stirred the water. ''Their leader. Shit. What can we do with them?''

''Technically, nothing. The NewMen got out of the building. Scavengers didn't break any laws.'' He closed his eyes briefly, and fidgeted at his chestpack medi-comp.

''No!'' McMartin roared. ''Not until you have finished the report. Then dose yourself into a coma for all I care.''

''It . . . hurts.''

McMartin smiled beneficently. ''Suffering is good for the spirit. Go on.''

''When the building collapsed, shock armor protected my men until we could get them out. I tried to stall until one of them died.''

McMartin raised a moist eyebrow. ''Yesss. That might have given you some leverage. What happened?''

''I just couldn't slow up the rescue enough. We do have one possibility. This man . . . Warrick.''

''What about him?''

Killinger's lipless mouth pulled back from his teeth in a grotesque parody of a smirk. ''That's not his real name.''

''No?'' McMartin's eyes glittered with interest. ''Then who is he?''

''The real Warrick was white. Died three years ago in a gang war with the Ortegas.''

''The Ortegas. A gang war. How quaint. You must have enjoyed that little unpleasantness.''

''Wrong branch of the family. I worked for Wu. Little bit after that, this nigger took over. Name of Aubry Knight.''

''You know him?''

Killinger's breath rasped more harshly. ''Yes,'' he hissed.

"I knew him. He crossed Luis, ended up in Death Valley Maximum Security Penitentiary. Murder, attempted rape. He escaped during the riots of '24."

McMartin rolled over in the water like a bloated pink walrus. He virtually glowed with pleasure, his air of irritation sloughing away. "Excellent. Excellent. By allying themselves with this criminal, the NewMen have shown their true colors. Excellent. I'm not sure that I could have arranged it any better myself." He made a motion with his upper body that was curiously like a man trying to sit up while floating. "You may anesthetize yourself, Marcel."

Killinger's fingers eagerly stroked his medi-comp controls. Almost instantly, his scarred face relaxed, and he sighed. "Oh." He giggled, then straightened himself upright again. "Shit yeah. That's *much* better."

"Good. Of course you understand that we want his body, alive if possible, to turn over to the federal authorities. If not, then dead will suffice, as long as his DNA scan matches. How long will it take you to get him?"

"That depends on the . . . ah, cash involved." There was a leading question in Killinger's slurring voice.

"The Great Man who we both serve considers this of paramount value. Consider yourself on Carte Blanche. The money will be routed through the usual channels. This matter must come to a conclusion before July."

McMartin switched off the live broadcast and clicked in a different video.

The air wavered, and opened on a new vista.

The Omniscan took a long, majestic scan of a crowd, pulling back and back until they were in the rear of the auditorium. The auditorium overflowed earnest faces. There was no easy method of categorizing the audience. They were young and old, male and female, white and black and brown. They watched and listened to the flawless hologram at the front of the auditorium.

"—this great land of ours? Your hearts hold the answer! Your hands hold the power! We have tolerated *sin* in our midst for far too long. In the eyes of the Lord, America has become Sodom, has surpassed Gomorrah. And we are being punished. Punished for tolerating perverts in our midst—using Harris's tame sodomites for murder and terrorism. We wonder why Swarna and the PanAfricans sell uranium to the Soviets? They have every reason to hate us! It is the Gorgons who slew Swarna's half brother, and all the world knows it! As long as we support such filth and immorality, disease will ravage our country, our wives and children. Inflation and economic chaos will destroy our lives, our hopes, the dreams of our forefathers.''

The scan moved up to the podium, to the projection of Sterling DeLacourte.

DeLacourte's iron-gray hair was gloriously leonine. On other men such a mane might have seemed affected. On DeLacourte it evoked a sense of the biblical, conjured images of heroes from a simpler, sterner, less forgiving time.

To the right of the projection stood two of his advisors, in the flesh. They were quiet, dark-garbed men who had resigned from the current administration to join his campaign. To the left was a projection of his lovely wife Gretchen. It flickered weakly.

"Damn," McMartin snarled. "The Montana feed is off again."

The three-dimensional shadows of DeLacourte and his wife shared smiles. He turned back to the audience. "I will not allow this country to sink into the slime."

McMartin diddled the Omnivision control key chained around his neck. The room around them disappeared. The flotation pool disappeared. Suddenly McMartin and Killinger were *there*, at the rally, surrounded by DeLacourte's followers. They zoomed up until they were seated in the front row, until every theatrical flip of DeLacourte's hair was an assault on their sensibilities.

"The lives of my family, my wife, my child, are at stake. I pledge the last drop of my blood in this holy war. I give you a challenge. This country belongs to the children of the Bible. Old Testament, New Testament, Christian, and Jew. The men and women who built her and love her and revile the flood of filth as I do. In my heart, I know that any one of you would give his life to purify this country. I ask only the chance to make that sacrifice myself. This is the ultimate contest, with the ultimate prize: the soul of every man, woman, and child on this planet. Today, as in the time of Moses, what we need is a strong man to run the race. 'His going forth is from the end of heaven, and his circuit unto the ends of it: and there is nothing hid from the heat thereof!' "

He paused, panting more with excitement than exertion. "Such battles are not easily won. In another time, another day, victory would have demanded your lives, your blood. Today, by the glorious grace of God, all I demand is your votes!"

The crowd roared thunderously.

McMartin switched the Omnivision off again. The scene dwindled, the audience faded and shriveled into a dark shadow, finally dying altogether.

McMartin splashed in the pool, paddling himself around. "This present business must be resolved before the convention, Marcel. If for a moment I thought that you weren't the man to do this, I would find someone else. I hope you believe me."

"I know the timetable."

"Good. Good. Then, I think that you have some medical business to attend to. I wouldn't want to detain you."

Killinger spun his wheelchair around and purred out of the room, late for his appointment with the surgeons. The door clicked shut behind him.

Good man, McMartin thought.

But that was what it would take. A lot of good, hard men, willing to do whatever it took to make this country great again.

Whatever it took.

CHAPTER FOUR

His Bones the Bars

Wednesday, May 17

"—This is the beauty, the strength, the glory of our accomplishment—"

"—The world beyond cannot, will never understand—"

"—removal of the primitive gonads. Removal of a quantity of the third germ layer, that which lies between the ectoderm and entoderm. Called the mesenchyme, this undifferentiated tissue gives rise to the urogenital system, the lymphatic system, the heart—"

Medusa-16 sat in the darkened arena, passively absorbing the four tracks of sound, eyes closed even though brilliant images flashed through his mind. The computer leads tapping into his skull provided sound and image, fed information more quickly and efficiently than any form of reading or aural input.

He existed in a realm outside ordinary time, ordinary sensation. 16, with a dozen of his "brothers," was deep in Alpha-Theta synch, assimilating raw computer input.

The headset synchronizer monitored his brain waves, dominating them with pulses of light and sound, forcing them into the most favorable rhythms for effortless learning.

The images were absolutely real, in color and depth and sensation. He felt the flash of cold as a male fetus's temperature was lowered to near freezing. Felt the pressure of the knife blade as cells were trimmed away, removed to a sterile growth chamber.

And there (with a perfectly timed trill of beta rhythms)

16 felt a surge of pride as the cells were hormonally stimulated into a new fetus, this one female.

The tiny, pulsing curl of pink flesh grew in time-lapse, so real that 16 could have reached out to touch, to feel, to wonder. The thought alone gave 16 any angle he wished, examining, searching, struggling to understand this, the next step in the Project.

Tissue, mesenchyme tissue, was implanted in the belly of the first fetus. A sliver of semipermeable membrane separated it from the rest of the body. And here, the whisper of voices rose back to his consciousness:

"—Such a miracle, such an unparalleled act of creation—"

"—There are those who would destroy you, as you were rejected by your parents, hated by the parents who should have loved—"

"—membrane will allow nutrients in and wastes out, while simultaneously projecting the hormonal milieu to continue the development of the second set of internal and external genitals—"

16 remembered the rest. That membrane would dissolve soon after birth, to allow sharing of hormones. The result? An artificially created, bi-fertile hermaphrodite with two ovaries, two testes.

16 took pride: *he* had not been created, merely modified. His ovaries were *his*, although his vagina had been created by the stroke of a scalpel. He was special, special in mind and body, due partially to the effects of Cyloxibin, and partially to the regimen imposed by the NewMan doctors and trainers, under the watchful eye of Quint.

Soon, 16 would be told why. Told the secrets that would make the world fit together as a cohesive whole. Until then, 16 would grow, and learn, and practice the arts of death.

And dream . . .

The framework of steel and plastic rose thirty floors above the wet, glistening streets of Los Angeles. For the present, it was nothing but a maze of girders riveted together at right angles. There were no walls, no floors save for small square elevator landings for the twin lifts.

For now, the high-rise was mere bones. The flesh would knit later.

Aubry Knight stood at the very top, at the crosspoint of two naked steel and magnesium beams. The wind plucked at his hair, the rain chilled his skin through his light jacket. Peering west he could see out over the Maze, lit now by the orangish radiance of the setting sun.

Four years ago, the Great Los Angeles Quake had ripped through the inner city, leaving torn flesh and shattered dreams in its wake.

The firestorm that followed had done more damage than the original quake. Businesses fled west to the beaches, and south as far as San Diego. Ten square miles of central Los Angeles was simply cordoned off. The poor and the homeless gravitated there like silt settling through water. Ten months later, the Maze had been proclaimed the worst and most shameful ghetto in the United States.

To the east and west, the gleaming skeletons of new buildings rose from the ruins. From three hundred feet above street level, he could see them clearly. They seemed a menagerie of magical creatures awakening to phantasmal life.

But if he closed his eyes, he was back in the caves, back in Death Valley's underground hell. His blood roared with apomorphine. Nausea was a gripping fist: squeezing, emptying his stomach again and again. The faces of the men who had raped his mind flared like bonfires in the deepest night. There was no escape from them, no escape from the prison he carried within him: his dreams the walls and warden, his bones the bars.

The steel beneath his feet vibrated as one of the elevator cars rose up the side of the building. It jostled to a halt, revealing one of Aubry's chief advisors, Leo Baker.

The organizational genius didn't walk out along the naked girder. He merely stood at the elevator deck as the doors closed and it sank back out of sight.

Aubry saw Leo, but didn't acknowledge. He breathed deeply, let the adrenaline purify him, drive the goddamned dreams farther underground. He was tired. Soon he would have to sleep.

Finally he spoke. "What's the news, Leo?"

Leo was the shorter of Aubry's two lieutenants. He was a round man with a wrinkled face that bore so many scars that at times it appeared quilted. He peered down through the webbing of girders, and looked a little green. "Bloodeagle and the NewMen made their way out. They have a cell in San Diego. They'll be safe for the time being."

"Righteous." Aubry crossed the beams as if strolling across a sidewalk. Leo watched him nervously, chewing at a thick wad of tobacco. He almost swallowed it as Aubry jumped from one girder to another, spun and balanced. He grinned at them.

"Ah, boss . . ." Leo flinched. "Do we have to talk about it up here? Why don't you come on down . . . ?"

"I like it up here." Aubry laughed flatly. "The tunnels get close." He jumped up and gripped one of the overhead beams. For a moment he pretended that his fingers slipped on the wet steel. He dangled from one hand. He was tired. Why the hell wouldn't his body feel the fatigue? It was as if the mind was one creature, the flesh another. "Go ahead. Tell me about the haggling?"

"The contractors offered fifty percent. Pacific Construction has to pull at least half of their work force from within the Maze, or through the Scavengers." Leo forced a smile as Aubry handwalked the underside of the beam. "We got the license while nobody wanted it. Now that business is moving back in . . .

"We owe you a lot, Aubry. You, and Promise."

Aubry's face creased bitterly. "Yeah, right. Me and Promise." He dropped down to the beam, his footing as secure as suction cups on glass. He was silent for a while, looking out and up into the night. The rain pattered against his face, but he didn't blink. Aubry Knight stood there as if he had grown out of the girder, as if he shared a unity with the elements.

"You're one of us."

Aubry's face held no answers, but seemed sad. The vigor and false gaiety dissolved. What there was in its place was something that bit more fiercely than the wind.

"I died in Death Valley," Aubry answered numbly.

"Let it go, Aubry. For God's sake."

He pointed up into the night sky. "Up there, man. Right now, while we're talking. Men are Nullboxing. Someone's getting ready to go against the champ. I can't ever do that. I was born to do that. It's all I can do, really—"

"That's bullshit. You've expanded Scavenger operations north and east—"

"Promise did all of that. I just sat and nodded my head, man. I don't have the skull for that kind of stuff. I teach a few drills, lead the work crews sometimes . . . you need her more than you need me—" Suddenly his face and voice changed. "Hey, forget it. Just brooding, you know? Go on down. I won't be long." Leo retreated from the cold. The elevator gate clanged behind him.

Slowly Aubry's head dropped. Perhaps he didn't deserve the stars, the ultimate escape from Earth's jealous grip. Never would he pit his skills against other Nullboxers.

He hadn't been a fighter. He'd been a killer, and it was no use trying to pretty that behind labels.

A soldier in Luis Ortega's ungodly army. A skulker in darkness, the evil will of a twisted mind made flesh. And the more that Aubry struggled to free himself from that web, the tighter it clutched at him. . . .

He had tried to leave, to find legal outlet for his awesome skills. But before he could even complete his Nullboxing training, Luis came after him.

What followed nearly destroyed his remaining humanity. Years in the worst prisons in America. His only friends had been brutally murdered. His efforts to avenge them led him to a chair in an empty room with a holoscreen, and smiling doctors who grafted a crippling, reflexive nausea onto his anger. More betrayals, more double crosses. And, after he escaped, another web of lies that led to an inescapable confrontation with his tormentors.

And at the end, Luis Ortega was dead, the Family itself in ruins. All it had cost was hundreds of innocent Scavengers.

We owe you a lot, Aubry. . . .

What a joke. Even when he tried to do something

positive, distributing Cyloxibin free to the public, it had backfired hideously.

Hell. He didn't even know why he was still alive. Why he had been born with such a twisted, savage skill. Why his strength and speed and pain thresholds were so much greater than those of other men.

Why he lived on when better men preceded him into the great darkness.

The second elevator gate folded back and Promise was there.

She was tall for a woman, but her eyes barely came to his chin. Her hair was shoulder-length, and trailed dark inches beneath her rain cowl. Sometimes she made it stand up away from her head, and sometimes it fell in an ebon cascade. Occasionally it still sparkled when she was happy, or mischievous. Most especially when she danced.

He came to her, walking along the beam as if it were a sidewalk. She folded him into her arms, and together they looked out over the city. The sun was setting out behind the Century Towers fifteen miles west. The new central business district. It was there that the nerve center of Los Angeles had fled after the quake and economic collapse.

The sunset was a thing of dense, broken clouds, splashed with burnt umber. The first few stars already twinkled in the gloom. A few lights flared in the skeletons of the new buildings. To Aubry, the night seemed especially beautiful, and that thought depressed him as well. So many lives gone. So many eyes closed, never to see another sunset.

And Aubry Knight lived on.

He squeezed her. For the ones who had gone before.

"Come down for communal supper, Aubry." Her voice was golden to him. He should have felt warm. Safe.

Why the chill?

"Thinking about Nullboxing?"

He nodded.

She pressed herself against him more tightly.

"Come down." The wind plucked at her hair, and as he bent to kiss her again, the left side of her face sparkled. He tried not to notice the diminution of color and shape control that had once come so easily to her. When he concentrated on what he *had*, as opposed to what he had *lost*, it eased the pain.

"Let's go," he said finally, and together they entered the elevator.

It jostled once, then began to sink. They shared it in silence. An uneasy mixture of joy and sorrow welled within Aubry, and he was unsure which was winning the battle.

The elevator hit the street level and paused. Aubry thumbprinted the optical scan and the lift continued to sink.

The municipal construction men could not enter the private Scavenger tunnels.

"We can't hold this," Promise said softly. "The city's coming back. The utilities and maintenance people have returned."

"We've got some rights."

Promise squeezed him tightly. "I've done everything I could. The Scavengers will end up owning property here. Legal ownership. The lawyers will get richer than we will, but we won't end up destitute. You didn't think that they could live down in the tunnels forever, did you?"

Aubry sighed as the elevator continued to sink. "I know. I'm just not looking forward to it, that's all. Crazy, isn't it? We fought like hell to make us legit, and now I'm afraid of it happening."

The platform jostled to a halt, and the face of a tall, moonfaced man greeted them. His face could have held another nose without seeming crowded at all. Aubry said "Quarry," and embraced his lieutenant. "I didn't expect to see you back from San Diego so quickly. Did all of them make it?"

"The Minotaur didn't. He had lost too much blood."

Aubry nodded. "At least he didn't die in one of the camps. And the rest of them?"

"Fine." He tore a scrap of paper off his clipboard. "We barter for these medical supplies tomorrow. We need antibiotics, and a new ultrasound modulator. If you can find the components at Free Market, I can cobble it to-

gether. I'd prefer that. I don't feel comfortable when the
government has a complete inventory of our assets.''

Aubry laughed. "Can't imagine why." He folded the
paper and slipped it into his pocket as he got into the cart.
With a slight bump, it set off along the track.

"Legitimate. It's hard to believe, isn't it?" He smiled
wistfully. "I wish Warrick were here to see it."

"This was his dream," Promise said. Aubry turned to
look at her, sighing at the long cool curve of her neck, the
fineness of her nose and eyes. They combined the sensitivity of an Asian with the raw sensuality of African features.
If nothing else, if no other part of his life had ever
amounted to anything, this glorious woman's love compensated for a world of disappointment.

The cart passed the former living quarters of the Scavengers. In these side rooms, twisted corridors, and dark
vaults beneath subterranean Los Angeles, the battle against
the Ortegas had raged.

Quarry clucked worriedly. "We found another clutch of
squatters."

"Not a real concern," Promise said. "Take a note to
cut back on work in the Sears building. The Reclamation
Code of '25 gives us the right to the Mall. That is it.
Aubry doesn't want to sink time and energy into rebuilding
what we can't hold. Right, hon?"

He heard her, but the words seemed far off, tinny
echoes. *The city is coming back. What the hell happens to
me?*

"Aubry? Did you hear me?" Quarry and Promise exchanged glances, and Aubry only caught their expressions
out of the corner of his eye. They were worried about him,
and he wasn't surprised.

He was worried, too.

It was wonderful to see the life, the vitality and enthusi-
asm in the tunnels. Goods were being ferried in from the
market, purchased with Scavenger labor. Kevin Warrick's
original promise to employers and employees was still
alive, still simple and consistent: an honest day's work for
an honest day's pay.

The Scavengers operated on a simple principle: anyone who was willing to work, could work. Compensation in goods, services, cash, or trade union Service Marks depended entirely upon the intensity, duration, and quality of individual efforts.

The Scavengers represented hope. The City of Angels had abandoned her heartland and fled west to the beaches and south along the coast, creating a new business district rather than bothering to rebuild what had been.

No longer did Scavengers live in the dank corridors beneath buildings, although there was still much work to be done there. Now, the rebuilding of Los Angeles was almost finished, and Aubry sought to find training for his people. One day soon the Maze would be an ugly memory.

It was almost that now: disease and violence no longer made her night streets an abattoir. A few Thai-VI victims still hid in shadowed rooms, but as in other parts of the city, and in other cities all over the world, the dreaded venereal leprosy was almost exclusively confined to camps and isolated security areas. The dreaded Thai-VI Spiders no longer haunted the streets, playing their loathsome game of sexual "tag."

The Maze now had industries other than prostitution and drugs. Still perhaps the worst and most shameful ghetto in America, it was no longer the utter hell that it had been following the firestorm of '24.

And if a measure of that growth could be attributed to the tireless efforts of Aubry Knight and his partner/mate/lover Promise, then so be it.

Aubry looked at her without shifting his head. Damn, she was lovely. An unpleasant question remained: What were they to each other? It was hard to say sometimes. Did he truly feel love, or just the effects of the Cyloxibin mushroom? And was there a difference?

Or something else? He scanned his past, finding little help there, few images of peace or contentment, let alone affection.

Then, of course, there was the Dead Zone, where the horrors of Death Valley had warped the locks he kept on his memory, and the raw sewage of his past oozed up around the edges of the seals.

He didn't want to look. He really didn't. But there was morbid fascination with the endless black halls that closed in on him. *With the torn bodies of his friends, crawling eternally in the darkness, their hands outstretched—*

(God, no. Shut that away—)

—to him, "help us," they say, hands and faces grimed with their own blood. "Help—"

(In the name of heaven. Anything but that. Even the nausea. He ground his knuckles against his temples, and the faces and voices dissolved into a solution of that dandy universal solvent, self-inflicted pain.)

The cart lurched to a halt, and Aubry snapped out of his trance. Quarry smiled uncertainly. Promise held out her hand. "Help me from the cart. Pretend you're a gentleman."

Aubry had to laugh, and the ugly images faded again. For a while.

"This way, Aubry."

"The dining room is over at the other end . . ." he protested weakly.

"It's being remodeled," she said, still hiding that grin. "We're meeting over in the Blue Room." Aubry shut down his protest. This was the most beautiful area in the Mall, possibly the loveliest in the entire Maze. When the economy began to work again, when the Mall began to interact with the outside world, then people might come in for gracious meals and shopping. The business offices might thrive again. One day . . .

Hopefully one day soon.

The Blue Room had been planned as a luxury restaurant before the firestorm, and its refurbishing had been a special pet project by Promise and the others. They had actually kept Aubry at a distance.

But now . . .

The usual glowing plastic lightsquares weren't in evidence. The lighting was supplied totally by candles, and the whole room had a soft glow that warmed him in places so numb he hadn't felt the cold.

The candlelight reflected back from the walls and ceiling. Promise had wrought a miracle. There were busts in the lobby, and bas relief copper sculpture, paintings with a dominant thread of gold running through them. The room was gilded, and Aubry caught his breath. The tables were arranged in an isosceles triangle clearly pointing to a seat of honor. He turned to them. "What . . . ?"

"Three years," Leo said warmly. "Three years since you came back to us. Since you came to carry on and push forward what Kevin started. This is just our way of saying 'thank you.' "

He turned to Promise. "You knew?"

"I *planned*, love."

Sheepishly, Aubry took his place at the head table. As he stood there, four hundred and twelve Scavengers came to their feet and faced him.

Aubry looked out at them, and tried to find words. "I never thought . . ." The doubts, the fears, receded. They still spoke, not so urgently now, their flames cooled for the moment.

Promise kissed him with embarrassing thoroughness, and his people . . .

His people!

. . . applauded roundly, and the feast began.

"Are you coming to bed soon?"

"Soon," Aubry said. "I'm working out some drills for tomorrow's class." He sat in full lotus, knees flat on the tiled floor. He answered Promise without disturbing the meditative state that had taken him only a moment to swim into. That was how it felt. Swimming into an infinitely deep and dark black eye.

And in there, the water was the same temperature as his skin. His sense of identity began to drift away. And there, in a room that was dark and private, he met once again with his friend and teacher Kevin Warrick.

Thin, almost unhealthily gaunt, with piercing eyes and jutting cheekbones. Warrick looked much as he had on the last day of his life. A man old but utterly unbowed by life. Circumstances be damned: Warrick was the only human being in this life who had ever beaten Aubry in fair combat.

"Warrick . . ."

And as always, he was there.

Perhaps, as Promise maintained, there was truly a psychic connection between Aubry and the dead man. Or perhaps, as Aubry believed, the answers lay in the same mind that framed the questions. Either might have been true. All that he knew for certain was that there was comfort in the quiet conversations he conducted with the old man. Comfort, and peace.

For now, phantasm or delusion or mirage, the image of Warrick floated before him.

"Should I have helped the NewMen?" Aubry's brow furrowed. "I don't know. I don't know why I did it. I'm . . . confused." Even to himself, his voice was as plaintive as that of a child. "Did I do the right thing?" Aubry waited in the dark, and the cold. A very faint tickle of moving air played against his skin.

You did what you had to do, Warrick answered finally. *Whatever the motivations, the actions were correct. Don't ask so many questions of yourself. You don't have the answers. There are no answers. Only actions.*

Aubry thought quietly. Actions. If action helped him forget, then action was good.

He opened his eyes, flickered his gaze sideways to see Promise in the doorway of his workout room, watching him silently.

Aubry put his palms flat on the floor. He lifted his crossed legs from the ground, uncrossed them and slid down into a complete split. The rusty tug in his hamstrings reminded him that he had not done his exercises for forty-eight hours. Other than that, he was able to circle his body around almost effortlessly. The thick muscles in his legs and midsection flowed like oiled cables, gave no resistance at all. This feeling, and the ones that would follow shortly, he treasured above all others in his life.

He spun to his feet, and leapt into the air. His entire body flattened into a kick that was so fast and precise that the air popped. He landed lightly, spun and kicked, spun—

And Warrick was there with him, slashing at him with the *bo* staff. Striking and slashing, goading Aubry on and on. Ever reminding him that he must breathe smoothly. That he must release tension into the movement, not hold it in his muscles. And continuously, unceasingly challenging him to channel his emotions into an undifferentiated white light, a pure essence. That essence and that alone enabled his movement to be an expression of Self, and not merely a reaction to external stimulus.

Somewhere during that time, Aubry the man and Aubry the movement lost their distinctions. He stopped, pivoting. Promise was gone from the doorway. He listened carefully, sweat drooling down his forehead, his beard, his chest, pooling at his feet.

She was asleep.

Aubry folded back to the lotus position, and listened to his heartbeat. Five minutes later it was calm, had regained its customary rhythm of thirty-five beats per minute.

Promise was still asleep, and there was no sound from the world around him. Silently Aubry lifted one of the rectangular floor tiles. The floor was hollowed beneath, and in the hollow lay a package wrapped in oilskin. When he unfolded and emptied it, it yielded an ancient book.

Aubry hitched himself over closer to the lightsquare and opened the volume to the halfway point, where he had stopped the night before.

Slowly, laboriously, he ran his heavy finger under the words, shaping them, sounding them as carefully as possible. It hurt his head. His damp finger made marks along the page as he read.

There were pictures, and that made it easier to keep interested. And there were funny parts that made him smile, sometimes. But it was so hard. For three years he had struggled, reclaiming what little he knew of reading, pushing on. It would have been easier if he had been able to ask for help, but he couldn't do that. Just couldn't.

He squeezed his eyes shut, warding off a headache. Here was a part that he liked. He raised his voice a little, speaking nervously at first, then with greater confidence:

"The sun was shining on the sea,
Shining with all his might:
He did his very best to make
The billows smooth and bright—
And this was odd, because it was
The middle of the night . . ."

Promise awoke, and rolled over.

Aubry was shaking, eyelids closed but fluttering. She ran her hand over his forehead, wiping away warm, sticky sweat. His hand reached out for hers, and gripped with feverish strength.

He muttered something unintelligible, then rolled over and settled in.

Finally his body relaxed as tension seemed to leave him in a great sigh.

She lay there, watching the rise and fall of his great shoulders, and heard him mutter something under his breath. For a moment she considered shaking him, finding out exactly what he meant, then decided against it. It had to be nonsense. Weird, though.

It had sounded like *"O oysters come and walk with us—"*

Nutty. Promise lay back and closed her eyes. Within a few minutes she was asleep again.

CHAPTER FIVE

Free Market

Thursday, May 18

To Promise, the sights and smells of Free Market day made the rest of the week worthwhile. The rich, heavy aroma of fresh cooked meat and breads was intoxicating. It was good to smell pork and beef again. For a while, strange dishes with Spanish and Korean names had been Maze staples. And for that same while, for some strange reason, dogs and stray cats had shunned the Maze. Curious.

Hundreds of colored pennants vied for attention. Makeshift wooden and plastic booths titillated the senses.

A tiny half-naked Chinese infant ran past, bare bottom shining. Its mother, a bird of paradise Exotic, ran close behind, her rainbow scalp feathers ruffling in the wind. Promise spun to avoid them, laughter bubbling from her throat.

On Market day, the Maze was no longer a limping invalid of a community. Today it was a vibrant, living organism, with a rhythm and power all its own.

The Market spread over a four-city-block area in the devastated Pershing Square district. The Scavenger booth was the largest in the Market, neatly bracketed by two billboards. The one at the left encouraging all to vote for smiling, bespectacled President Harris. At left, a woman in the kind of indeterminate uniform that suggested nurse or nun with equal facility encouraged unwed or reluctant mothers to freeze their unborn children for future adoption at Xenon cryonurseries.

At Free Market one could find food and drink, repaired

clocks and mechanical parts, antiques, and handicrafts and endless bric-a-brac. Amid the endless heaps of goods were odds and ends crafted by a million agile minds.

Promise moved among the booths, calling the vendors by name as they greeted her in kind. She spun as something hard and square-cornered bumped her backside.

"I'm sorry, Promise . . ." An old woman draped in rags pulled back a cart bearing her entire stock of worldly possessions. The woman resembled a withered, skinned apple: deep wrinkles, and dry, cracked skin bleached by exposure. She had no teeth left, but a skewed sort of humor still glinted in her hazel eyes.

"Good morning, Hilda." Promise gave herself two points for plucking the elusive name from her memory. Hilda's shopping cart brimmed with twists of wire and broken metal parts. The entire mess was worthless, but almost certainly the fruit of an honest day's labor. The old woman had tried.

"I have . . . things. Here for you." The woman cackled to herself and dug into the cart. She fiddled among the objects until she found something about the size of a human head. Glass tubes and coiled springs popped out of it in bizarre configurations. Promise couldn't tell the difference between design eccentricities and sheer metal fatigue.

"See? See? I told you."

"Yes, Hilda. So you did." Promise held it up. What had the old woman said? And when had she said it? Damned if Promise could remember. She had to be careful here. Hilda would be terribly hurt if Promise didn't remember every detail of their last conversation.

"Why . . . it's . . . just what you said. I'm speechless." What the hell was it? A clock? A potato-juice-powered radio? She really couldn't say. "It's . . . you really don't see one of these every day, that's for sure. And it's in . . . wonderful shape." She tilted it onto its side, wincing as grit streamed out of a crack.

"Well. Why don't you go over to our booth and tell Mira 'Blue twelve.' She'll take care of you." She gave the object a final rattle and handed it back. "And give her this. I'm sure she'll love it."

She laughed to herself as the old woman doddered off to the Scavenger booth.

At the east end of the Free Market were a row of employment shells. The busy prefab boxes were sponsored by companies dedicated to developing the Maze's labor pool. It was doubtful if General Electric and Consolidated Fusion would recruit, but Human Services people would be plentiful.

At the moment, the line was a sea of faces, some desperate, some optimistic. The booths listed opportunities in massage and interactive therapy, legal prostitution, domestic assistance and all of the other high-touch services that machines could not provide. Human Services specialized in listing and accommodating those areas where untrained adults could find employment.

She scanned the lines, feeling satisfaction. She had helped make this possible. As her gaze continued to move, she saw the play area on the far side of the employment booths. In it children dangled pendulously from swings, chittering like monkeys. Their joyful screams filled the air as they yo-yo'd about.

There were many, many children about two years old. An explosion.

Suddenly Promise was oppressively aware of the vast number of couples. They held hands, wound their arms around each other, carried their children. Men and women in endless pairs, and more than half of them wore the tiny gold Cyloxibin mushroom pendants, openly proclaiming themselves bonded '' 'shroomheads.'' The spores were available free on folded squares of blotter paper, passed out by the tens of thousands. The mushrooms were distributed fresh and dried. They grew wild all over California.

It was too late to stamp them out. The risks to unborn children discouraged millions. Millions more ignored those risks, eager to indulge in the most powerful and bizarre hallucinogen yet discovered or created by man.

Even now, three years after her last dose, Promise still experienced flashbacks. Moments when making love was so explosively powerful that it singed a hole through her reality. Those moments left her tumbling in a void, falling and falling, alone yet enfolded by the love of her life.

She wrenched herself from her reverie, and searched the

faces of their tiny children. How many of them would be victims of the mushroom's dark gift? One percent? Three? It depended on who you listened to.

Promise closed her eyes, shutting out the young faces. The sounds of their high, sweet voices still fluttered at her ears. Unconsciously, her fingers pressed against her flat dancer's stomach.

The doctors swore there was nothing wrong. That the miscarriage she had suffered in Terra Buena three years before had not damaged her womb. She laughed bitterly. A woman in harmony with her body understood herself as no doctor could, to a depth that machines and chemical tests cannot reach. She knew there would be no more children for her.

Perhaps it was the long years of chemical birth control. Or the abortions. Sometimes, alone in her room, Promise suffered bloody visions. A mountain of torn fetuses weighed on her conscience. How many had there been? If she counted the menstrual extractions, there was literally no way to know. The fetuses were the unwanted children of men whose names had long since faded from memory. Perhaps her body had finally revolted. Three years before, ravaged by Cyloxibin fever, Promise had ripped the birth control implant from her arm. Her body made one final, herculean effort to give her a child.

A healthy girl child. Or a boy. A healthy, happy child, who would laugh when she coddled it, would need her with all of its heart and spirit. Someone who would know nothing of her past, would care only that she was *Momma*.

And through that caring, ease her painful memories.

Your past is stained. But here is new life, and through it, what has occurred may be undone. A life ill-lived might begin anew.

That was the dream, the thing that might have been. A bullet intended for Aubry had shaken her from that dream, and simultaneously terminated the life within her.

It left an unending emptiness, an eternal lack of deep connection when she made love to Aubry. Physical release she could have, but something was missing, would always be missing. At times like this the pain surged through her undiluted.

A hand touched her on the shoulder, and Promise turned, hoping that it wasn't Hilda again.

It wasn't. It was one of the Mazies, the barely post-pubescent youngsters who found employment outside in the straight world, doing everything, anything. Prostitution had been legal in California since the turn of the century, another concession to the state's endless hunger for revenue. Promise had lived in that world for seven years. Those years had brought her teetering to the very edge of sanity. She had never quite tipped over.

The girl's face was still young, and fresh, still innocent with youth. Her hair was a dusty blond, clipped short. The hollows beneath her eyes were the only traces of fatigue. Her ready smile was purest vinyl. Promise wanted to reach out and shake her.

Get out of the trap. I know what you're doing, and I know what it's going to cost you. Believe me. You can't afford to pay.

"My name is Rose. I need to talk with you."

"What about?"

"Your man."

"Warrick?" Promise's eyes narrowed.

"Warrick is dead," the girl said. "I heard them say it. And Aubry Knight is about to be."

Promise frowned. She and Aubry knew that the charade wouldn't hold up forever. She could only hope there was still time to repair the damage. If not . . .

"All right," Promise said reluctantly. "Come with me."

Aubry sat at the council table, flanked by Leo and Quarry. His enormous chest moved slowly with the rhythm of his breathing, hands folded placidly in front of him. Impassive, he watched and listened as Rose told her story.

"I provide . . . body services for McMartin."

"Who's he?" Aubry's voice was neutral. Promise stood just behind him, hating the sound of it. It irked her when he made his normally deep, mellifluous voice hollow and flat. She couldn't read anything in its timbre. His eyes had darkened almost to black.

"McMartin Cryogenics," Rose whispered nervously.

"And there's another man who works for him, named Marcel Killinger. He's supposed to be head of an independent Merc unit, but he really works for McMartin."

Only now did Aubry's face show emotion: wariness. "Killinger again," he said quietly. "I should have known we weren't through with each other."

Rose clinched her hands into little fists, her voice urgent. "You hurt Killinger. They were pretty amazed at that, 'cause he was wearing armor. He has a real hard-on for you."

Promise looked at Aubry questioningly.

"Years back," Aubry said. "Right after I joined the Ortegas. Killinger had a real problem with me coming up so fast. Switched Families, went to work for Wu. I didn't know he'd gone indie."

"They have a federal bounty, Mr. Knight."

"Bastards," Leo said. "That gives Killinger a free hand."

"That's what they want," Rose said. "They don't want you back in jail. They want you dead, as a warning to anyone else who might want to help NewMen."

"Is that right." Aubry closed his eyes for a few moments, thinking. "Why are you getting in the middle of this?"

Rose dropped her eyes shyly. "The Scavengers helped me after the quake. I was burning up with fever, and they brought in medicine. I can't repay what I owe. This is the closest I can come."

One of the Scavenger women escorted the girl out.

And what now?

"Aubry . . ." Leo began.

Aubry waved his hand, demanding silence. "That's the game. It's over. It was gonna happen sooner or later. It's not like I can lose myself in a crowd. I can't say I'm not Aubry Knight. I can't prove I'm not guilty of murder."

Quarry stood, and all eyes went to him. "Aubry. You know that we would fight for you." Everyone at the table nodded. "Unfortunately, this isn't the Ortegas. This is a federal warrant. What the hell are we supposed to do?"

"There isn't much I can do but leave." He looked out at them, the only family he had ever had, and bowed his head.

Promise reached out and took his hand. Of course there

was nothing for the two of them to say to each other. She would go where he went. There was no choice for her.

She smiled to the two men at Aubry's sides. "I know where we can go. Maybe you can already guess. If not, there's no need to weigh you down with information you don't need. We'll come back if we can."

The majority of the things Promise wanted to take lay close by one another. A few items of clothing, an extra pair of shoes. A few reminders of their life among the Scavengers.

On the other side of the room, Aubry packed a duffel bag. He paused for a moment, and turned to face her. "Did I play it right?"

She smiled, coming to him. She pressed herself against his body so that she could hear the slow thunder of his heartbeat. "You did the only thing. It will be all right. Besides—" She looked up at him, and kissed him firmly. "It's high time that you met my family."

The fuel cell of their electric car would take them five hundred miles before it needed recharging with liquid hydrogen and oxygen. They would make connections for food and shelter along the way. If it became necessary to ditch the car, they could, and would. Until then, safe transport, with forged papers, was theirs.

Leo looked into Promise's eyes for a long moment, then closed his own. "I'm so damned sorry."

"There's nothing to do, Leo."

"If there's anything you need . . ." The unfinished offer hung in the air unanswered, unanswerable. "Go with God, both of you."

They nodded, and the side of the garage rolled up. With a rolling purr the engine began to turn.

The sun would be up in a few hours. By then they would be on their way.

"Be well," Leo said. "Survive."

"That's all I know how to do." Aubry's mouth twisted in a grin, and he clasped Leo's hand. "Good-bye."

They rolled out into the early morning. They were forty

miles north of the Maze, out past the San Fernando Valley. Their papers would get them as far as San Francisco, and from there . . .

Time would tell.

CHAPTER SIX

Rose

Friday, May 19

With a quiet whirr, the folding door between McMartin's pool and living room slid open. Rose stepped through gingerly. The polished wooden deck around the pool tingled her bare feet.

McMartin's bulk hung suspended in the pool. Fractured light from the faceted plastic dome in the ceiling cast a kaleidoscope of lazily rotating colors on his pale acres of skin. He made a lazy flip, dipping beneath the saturated glycerin solution, then surfaced again. He stared at her as he came up. Although the fluid ran into his small, dark eyes, he didn't blink. One globular hand reached to the floating tray eternally in front of him, and scooped a handful of cold ham mousse, the pinkish gelatin glistening in his hand before he smeared it into his mouth.

"Rose," he said placidly. She walked around the edge of the pool, watching him from the corner of her eye. Did he know? How could he . . . ?

McMartin seemed to know many things that no one should know, and used facts with the precision of a surgeon. She hoped that she hadn't made a mistake. She couldn't afford to lose her job.

"Rose," he repeated. "Didn't you hear me?"

"I'm sorry, sir." She looked nervously about. Where were the other girls?

He ignored her question. "I want you to check the thermostat. It isn't sampling often enough. Maybe the pump assembly is malfunctioning. It's been half a degree off all day.'' He giggled, and plucked a stuffed blue crab shell from the crowded tray, examined and rejected it in favor of a crispy black mint-barbecued leg of lamb.

She checked the bank of digital displays. Everything seemed in order, but she couldn't tell *him* that. McMartin would certainly claim that his skin was more sensitive than any mechanical probe.

"It must be broken, sir. Nothing shows up wrong. I'll make a note to have it checked.''

"Yes.'' He giggled again. "You do that. Half a degree is totally unacceptable. My skin is *so* sensitive. Thank you, sweet mouse.''

Rose slipped a latex cap over her finger-length hair.

Something was wrong, she could feel it. Usually, he would vibrate with eagerness, waiting for Rose and the other Mazies to minister to his needs. To massage him in the water, to roll him onto his back in the thickened water. Kneading and stroking and pleasuring him. He would hang in the water like a Portuguese man-of-war, groaning and petting one or another of them. Pulling them close to his obscenely lush mouth for a foul, thick-tongued kiss.

Today none of the other girls was there. He looked at her with all sexual interest submerged. There was no hunger visible in his eyes. At least, nothing she could see on the surface. No interest, no feeling. Just an emptiness. Rose shuddered.

She stepped into the water.

She loved its buoyancy, its divine warmth. It would have been heavenly but for the presence of McMartin. He was a motionless, swollen blob of a Golem in the center of a room-sized flotation tank.

There were times when she wished that she could merely hang there, by herself. Just let her troubles drift away in the same fluid that supported her weight.

She had to remember that this was business, and only business. What she thought, or felt, or wanted, meant nothing at all to McMartin.

She wiggled eellike through the slime.

He watched her approach, motionless save for a bovine chewing motion.

She treaded water in front of him. "Where are the others?"

"None but you today, my dear," he whispered. "But that's all right. You're my favorite, you know."

She smiled modestly, suppressing a shudder. *He knows. Dear Lord, he knows.* . . .

She began to wipe him off. The heavy artificial sponges helped remove the slick of brownish fungus that always formed on him.

It was much harder without the other girls to help. Not just in terms of shared exertion. *Misery loves company.* There was a shared disgust, a private joking that made things tolerable if not pleasant.

He opened his mouth. Rose scrubbed his teeth for him. His little black eyes watched her every movement as she removed the plaque. He hawked and spit into the water. The constant whirlpool flushed it away, as it did all his body wastes.

"Where were you last night?" he asked mildly.

"At home, sir." From a bag at her waist Rose extracted a pair of clippers, cutting his fingernails. The pale curls of soft tissue were swept away in the current.

"Did you feel DeLacourte's address?"

Damn! She should have known he would ask. The only politic thing to say was yes.

"Of course." She paused, trying to anticipate his emotional needs. "He's a very great man."

"Indeed he is," McMartin said, as if truly interested in her opinion. "What did you think of his final statements?" He smiled benignly.

Her mind scrambled. What had DeLacourte's closing statements been the last few weeks? Always, on . . .

"Gorgon? The special antiterrorist force? I . . . don't know about things like that. The President says they're necessary."

McMartin frowned. "Yes, I've heard him say that. But they're assassins, dear. They came within a hair of killing the legitimate head of a foreign power. *Did* blow his

brother into kitty kibble. Everyone knows it, and everyone
pretends it isn't true. Disgusting.''

"I don't know, sir. I've never had a problem with
them . . ." She began to tremble, and fought to conceal it.
Being this close to him, alone for the first time, she was
suddenly terribly aware of the immensity of his body. He
was HUGE, by far the largest human being she had ever
seen. And his constant immersion in the flotation tank had
caused muscle atrophy: he seemed to be a bag of human
pus. In her darker fantasies he loomed translucent, the
pulsing sacks of his organs suspended in warm, clotted
jelly.

McMartin performed a lazy breaststroke, and tremors
shivered through the sludgy water.

"I want to watch the tape again."

"Yes, sir."

"And while we do . . ." He clapped his hands, and the
Omnivision holo lit up. The image of Sterling DeLacourte
appeared above their heads. McMartin rolled onto his
back. "And while I watch, take care of me, my dear."

She smiled, curling her lips into a lie. She swam up in
between the grotesquely swollen thighs, searching.

McMartin hiccoughed with sudden pleasure as she reached
her goal.

"—Harris a bad man, I'm saying he's a dupe. The men
who control him are no more than cowards and frauds—"

The words became muffled as Rose bobbed below the
surface of the water.

"I do not advocate violence, and yet this is the only
language these people understand. I am a man of peace,
and yet the filthy homosexuals—man shall not lie with
man! This is clearly stated in the Bible. Why then does our
government protect this filth, use them to destabilize foreign regimes. We claim that the PanAfricans are our
enemies—we have made them so, with terrorism of our
own . . ."

McMartin was beginning to breathe a little harder now.
Rose gulped air, keeping him excited with her hands, and
dove back beneath the surface.

"And if we tolerate this degeneracy—"

McMartin was growing too excited. His thighs pressed against the sides of her head, and the pressure grew crushing. She panicked, trying to pull away, but couldn't move. She thrashed her legs desperately as her lungs screamed for air.

No! Please . . .

The enormous thighs kept her pinned. Her lungs, desperate, aching now, spasmed and sucked in thick, warm water. Adrenaline exploded in her body and for a few seconds she was supernormally strong. Blind terror, fear of imminent death, gave her the strength of a giantess. She struggled insanely to drag in a single mouthful of air. His hands were on her head. She twisted, trying to bite the flabby thighs, to fight, to survive, or failing that to commit one last desperately defiant act.

Her efforts meant nothing to him. Almost tenderly, McMartin's gelatinous body smothered her motions. The roaring in her ears was all-consuming. And then there was no more thought at all.

A door at the edge of the pool slid back, and Killinger appeared.

"It's over?"

"Yes." McMartin's thick tongue slid out, licking a slick of dried salt from his lips. "Actually, it was quite good. It . . . touched that moment, Marcel. It seemed to last forever." His eyes were sleepily half-lidded. "I want you to run a risk analysis—I wouldn't mind having this arranged on a regular basis. Ah well." His eyes snapped open, and he was viciously alert. "Business before pleasure." He kicked at Rose's body and it rolled limply in the water. It floated slowly, sadly toward the rim of the pool.

Rose's body floated facedown in the swirling water, pink buttocks bobbing gently as the foam swirled away around her. Killinger took a pole from the wall. He was moving stiffly, as if the ultrasound knives and electronic-pulse cauterizers and tissue growth accelerators had not yet returned him to the one hundred percent mark. He extended a wire loop from the end, and slipped it around Rose's head, drawing her to the edge of the pool.

"It's almost time for your report, isn't it?" Killinger grinned at him. "What would DeLacourte say if he knew about you?"

"He won't know. He is a good man. A holy man, whose cause is just." McMartin shrugged. "If my reasons aren't the same as his, well, that's too bad." McMartin waved his arms and legs, propelling himself to the edge of the pool. He paddled over to the side of the pool and smiled up at Killinger.

"Never," McMartin said. He smiled, showing short, pearl-white rows of teeth. "Never suggest such a thing again. Never let me know that such a thought has crossed your mind."

Killinger started to speak, and then caught himself. The smile was not the smile of a man, it was the smile of a rabid animal whose lips curled up at the moment before attack. His neck rippled with tension. Killinger had wandered very close to a line, and his task now was to keep from teetering off.

"I . . . didn't mean anything by that."

McMartin reached up, took Killinger's hand with a hand softer than a baby's. "I'm sure you didn't, my dear." McMartin sighed vastly, and paddled back. "But you must purge such thoughts. I am vulnerable to sins of the flesh. And such a nice lot of flesh, don't you think?"

He laughed tonelessly and dove under the surface of the water like a bloated otter.

Killinger wiped the slime from his hand. He was trembling, and hated himself for it. Suddenly Killinger wanted nothing more than to get the hell out. Teasing McMartin made about as much sense as getting a blowjob from a rattlesnake.

McMartin surfaced, streaming water from mouth and nose. "I am but a simple servant. Flawed, human. In need of salvation. A man like DeLacourte needs his flawed human vessels, don't you think?"

"Yeah. Sure. I guess." *Get me out of here.*

"Good. Now get this shit out of here. Now."

McMartin watched Killinger haul Rose's body from the

room, and smiled in satisfaction. Fear worked quite well in controlling the lower types, yes it did.

Now, then. It was necessary to gather his thoughts. It occurred to him, almost belatedly, that it was fear that controlled him as well.

Perhaps, to a man like DeLacourte, even he, McMartin, was one of the lower types. Merely a creature of base flesh. McMartin looked at his vast, pink body bobbling in the glycerin, and smiled with satisfaction. He nudged his floating tray over nearer to him, and poured himself a giant shot of tequila. Before he tossed it back, he licked a bit of the salty fungus from his shoulder.

He giggled as the tequila burned its way down.

Flesh, yes.

But such a *nice* lot of flesh . . .

CHAPTER SEVEN

The Gray Man

Monday, May 22

The black limousine broke away from the black glass spires lining the Madison Avenue Compway and turned onto Sixth Street. From here, the beacons would bring it into the garage. Jack Hands didn't really need to think about the process at all, could allow his mind to drift. At the moment, his thoughts were concentrated on the man in the back seat of the car he drove. The man who just might be the next President of the United States.

Jack Hands had known this man for ten years. Had driven and served him as personal secretary all over America and Europe. He wondered whether there was any force on Earth sufficient to prevent that dream from becoming reality.

The power wielded here, on Madison Avenue, was different from Washington, but Jack Hands had never become inured to it.

Here, in a twenty- by four-block area, all the communications in America were gathered into the single most complicated switchboard in the world. All five national broadcasting networks operated from here, the major sensie lines stretched out across the country with their direct-induction overloads. The major magazines of the country had their executive offices here. The estimated two million people who created, processed, conducted, built, manipulated, interpreted, destroyed, and controlled the minds and media of the country. Their names and faces were rarely known to the public, but more than any elected officials, they actually helmed the good ship America.

He looked into the rear seat, through the tiny sliver of partitioned glass unobscured by curtains. Sterling DeLacourte was, as usual, talking to the flat telescreen in the back seat. Talking, arranging, dealing with. Most people, even his business associates, dealt with DeLacourte only through holo. Hands felt a special cachet in knowing the Prophet in the flesh. So to speak.

DeLacourte. *Time* magazine had cynically echoed his followers, calling him ''America's Ambassador to the Lord.'' That was OK by Hands. He figured it was OK by most of America, too.

He turned the limo into the drive, and slid down into the parking garage. The rumble of its ground-effect skirt died as the turbines slowed. The limo settled onto its hydraulics without a bump. Jack unsnapped his safety harness and stepped out.

Jack Hands took a metal rod from his pocket. He clicked a button at the base and swept it around as it telescoped into a half meter of antenna. The digital meter built into the handle didn't twitch: there was no electronic surveillance. Once within the offices of TriNet, they would be even more secure. This was DeLacourte's private world, more so than his thirty-room mansion in Connecticut. More than his five-bedroom suite in East Manhattan in the Perfumed Stockade. Even more than the yacht anchored four miles off the Florida Keys.

Jack pressed his wristwatch against the door handle, and it popped open.

Sterling DeLacourte was only an inch over six feet, but gave the impression of greater height. He was as slender as a whisper, but carried himself with the mass of a giant. Crowds parted for him like the Red Sea.

There might have been a hundred generations of holy crusaders in his blood. He had a long, immaculately tailored head of gray hair. His eyes were piercingly blue. His face was roughly hewn, a work of flat planes that caught the Omnivision receptors perfectly. He seemed a man of infinite strength. It was possible to draw any conclusion, sustain any impression one desired of DeLacourte. Sensuality, austerity, power, the kindly father, the stern disciplinarian, the unyielding apostle. Or the magnate, sole owner of the greatest independent satellite network in the world.

Sterling DeLacourte.

"Jack," DeLacourte said slowly, moving his head with that slightly mechanical movement he sometimes used when not before the cameras. "For the next few months, I would like you to use manual override when in the city. After that"—his even, white teeth gleamed—"we'll be on the Presidential Network. More carefully monitored."

"Than the Executive?"

"Yes." His eyes narrowed. "Yaounde. Two days ago. A Vice President of Union Carbide had his onboard overridden. Before the chauffeur regained control, the defenses had been invaded. He was kidnapped. They found the chauffeur's body this morning."

"Yes, sir, I've prepared an update for you."

"Good man." DeLacourte's eyes were focused elsewhere, his mind distracted. "We are heading into deeper waters, you know. We must be more careful. There are forces afoot . . . which would stop me. If they could."

"They can't."

"Perhaps not, but the people of this nation must make their choice in an environment untainted by emotional hysteria."

"I understand, sir."

"Very good." DeLacourte walked toward the waiting elevator. Jack watched him move. There was something in the man, something that gave Jack a feeling of peace.

Peace in these troubled times . . .

No small thing, that.

The elevator door slid shut behind them, and Hands waited for him to speak. "Jack," he said, "I want the subliminals on the broadcast used more effectively, especially the subsonics. Blend them with the organ music."

Hands blinked, switching modes from driver to executive officer. To his knowledge, his relationship to DeLacourte was virtually unique outside of the military. "Yes, sir."

"These are troubled times. Indecency, immorality, and

homosexuality swamp our nation. To think that weakling Harris actually uses this filth in illegal operations abroad.'' He paused. "What is the status of the Yaounde kidnapping?"

"There's been no official statement . . ."

"But?" The question hung in the air between them like a bloody sun at dusk.

"Unofficially, Gorgon has already been deployed. Premier Swarna has disclaimed all connection with the kidnappers, but any intrusion into the PanAfrican Republic is still skirting an act of war."

DeLacourte grimaced. "An abomination. To think that America forces other nations to submit to this shame. That the safety of our citizens should rest in the hands of these . . . perverts." For a moment the executive overrode the Prophet. "Who is our man on assignment?"

"Marina Batiste. She's good. She did our six-part series on the NewMen last year. She's actually gotten Gorgon to cooperate with her."

"Amazing. I thought they hated women." He stopped for a moment, thinking. "I want to change the sermon for the day. Take a note, Jack."

Hands triggered the solid-state recorder built into the collar of his coat. In one sense, the recorder was unnecessary: he invariably remembered everything he said, heard, or saw from the moment he awoke in the morning until he fell asleep at night.

"Remind them that Satan often creates crises, so that his tools may insinuate themselves into our trust. For Gorgon to dispose of an evil proves nothing, for they themselves are a greater, more insidious evil. If Harris cannot see that this is sapping the moral fiber of our country . . . et cetera. Download that to secretarial, have them send me a draft by two o'clock."

"Yes, sir."

The tube shushed to a stop, and DeLacourte stepped out into the offices of TriNet. They were designed as a series of concentric circles. The elevator opened near the very center, across the hall from the door with the sterling silver letters "S.D." on the door. Executive, junior executive, and secretarial offices emanated outward from the center like the spokes of a wheel.

The high chittering sound of conversation, the purr of a coffeebot making the caffeine rounds, and the mingled soundtracks of a dozen Omnivision broadcasts from a dozen different offices melted into a buzz. The buzz died completely as his employees absorbed the presence of the Gray Man.

There was a general chorus of "Hello, Mr. DeLacourte" and "Good morning, Mr. DeLacourte" as he turned right and strode the length of the hall. He answered every nod, every cheery greeting with the same, although Hands knew that DeLacourte's mind was miles away. That was an aspect of DeLacourte that Jack Hands respected highly: his mind was dual-track. He could think about one thing, and converse on another. Amend that: *multi*-track, like a human Omnivision. Hands was never entirely sure when or where his employer's mind wandered, into what strange reaches . . .

DeLacourte reached the end of the hall. The door slid back, revealing a conference room with a dozen chairs, all but three of them already occupied. The Gray Man nodded perfunctorily to the men and women seated, and took his place at the head of the table. .

Hands seated himself to DeLacourte's right, and waited. DeLacourte spent a moment looking through the day's agenda on the video plate built into the desk. This was, Hands knew, more to give the board a chance to adjust themselves to DeLacourte's presence than anything else. Strange: no matter how much time anyone spent around him, there was just . . . something about him. One never quite acclimated to Sterling DeLacourte. There was something unnerving about him physically.

For instance (and he was almost ashamed to admit that it bothered him), it was odd that DeLacourte looked *younger* in person than he did on the Omni. When had he first noticed that? Two years ago, perhaps, when DeLacourte ceased appearing in public? There were other disturbing things as well. Other reasons for his associates to feel uncomfortable around the Gray Man. He squelched the speculations instantly.

Jack Hands had opinions, but he kept them to himself. Sterling DeLacourte scared people because he knew them. *Knew* them—not just their habits and foibles, the things that an armada of private investigators and computer jockeys might unearth. He knew them as if he had made them. As if he had God's area code in his pocket dialer.

He shut that thought down. He would find nothing useful up that route.

"Gentlemen," DeLacourte began. "Advertising revenues are up one point four percent from last quarter. I recall a somewhat higher estimate. Can you explain this to me?"

Carter stood. Although an inch taller than DeLacourte, he seemed somehow much smaller. "The majors have shifted their schedules, sir. A direct response to our aggressive programming practices. In a way it's a compliment: all four of them are running scared. They know that they can't stop us. They've reached their point of inefficiency. We're still growing. As we get closer to the National Convention in two months, our viewership will polarize and then expand. We're winning, and they know it."

"Those don't look like winning numbers to me," DeLacourte said neutrally.

Carter cleared his throat almost apologetically. "The numbers don't tell everything. I would like to direct your attention to the semantic differential—" Carter dropped a clear plastic card into the arm slot of his chair, and punched in a priority code. A mountain range of spike graphs appeared, each segment labeled with the name of a different candidate. "The s.d. is the best research tool we have. We interviewed over a hundred thousand registered voters. We used paired phrases like 'weak-strong,' 'tense-relaxed,' 'decisive-ambivalent,' and had our subjects describe their ideal candidate on a scale of one to seven in each of these areas. From this information we plotted *this* line, representing the Ideal Presidential Candidate. We then asked them to evaluate each of the six front-running candidates."

"Including the incumbent?" DeLacourte asked.

"Of course. If they thought Roland Harris was very brave, for instance, they would give him a seven along the cowardice-bravery line." A ghost mountain range appeared, floating in front of the "real," multicolored ranges representing the other candidates.

"The gap between your line"—with a touch of his

finger, a blue range moved to the front of the floating exhibit—''and the Ideal line represents the personality traits you should try to improve. Note that, for you, the greatest gap is between 'aristocrat-common man.' This is a tricky call, because while the public wants the trappings of royalty, they resent a leader's life appearing too easy.''

Carter removed his wire frames. ''Frankly, sir, there is a public perception that you have experienced insufficient personal suffering in your climb to the top. Everything seems to have come too easily to you.''

A dry smile wormed its slow way onto DeLacourte's face. ''And what would you suggest, Mr. Carter? Prostate cancer, perhaps?''

Carter peered into his master's eyes, suddenly very uncomfortable. ''I—uh, I don't have the answers, sir. Our image consultants are ready to work on this area immediately. However, what I wanted you to notice is that with the exception of President Roland Harris, and Republican front-runner Sloan Hittleman, you have the most favorable profile. That's . . . that's all, sir.''

''Thank you, Mr. Carter. I will reserve judgment for another week. May I remind you all that we demographically dominate three states where revenues have actually *dropped*. This calls for a reexamination of our methods. I hope we are together on this.'' Carter nodded as if his collar were too tight, and sat down.

''Mr. Talbot.''

A short round man with a peeling sunburn stood. ''The ratings on the Los Angeles affair were good, but as you suggested, we kept coverage to a minimum.''

''An unfortunate necessity. Of course the other networks picked it up.''

''And the independents, and the hard services as well. They're having a field day with the Merc claim to act in your behalf.''

DeLacourte frowned. ''Yes . . . I want to slot an editorial. We need to be sure that the public sees that these people are not my puppets: I am merely in tune with the times. I abhor such regrettable acts, but more abhorrent is the fact that good and decent men would behave in such a manner. Even good men can resort to violence when inundated by . . ."

DeLacourte paused and flashed his teeth in a brief smile. "Am I understood?"

"Absolutely, sir."

"Now, then: we have three different profit projections. The central question seems to be one of original programming versus buying rerun material . . ."

Three-quarters of an hour later the other men filed out, leaving only DeLacourte and Jack Hands.

DeLacourte leaned back in his chair, folding his hands over his belt. "Satisfactory. There is too much to do, Jack, and so little time. Satan never tires in his efforts. He has so many hands, and it sometimes seems that the Lord has only these two." His smile brightened. "Now give me five minutes with my family, then we can pump in the feed from the West Coast."

"Yes, sir. Should I leave the room?"

"No, I'll shield you. I have no secrets."

Again he smiled, and Hands was overcome with a wave of affection.

The room darkened, and the table disappeared. Suddenly they were in the Rockies, in DeLacourte's retreat just outside Denver. It was remarkable how vivid the image was. He could almost smell the trees, the cool, gentle winds blowing down through the mountains.

He waited, an invisible man in the valley, as DeLacourte's wife and child appeared.

Where was the broadcast/projection apparatus? Obviously, here in New York it could be built into the walls themselves. Where was it in Colorado?

Gretchen DeLacourte carried herself with that lightness and confidence that seemed to come more from breeding than education. She was about five and a half feet tall, with auburn hair that the Colorado sunlight flamed into gold. At Gretchen DeLacourte's age, a woman's beauty is less a product of genes than experience and attitude. She had a simple strength and dignity that made his heart ache.

At Mrs. DeLacourte's age . . . Hands caught his thoughts wandering. There it was again, the uneasy sensation that his master was getting *younger*. When had that impression begun? For all of his extraordinary memory, Hands wasn't sure. Certainly no more than three years.

God had never seen fit to bless the DeLacourtes' thirty-year marriage with natural children, so at last they had adopted a fetus from Xenon Cryonurseries. Eight-year-old Conley was the prototype of every towheaded barefoot boy who ever ran laughing through tall, wet grass. He came with his mother now. In holding her hand, he seemed to steal some of the sobriety from her face.

Hands hung back, watching as DeLacourte and his family met. They came within inches of touching, but halted there, reluctant to spoil the illusion. Gretchen smiled warmly. "You look tired, Sterling."

"There is so much to do. The West Coast fiasco."

"Yes." Dark lines formed at the corners of her eyes. For Hands, Gretchen DeLacourte stirred all of the right urges: protectiveness, admiration, loyalty, a smattering of lust. With such a woman to stand beside him, how could DeLacourte lose? "What can be done about it?"

"I don't know. I don't disapprove of the intentions, just their methods. My message is a vital one, but the ones most desperate for my message are often guilty of imprudence. I want to stop the violence without losing the faithful." He smiled to her, their lips only inches apart. "Do you suppose that it has always been like this?"

"If you speak loudly enough for all to hear, some will be deafened. If your light shines brightly enough for all to see, some will be blinded." His fingers brushed the spectral golden strands of her hair. "I love you."

"I love you." He knelt, and stretched his arms out to Conley. The boy reached out, and their hands overlapped a little. Conley giggled and pulled back until their fingers just barely touched. "Father."

"Conley. Are you enjoying your stay?"

"It's OK, sir . . . but I wish that you were here. When do you think you'll be able to come out? Or when can we come out there?"

"Soon, Conley. Soon. I just wanted your mother to have a chance to get away from everything. Soon."

The boy fidgeted, then couldn't resist the urge anymore. He reached up to hug his father, oblivious to the fact that his arms sank into the hologram. The illusion of contact was enough. DeLacourte stood. He wiped at his face. "I miss the two of you so much. It's so hard sometimes." He turned to Gretchen. "Darling—as soon as you feel rested, please come back. I need you here. All of the preparations for the Democratic National Convention are draining me."

"I understand. We can be on the next shuttle out—"

"Another day, at least. Please. I need your strength. Store a little more of it up for me."

"All right."

The image faded, and for a time DeLacourte stood staring at the space where his wife and child had stood. He turned to Hands, tears streaking his cheeks. "That's what it's about," he said huskily. "My wife, my boy. If something isn't done, there won't be a world for Conley to grow up in. By God, I'm not going to let that happen."

Hands nodded quietly, and said nothing as the conference room reappeared.

DeLacourte dried his face. "Now," he said. "Get me McMartin."

DeLacourte sat back in his chair, waiting as the room rippled. Their chairs balanced impossibly on the surface of McMartin's pool. The grotesquely obese man reminded Jack Hands of nothing so much as a flesh-colored gelatin.

Or the most bloated walrus who ever lived.

Anything but an ordinary human being. That, McMartin didn't remind him of at all. That the world should be in such a state that a man like DeLacourte needed an abomination like McMartin . . .

"Yes, sir."

"Things got out of hand, didn't they? I want to know why."

"The Scavengers intervened."

"Scavengers? What the devil?"

"A group that expanded after the '24 quake. They have squatter's rights on a couple of square blocks of Old Downtown. Selling it back to the city now in exchange for employment benefits, other things. Their leader, an escaped convict named Aubry Knight, interceded."

McMartin bobbled around in the water a little, waving his hands to locomote.

"So the NewMen got away? I see. I suppose I should praise the Lord there wasn't more bloodshed."

"There will be if we get our hands on Knight. He seems to have vanished."

"I am only interested in the pervert filth."

"Sir—if you want the NewMen stamped out, we have to isolate them, make sure that anyone contemplating aid to them is aware of the consequences. The very grave consequences."

"Good, then. By God, you will follow the letter of the law. You offer quarter when possible. And if death is necessary—I expect them to be killed like men. Animals they may be, but we are men. There must be no confusion in the public mind, do you understand?"

"Yes, sir."

"One more thing—" Was it Hands's imagination, or did DeLacourte's voice waver? "The last special you sent was too short-term."

McMartin's eyes went sleepy. "The human body has certain . . . adaptive capabilities."

"You're being paid enough to compensate," DeLacourte said. There was an edge of tension in his voice.

"Yes . . . I can accommodate that. Certainly. Well, my friend, we will speak soon." McMartin's picture faded.

DeLacourte turned to Hands. "I . . . trust you, Jack. Where I go, there is room for those I trust. And only those. Remember that."

"Yes, sir."

"Leave me now."

Hands left the room. There was a speech to oversee, and business to attend to. But he couldn't help a final glance back at DeLacourte. His master sat at the table, staring off into space. Thinking perhaps of the presidency. Or of the thousand thousand concerns of his network. Or of a ragtag group of hoboes called Scavengers.

Or of something that would be delivered soon, something of greater durability than a previous shipment.

CHAPTER EIGHT

Rest Stop

Tuesday, May 23

The rainfall on the Canadian Compway left thick greasy streaks on their windscreen. Their windshield wipers flagged back and forth sluggishly, slushing aside distorting sheets of wet. Yellow highway lights curved like sickles over the road. As their car cruised north, it was alternately bathed in filtered amber light and plunged into deep shadow.

Aubry checked his charge meter, compared it to the beacon readout. The display wavered in the red, but wasn't solid yet: there was still a decent margin of safety.

He turned off the compway, switching back to manual for a few hundred yards before cruising into the driveway of a service station. The station was old, a prefabricated shell overhanging a series of nested boxes: office, garage, storage. Though the office windows were darkened, green light crawled up their beacon antenna.

"They have to be open," Aubry muttered, searching for signs of life. "Can't broadcast if you're not open . . ." Still, he sounded doubtful. The only visible light was in the service bay.

As he cruised to a halt, the turbines automatically slowed. The car settled to the ground with barely a shush. The coiled bumpers absorbed most of the shock, but Promise woke anyway. Her thin, heat-reflective cocoon of blankets crackled as she stirred.

"Baby . . . where are we?"

Aubry drew his coat tighter as the rain died to a thin

mist. The silence was almost alarming. Without the purr of the engine, or the slow beat of the windshield wipers, there was no sound at all. How many times had he experienced silence? In every remembered moment of his life there had always been a background hum of some kind.

The clouds parted, and the moon showed as a dim, shallow crescent low on the horizon, hidden by clusters of pine. The pale glow of the service station was the only available light.

"We're near Lake Shasta. About a hundred miles south of Oregon. I figured we'd camp here tonight, and go on in the morning."

Promise yawned sleepily. She rubbed at her eyes and pulled herself out of the car. "Is this place deserted . . . ?"

The office door creaked open, and a man appeared. He was in his fifties, and time rested a heavy hand on his shoulders. His body was shaped like a sweet potato, and there wasn't enough straggly gray hair on his head to cover the bald spot. The potato analogy extended to his facial features. His nose was bulbous and peeling, disproportionately larger than the rest of his face. But he seemed clean, and friendly, with a ready smile. His arms were outstretched.

"Evenin', folks." He peered at their vehicle. "Whee, now—you got a bit of an antique there, don't you?"

" '04. One of the first floaters," Promise said proudly. "Costs to maintain it, but I say you don't throw something away if it's been good to you. My family's gotten a lot of service from this one."

The man bent to peer at the car. Aubry saw the name Courtney emblazoned on a label above his right shirt pocket. A thin gold chain dangled a tiny mushroom. Aubry quickly repressed his nervous grin. When Courtney saw that it had caught Aubry's eye, he folded his collar over it. "Well— you'd use an alpha cell in that, right? Got just the thing."

"That's what the beacon said."

"Good things. Be out of business without them."

Promise and Aubry walked with him as he moved back into the dark cavity of his service port. It was filled with tanks, boxes, and twisted hoses that sprouted from the walls and the ground in endless profusion. Courtney pointed them out, naming each energy source almost absently. "Gas, Gasohol, Elpegee, meth, alpha-omega energy cells. Solar chargers, So many damn models on the market, hard to find your poison. You came to the right place."

He trundled a cart over to the stack of energy cells, each cached in its own dust-free niche. Aubry was mildly surprised. He expected to see dirt. Instead, the garage was a tidily kept workspace bristling with tools and the instruments of a mechanic's craft.

"Shasta Lake far from here?"

"Nope—about sixteen miles up Westly here," the old man said, pointing. He counted down a stack of batteries and sighed with pleasure. "Here's what you need." He pulled out a box about the size of a human torso from its stack, and clicked it into the cart. "What brings you folks up this way?" He cocked his head sideways. "Not visiting relatives are you? Had some folks through a little earlier, on their way to Hoopa."

Aubry's ears perked up. "Hoopa? The Spider camp?"

"Used to be an Indian reservation till the Feds sold it off. It's west, off the 299. Yeah, most of the Spiders in the western U.S. are out there. Hear it's hell. They say if the wind blows the wrong way, you can smell it in Eureka." He grinned through stumpy brown teeth. "Probably bullshit."

The cart hummed as he guided it over to their car. "Spiders, not more'n a hundred miles from here. Thousands of 'em."

"And what do you think about that?" Aubry voiced his query cautiously.

The old man took his time in answering, and for a while Aubry thought he wasn't going to answer at all. "You know, sometimes I listen to DeLacourte on the holo and I think the man is just another Bible-thumper. Other times . . . I dunno." He undid the catch, and unscrewed the latch on the energy cell. "Pop that on the inside, will you?"

"Sorry." Aubry undid the cell catch on the dashboard.

"Then, you know, I look at what's happened to our country. Not just California. Not just the quake. Hell, we healed from that. That wasn't the worst. We don't believe in what we used to believe. And I'm not sure we believe in the future. And we don't like where we are. Hell of a thing, ain't it? Ah.'' He pulled the old cell straight out into the replacement cart, pivoted the cart and aligned it. With a click, he hooked the other cell into the track. At the touch of a button, it began to ease itself in.

''Courtney?'' The voice came from over by the door. Aubry turned, and hissed under his breath at the woman coming across the lot. Rain was falling in a light mist now, and she seemed like something from a holo ad promoting euphorics. She wore a shawl over her head, so Aubry couldn't tell the color of her hair, but her face was a calm melding of gentle ovals. She looked at him, and he sensed that the peace he saw there was a new thing, something which had eluded her for years.

She embraced Courtney, and whispered something in his ear. Aubry thought she nibbled it as well. Then she laughed in a surprisingly low voice. ''We weren't expecting any more business tonight.''

''Ah . . . I can understand that.''

''Think you'll be staying long?'' She rubbed against Courtney like a kitten begging for a saucer of milk.

''Just a few more minutes,'' Promise assured her, then sidled up to Aubry, and whispered ''mushroom.'' For a moment the folds of fabric protecting the young woman from the mist parted, and Aubry saw the chain with the mushroom emblem.

Courtney kissed her, and she smiled shyly to Aubry and Promise, then returned to the station. Courtney cleared his throat and grinned crookedly. ''Sylvie and I live out here by ourselves. Not much happening. Don't see a lot of people. I like it like that. The cities aren't much to crow about.''

Aubry nodded agreement.

''Where you folks from?''

''Los Angeles.''

''Yeah. Big mess down there. You hear about it?''

''Lots of messes. Which one are you interested in?''

''Some big NewMan group shot it out with the police. Some con helped them escape, and they're after him.'' The old man averted his face, turning to touch fire to his pipe. "His picture's been all over the Omnivision. Reward, and everything." He shook the match and dropped it to the ground, where it died with a hiss. "Hell, I don't have nothin' against faggots if they keep their hands to themselves. But between them, and the Spiders, and everything else, maybe DeLacourte makes sense. . . ."

He clicked the battery into place, and gazed out over the trees. There was a distant glow on the western horizon. A city over there, somewhere. "And maybe he don't. Not everything new is bad. Maybe the Bible is the answer. Dunno. Mebbe it's just the question." He chuckled to himself and unconsciously stroked his pendant as he shuffled over to his register. "How you paying for this?"

"Good trade Marks."

The old man nodded. "Sounds right to this one, I'll tell you." The computer ran a series of numbers, giving a market quote. "Be twenty-seven on the trade. Make it twenty."

"Wha—?"

"Oh, I got a lot to be happy for. Them mushrooms is one of 'em. Ain't got no kids, so I don't know about that part of it. Don't suppose I'll ever get to meet the people made it possible for Sylvie and me . . ." Courtney grinned again, and he looked wistfully at the cozy office; the darkened windows seemed to beckon him. "But I do what I can to pass on the favor. Say. You folks ever meet up with this Aubry Knight, you thank him for me."

Aubry gave him a thirty note, and the old man ran it through his machine. It checked the serial number and encoded trade history, found it to be valid. It tagged the date and location, and gave him the okay.

"Good enough." The old man turned to them as they went back to the car. "You know, these roads don't get traveled much. I'd think that a man traveling on 'em, staying to his own business, could have quite a bit of trouble pass right over him without making a squeak."

"Sounds like the kind we want."

"Figured as much. You look like nice folks. You drive real safe, now, hear?"

Aubry started the engine, felt the whine of power as the

ground-effect shield lifted them up. In his rearview, he could see the old man squint after them for a minute, then turn, and with a surprisingly vigorous step return to the station.

Aubry scratched his beard nervously. "Think he'll talk?"

"Sweetheart, you must be blind, deaf, and dumb."

They drove up Westly Road for a time. Aubry finally pulled off at a sign which declared Shasta Lake only a mile distant. There were no lights, and the road was unpaved. They pulled off and hummed beneath a stand of trees.

The seats reclined. Aubry pushed himself back into them, and sighed. He just wanted to close his eyes for a while, to rest, and abandon his worry.

"I could drive," Promise said softly.

"And you will, tomorrow. But right now I just . . ." He searched his mind. *You can tell the truth to her. If not Promise, who?*

Promise leaned her head against his shoulder. "You're going to have to learn to trust. My family is very close."

"Tell me more about them?"

"They are good women." She kissed his ear and cuddled in close. "They log, and they farm, and they live simple lives. They love the earth, and the sky, and the miracle of birth." Promise's hand was tight on his arm, and her voice was sad. "That was all most of us cared about, once upon a time. Things got kind of complicated. Worshipping the Goddess, the Earth Mother, became 'witchcraft.' "

"Wasn't it?"

"Define your terms. Most of the great pagan festivals are still with us today—disguised as 'Christian' holidays."

"Bullshit."

"Truth. Yule is called Christmas, Ostara is Easter, Harvest Home is Thanksgiving. My mothers gathered the remnants of as many women's mysteries as they could find: dance, ritual, poetry, whatever they could find. They wove them together. It was . . . simple, and direct, and beautiful. I could have stayed, but didn't. I'm glad, because I wouldn't have met you."

He tousled her hair with thick fingers.

"They'll like you—"

"I thought you said that they don't like men?"

"You're not men. You're my Aubry." She giggled, and burrowed closer. "They choose to live without them. There's a difference. And they're just one of the communes. There are six, and some of them have male participants. Fathers, husbands . . ."

"Slaves."

She laughed ruefully. "No, not really. There are men who want to be dominated by women, and some of them have useful skills. If they want to come and work in the communes and are admitted, then . . ." She shrugged. "But they're not sought out, and rarely encouraged. The communes aren't about dominance."

"I'll have to see for myself. I've never seen anything other than dominance. We'll see."

They held each other for a time, and he heard her whisper, "God. It's been so long."

"Since you left?"

"I disgraced them so . . . I just hope." She was silent for a time, and Aubry was content just to hold her. "We'll find a place," Promise said finally. "Somewhere. I can't believe that we could love each other like this, unless there was a way to be together."

The night was cold outside. Inside the car, locked in each other's arms, there was warmth. Aubry watched the trees swaying gently in the wind. "I don't think anyone is following us. I hope not." He thought of the automatic shotgun cached beneath the rear seat. "I . . . don't want to fight if I don't have to."

"You don't. Not anymore."

She pulled his head down on her shoulder, and together, they waited for dawn.

CHAPTER NINE

Ephesus

Wednesday, May 24

Aubry felt utterly vulnerable.

The road was too open. As far as he could see there wasn't a single microwave tower, house, or so much as a lettered sign. All about him was a rolling, flowing, enveloping emerald tangle. Flowers exploded in all colors but shaded toward blue and yellow. It made his head feel light and hollow.

The very air smelled different. Without walls or sharp angles his sense of perspective lurched out of synch. Shadows were black caverns leading to nameless mysteries. The wind-whipped branches seemed phantasmal arms. They beckoned to him, whispered mockingly, laughed at his insecurity. Something deep and central to his being raced out of control.

With the floater's plastic hood down, the wind ruffled Promise's hair into a dark, fluffy mass. She pushed herself back into the seat and sniffed deeply. Her smile deepened with every passing mile.

"My home," she whispered.

"What?"

A row of bright orange flowers flashed by, leaned out over the road as if trying to touch him. Promise stretched out a hand, and the blossoms were just inches out of reach. "This is my home, and I've been away too long."

They were still traveling back roads, had avoided San Francisco and Eugene, heading northwest into Tillamook County.

"In my entire life, I've never seen so much green."

"Douglas fir," Promise murmured, pointing lazily at one of the passing giants. Her gaze skipped from tree to tree. "Cedar, hemlock, spruce . . ."

"How come you know so damn much?"

"I was *raised* here." She laughed. "God, it's like crawling back into the womb."

"I've felt like that before. Usually just before you get a headache."

"Liar."

"True." Aubry swerved the car hard. A brown- and white-dappled shape burst from the roadside, freezing suddenly in the center of the road. "Damn!" He spun the wheel, barely managing to avoid a tree as he skidded onto the shoulder.

"What in the hell was—"

Promise laughed delightedly. "A deer, dear. You know, an animal." It twitched its tail for an instant, then disappeared into the thick brush on the far side.

Aubry's grip on the wheel was fierce. "I know what animals are."

Promise leaned her head against his arm. "My proud city brat. You know as much about wildlife as I did about 'tube scheds when I first went to Vegas."

He was still watching the forest, peering after the whitetail as it disappeared into the brush. The forest healed up after it, leaving no trace of its passage. "Is it going to rain chipmunks next, or what?"

"Used to. If things haven't changed in ten years, you might have to look out for Bambi's friends, yes."

"Just wonderful." Aubry grimaced and lifted the car from the ditch, spitting chips of gravel into the air as he headed back up the road.

Oregon's northwest region flooded his senses with unfamiliar sights and sounds. His head buzzed painfully, hovering near sensory overload. The low morning sun blazed against banks of fluffy, towering cumulonimbus. The wall of trees hammered its light into thin, twisted shadows.

Aubry reached out, finding warmth and comfort in Promise's hand.

Fifty meters around a bend, a wire fence blocked the road. A painted square of sheet metal above it read simply: "Ephesus. Private land. You may pass no farther without permission or appointment. Please use the callbox."

Promise hopped out of the car, stretching like a big brown cat. She growled and grinned to herself. "We're here."

He loved to watch her move, especially when she was working the kinks out of her dancer's body. She got kinks in the most interesting places.

Aubry forced his mind to quiet, opened his senses. To the north, river sounds filtered gently through the trees. There were other, smaller, animal sounds around them. Somewhere in the distance, a piece of heavy equipment thrummed against the ground.

"What does 'Ephesus' mean?"

"It was a city in Anatolia where the two major tribes of Amazons met. One from Lydia, the other from Asia Minor. They worshipped at the temple of the Goddess Artemis." Promise ran her hands along the gate, humming to herself. "The gate wasn't here when I left," she said quietly. "It might as well have been. It feels right. The nails were hammered in. This wire was twisted by hand."

"That some kind of virtue up here?"

She made a face at him. "The Sisterhood believes that we have forgotten a lot of the simple virtues. The simple pleasures."

"Like men?"

"Can't get any simpler than them, yes. Be polite. They have no obligation to take me back, you know."

There was a voicebox attached high in the corner of the fence, an ancient telephone system with a punch dial. Promise lifted it.

She spoke with quiet reverence, exuding a strength that was unlike anything Aubry had seen in her before. She drew herself up until she had the very last hair of her five nine, and spoke.

"Greetings. Promise, egg mother Freleng brood six. I request entrance for myself and a guest."

For several seconds there was no reply. Then an answer

crackled back over the speaker, more clearly than he would have expected given the primitiveness of the surroundings. "Our records show that daughter Promise, sixth brood Lord Mother Ariane—"

Promise's eyebrows raised, and she hissed something under her breath that Aubry couldn't hear.

"—has been dead for ten years. Entrance denied." The line clicked off with a dull buzz.

Promise stood, and her mouth went slack. With a shaking hand, she replaced the receiver on the hook.

"No," she whispered. The wind stirred the fringes of her hair, and her emotional control slipped. Her hair flared red, some of its glory stolen by the bright, cool sunlight. "They can't."

"Can't what?"

She turned to him, panic-stricken. "When I left, when I ran away, my mother pronounced me dead. I have no right of sanctuary."

Aubry slammed his hand against the gate. "Damn! What is this? Are they worried you might contaminate them, or what?"

All of the life and joy suddenly drained out of her face. Promise folded, sitting heavily in the middle of the road. "I knew that it hurt her, but I . . ."

She looked up at him. "I'm not sure anymore, Aubry. If they declared me dead . . ."

"Just for leaving? I don't get it. Most parents are *glad* when their brats leave."

"Be quiet. Please. Just let me think."

"Think, my butt." Aubry pulled his toolbox from the back of the car and extracted a thick-handled, scissorlike device. The chain sealing the gate was half-inch tempered steel, but no match for the jaws of the Scavenger bolt cutters.

"You can't do that," Promise said miserably, but there was no real warning in her voice, only a meld of fear and hope.

"It's harder to say 'no' when you're staring in someone's eyes."

Promise stretched out a hand, and Aubry pulled her

lightly from the ground. "That may not be the best idea you've ever had."

Aubry swung the gate open and back, and scanned the road. "No alarm, nothing. Let's go."

They climbed back into the hovercar. Aubry gave Promise one hard glance, then lifted the car from the ground and continued on.

The road beyond the gate was narrower, hemmed in on all sides by the magnificent rise of trees and vines, the riot of color. The young sun played peek-a-boo behind them, and Aubry tensed.

The road made a lazy L-turn ahead. As Aubry cleared it, he saw a red, rubber-tired truck slewed sideways across the road. His tensed muscles barely responded in time. To either side was a steep ditch. There was no way to go around it.

Aubry's nerve endings itched. "Ambush," he muttered. "What now?"

"Prayer might be appropriate." Promise pushed herself from the car, and out onto the road. "Hello?"

She called it hopefully, and raised her hands into the air. "Promise. Egg mother Ariane brood six. Regardless of what the computer says, I am alive. I request sanctuary."

There was a long pause, and then three women appeared from the woods to either side. Two of them carried rifles at port arms.

The third caught Aubry's attention. Her dark red hair was as short as a boy's. She carried no weapon in her hands, and yet radiated a kind of assurance that Aubry recognized instantly. Her feet moved in hypnotically fluid flat-footed shuffles.

Despite the situation, Aubry smiled.

"Let me do the talking," Promise whispered.

"You were denied entrance," the redhead said tersely. "You are now ordered to leave. This is private land."

The unarmed woman faced Promise. Aubry was startled by their similarities. Her skin was much paler than Promise's light chocolate, but they were the same height, and had a similar Eurasian cast to the eyes. The basic bone structure was almost identical, although there was more fat padding on Promise's body.

"Jenna . . . ?" Promise said uncertainly. She stared into the redhead's face, searching, recognizing. The woman's face didn't flicker.

"You will leave. You have sixty seconds, after which time we will eject you physically."

"Jenna . . ." It was a whisper this time. "You're brood seven. I'm brood six. The rules couldn't have changed so much. I'm your elder sister. I need sanctuary. I am a woman of the People. I was born here, and I have returned. When I left I took nothing of value. I violated no structure. Whatever has changed since I left, *I did no wrong*." Promise's voice was haggard, reminding Aubry of another, more desperate, woman he had known three years before. "Turning me away is the same as condemning me to death. Are you willing to take that responsibility? Because if you are, what is the difference between you and them?"

Jenna's eyes moved from Promise to Aubry and back again. "And this. This is yours?"

"Yes."

"Even if we extended it to you, we would owe no man sanctuary." She turned to Aubry again. "He's a big one. True. But we have enough strong backs."

Promise gripped Aubry's arm. "I love him. We love each other." Jenna's face remained impassive. Promise's voice became desperate. "He was the father of my child."

At last, a flicker of interest lit that face. "Was?"

"The child died in my womb."

"Weak seed," Jenna sniffed.

Aubry tensed, anger beginning to boil, an anger swiftly squelched by thousands of hours of disciplined practice.

Promise displayed no change of emotion. "It was the result of a bullet wound. He was fighting for my life."

For the first time, Jenna spoke directly to Aubry. "You are a fighter?"

"The best you've ever seen," Aubry said simply. For the first time, the corners of Jenna's mouth curled up in a smile. A speculative smile, he noted.

"If you are a lost daughter, what gifts do you bring?"

Promise scurried back to the hovercar, pulled two boxes

from the back. "I have gifts for the Matriarch. We bring skills. I have learned the dances of the outer world, and can teach. We can offer favorable trade with the Scavengers."

"The Scavengers? What is your connection with them?"

Promise touched Aubry's shoulder. "He is Warrick."

Jenna's smile broadened. "More interesting all the time. Well, brood sister. I'm going to give you an opportunity to present your own case. You will ride in the truck. I will sit with Warrick."

Jenna raised her arm, and two more women emerged from the trees. Aubry cursed himself. He hadn't seen them, hadn't even suspected that they might be there. The forest was disorienting.

Aubry shrugged, and climbed into the passenger side.

Promise looked at him once, skittishly, then followed the other women into the red truck.

Jenna flowed into the seat next to him.

Aubry switched on the turbines, lifting it from the ground.

"Just hover? Does it float?"

"Old model," Aubry said.

"Should have known." The truck ahead of them began to move.

"Warrick," Jenna repeated. "Or Aubry Knight."

"You've heard of me?"

"The way your name has been up and down the coast? Don't kid yourself. No decent pictures, though. They didn't get the beard." She gave a tight little laugh. "You really put a bug in DeLacourte's basket. That wins you a few points right there."

The truck ahead of them began to accelerate. Jenna waited until they hit a wider part of the road, and then said, "Go ahead and pass them." Aubry wove expertly, pacing and then passing.

"They say you're very dangerous, Knight—armed or unarmed. What form did you study?"

"Nullboxing. Streetfighting."

"Nonclassical, then."

Aubry watched her from the corner of his eye. There was strength in her. Her body fat content was low: her breasts were small, the muscles of her neck wiry. Her fingers lay quietly in her lap. They were long and square-tipped, and had weapon-nature. There was no callus on the palms or abrasion of the knuckles. No thickened skin along the side of the hands. A slight bruise above her eyebrow. She sat erect but relaxed in her seat, as if suspended by a string from above.

"Aikido?" he asked. "At least three-dan. And you studied some form of boxing. Pa-kua?"

"Hsing-i," she said happily. "You're good. Fourth-dan Aikido. Mistress of Durga."

"Durga?" He searched his memory, and could find nothing that matched the word, not a flicker of an image. "I've never heard of it."

"Don't worry. You wouldn't have. If you're allowed to stay, though . . ."

"I'd like that," he said, curiosity piqued.

"I'm here with you for a reason," she said finally. "I don't know why Promise ran away. I don't know why she returned. I don't know why the Matriarch declared her dead. My duty is to protect the Sisterhood, and I'm stretching my authority to bring you in."

"I could say 'thank you,' but I get the feeling that's not what you're looking for."

"You can screw it up for the both of you," Jenna said bluntly. "Make a right here." She pointed her thumb down a small road.

Aubry made the turn sharply, pleased with the way the vintage car handled the unpaved road. "Screw things up. All right. How?"

Jenna's eyes flashed, and for a moment she was nothing like the slight, pleasant woman who sat on the seat an instant before. "You're not welcome here. Don't forget that. Now. Ever. If you are allowed to stay, it will be purely for Promise's sake. If she is allowed to stay it will be purely an act of charity."

"What did she do that was so bad? She just wanted to peek around outside. What's everyone so scared of?"

Jenna was quiet as they bumped along. Now they began to pass more people, all of them women. They were engaged in light work along the roads, planting seedlings, chopping back brush. They all looked sturdy and strong, if tending toward a rather unappealing beefiness.

"This may be difficult for you to understand," Jenna said quietly, "but I'll try to explain it, since your lives may depend upon it. This commune is almost fifty years old. Suzette Freleng, who founded it, was a clinical psychiatrist who conducted a women's consciousness-raising group that dealt with rape and physical abuse. She created this retreat, away from men, away from any connection to a male-dominated world. The retreat became more popular than she had ever anticipated. Soon it was world renowned, and other women bought up the adjoining land. Farming and especially logging were initiated, and by 1985 the commune was self-sufficient."

"So they hid themselves away. They wouldn't be the first, I guess. What has that got to do with me?"

Jenna's smile was more strained. "If you're going to understand, you'll have to listen. You have no idea what it is to live in a society . . ." She paused, examined his profile again. "No, maybe you do," she said quietly. "There may not be much difference between being a woman and being black. The power is in the hands of white males."

"I know some pretty powerless white males, but go ahead anyway."

"Women came, and continued to come. Almost all were feminists. Lesbianism is the ultimate expression of a feminist philosophy, so that was the dominant form of relationship. By the 1990s we had achieved a kind of notoriety, and more money poured in—it was seen as a model, nonmale society."

"Wasn't that about the time the pseudobaby thing happened?"

She laughed bitterly. "Pseudobabies. A baby is a baby. Artificial insemination didn't produce 'pseudobabies.' Nobody even coined the term until enough women were doing it alone, without husbands or boyfriends, to threaten a few precious egos."

"And the artificial wombs. That's a big chunk of the public's problem with the NewMan Nation."

"It's all nonsense. Ariane Cotonou's ACT—the Alternative Conception Technologies—changed everything. Artificial insemination had been possible and practical for a long time. Induced parthenogenesis, egg fusion, and by the 'teens, the beginning of a practical cloning technology. Dr. Cotonou refined the cryogenics, made a large-scale approach more practical. The commune gave women the freedom, and ACT gave them the choice. For the first time in human history, men and women are in total control of their own sex organs. What's so wrong with that?"

"How many women do you have here?"

"There are fifty thousand women in the various communes."

"All lesbian?"

"About two-thirds. The rest, avowed feminists. There are about a thousand men."

"Then what's the problem with me?"

She looked at him objectively. "You're not a submissive."

"Damned right."

"But . . . somehow I don't think you dominate Promise either."

"Why would I want to?"

"No sane man would. That doesn't seem to stop many of you. My point is that we get about a thousand 'immigrants' a year—rape victims, or victims of brutal relationships. They come here to get away from the system that allows . . . *encourages* these kind of actions. The men here are submissives, most of them believing in female dominance. Why do I have the feeling you aren't into shackles and silk?"

Aubry snorted.

"You're likely to be intimidating to some of them. If they get upset enough, there could be trouble."

"You're not intimidated by me, are you." It was more a statement than a question.

"I'm not intimidated by anybody."

Aubry relaxed. "You know something, Jenna, I really hope we're going to be friends." She indicated a right turn and he took it smoothly. "Just how good are you?"

"It's not how good I am. It's how good Durga is."

"How good is it?"

"You can't take me. I guarantee it."

Aubry hunched over the wheel, grinning. "I can hardly wait."

As they came closer to the center of the camp, there were more dwellings. They were wooden, and looked sturdy, lovingly crafted, and handmade. It suddenly hit Aubry that he had seen no machines.

"It's a chance to start over," Jenna explained simply. "Like I said, a lot of these women had been brutalized by the outside world. They had accepted the roles given them by men, and only rejected it when it became threatening to their lives or spirits. Working with nature, living with nature, helps them get back to their original selves."

"I . . . don't know much about that."

"What *do* you know about, Aubry Knight?"

Some of the women stopped their work and gazed curiously at the car as it passed. If they saw Aubry first, their faces tensed until they saw Jenna. If they saw Jenna first, their attitude toward Aubry was very nearly one of contempt.

The women filled a full spectrum of physical types, except that none seemed cosmetically beautiful. There were strong, healthy bodies and good strong features. Bronzed limbs glistened in the morning light as they hefted and carried. Voices lifted in song and laughter as women helped each other, pausing in their labors for a moment to watch the car cruise past.

Once again, Aubry was the outsider, unneeded and unwanted here.

There, for a moment, he saw a man's face. A man and a woman struggled together to lift a piece of furniture. It looked handmade, and newly painted or stained. The man was stripped to the waist, sweating, his belly protruding over his belt by inches. His heavy dark beard was smeared with dust. The woman on the other end of the couch was also heavy, but moved more lightly and freely. She was easily stronger than the man.

They pulled into an oval arrangement of buildings. This appeared to be the center of the camp. Here there were more vehicles parked and more citizens in evidence.

"First left," Jenna said, directing him to turn between two large buildings, one of which was still half-bare wooden arches.

The dormitories didn't intrude, didn't impose themselves on their surroundings. They fit in, the trees and the flower beds an organic part of the entire rather than something stuck in like cloves in a ham.

It was pleasing, soothing, and Aubry felt his relaxation deepen. No. Wait . . . this was no time to relax. He was not among friends. To relax now could well be fatal.

Jenna pointed, and Aubry brought the hovercar in to a landing in front of a very plain, rectangular wooden building. There were places for cars here, though, and charging posts. He nosed the vehicle up to the post, and engaged it, happy to see the LCD flicker as the charge began to run.

If they had to leave, at least they would be able to go on a full charge. That meant something.

The windows of the building were stained-glass madonnas, the same basic theme reproduced in a dozen races and cultural milieus.

A group of laughing, joyously dusty children darted by, playing some swarming variation of tag. One of them, a freckled blond about six years old, stuck out his (her? It was difficult to tell. There was no obvious gender identification.) tongue at Jenna, and then dashed away giggling.

Aubry stepped out of the car, waiting as the truck pulled up sideways. Promise exited stiffly.

Jenna placed her hand on Promise's shoulder, and for a moment the two women formed mirror-images of each other.

Jenna was the wirier of the two, built almost like a bodybuilder. She probably outweighed Promise by twenty pounds.

One obvious conclusion was that Promise and Jenna shared the same basic bone structure. The difference: Promise had built her body for appearance. Jenna, for function.
Function.

That was one of the things had had niggled at him since first entering the camp. Very little of what he saw seemed to be there for raw appearance. There was no makeup worn by any of the women, their clothing was strictly functional.

In a way it was surprising, but then again in that aspect they resembled Scavengers. Although he was used to the Scavenger women, some small part of him, rather petulantly perhaps, wished that these women could have been a bit more, well, *decorative*.

He gave a mental shrug and embraced Promise.

She seemed dazed, disoriented.

"It hasn't changed," she said quietly. "New buildings on the perimeter. And three new camps to the north. But aside from that, I feel like a decade just dissolved."

Aubry felt the first bare bones of adjustment. Survival in the city meant growing solid, dense, armor-plated. But in order to thrive here he would have to expand, to encompass and interact with the natural forces around him.

At the moment, Promise seemed to be having more problem than he was. Her shoulders were hunched, her fingers knitted together tightly.

An overalled work party passed them, heartily singing a song whose lyrics he couldn't quite catch, although there was something in one of the verses about ". . . *they'll find a rapist slaughtered in the morning* . . ."

He heard them before they saw him, and when they did they quieted. One of them spat into the dust near his feet, and another turned away, eyes suddenly frozen with fear.

Jenna called to them, and they stopped. She walked over, and whispered a few words, her arms wrapped around their shoulders. They all laughed together, and the work party continued on its way.

"What did you say to them?" Aubry asked curiously.

"Oh, I just said that if you got out of line you'd be singing contralto. Nothing much."

"Nice lady."

"I get the job done. Two of those women were rape victims. One of them was mute with psychotic shock when she came here." Her eyes were suddenly very hard, and Aubry felt blistered by the intensity. "It's a hell of a world you made out there, mister."

"Me? I didn't make it."

"You're a part of it. You're a part of the process. If you're not part of the answer, you're part of the problem.

And for too many women here, the only answer is being totally away from anyone like you.''

Promise huddled closer to him, and they entered the low-ceilinged administration building.

The halls were decorated with paintings, most of them simple, delicately executed nature studies. Several were pictures of animals protecting or nursing their children. The tones tended to be earth tones, golds and browns and greens.

There were smaller offices along the hallway, each with a small clutch of women working, filing, operating a few computer stations. In a play area at a corner of the office, several small children wrestled, built a cathedral from magnetic blocks, or read.

The level of technology was very low. He noticed solar cell flags out the windows, and reckoned that little of the camp's power came in from the outside.

A door at the end of the hallway opened as they reached it, and a woman in a neat, dark suit greeted them. Her eyes flickered over Aubry quickly. As they did, her expression resembled that of a woman discovering a dead cat beneath her floorboards. She moved on to Promise.

The woman was apparently in her early forties, with an unlined and unpainted, somewhat severe face. "You are Promise?"

Promise nodded shyly.

"I am Dasha. We'll need to get your fingerprints. You've been declared dead for almost ten years.''

Promise nodded. Her fingers were inked, and transferred to clear plastic slides.

Aubry felt like he'd stepped into a time machine. Everything was so unbelievably primitive!

Dasha compared Promise's prints to those in a card file, hawing over the results.

"Can I . . . may I see my mother?"

"No," Dasha said bluntly. "She has already said that she does not wish to see you, or speak to you. Your prints match.''

She glared at Aubry again, and her shoulders tightened. "You and . . . he may stay for two meals, and may spend the night in one of the peripheral barracks. We will help you make contacts if you need them. You must leave in the morning.''

"I . . . why?" Her voice was a painful whisper. "Why are you doing this to me?"

Dasha's eyes were cold. "You know why. You broke your mother's heart when you left. No word. No communication. You were to take the role Jenna now holds."

"I'm not a warrior," she said meekly.

"You are your mother's child, you were trained in our mysteries, and you abandoned them," Dasha said coldly. "And you ran away with that man."

"Jamie," she said numbly. "I was in love. I had to run. I would never have gotten council approval."

"And for good reason," Dasha said haughtily. "Tell me—how did it work out? I assume that this Jamie was different from the others. Tell me how wonderful everything was."

Promise lowered her head. "I was eighteen. I was in love. I did something foolish. I'm back, and I want to present my mate to the council."

"No," Dasha said. "You may eat, and use our research facilities, and you may leave in the morning. And that is all." She rustled the release form, and held it out. "Now. If you will sign here . . ."

Choking back her tears, Promise did. Jenna stood, not watching, hands clasped behind her back.

Out of the corner of her eye Dasha caught Aubry's glance, and she smiled with mock kindness. "On the other hand, if you would care to renounce this . . . man, perhaps your suit would be considered more favorably."

Promise broke the tip of the pen, tearing the paper. She pushed the paper back across the desk.

CHAPTER TEN

Dance of Life

6:00 P.M.

"Colleen! Colleen!" The cries shook the dining hall. A large woman, over six feet and in no way petite, took the raised dais in the center, and someone handed her a guitar. She grinned like a jack-o'-lantern, dropped her voice into a gravelly bass rumble, and sang:

> *"Oh, Susan B., don't bother waiting up for me.*
> *I'm going out with the boys, for a little . . . fun.*
> *Lock all the doors before you do your chores,*
> *Don't let any strangers in, and get the dishes done."*

Promise sat quietly in the dining hall, absorbing her surroundings. It was not yet time to make a move. Aubry sat beside her, as tense as a coiled snake. He ate without a sound, his shoulders hunched, with that familiar *I'm not really here* expression on his face.

The guitarist raised her pitch to its normal level, and sang a reply to the previous lines:

> *"Sorry, darling Charlie, but I've got a date to keep.*
> *The other girls are waiting, I can hear the car horns*
> *beep.*
> *When you read the morning papers, dear, don't let it*
> *shake your sleep,*
> *That they found some rapist slaughtered in the morn-*
> *ing . . ."*

The music and laughter of the evening had not been lost on either of them. They were separate from the hundred or so women and five men in the room. They were not yet a part of Ephesus.

Promise's eyes searched the room, looking to see if her mother was there. No. No sign of her, and there were no empty seats at any of the tables.

There was no rigid sense of organization, so in that sense things had not changed in her absence.

The sisters sat in groups and clumps, a hundred laughing, happy faces. Many were paired with lovers, all were grouped with friends. All but Promise and Aubry.

The kettles of gumbo had emptied and filled again, and a mixed gender team carried them back to a kitchen in the rear of the lodge for refilling.

Aubry was being pointedly ignored. Occasionally a woman would glance at him, eye him speculatively, then turn and whisper to a friend or lover. Derisive laughter would follow. She knew Aubry could cope with fear, or hatred, or even contempt. But derision was a totally new experience, and he had no frame of reference from which to understand it.

"Wait, love," she whispered. "Our turn will come."

"I don't know how much more of this I can take." His big hands were tensing and untensing as if they longed for something to break. There was nothing for Aubry to focus his discomfort on. Nothing to do but bide his time and wait.

He leaned to whisper in her ear. "Isn't there a ritual of challenge here? You said something about that."

"Yes, for the position of combat mistress," she whispered in reply. "But you have to be a woman, and you have to be a member of the family."

"Then you could challenge Jenna if they readmitted you?" His eyes narrowed.

"Aubry. Jenna and I went through that, years ago. It was no contest, and she's had ten years to get better. She wouldn't be who and where she is if she wasn't superb."

Aubry grunted, and continued to eat.

They were alone at their table, last to be served. The

food was as good as her memory had suggested. The protein was mostly fish, and that was secondary to the pasta shells that formed two-thirds of the course.

Next to that were plentiful leafy vegetables, and ice-cold water. It was simple, and nourishing, and she loved it. Aubry chewed every bite as if searching for lumps of poison.

It was almost funny.

A gust of sudden laughter took her mind back to the song rocking the room. Again the singer lowered her voice, and scowled:

> "Oh, Susan B., have some beer in the fridge for me,
>   Are you putting on weight again? Your arms look
>   thick.
>   If all that exercise did nothing I'm not surprised
>   When will you get tired of this fitness kick?"

And this time, fully half of the women in the room joined her in the retort:

> "Never, darling Charlie, for this isn't flab, but meat
>   Six months of heavy training now,
>   And three months on the street.
>   And after years of running, yes revenge is very sweet
>   And they'll find some rapist slaughtered in the morn-
>   ing . . ."

For her, the meal and the music and the company were intoxicating. It was amazing how easy it was to slip back into the rhythms, almost as if she had never been away. She felt herself shrinking. Once more she was a child, a girl who still had sensation on the left side of her body, who laughed and played with her friends, still knowing no world outside the communes. Still playing wondering child-ish games of what-if.

And now . . .

But for Aubry, she could disappear back into this world without a backward glance. The old ties were still binding.

Why not? Aubry could survive without you better than he can with you. He could disappear back into the slums of any of a dozen cities, and survive. Thrive. He only stayed with the Scavengers because he knew that you needed him. These are your people. They would forgive you if you didn't have Aubry with you. . . .

But even as she thought it, she knew it for the lie it was. Aubry was her man, and she could no more leave him than she could shed her skin.

Her Plastiskin sparkled briefly, mockingly.

At the front of the room the song was concluding, the wife's final mocking words being sung as sweetly as a lullaby:

> *"Never, darling Charlie, do you hear one word I say*
> *And well I know the kind of games you play when*
> *you're away.*
> *It wouldn't much surprise me if you don't come home*
> *by day*
> *And I find that I'm a widow in the morning."*

The women applauded and cheered and stomped as the guitarist took her bow, and the food trays were cleaned away.

Promise didn't know her, at least was not sure that she remembered her. She had the vaguest memory of a chubby twelve-year-old named Colleen. The smile was similar but the memory could easily be faulty.

"My second song this evening is about Mother Eve. We all know Mother Eve, don't we? Sure. She brought sin into the world!" The crowd laughed and hooted appreciatively.

Colleen drew a thin, dark cigar from her shirt pocket and lit it, inhaling with relish before exhaling a thin plume of smoke into the air.

"Well, it hit me that all Mother Eve did was bring an awareness of dyin' into the world. And with that awareness, people starting doing things—"

She struck a chord on the guitar. "They started building—" and she struck another chord, "and having babies—" Colleen grinned as her fingers wrung music from the strings.

"—and loving each other like crazy, 'cause that's what

there is to do in this world. Leave it a little better off than you found it, and love each other like crazy.

"And Mother Eve gave us all of the good things that we have, because she had the courage to go and *do* while Adam was busy playing with himself. She gave us courage, and curiosity, and everything. And Men took that story and twisted it around, and used it against us, tried to make us ashamed that we were the thinkers and the doers, and tried to make us more passive. Well—"

She launched into her song then, and Promise remembered it. The first verse was about Mother Eve, and before she had gotten two lines into it a dozen voices had joined her, and the rafters shook with song.

By the second verse, which was equally raucous, Promise had joined in. This one dealt with a male scholar's speculation that Joan of Arc may have been a boy. That one was stood on its ear by a complementary, shamelessly bawdy verse suggesting that Napoleon Bonaparte was a woman.

Aubry rolled his eyes and sighed. Two more women joined Colleen on the stage, and all carried string instruments. Promise gripped Aubry's hand. "This is it. This is what we're waiting for."

"What?"

"The dancing is about to begin."

The music rose to the highest cross-beams in the room, and, in a way that Promise only dimly understood, completed her transition to the past. She didn't feel anything of herself, didn't feel anything of the past years.

One at a time the women stood, and danced around the room joyously. It was Ephesus's tribal dance, an offshoot of the same root that produced Durga, a remnant of an earth magic from prehistoric India. They reveled in their own feelings and in the very aliveness of their sisters; together, they celebrated their bodies.

Promise remembered. It was entirely too easy to remember. Suddenly she was a girl again, innocent again, with all of her life ahead of her, feeling her body move to the music, riding the music, knowing that she had a special connection with it that none of her sisters enjoyed. She took that knowledge, turned it around and around in her head until it emerged as a decision.

The chain of the dance went on, and as it passed their table, Promise rose and joined it. She had a last and final image of Aubry looking after her, eyes ablaze, taking in the twist and undulation of her body, and she knew again how the natural expression of her body's potential was that which was sensuous, or sexual. It didn't have to be the overemphasized bump-and-grind of a stripper, or the desperate, shallow sexuality of a prostitute.

It was there, it was there in the natural polarity of man and woman. Perhaps it was her sense of this that had eventually driven her away from her sisters. It she would be a whole woman, she must have a whole man.

Her body moved as if each sway, each moment of movement to the beat, started somewhere deep inside her, somewhere inviolate and untouched by life. Aubry claimed his Nullboxing movement originated in such a place.

She threw her head back and moved, aware that as she did, all eyes in the room were on her, moving with her. As she reached the front of the room she stayed there, and danced for them as she had never danced before.

There was music, and there was space, and there was her mind and her nervous system. And within that matrix she plied her craft. Transitory art, impermanent gift to the world. A fleeting touch, a suggestion of life beyond struggle, gift given with no thought of survival.

Primal woman.

She could smell herself as she moved, as her sweat began to flow. As slowly, the other women and men in the room began to clap their hands together. A low cry of appreciation rang out as she pushed beyond and beyond. The room spun, everything coming together now.

Now there was no time, and she had never been away.

And yet all the pain of her separation, all of the months and years wandering in the world. The hundreds of men that she had taken to her bed, in search of . . .

What?

Aubry? In search of someone who could make her feel complete, as she tried to make him feel? And if that was what she truly needed, then who could say that it was wrong? Who could say that her life, as her dance, in not concealing itself and its deepest mysteries from her diadic opposite, was less than they had asked of her, less than her family required it be.

Everything, every fear, every joy, every hope of her life was there in that dance. She swirled and leapt, every follicle of her hair, every flicker of her finger utterly alive.

And as she danced, her hands went to her clothing and tore them free, scattered them to the winds. Naked to their eyes she danced before them.

Durga, the dance of life.

There was an almost wolflike howl of approval as the smell of her sweat and passion rose in the air. She clicked her teeth, triggering the microprocessor implanted within her jawbone.

The Plastiskin erupted into fire, and the room went silent.

The musicians ceased to play, and all eyes were upon her.

There was a blur, an accelerating whirl, dizzying, maddening, hallucinogenic . . .

And then she was still, in a womb of motion. The rest of the world spun, but she was still, calm. She breathed in, and the world fluxed. She breathed out, and the world receded.

Everything was motionless. Now she was here, and now there, and in between there was nothing but feeling, nothing but a flare of emotion. At last she spiraled down on her left knee and the ball of her right foot, her arms extended beseechingly.

She stood slowly. There was still no sound from the room around her. Her hands rested lightly on her hips. She looked out at them.

"I am woman," she said. "I am you. I am what you made me, and you are my sisters. If you would curse me for loving, then there is no love. If you would curse me for needing, then drown your children. If you would reject my man without knowing him, then you are as guilty as any witch-burner. I have always carried you in my heart as the strongest and most wonderful family anyone could have. I beg you. Do not soil that memory. Forgive me. Take me back. Give my love a chance.''

Slowly, still without a sound from the assembly, Promise pulled her clothes over a body gleaming with sweat, and stepped down.

Subtly at first, then with growing fervor, a sound like *hyunn-huh! hyunn-huh!* began to fill the room, swelling and blossoming, until every throat carried it. Promise didn't hear it. She saw only Aubry, and the twin tracks of tears on his beautiful face, and the love that shone in his eyes for her.

And her love for him burned within her with every step as she passed the rows of women as they looked at her, looked at him.

And in their eyes, there was no longer contempt or amusement. And when he took her into his arms, and kissed her deeply, there was nothing in the world for either of them but the sound of the hands clapping, and feet stamping, and the love of her family, and the love of her man.

It was, for Promise, the happiest moment of her life.

CHAPTER ELEVEN

Gorgon

Thursday, May 25

Marina Batiste was on the riverbank, in sight of the bridge now. She pulled herself up a few cold, wet inches at a time. If she allowed herself to think about it, she was miserably uncomfortable. She didn't allow it—not while there was a job to be done.

She made out the individual figures of the "Nigerian Liberation Front" cardboard revolutionaries as they patrolled the Dja Bridge, wasplike infrared/laser-sighted machine pistols at the ready. According to Quint and Ibumi, the bridge was a cantilever span, twelve hundred feet long, the longest bridge in Cameroon.

Her body was blackened with heat-reflective makeup. Neither visual nor thermal scan would pick her up. As silent as a night cloud, she wiggled in closer, trusting the automatic focus on her portable holo rig.

"I count eight men," she subvocalized. The transmitter anchored in her jawbone would pick up anything louder than a thought, broadcasting it tightbeam to a computer-assisted receiver some thousand yards away. There, it was recorded for future broadcast on TriNet. Always assuming that she survived to bring it back.

Security was everything: in all of southern Africa, that area controlled and united under Swarna's PanAfrican flag, there was no safe haven for Gorgon or anyone associated with them. Covering this operation for TriNet meant that Marina was a very long way from friends. Curiously, that idea pierced the normal veil of dispassion that masked her fear. She was the only woman, the only *outsider*, ever to have the opportunity to watch Gorgon make a kill.

Perhaps it was only the adrenaline of fear, but her heart jackhammered in her chest.

The receiver whispered in her ear: "One more man. Need visual." That was Ibumi's dry rasp, and it made her skin crawl. Ibumi was second in command, Quint's lover, and as spooky a human being as she'd ever met. Ibumi was Swahili, his family American for three generations.

She crawled a little closer, near the no-man's-land Quint had established for her. *"Come closer than the tip of the rock's shadow,"* his voice echoed grimly in her ears, *"and I'll kill you myself."*

Finally, she had her vantage point. From here, she could see the bridge, the guards, and the limousine containing four frightened people. Officials from Union Carbide, and the multinational Energy trade union. They were huddled inside, bound hand and foot.

They would die in—Marina checked her watch—twenty-two minutes unless Energy put pressure on President Harris to meet with Swarna. It would never happen. Harris's official position was nonrecognition of the PanAfricans, a policy strengthened through economic sanctions and support of northern guerrilla forces. And an abortive assassination attempt which America denied in public and cursed in private.

The assassination of Swarna could have worked, destabilizing the twenty-year-old black nation. Only Swarna could hold the PanAfricans together, a man as charismatic and invaluable to his movement as Fidel Castro had been to his. And the assassination, so brilliantly schemed, had been leaked to the American press by traitors within the State Department, the mission forced to abort in midstride. An embarrassing, expensive failure.

Actions like the ones on the bridge were Swarna's way of striking back. A little war of nerves. The Nigerian Liberation Front, a puppet group, kidnapped Energy officials. Swarna could disavow their actions, but refuse to intervene. By an odd coincidence, their demands coincided with Swarna's needs.

Surprise, surprise.

"Nine. Contact made. In car with hostages. Proceed?"

Snipers were in place on the hills to either side, and they would make their move shortly. Unless they deactivated the explosives first, such a move would be murder and suicide.

Marina peered through her holocamera's night-vision scope. A Gorgon was moving into position just east of the bridge. She focused in on his weapon, tugging her memory until the right facts surfaced. The man carried an Armasault AT-14 semiautomatic rifle and peered down at the bridge. Firing 1200 particle/liquid explosive shock antipersonnel or armor-piercing rounds per minute, the Armasault was custom-made for Gorgon. It was configured with either vibration-sensitive geophones or an advanced ambient light nightscope, both AI enhanced for accurate location of targets. According to Quint, the starlight sensitive devices were infinitely preferable to the revolutionaries' infrared, because IR is detectable. The Liberation Front snipers might as well send up flares advertising their positions.

There were the packages. Twenty pounds of high explosive at either end of the bridge, to be triggered by . . .

She focused again, and breathed a sigh of relief. A slender radio aerial rising from a package next to the explosives. Just as Quint had said in the briefing. Radio controlled. Probably a manual backup.

"Ready," her earphones whispered. *"Blackout in forty seconds."*

Marina lay back against the hill for a moment, breathing hard and gathering her nerves into a usable bundle. They would only get one shot at this, and that would be it.

Thirty seconds.

Marina was five feet and ten inches of wiry, Arizona-raised Latina. She had covered every nasty job that Sterling DeLacourte's TriNet handed her, working for six years for an opportunity like this one. When she closed her eyes she could see Cronkites and Pulitzers dancing a fast waltz.

Movement.

She focused in on the limousine.

She could see only the barest outlines, but a moment later the computer identified the profile, flashed online with a name and a short bio. *There* was Larusa, the Canadian mercenary, and there Lancaster, from Newfoundland. And there . . . that profile. There was too much shadow, too little detail, and the computer couldn't make it.

Insufficient data.

Aguiyi, officer in charge of the Nigerian Liberation Front forces, strained to pierce the darkness. Every muscle was knotted, and burned with tension. His stomach was an acid ruin.

Only two years before he had been a colonel in the regime which had cemented shattered southern Africa into one of the most powerful forces in the world—one which certainly intimidated the hell out of the West. When Swarna's covert operations division drummed him from the army and set up a new identity as a terrorist, he had been uncertain of his willingness to serve in this new and unique capacity. But in the past twenty-four months he had lived in a shadow world, with its attendant terrors and dark rewards. He had discovered things about himself that he had never admitted before.

If a message did not come over the radio in five minutes, he would be allowed, no, *expected* to go to work on one of the prisoners.

This he hoped for. The three men and one woman who composed the party from Union Carbide and International 108 were as docile as whipped dogs. The woman. Now, she seemed interesting. He heard her muffled cry from within the car: Carter was amusing himself with her even now. Perhaps, as the Englishman claimed, she was secretly excited by the kidnapping. Perhaps she hoped that she would have something to exchange for her life.

Well, he and his men would take her up on that. Afterward, of course, they would pull her tongue out with fishhooks and laugh as she choked on her own blood, but why let that spoil their fun?

There were two men at either end of the bridge at the moment, and they paced constantly.

There had been rumors that the Americans would try a rescue effort, but he laughed at that. The Americans were crippled giants, holding no true world power. They dared not wage open war against Swarna—the mineral resources of the African continent were coveted by the Soviets as well, and it would take little to push the PanAfricans into the Soviet orbit.

Oh, there had been a few abortive military actions, but no official American military forces had been engaged. Only Gorgon, with its odd paramilitary status, had been employed, and that in an indirect manner.

No mind. This situation would resolve on the diplomatic level. He sincerely hoped Harris would refuse to meet with Swarna, and that no other release arrangements would be made. At least for eight hours. It would give them a chance for the woman . . .

Nandela, the communications man, squatted near the car with his radio unit on, scanning. He looked over to Aguiyi, his broad, dark face impassive.

"Soon. Another rumor, though. A Swiss shuttle made an irregular landing at an airfield thirty miles from here twelve hours ago."

"And?"

"I merely find it . . . interesting. We were not able to match the registration with any Swiss vehicle. It may mean nothing, or . . ."

"Five minutes, my friend . . ."

Nandela frowned. "I can't get the rest of the broadcast." He jiggled a switch on the ancient apparatus. "That's funny, I'm not getting any station at all."

"Try—"

With a sharp crack, the car window spiderwebbed with cracks, a neat bullet hole in the center. Carter's hands slapped over his face. He screamed wetly and slid down out of sight.

"Damn!" Aguiyi screamed, furious. Nandela peeked up

over the railing. "I—" His head snapped back violently and he fell back, a round hole punched neatly between his eyes.

Bastards! Bastards! He had warned them, he had warned them all. So be it. Let the consequences be on their heads; if they couldn't pay the ransom he demanded, they would get back charred corpses.

He screwed down the safety knob on the transmitter, mumbled a prayer to gods unacknowledged since childhood, and pressed the button.

Nothing.

He screamed now. Bullets spattered around him, but it was merely a covering fire to keep the rebels pinned. The real action would take place within a few moments.

Well, he could still take those goddamned executives with him. He turned, and began wiggling toward the car on his belly. From where he was now, he could see two of his men at the far end of the bridge, facedown, unmoving.

Damn! Damn! What had gone wrong?

Only a few more yards . . .

Then with barely a sound, a figure flowed over the lip of the bridge railing, a solid shadow, night-black and almost invisible in the dark. The shape was almost six and a half feet tall, impossibly massive.

Aguiyi recognized it. No one who had been exposed to American Omnivision—even if it was only flatscreen monochrome—could fail to identify the figure.

Gorgon. A leering Gorgon gas mask obscured face and throat, its machine pistol aimed directly at him. A second Gorgon appeared next to him, moving silently. The two stood very close together.

Aguiyi's machine pistol was aimed at the fuel tank of the limousine. Even in death, his finger could contract, spewing tracer rounds into the tank, a fireball into the air.

Very well. He knew these Gorgons. He knew their weakness. The man Quint, their leader, was insane. Aguiyi might yet survive.

He bent, and laid his pistol on the ground.

The larger Gorgon's machine pistol remained aimed at

him, and to Aguiyi, its bore seemed larger than the moon, than the sun, was a gaping maw swelling to swallow him.

Could he have been wrong? No. It was . . .

The Gorgon turned, and handed his gun to the other man.

Gorgon took no prisoners, but Quint was said to be a fanatic about physical combat.

Aguiyi drew his knife, waiting. Smiling.

"Come, sissy boy," he hissed. "Come and die with a man."

The Gorgon was impassive, unmoving.

Aguiyi hurled himself, knife first. Aguiyi saw the blade appear in his opponent's hand as if by magic, but there was no time to change directions or adjust. The edge of Quint's left hand smashed into Aguiyi's forearm, shattering the ulna and radius like glass rods. Quint's right hand flickered.

Pain blossomed in the terrorist's throat. His lungs spasmed, fighting for air and sucking blood. He collapsed, feeling his life pumping from a pierced trachea, trying to seal the hole with his fingers, knowing the horror of certain death.

The two Gorgons exchanged a quick handslap.

Aguiyi's lips moved, but the only sound was a wet hiss. *"Kill me."*

The larger Gorgon looked at him, face and emotions hidden behind the mask. He bent down and wiped his blade on Aguiyi's shirt. "I already have," he said calmly, and he moved on.

The enormous dark shadow detached itself from Aguiyi's collapsing body and strode to the door of the limousine. Even as he did, other shapes were moving onto the bridge from both sides.

Silently, efficiently, the shapes disarmed the explosives, and checked the bodies of the dead.

One counterrevolutionary was still alive, crippled by a bullet in the shoulder. The second Gorgon bent and neatly sliced her throat. Her body flopped around for a few seconds before quieting.

The big man opened the door carefully. The four

hostages—arms bound behind their backs, eyes glazed with surprise and gratitude—looked up at him. The Gorgon paused, then pulled his face mask away. He had the eyes and golden beard of a Jesus, utterly at peace.

"I'm Quint," he said, his voice giving the lie to his face: it was without inflection, the voice of a dead man. "You are free."

Friday, May 26

"Incredible." DeLacourte clucked softly as the images faded into transparency.

He sat back, and looked carefully at the dark-haired woman seated across the stage from him. He drew a thin, yellow-wrapped cigar from a coat pocket and clipped off the tip.

"The new portable units are almost beyond belief. I assume . . ."

The woman seated across from DeLacourte measured her answer carefully. "Life-eye cameras on four of the Gorgons, including their leaders, Quint and Ibumi. Ibumi killed the woman. Sound and image equipment on the hill over the bridge. The rest was reconstructed by computer animation. My guess is that you can't tell where the real image ends and the computer takes over."

"What is your impression of Quint?"

She closed her eyes, thinking carefully. "Fanatic. Does things by the book, but then, he wrote the book. Walks around like two-legged death. He's too close to this Ibumi— even for lovers. It's like they're Siamese twins. Make a show out of groping each other in public. I think he's addicted to Ibumi's body, or something." She opened her eyes again, and they were clear as tinted glass. "Brilliant tactically. Utterly ruthless."

DeLacourte nodded approval. "Marina has done extraordinary work." Jack Hands lit his boss's cigar, then leaned over to whisper into his ear.

The tall, slender reporter sat quietly, waiting. She was pretty but not beautiful. Her mouth was generous, naturally pink, and offset the gray-blue of her eyes. Her freckles were darker, cheeks peeling a bit due to her recent exposure to the sun.

Finally, DeLacourte straightened and templed his hands together. "Ms. Batiste. I hope that you realize that due to the nature of your contract with us, we retain the right to decide what is to be done with this . . . admittedly remarkable account."

"I voluntarily signed an exclusive with you, Mr. DeLacourte. I keep my agreements—"

"I know you do," he injected paternally.

"But the public needs to see this." The latin inflection was a light, sweet syrup in her voice.

"Recent information actually . . . ah . . . links Gorgon with Swarna's terrorist attack itself. We were hoping that your operation would help to document such a connection."

She laughed. "That's a joke. You're seeing three miracles here. One, that the people from one-oh-eight got away with their lives. Two, that Gorgon would let a cameraperson wire them for the assault to make a coherent record of it. Three, that they would let a *woman* be a part of the effort. Miracles."

Marina paused. The tension in the air was palpable. When after twenty seconds there was no sound, no comment, she spoke again. "I see. The disk doesn't give you what you wanted. Christ—everybody knows that Gorgon was used as a tool to attack Swarna twice. If it hadn't been for that leak to the *Washington Post,* the second attempt would have blown him into as many pieces as his half brother. There's no evidence of collusion. It's a good disk, Mr. DeLacourte. The best I ever got, and you know it."

"You've had excellent stories in the past, Marina. Moonman, for instance."

"I got the story. I found Moonman, and interviewed him."

"I would have appreciated an opportunity to . . . speak with him."

"You wanted Moonman in prison, and that wasn't part of our deal."

"Yes. Well, it was never stated that your new tapes would be broadcast. Just paid for."

"You bastard," Marina said under her breath.

"And what you need to know is—is it going to make it onto the air?"

She nodded. The flame in her eyes was carefully screened.

"As you know, I am the head of TriNet. I would certainly never suppress an important, newsworthy story."

She waited, unimpressed. "But."

He nodded. "I think that you can have a grasp of the problems that I face. My career as a communications executive, my ambitions, obligations . . . indeed, even my own life is secondary to the needs of my country."

He drew on the thin cigar. Its coal flared in the dark like a glowing third eye. "I hope that you can see that."

"It's the truth," she said. "What I brought back for you, what I risked my life for, is the truth."

"Truth, Miss Batiste, is not always contained in facts. I'm sorry. Your contract will be paid in full. In fact, there is a generous bonus in this for you."

She stood, eyes alight. Her mouth opened. *Keep it. Keep your damned bonus.* . . . Then she looked again at DeLacourte's expression, vacant and empty as a moonlit pool, waiting without commitment for her response. Suddenly she felt a chill at the back of her neck, and knew that the last thing in the world she wanted was to anger this man.

"All right, Mr. DeLacourte." She put on a show of letting the air out of her lungs in a hiss. A beaten woman. "I . . . guess maybe I'm just stressed out. Hell, I could use a vacation. Now feels like a good time." She grinned at him, a carefully calculated smile containing just the right portion of yum-this-shit-tastes-good. "I think that bonus is just what I need."

She paused, as if embarrassed, and then backed out of the room.

"Weakling," DeLacourte said quietly. "That's why there has never been a woman in the White House. And never will be."

"Mr. DeLacourte, we need to begin work on the divestiture plan."

"Yes . . ."

Jack Hands flicked a toggle on his briefcase. A branching schematic overview of DeLacourte Enterprises appeared in the air before them. "All of the entertainment and communications arms must be modified. You can maintain a controlling interest in any of them, but not sit on their board of directors. And if you are elected, you won't be able to keep an active seat on the L-5 engineering plant. Too many government contracts. TransCon Shuttles is different, and we are still investigating. It is recommended that you discontinue your holo lecture series, and of course the Sunday services. You would be entirely too vulnerable to an opposition demand for equal time."

"Damned lot of nonsense. If a man has built up an empire, and controls it, isn't it reasonable for him to be more capable of running a country? That kind of thinking got us into the stinking hole we're in today."

"Yes, sir. I've been preparing a statement for you to deliver next month. I want you to approve what we have so far."

DeLacourte's eyes were open, but his mind wasn't in the room with Hands. It was somewhere else, dealing with another issue already. "I'm sure that everything is fine."

"In it," the aide continued, "we deal with the rumor about the 'Oath.' There have been whispers that if you are elected, you will never live to see the Oval Office."

"Fools." DeLacourte's eyes were half-lidded, almost as though he were drugged. "I don't care about that. I don't care about anything but this filth. It's all around us. It must be rooted out without hesitation. Without . . ."

For several seconds DeLacourte's mouth worked soundlessly, his large, dark eyes fixed on something in another place and time.

Hands cleared his throat politely. "Without mercy?"

"Yes. My wife is with me, and the American people are with me. Killing me will only strengthen their resolve. It will not matter. All that matters is the filth."

He turned and glared at the aide, and his eyes were fever-bright. "This sickness has rotted our core, and it must die. The waves of addiction and perversion that sweep our country—this must be the thrust of the speech, not my own miserable life. Mushrooms. The damned abominable mushrooms, promising paradise and delivering damnation . . .'' He slammed the side of his fist on the seat arm. ''How many souls lost? How many? Well, no more. There is an end. An end to it. And it comes now, I tell you.''

He pushed a button on the seat, and the branching outline delineating his holdings and the structure of his empire faded, and once again Quint's face appeared. Utterly defiant, as alive as if he stood there, knife in hand, challenging, daring.

''It ends,'' DeLacourte repeated.

The aide slowly closed his briefcase and stole from the room. Behind him, in the darkened theater, DeLacourte watched the rescue tape in reverse.

CHAPTER TWELVE

Dreams

9:23 A.M. Monday, May 29

The man in the pool was hideous, his body grotesquely inefficient, but Medusa-16 had no choice but to listen, and obey. Those were the orders, and the orders were to be obeyed. Could not even be questioned. Quint stood silent by the pool, gargantuan arms folded, blue eyes piercing and watchful. Next to him was his lover, Ibumi, black and implacable and always, always touching Quint.

The man in the pool smiled up at them, at the twenty Medusas who sat cross-legged upon the floor, watching with identical expressions of rapt attention.

They were of many races, but only one breed: healthy, strong-looking boys between the ages of ten and thirteen. Boy Scouts perhaps, with eager smiles and ready hands.

McMartin grinned mirthlessly at them, but 16 could not see the smile. He saw the teeth behind the smile, the impossibly huge body, the small black eyes, and was frightened.

"After the Fourth of July, you will be hunted," the fat man said. His black-marble eyes scanned the row of Medusas, and something that 16 registered only as hunger flickered in them. "And there is only one woman who can connect you with the NewMan Nation. Ariane Cotonou can destroy you, so you must destroy her first. This will be your first time away from each other. Your first time away from the Nation—"

And now Quint, giant, irresistible, spoke. The Medusas,

sitting in their four rows, turned to him, their eyes worshipful.

"You *will* succeed. The future of our people depends upon it. There is no alternative. It is the only reason you exist. You are NewMen! You are Gorgons! You are . . . Medusa!"

16 raised his arm, returned Quint's salute. He was a warrior! He would fight! Would kill the woman Cotonou! Would bear children for his people! This was who and what he was, and his feelings came last. So he had been told. So it was.

Wasn't it?

3:47 *P.M.*

With a scream like a dying giant, the poplar tree fell to earth. It thundered as its bark rent and the branches splintered and snapped away from the trunk.

Aubry had seen buildings die, had personally punched the button that triggered pounds of high explosive in their guts, but watching the tree fall touched something unexpected. He felt a moment of grief, combined with a surge of giddy power. *So high and mighty. We can bring you down!*

The last few feet of the descent were more sound than vision. The vibration slammed through the earth and rocked him to the core.

Crewmaster Glenda Wright rubbed her hands together and slapped Aubry on the back. "All right, muscles. Let's see what you can do."

She was a strong, stout woman with a weathered face. She might have been pretty if she had bothered to make that face up. She made no secret of the fact that she didn't give a damn.

The saws were ultra lightweight, motorized frameworks with strands of iron-molybdenum monofilament crystal wire running in an endless loop. The wire was insanely stronger than steel, and sharp enough to slice dust.

Aubry shouldered in next to the tree and began stripping away branches. A dozen other figures buzzed around the tree as well, carrying away the branches, clipping, judging, attaching the anchor pulleys.

A tow line dropped from overhead, and he grinned as they attached the bobbling teardrop of an immense golden helium balloon to the tree trunk. The gigantic yellow balloon was moored to an overhead span of cable running north and south, and ballasted with a series of interlocked iron rings. When the rings were released, the trunk groaned and rose up into the air, dangling between the balloon and the line like a grotesquely huge musical note.

The balloon rippled in the wind as the gears ground.

The crew applauded thunderously as the log moved north toward the mill. There were too many workers—in any commercial operation, salaries would have eaten up the profits. But then, Ephesus sought something far more elusive than profit: health.

Aubry stopped, wiping his arm across his mouth, shaking sweat droplets from his beard. They were about twelve miles north of the main camp, a decline nestled in the middle of the Tillamook Burn area in northern Oregon. A shallow fork of Trask River ran through the floor of the valley. This time of year, it was barely deep enough to moisten their boot soles.

Before letting him out with the crews, they had indoctrinated him, shown him the films and reconstructions of the "Burn," the most hideously costly fire in Oregonian history. That had been almost a century ago, and the area had been refoliated with a vengeance.

"We don't harvest trees here . . ." he had been told over and over again. "We rebuild human beings. Human beings who have been ravaged by the people who were supposed to love them. Protect them." Glenda looked at him pointedly.

"And if you can't hack that, get out. We don't need you here."

Aubry swallowed his ire, and shut up.

He still didn't quite fit in, but after a week, no one stared anymore. There were few smiles and fewer friendly words, but he didn't feel like King Kong.

It was gruelingly physical work, he had to admit that.

The terrain was rough, all of it, and there was no way to make that less of a problem without raping the woods.

So the women hiked up through the backwoods. And they scouted, and they marked trees. And they cared for the sick timber, and they planted new seedlings.

To the west, they plowed the ground, and made their harvests. And somewhere in all of it, people were being reborn.

It seemed like bullshit to him. Bullshit.

He sliced away a branch, and then another, and then clicked the saw off and slipped its safety sheath back on, looking at the branch in front of him. It was three inches thick, and he felt a flare of hatred toward it that was shocking.

Aubry grabbed it and pulled at it, feeling the give in the structure, feeling it yield and spring back like a living thing.

Didn't it know it was dead? Why did it resist? Why would it bother . . . ?

For no reason, all of the anger and frustration he felt was suddenly focused on this harmless piece of wood, this branch, already dying, its juices already slowing, growing viscous. He slammed at it with the side of his hand, and felt it crack. He snarled at it and wrenched fiercely, ripping it away from the bole of the tree with a single surge of strength.

He stopped, suddenly aware that he was being watched, that shocked eyes had witnessed the single act of violence.

Aubry sat on a stump, chewing on a piece of jerky.

Glenda came over to him, eyed him suspiciously. "This is the first time you've sat down today, mister. What are you trying to prove?"

Aubry looked up and said in a neutral voice, "Nothing. I'm not trying to prove anything. I just want to work. Is there anything wrong with that?"

She shook her head, and trudged back downhill.

His head hurt. He looked up at the sun, suddenly dizzy. The blinding yellow orb grew swollen, filled the sky, and suddenly—

A hand reached out of the sky, a hand slimed with

blood, and the face of Carl, teeth punched through lower lip, now crawling through the hallways of Death Valley, holding in his intestines with one hand as the other clawed him a few more inches forward. And Carl looked at him, eyes weary and numb with approaching death, and whispered: "You were our friend, Aubry. We needed you, and you let us die—"

He gasped, and ran. Ran up into the hills, trying to find some place to hide. The images were breaking through the blockade, through the mindshields that Warrick had helped him build. Suddenly, unbidden thoughts of Death Valley came back to him. All of the fear, all of the pain, all of the darkness, and the endless tunnels. His vision blackened at the periphery, and Aubry was suddenly half-blind, stumbling, the demons of night swarming out, baring their teeth in the light of day.

And Maxine. Images of that horrid night on the beach, when the woman he thought he loved had betrayed him. As every woman he had ever known had betrayed him . . .

No! That wasn't true. There was Promise. . . .

Yes. And if it weren't for those damned mushrooms, how long would it be . . .

He ran, the voices hammering their way through, the shields falling, peeling away from him. He screamed now, screamed like one of the dying trees. He ran, straight up the hill, sprinted until he felt his lungs were about to burst. His legs flamed.

There was nothing around him but walls, walls, and the darkness that hid death from him, and the screams of the shattered. . . .

Aubry ran into a tree headfirst, fell and sprang up again, smashing into the trunk with his bare fists, smashing until the blood ran from his hands and the bark flew in crimsoned chips.

He battered at it, smashing hands, knees, elbows, feet. . . .

And finally he slid down and lay exhausted upon the ground.

It had to mean something. All of it had to mean something. All of the pain had to fit in somewhere.

With the strength of the pain in his hands, he bore down, and forced the walls to retreat, the darkness to lift. Forced the door to close. Forced the ugly images to retreat again, to hide for a few more hours, hissing and coiling in the back of his mind.

Aubry gasped for air. Every night, Promise fought to teach him the dances of Ephesus, and every night he felt his body rebel. He *couldn't*. He just *couldn't*. He would look like such a fool, his great, muscular body twisting and mincing like a faggot. He just couldn't. . . .

"They said I'd find you here."

Aubry looked up into Promise's face. She examined the chipped tree bark. "We kill them," she said, "but we rarely torture them first."

He glared, his gaze sinking back to the ground.

"Come on. You're through for the day."

"How was the nursery?"

She smiled wistfully. "I still don't know if that duty was a reward or a punishment. I guess—" She took his hand as they walked down the side of the hill. "Aubry! Your hands . . ."

He jerked them away, hid their torn skin in his pockets. "It's nothing. Just training."

She stopped him there on the hill, and looked at his hands, his elbows, the torn, bloodied cloth on the knees of his pants.

"What are you doing to yourself?"

"Nothing. I'm fine." He pushed her to arm's length, hating himself for the lie. "I. Am. Fine. Read my lips."

Promise stopped, stood there as Aubry stalked back down the hill. He got a dozen steps before he stopped. She stood up there, above him and seemingly very fragile, her hands tucked into her coat pockets.

"Aubry," she said quietly. "Do you want to be here with me?"

"I want to be with you. I don't want to be here."

"I don't have anywhere else to offer you."

Aubry slammed the side of his hand into a tree. Promise tried to work up a smile. "There you go, beating up the trees again."

"Listen," Aubry said desperately. "I don't know where I want to be. I don't want to be in Ephesus." He slammed his hands against his chest, hard. "I don't want to be in here, either. I got no choice. Maybe nobody ever has a choice."

Promise walked down to him. "That's a pretty lousy reason for us to be together, Aubry."

"I need you," he whispered. He pulled her close. "I'm afraid, Promise. There's something wrong with me. Wrong with my head."

"Cyloxibin?"

"Death Valley. It isn't going away."

He pushed her away gently. His mouth opened, as if about to say something, then closed again.

He walked back down the mountainside without her.

Aubry stood on the tiny balcony overlooking the compound, watching the women going about their jobs and pleasures, strolling hand in hand or alone. A few, a very few, were with men, but they seemed too self-conscious to touch.

A string of children ran, laughing, under the balcony. Aubry turned to Promise, who sat up in bed, reading one of the reproductive clinic manuals.

"Does it say anything in there about male children?"

"What?"

"Haven't you noticed?" he said. "There are about six little girls for every boy around here. Doesn't that say something to you?"

Promise folded the book against her chest. "No. What should it say?"

Her eyes were guarded.

"How many ways are there of fixing that horserace? What do they do? Smother them at birth?"

Promise spoke very quietly, with great control. "Of course not. A child's gender can be guided in several ways, Aubry. . . ."

"Just what are they doing over there in the clinic?"

"We have to be careful," Promise said. "We're on probation here."

"Yeah, like Jenna said. I can screw things up."

Promise patted the bed beside her. "Let's not argue. Please."

Aubry looked at her, and wanted to be reasonable. Wanted to see things her way, but saw only red, felt the door in his mind wedging open.

"I'm getting out of here," he said.

"Aubry—you can't. You know that we're under quarantine. They'll never let you past the door."

You make me sick.

"Don't worry," he said gently. "I'll be all right."

Aubry walked back out to the balcony, grabbed the edge of the roof, and curled himself up.

From the roof, he could see west to the big oval of the central compound. Directly around him were the dormitories of the single women, and some of the paired living quarters. At the north end of the oval stood the dome of the reproductive clinic, next to the administration building. It drew his attention strongly, and as he focused his senses, Aubry heard conversations from that direction, and the sound of clinking metal.

And something else.

Aubry climbed over to the edge of the building and caught hold of a drain pipe, tested it, and crawled down as soundlessly as a spider. He dropped to the next roof, maintaining his crouch.

He took the two-story drop to gravel on the balls of his feet. He checked to make sure that he wasn't being watched, and raced across the compound, heading north for the clinic. He dove into shadow.

There was a stand of trees between him and the clinic, and something told him not to start out into it.

People worked out there, in the near darkness, and his curiosity was piqued.

They *looked* like men, but it was hard to tell. They wore genderless overalls, and had chunky wedges for bodies, but that was meaningless.

They were moving crates out of the clinic. Heavy crates.

One of them emitted a wisp of steam. Two workers conducted a hurried conversation, and back it went to the lab.

Steam? Or condensation?

He watched, unsure of what was happening, as the last of the boxes was loaded into a vehicle that he couldn't make out clearly.

Then with a hum, it rose from the ground. No prop wash, no landing or safety lights. Just up and away. It hovered for a moment as if orienting itself, and then took off to the south, a small, boxlike hovercraft that jetted thin trails of steam. It looked insulated. Stenciled on the side were the letters "MCF."

He couldn't see any more. The doors of the clinic closed, and Aubry suddenly felt very exposed. He wasn't supposed to be here, that he knew. He was risking his own and Promise's life by being here, and yet . . .

And yet . . .

Aubry faded back into the shadows, and disappeared.

CHAPTER THIRTEEN

Dance of Death

Ephesus was silent, at least so Aubry thought at first. As he flowed from one pocket of darkness to the next, he suddenly heard a steady, rhythmic thrumming from the southern end of the camp.

He slipped through the rear of the administration building, across another small courtyard, and through the shadows of the dining halls and the library. From there, he could make out a circular amphitheater.

The floor of the amphitheater was approximately thirty by thirty meters. Steps had been cut into the dirt, and layered with planks to make ten rows of riser seats. An empty wheelbarrow lay on its side at the south end, where pale strips of concrete had been poured and molded into more permanent seating.

There were no *ki-yas* or other violent explosions of breath, but thirty women moved combatively across the floor of the amphitheater. In pairs, they shifted through a succession of dance movements, swaying and weaving without music.

Fascinated, he crept closer.

Each of them held a tapered wooden dowel in an underhand grip. But they weren't attempting to stab or slash each other. Rather, the intention seemed to be to blend together, moving in such a way that the blades came as close to the partner's body as possible without touching. The motions were circular, and flowing.

He finally made out Jenna's figure, and the rest of it clicked into place. Durga.

The dance was very soothing to the eye, so that after a few minutes of watching the ebb and flow he had to stop and shake his head: he had been on the verge of falling asleep.

A minute later, the same thing happened again. He caught himself yawning for no apparent reason.

That alerted him: there was something hypnotic about the movement, something that deliberately lulled the senses. That was even more fascinating, and dangerous.

He crept through the shadows, and moved in closer.

Jenna's head snapped up from correcting one of the pairs of partners, and she stared out into the darkness, almost directly at him. She stared for ten seconds, then turned back to what she was doing.

Aubry made out another figure on the outskirts of the practice area. A very old woman sat there. Her hair was long and white, and her face seemed very serene. Her shoulders swayed slightly as she watched the rites of Durga.

The sight was mesmerizing, and somehow reminiscent of Promise's dance. The women meshed and then drew back from one another. They spun, and then one partner would break away, and plunge headfirst into the ground. With a beautifully fluid shoulder-roll, she was up again, and sprang back to the "attack." There was no counter, no attempt to block the knife. Only a twist of the hips to let the blade slip past and—

On the other side, someone whirled into the air, and came down in what should have been a bone-jarring fall. But the woman collapsed like a rag and rolled back up to her feet and back at the opponent.

It was a good workout. After five minutes the white-haired woman rose quietly and inclined her head to Jenna. Jenna raised her hands into the air and clapped twice. The thirty women ceased their rolling and tumbling. They turned, and bowed shallowly to the old woman.

She retreated from the field, disappearing into the shadows of the administration building.

Jenna clapped her hands again. The women all sat, backs straight, hands on knees, listening intently.

Jenna demonstrated a few movements, short curving

motions of the knife, and Aubry had the distinct impression that the movements were not attacks but entries, techniques utilized to bridge the gap, cross the "no-man's-land" between opponents. To move into killing range.

Then she clapped her hands again. The women stood, and dispersed, speaking in low voices.

Jenna sat, framed by the pools of light, and peered out into the darkness for a while, once again almost directly at Aubry.

Then she turned and sat on her heels, meditating for a moment. Aubry moved out silently, steadily, coming in directly behind her on the balls of his feet.

He stopped twenty paces away.

She rose from the sitting position in a sort of reverse-corkscrew movement, and ended facing Aubry. The knives gleaming in either hand were certainly not wooden.

"You watched," she said. She smiled bitterly. "Men are not allowed to watch the rites of Durga. In ancient times, those who did were blinded and hamstrung."

"Not castrated too?"

"What use would they be then?"

"Nice people. Is that what you're going to do to me?"

Jenna stood, and folded her arms. "I've heard a lot about you from Promise."

"What did she say?"

"Girl talk. You know. I've seen Nullboxing, and to tell you the truth, it doesn't look very practical."

"You haven't seen me."

Jenna shifted her head slightly to the side, and in that pose, she reminded him so very much of Promise. He felt a familiar twinge . . . but he wasn't supposed to feel that way toward anyone else, was he?

"I think I'd like to," she said. "Sometime."

"What about now?"

"I don't think so."

She turned, and picked her bag up, shouldering it.

"Yeah, well, I can understand why. From what I've seen of Durga, it wouldn't last more than a blink."

Jenna stopped, and turned, and her smile was razor-thin. "You quite literally don't know what you're talking about."

"Listen. That dance might be great to keep senile muggers from running amok. But, lady, when you talk about a real fight, that's a whole different thing."

"And where is the *life* in what you practice, Knight? I see beefy, hyperthyroid muscle boys twisting each other into zee-gee pretzels. The second-highest injury rate in professional sports. An average professional life span of seven years. An average participant age of twenty-three. That's one hell of an 'art.' A lot of room for personal growth, for self-expression."

Aubry crouched. "Come on. Right now. We can scale it down—why don't you educate me?"

"There's no attack in Durga," Jenna said.

"I saw attacks in practice. What crap is this?"

"We practice them so that our workouts can be more realistic. But attacks are not a part of the art."

Aubry shifted uneasily. "I have to attack you?"

Jenna nodded. "And be prepared for the consequences."

"Practice knives?"

"If you're afraid of the real thing. Don't worry." She smiled. "I have very good control."

"Oh, lady. You are definitely pushing."

"Come on, mister. Let's see your stuff."

Aubry picked up one of the wooden practice knives, hefted it carefully. He worked his fingers around it until he found the right grip, and then wiggled the tip to and fro a bit, testing the balance. Then he began to edge his way forward.

Jenna stood her ground. When Aubry was four feet away from her, he paused. How close was she going to let him get? What would her move be?

Slowly, in perfect balance, Aubry moved forward into her sphere of control. Jenna slid back at the same speed. Aubry increased speed slightly, and Jenna matched it.

He stopped. All right. Purely defensive art, with a high level of sensitivity, and a structure that compensated for inferior strength, durability, and burst speed. Durga would rely on endurance, flexibility, and the ability to "fit-in" with an opponent's body. Right now, she was attempting to lead him off balance. If he never went off balance, never overcommitted, she would have no opening for a technique. Yet if he never went off balance, there could be no committed attack, and she could continue to blend with him.

Well. No way to resolve this combatively. Hell with it—what if I just look at it as an opportunity for a workout?

Worth a try.

Aubry exploded. Jenna barely twisted aside, her relaxed expression tightening with shock. Her knives were used primarily to deflect his arms and legs—that is, would have, if he had committed enough of his mass to lose control. But even at the explosive speed he used, there was never true contact.

Aubry backed off, grinning. "You're pretty good."

"Reciprocal judgment reserved," she said. She was panting a bit. So. Her cardiovascular conditioning was not extreme.

Or was that another trap?

Aubry darted in, broke rhythm and direction, and threw his first committed technique, a hooking kick that flashed a heel toward her head.

Jenna went under it, swept his standing leg, and coiled away as Aubry went down in a ball. He rolled as if the contraction were his idea and not hers, and swept *her* as she rose.

There it was. The arms were too dangerous. The legs were far more vulnerable—

But her roll was as much a feint as Aubry's, and she came at him along the ground now, slashing in a blind frenzy.

Correction: a *controlled* frenzy, thank you. Aubry timed her movement, feinted to the head with his bunched fingertips, dropped and feinted a sweep, and watched her reaction.

She was a move ahead. Three-move timing, very sophisticated, more like Tai Chi than any Japanese art. In order to stop her, he would have to damage her physical structure, and that he was unwilling to do.

Unless—

Aubry drew one of her blades down with a kick to the

shin, then shifted his shoulder as if about to throw a punch. When the blade came up he trapped her hand with his right. Her left hand sliced across as his fingers closed. Aubry released, and swept her feet. As she went to the ground, he disarmed the first knife, feinted a kick to the jaw, and then began a roll away. He reversed direction, catching the second knife on the sole of his right shoe as it flashed in. With the left heel he tapped her diaphragm.

She surprised him, keeping her composure with the breath slammed from her lungs, and the blade was at his groin—he smacked the inside of her elbow with a knuckle, and she dropped the knife from a suddenly nerveless hand.

Jenna's elbow jackknifed, clipping his jaw. Aubry rolled back, and shook his head, grinning.

Jenna came to her feet, holding one of the knives in a reverse grip, in classic "ice pick" configuration.

She was angry. At least she was breathing hard now, and her eyes were bright, and there was the slightest edge of a fighting smile on her lips. . . .

"Next clash, you're going to get hurt," Aubry said quietly. "I think we should stop now. You're very, very good."

Jenna inclined her head. She was still breathing hard. She watched him carefully.

"I've talked to Promise," she said. "She's been trying to teach you the dances. She says you aren't learning."

"They're not me," he said bluntly.

She looked at him, and at last he saw beyond the words, beyond the postures. For that moment, she was a woman interested in him as a man, and neither of them knew how to handle it. Jenna spoke first. "Come on. Come with me." She slipped her knife into her belt, and led the way.

They walked up a winding path behind the complex, and up the hill. He wished that she would slip, or falter, or weaken, something that would give him an excuse to touch her. He watched her legs work under the denim, and couldn't help comparing them to Promise's dancer's legs. Jenna's calf muscles were more pronounced, and moonlight glinted on her ankles as she walked. He caught his breath. He had a woman who was, in essence, Jenna with a different history. There was no reason to the attraction.

But reason never had much to do with it, anyway.

She stopped on a leveled shelf of earth where a circular amphitheater stretched back to the tree line. Aubry looked out; from here he could see the camp, the lumber mill, the hoist, and part of Marjo Valley. Above it, to the north, was the broken line of Flint Ridge. The swollen orb of the helium balloon rose over the valley like a demon, bobbling slightly in the wind.

"Marjo," she said. "We bought it with money and sweat. For most of us, it's the only home we want. For many, the only home we have. For some, the only home we've ever known. We live simply. That may be technology's greatest gift—giving us back the simplicity." She reached out and touched him, and he felt the electricity. He knew that she felt it too. Something in her eyes begged him not to take advantage of what he knew.

There was honor at stake here. He could have her if he really wanted, but that would ruin something else. Something that was more fragile, more delicate. Perhaps even more valuable.

Friendship.

"There isn't any magic out there anymore," she said. "We've figured everything out. Here, there's still a little of it. But you can't think about it. You have to just feel it. That's the magic. It's the magic of feeling. The first time you watch a child being born. Of watching someone weak become strong. Of watching things grow. Do you know what I'm saying?"

"I'm not sure." *Stop playing games. Either touch me, really touch me, or don't . . .*

"You say that the dances aren't you."

"They make me feel like some kind of faggot."

"Because they ask you to be feminine? That part of you is there. Just as the masculine is in me."

"Bullshit. Your whole art is based on evasion. There isn't a confrontational moment in the entire thing. In Chinese terms, it's all Yin."

"The dance and the fighting art are the same thing. Promise never understood that, not really. In the Indus Valley, the Mistresses of Durga practiced their art right under the noses of their men. She's the greatest dancer we ever produced, and she should have been Mistress. She ran from her 'masculine' emotions like you're running from the 'feminine.' It's all garbage. I just hope to the Goddess that the human race has time to learn that."

Aubry was silent.

"We're orphans," Jenna said sadly. "America is a nation of bastard mongrel children in a beautiful land that isn't really ours. The American Indians are the only ones with a real tradition here, and we've done everything we can to destroy them. We're a thousand different sub-cultures trying to survive with each other. The women here have nothing in the outside world, so we're making our culture from scratch."

"You can't do that. . . ." Aubry said, confused. "You can't just create yourself."

"Why the hell not?" Her voice became urgent. "You contain both hard and soft, Aubry. What good would your strength be without your flexibility?"

"Not a lot," he admitted. "But I'm no dancer. . . ."

"You move beautifully." They were very close together. "I'm trying to save you. I'm trying to give you a chance."

"Why do you care?"

She backed away. "Shit. You're hopeless." She took two more paces away. "Listen, mister, I can care about you without wanting what's in your pants."

"Then you have no interest at all?"

"You belong to my sister," she said simply. "It doesn't matter what I'm interested in. Or what I want. My honor is more important."

"All right," he said. "Let's leave it at that. What do I do?"

"Learn to lose."

"I lost, once."

"And what happened?"

"He became my teacher. My friend."

"That's just more macho buddy-buddy *yes sifu* bullshit. So you lost! So what! The strength is in you, or it isn't.

What are you so damned scared of? That you might be human? That you might be weak?'' She was yelling at him now. ''Well, if you live long enough, you'll find out what weak is, believe me. And if you're lucky, you'll have enough people who love you to help you through that time, but you never will if you can't be a goddamned human being.''

''I don't have to be weak.''

''I suppose you don't have to get old either?''

Aubry's answer was very quiet. ''Not if I die first.''

Jenna stared at him, then turned her back. ''Every tree out there is stronger than you. But you can kill it, or insects can kill it, or fire, or weather, or time. If you can't bend, you are going to break, Aubry. And that would be a shame. You . . .'' There was a catch in her voice, and she sighed. ''Promise loves you very much.''

''She has to. Cyloxibin does that.''

''God,'' she said numbly. ''You have to be the most frightened man I've ever met. You're dangerous as hell.''

She walked back down the path a few steps, then stopped. ''Good night, Aubry,'' she said, and then took another step. She stopped. ''And if you weren't with Promise . . . maybe I'd try to save you from yourself. You don't know yourself yet. Not at all. I hope you have time left. I hope we all have enough time.'' Then she was gone.

Aubry stayed up on the mountainside long after she was gone, listening to the quiet sounds, watching the stars.

He had never realized that the sky was so damned *large*.

CHAPTER FOURTEEN

Courtney

Promise lay on her stomach, awake but unmoving. The gauzy veil suspended from the ceiling fluttered in the early morning breeze. It obscured her expression. She watched as Aubry climbed in the window.

"Where've you been?"

"Thinking." He ran a thumbnail under his boot fasteners, and slipped them off as they fell into halves. "Thinking about a lot of things."

Promise lifted herself up from the bed, pulled the thin blanket up to cover her nakedness. "Anything that you want to talk about?"

"Not now. Not yet." Aubry sat on the edge of the bed, and barely reacted when she snaked her arms around him. "Do you ever wonder?" he whispered.

"Wonder what?" She kissed his ear, nibbled at the heavy lobes.

"Wonder if we really love each other." Even the effort to speak the words was gigantic. His body thundered its response to her overtures, all hormonal systems going for broke. He felt as if he was squatting atop an erupting volcano. He wanted nothing but to hold Promise, to bend her back against the mattress and join their bodies together.

He began to sweat, trembling with the effort not to move.

"I don't care," she said. "I don't care what caused it, or what feeds it. I'm sure that I'm happy with you. Aren't you happy . . ."

"I don't know," he said huskily. "I wish to hell that I did. I have a beautiful woman who can't keep her hands off me—'' and here he smiled. Some of his control broke, and he pulled her back onto the bed. ''And all I can think about is whether or not she would have loved me if it weren't for that damned drug.''

Promise pulled him onto his back, squatted atop him and began unbuckling his belt. She bared her fine, small teeth at him. ''Shut up,'' she said. She pulled his underpants away, and arched up onto her knees. ''I don't care if it was drugs, or fate, or an act of Congress.'' She held her breath and settled down on top of him. Suddenly all of his thoughts and concerns vanished. The only reality was the searing heat their bodies generated, and the thunder of his heart as she bent over him and fused their mouths together.

Tuesday, May 30

It was almost dawning when they stopped, when Aubry disentangled himself from her arms and stood naked in the room, watching the sun's first pale pink brush strokes along the horizon.

Promise lay watching him. Finally he. felt the intensity of her stare, and turned.

''Come on,'' she said. ''I want to try something.''

He grinned, and reached for her again.

''No, monomind, not that. Slip into your overalls. I want you out of here.''

''Why?''

''No questions. Let's just go.''

Aubry sighed. Whatever it was that she had in mind, he had a feeling that it wasn't going to be fun.

He dressed hurriedly and they went downstairs. They unhitched the car from the charging post. She wouldn't let him drive, just pushed him to the passenger side.

Something was wrong. Aubry did what she asked, went where he was told, but knew on some level that he was imprisoned. It didn't matter how pretty the prison was, how much love he was surrounded by.

He had no choice. And that one thing turned Heaven into Hell.

She drove him up over the wooden bridge, and into the

woods a mile or two. The road got uncomfortably rough, even through the air-cushion. At one point the dust and dirt blown up by the ground-effect skirt obscured their view. Promise pulled over to the side and stopped.

"OK. Down here." She took his hand and led him down a path to the water. It gurgled at him as he approached. The trees formed a canopy that shielded it from even the slight warmth of the morning sun.

"Why here? It's cold."

"And going to be colder. I want you to take off your overalls."

He squinted. "You *what*?"

She laughed. "I know. It's crazy, and it's uncomfortable, and you'll hate it. You'll never feel more vulnerable. I think it might be just what you need."

"You first."

"Ah-ah-ah. I'm not the one who has to dance in two nights."

"Yeah, well, if I don't believe you ever did it, I'm not gonna do it."

She stared at him for a minute, and then stripped. Her body was not as tight and muscular as Jenna's, but it seemed to have been made to show and to hold, and just watching it now fanned the flames to new life.

After the drug, and the time in prison, and the severity of Nullboxing training, he couldn't remember whether he used to feel like this or not. What was real? What was created by that damned drug?

Promise tiptoed into the stream, gritting her teeth as the freezing water splashed over her calves. "All right," she chattered. "Now you."

Aubry cursed under his breath and stripped his overalls off.

"You can either get in here a half inch at a time, or take the plunge."

Teeth clinched, he waded out until the water was to the middle of his massive thighs, almost lapping at his genitals.

Christ, did he feel ridiculous.

"Open yourself," she said. "Just dance what you feel."

"I feel like a foolsicle. Can I put my clothes back on, please?"

She laughed up to him, kissed at his mouth. "Not yet. Come on. Try."

Aubry gritted his teeth and spread his arms twirling around in a circle. Water splashed up between his legs, and he felt himself shrivel.

"Lose your balance and catch it . . ."

Aubry tried to relax and summon Warrick's face, but his friend's spirit seemed to belong to a land of steel towers. Here, in the mountains and valleys, in the world of dizzying greens and browns, Warrick and his strength was impossibly distant.

"Relax!"

Finally he did, and his ankle turned on a stone. He almost fell. Promise danced like a sprite in front of him, seemingly oblivious to the cold.

He stopped, and watched her, and tried again, and stepped on a broken branch under the water, jabbing his foot.

He stopped again, and this time he couldn't make himself move. "This is idiotic," he rasped.

She didn't laugh this time, eyes sad. The morning sunlight filtered through the trees, split into a thousand gentle beams, spotting their faces and bodies. "Aubry. I'm just trying to help."

"I know what you're trying to do—I just don't know what I want. For three years I've tried to be something that I'm not, and I'm *just not cutting it!*" The last four words were a scream.

"I'm not a builder, I'm not a leader, and I'm not a dancer. I'm a fighter. Put me in a Scavenger's suit and I'm a fighter pretending to be a Scavenger. Strip off my clothes and have me dance naked in a stream, and I'm a fighter stumbling naked through the water, and that's all, damn it."

He shook himself, grimacing, and stalked out of the water.

"Aubry . . ." she called after him.

"I'm sorry," he said as he pulled his clothes on. "I'm just not cut out for this. I've tried, damn it. I'm getting out of here. I—"

She stood in the stream, face a luminous oval masked

unevenly by shadow. He thought that she was going to have something more to say, but she didn't.

"They said that you might be able to stay if it wasn't for me. All right. Stay. I'm getting out."

Her voice was a bare whisper. "Where are you going?"

"I don't know." He sealed his boots and stood. She watched him, and their gaze met for a long moment. Too long, and he felt every fiber of his body reach out to her. He fought with all of his mind to resist. "I don't know. I have to think."

Without another word he disappeared into the woods.

Promise sank to her knees in the water, and began to cry.

Courtney Willis tinkered with the controls on the dashboard of the Mazda-Chrysler Tetra, nodding with satisfaction as the display shifted.

He still remembered cars it was actually possible to *fix*. Now, you just replaced parts. Once, you could pound out the bumpers rather than just put on a new one. Jury-rig an alternator rather than replace the entire modular electrical system. Adjust a carburetor rather than replace the computer chip that controlled the input.

Those had been simpler days, and his father had told him of even more basic ones: times when a car could literally be built from scratch, with no more education than a young man could pick up hanging around the shop.

In some ways, Courtney had to admit he had it easier. An enterprising mechanic could enter the desired specs— cost, performance, durability, ease of construction—into a computer tied to the automotive database in Michigan. One characteristic at a time, the machine allowed you to design your own car from the wheels up, complete with holographic instruction playbacks that made assembly disgustingly simple. Today, any idiot could design his own car. It would be unique to his temperament, and outperform anything a team of engineers could have cobbled together only thirty years earlier.

It wasn't fair, damn it.

Just the same, he liked the dashboards.

Well, really, there *were* no dashboards. All of the instrumentation and even the windshield on this new model were holo display.

From the outside, the craft looked like a black bullet sliced lengthwise. A little chilling to see it sliding down out of the sky—you didn't see many tru-flight vehicles up in Oregon.

And the man who stepped out of it bothered him, too. No taller than average, no wider than average, but there was something about him that set Courtney's teeth on edge.

The man wore leather, all leather, and he squeaked when he walked, damn it.

The man watched from behind wraparound sunglasses, sat in the corner of the garage and watched every motion. The skin on his face looked *fake*. He didn't know how else to put it. Fake, or maybe dead.

When his wife Sylvie came out to bring him a beer, the man hadn't looked at her, for which Courtney felt a mixture of relief and curiosity. Most men stared at Sylvie.

Maybe he was gay. Yeah. That might have been it.

But something made him nervous anyway, and he worked on the adjustment of the holo. The projection mechanism combined map coordinates with infrared and radar scan, giving perfect tracking and navigation in any weather conditions. For some reason, even that made Courtney feel a little uneasy.

The dashboard display needed so little readjustment. It hardly seemed worth the stop.

Unless . . .

Unless he didn't need service at all. His batteries and fuel cells were fully charged, and there were no gross malfunctions of any main or auxiliary circuit. Why did this man, in his incredibly expensive vehicle, end up at an off-road service station?

Courtney began to sweat.

He closed the door on the car, and turned around. "Well, that's about all that I can do for it. The resolution is better by maybe five percent."

"That's quite enough," the man said. "Thank you." His voice was quiet.

"How will you be paying for this?"

"Credit Marks. You take them, don't you?"

"Yes," he answered carefully. "But I don't see many of them these days."

"You saw one last week," the man said casually.

"I did?"

"Um-hum." The man held out two bills to Courtney. His every movement measured, Courtney took them. He started to run them through the cashequiter

"Oh, they're good enough. Just like the one last week. It came from the Buenos Aires Mint to San Cristobal, then Toronto. Then it bounced around in the States for a while before it hit Los Angeles. Ended up in the hands of a man calls himself Warrick. Or Aubry Knight. Those names sound familiar?"

"Nope. Hear a lot of names."

"In a little backwater shit place like this? Somehow I don't find that believable." The man took a freezecard image clipped out of a holo broadcast, and held it up to Courtney. "You remember him now?"

"Yes. I think I do."

"That's better. Much better." With a flip like a magician making a card disappear, the man returned the freeze to his jacket. A pair of trade notes appeared in their place. Courtney gasped at the denominations.

"We're very friendly people, and those who help us end up on top. It's really as simple as that."

Courtney swallowed hard. "Ain't really got nothing to tell you."

"I think you're lying," the man whispered, reaching out as if to caress Courtney's hand.

Human bone and muscle couldn't create the kind of pressure that Courtney felt next. It was as if his hand was caught in a vise. He tried not to scream, because if he screamed, then Sylvie would come out of the house, and if she did then—

But he couldn't hold it any longer, and he did scream, and the man released his hand.

Courtney fell to the ground, entire body flaming with the pain. "I . . . they said they were from Los Angeles. They were driving an '04 hovercar. Toyota, I think."

"Yes. What else?"

Courtney thought desperately. "They asked where Shasta Lake was."

"Is that where they were headed?"

"Said they might camp there. Go on in the morning."

"Go on to where?"

"They didn't say. Honest, they didn't say."

"Honest?" The man laughed. "On your honor? You had your chance to be honorable. You decided to side with scum."

The man knelt down next to him, Courtney curled into a ball, clutching what remained of his hand. The bones were pulp, fragments twisting through to the surface. Blood drooled from what was left. "Anything," he heard himself babble. "I'll tell you anything."

"I'm sure you will." The man stood, and smiled benevolently. He suddenly lashed out with a toe, connecting with Courtney's knee. The pain was incredible. "Just so you won't wander off while I disconnect your beacon. We don't want to be disturbed now, do we?"

There was a sudden scream, and Courtney heard the sound of his front door slapping open.

"Don't move." It was Sylvie's voice.

Don't. Get out of here. . . . He tried to say the words, but pain had frozen his vocal cords.

The stranger laughed. "Now why don't you put that down, little lady?"

Courtney wiggled around until he faced the house. Sylvie was on the steps, the Remington pump nestled against her shoulder, barrel aimed precisely at the stranger's face.

"You get away from him," she said, her voice on the edge of cracking.

The stranger laughed again. "This is all just a misunderstanding. I'm sure we can work something out—"

He was turning sideways, and Courtney saw that his right hand, hidden from Sylvie, was reaching into the coat—

There was a sudden roar, and one of the Tetra's windows exploded. Before anyone could move, Sylvie had shifted the barrel again, and the stranger was no longer smiling.

"Next shot's right between the eyes," she said. "Law's on the way, mister. Always takes 'em too long to get here, so if you take off right *now* I might decide it's less trouble to let you go than to shoot you or try to keep you covered for a half hour. *Get*."

The stranger's hand dropped away from his pocket, and he nodded, smiling sickly. He swung into the car. It started with the first touch of the ignition, and lifted away, blasting them with dust.

Sylvie ran to her husband, who was beginning to lift himself from the ground.

"Damn nice car," he said, nursing his hand. "Wasn't the car's fault." The blood was draining from his face as he stood. "Should have shot him in the leg." And he collapsed against her.

Killinger was hovering at two thousand feet when the rest of his unit caught up. They were specks at first, almost invisible in the afternoon sunlight. Then a dozen of them materialized. All were encapsulated, so that it would be impossible to see who or what was within.

The first vehicle wagged its fins in salute. The radio crackled. "Sir?"

"Nothing," he said irritably. "They didn't know anything."

Killinger tamped his anger down. It was unprofessional. Later, after this was all over, he would come back and take care of those two. "Knight has disappeared for now. Fortunately we have business farther north, or my trip would be for nothing. Are the incendiary units in place around Marjo?"

"Yes, sir."

"Well, then." He sighed in satisfaction. "Let's go and pay those bitches a little visit. It's time the Medusas got their test run."

CHAPTER FIFTEEN

Ariane

Tuesday, May 30

''No, I haven't seen him since this morning. Why?''

Promise smiled uncertainly. Why indeed? If Aubry wanted to go off by himself and sulk, that was his option. If only it wasn't so damned important. If only . . .

Promise left the administration building and stepped out into the oval. All around her, the life of the encampment was in full swing. Women were working at a myriad of large and small tasks. The new eastern dining hall was almost complete. There, to the south, the concrete foundation for a new amphitheater was being poured even as she walked.

She strolled the center lane, forcing Aubry from her mind. She loved him. Her body screamed for him when she woke in the morning, when the empty sheets caressed her skin at night. But perhaps he was right. Perhaps a chemical could create a bond that shouldn't have existed in the first place.

And is love enough? Is it enough to want someone right down to your marrow? Or are other things as important, perhaps more important . . . ?

Perhaps it was time for them to find out.

The smiles that she received from the passing women were genuine. In no way were they ingratiating, imploring, expectant, cajoling. They were a genuine emotional embrace. They were faces that said ''welcome,'' and voices that echoed the thought.

Perhaps, just perhaps . . .

Her own jobs in administration and nursing were undemanding, but held a certain potential. If she were to stay. If she renounced the outside world, then there would be more responsibility, and a position of greater importance. Her administrative skills, gained in tenure with the Scavengers, would be of great use to Ephesus. They had let her know that in no uncertain terms.

But for now she just walked, looking.

There were so few men here. How did that make her feel? How did it feel to live in a world dominated by women, after spending the ten years of her life in a world where men controlled almost everything.

Peaceful. Frightening. Exhilarating. Her own strength was challenged, rose to the call. It was . . .

It was home.

Dinner time, and still Aubry had not appeared. Their hovercar was still there. Aubry hadn't removed any of his belongings from the room. Promise sat on the edge of the bed, and looked at his things. She picked up one of the shirts he had worn the day before. She smelled it, inhaled deeply. His natural spicy scent burst on her senses.

Her body ached for him. She bit her lip, trembling. Was it right to want someone so badly? Was it healthy? She didn't know, and, in part, did not care. It was the way that she felt, and there was nothing to be done about that.

But she could affect what she did with the realization.

Promise walked to the window, and looked out over the valley of Ephesus. Why had she come back here? What was it that the outside world lacked for her?

The domes of the houses, the evening lights just beginning to glow, all of these were good things, warming things, but they had not been in her mind.

There was one reason, one clear and obvious reason, something that had yet to be resolved.

She left the room, crossing the courtyard to Bioworks, the northernmost building on the oval.

The building was a little cooler than the air outside. The

halls were striped with gleaming plastic, more than any of the other buildings. Here there was more metal than wood, and the lighting seemed almost pointedly artificial. The floor beneath her purred with odd vibrations.

Her feet felt heavy here, as if she were trespassing. A woman in a lab coat brushed by her in the halls. Promise smiled, and turned to let her pass. There was an entirely different feeling here in this place, and she wasn't sure what it was. The stained glass and the wood were decoys. The pattern of color on the ground, focused as if by a rotating jewel, softened every angle, somehow made it difficult to think.

She scanned the pegboard at the end of the hall listing assignments.

The names ran horizontally, each of them engraved on a tiny wooden rectangle and pegged at their daily assignment. She scanned them, searching for something.

A. COTONOU. It wasn't larger or more prominent than any of the other tags, but then she wouldn't have expected it to be. But there was the name, Promise couldn't have forgotten it in a hundred years. Ariane was here.

Promise peered up the stairway leading to the second floor, and sighed. She could have walked right up without a problem. But Ariane was in the basement, in a higher-security section. She couldn't get admittance without a passkey. There was no way to fake her way through. Everyone knew everyone else by sight. The only thing she could do was wait. She tried three doors before she found one that was open. Within, two lab coats were hanging on hooks. She slipped one on, warmed instantly by the heat-reflective cloth.

Back in the hall again, she sank her head into her hands, and waited.

Forty minutes later, the elevator chimed. Promise carefully scanned the emerging group. They numbered six women, trim and healthy and talking quietly to one another. Promise searched their faces. Could her mother have changed so in ten years? No . . . but she rose as they exited, and stood at the nearby water fountain, as if ignoring them. As the last of them walked past she slipped into the elevator before the door closed.

Unbidden, the elevator sank slowly, and touched bottom with a sigh. The colored lights at the top of the door frame washed from green to gold, and then the door hissed open.

It was actually chilly in this part of the building, making the insulated lab coat a necessity. The lights were skewed somehow. Promise peered through the long, low windows into the various labs where secret, tender miracles were being wrought. Each of the separate rooms was filled with glistening metal and crystal. One bank of walls was partitioned into hundreds of small slots, like safe deposit boxes. Each had a green glass window. The doors into the rooms were locked.

There were two operating rooms at the far end of the hall, and neither was occupied. Promise slipped into one.

Something inside her wanted to cry. It was here, or in a room much like this one, where she had been conceived. Was this where Ariane and her technicians had worked their gentle magic with Suzette Freleng's ancient, frozen eggs?

From a rack to her left she extracted a slender glass pipette, and held it up to the light. Had this been part of the process? And had the frozen egg been transported in one of these to the next room, to undergo the delicate manipulations that would fuse them with one of Ariane's? Then was the resulting fertilized ovum implanted into her mother's uterine wall? She was the child of two women, but one had died long before Promise was born. Promise had always paid most honor to one, and now needed so much to . . .

"This is the place."

Promise turned, flushed with embarrassment.

The woman who stood in the doorway was inches shorter than Promise, her skin fractionally lighter. Her hair was long, and very white. She was stout now, and, from the mixed Polynesian lines in her face, looked as if she would have been more at home in a sarong than a lab coat. Time and a slowing metabolic rate had stolen the muscle from her body. She carried a white plastic clipboard tight against her chest.

"You're wearing glasses," Promise said lamely.

Ariane studied her, harsh words hovering near the surface. She took the gold frames off, folded them, slipped them into a breast pocket. "Yes. I suppose I could have had corrective surgery, or optical feedback training. I've never liked the idea of little plastic chips floating on my eyeballs."

Promise tried to laugh, but the best she could manage was a smile. "I had to see you." The air conditioner whispered a breath of cold air against the back of her neck.

"Why?"

Tears were close now. "I wanted to see my mother. There was a time when I could run to you when I hurt. If I skinned a knee, you were there. If I stumbled, you were there to pick me up."

"That was a long time ago, Promise. You decided to leave. You knew the cost."

"And you knew the cost of staying! Did you really think that I would be satisfied just reading and scanning the outside world?"

"No. We're not perfect here." She plucked the pipette from Promise's hand, and slipped it back into the rack. "We make mistakes. We feel fear. We make rules to protect ourselves. We know what happened to you when you left."

"You knew?"

Ariane's expression was almost scornful. "Can you really believe that I wouldn't care?"

"I think I want to come back."

"You were told that the option was open."

"Just . . . let the decision be one of love, not need. Please." Promise took a step toward the woman who stood clipboard pressed to her chest like a shield. "Please let me decide. Everything I did in the outside world I did to survive."

"You think that I can't understand survival?" Promise stepped closer, into the light. Her mother looked much older than she remembered, as if more than mere years had crept into the equation. Some poison of the soul, perhaps. Her facial skin looked doughy and too malleable, like someone who has made one too many concessions to necessity.

"I built all of this."

"And it's beautiful."

"Is it? It was meant for women, as a refuge from the filth of men. And it was structured as a democratic society. If only I'd known how deeply the poison has seeped."

"What do you mean?"

"I tried to build something strong and good here. My patents brought in money—more money than I would ever need. If I'd only known." She shook her head, for a moment seemingly unaware that Promise was even in the room. "I wanted to give life. To extend life. My God. That man can twist anything."

"What man?"

Ariane caught herself. "Men." She looked up at Promise again, eyes bright. "You were my daughter. You were to follow my work. We taught you to dance, and you gave it to men. We taught you love, and you whored yourself for men."

"And women," Promise breathed. "Women paid me, just like men. And they treated me no better."

"Corrupted women!" Dr. Cotonou screamed.

"Then the entire species is corrupted," Promise said quietly. "Then mothers corrupt their children in the cradle. Who was it who said 'give me a child for the first five years, and you can have him thereafter'? That's the mother's role. If we've so abdicated responsibility, what sense does it make to blame men for that? Why not just consider it a basic flaw in the species and give the damn planet back to the roaches?"

"I won't debate with you, Promise. You asked sanctuary, and it was granted. You asked for your man to have an opportunity to prove himself to us. He did work with us, that is clear. And he was given an opportunity to dance. If he takes it, there will be a vote. I can't interfere."

"Not pro or con."

"No. Neither pro nor con. Heaven help me." She held the door back. "I have to ask you to leave."

Promise walked out past her, past the little woman who seemed terribly bowed by age and time, as if staggering under a burden she dared not share.

"Mother . . ."

"Go on now," Ariane whispered.

As Promise passed through the door she turned, and hugged her, kissing Ariane's face desperately, hoping for a response. Any response.

"Go, now."

Promise turned and left.

The dinner was delicious, but Promise's tastebuds simply weren't in gear. She couldn't enjoy it at all. The tastes made it as far as her conscious mind, but not to her pleasure centers.

She listened to the blur of conversations in the room, feeling guilt atop the loss. Aubry was gone. He had left his things, and just gone. He was through with her, with *them*.

The grief was so strong that she could barely move. She found herself staring at her fork for long moments, until Jenna came to her.

"Are you all right? You haven't eaten much. I've watched."

"I'm fine. Just frightened. Just . . ."

Jenna sat, and took Promise's hand in her own. "If it's over, it is."

Promise slid her own hand free. "You wouldn't understand. Everyone acts as if he's doing me a favor to go away. Jenna . . . I love him. I only loved one other man, and he betrayed me. Aubry never has. He saved my life. He gave me my child. I . . ." Promise buried her face in her hands, and wept.

Jenna watched her, face betraying no emotion. Finally, she spoke. "I think that I can understand. He's a lot of man, Promise. I'd be lying if I said I wasn't attracted."

Startled, Promise glanced up. "You?"

She nodded. "Nothing happened, or would have happened. You're my sister. He's your man. And we both knew the score. But the feeling was there."

"I didn't think you liked men."

"Most men are little boys. When they don't get what they want from life, they have their women stroke them, let them feel that life is against them. I just didn't feel that from Aubry. He's a man, and most aren't. What he *isn't* is a whole human being.''

"What . . . ?"

"It's just an observation. He is the most dangerous fighter I've ever seen. I couldn't kill him with a hand grenade in a locked room. He could have broken every bone in my body without effort, just by breaking the rhythm of the flow. But he didn't. He let me have my honor. But that isn't enough. He doesn't know that *he* is the power. Oh, it's the Nullboxing. Or it's this man Warrick. But Aubry can't see who Aubry is. And so he'll keep searching until he finds someone who'll show him. By killing him.''

Promise dropped her fork onto her plate. "I don't think I'm hungry.''

"I don't blame you." Jenna straightened her back. She changed the subject without artifice. "Dancing tonight. Three of the girls are making their debut.''

Promise sighed, and leaned back against the cushions.

The places were cleared, and Promise drew herself up and back. Why inflict her private demons on others?

The three girls appeared, greeted by a polite round of applause as they stepped onto the stage. They wore gray tights that were so sheer they made silk seem like burlap, and clung to their young bodies like a spray of moondust. Promise was transported. She remembered her own moment, so many years before, making her first appearance here, the butterflies swarming in her stomach.

The girls began to move.

Shyly at first, the barest tilt of their heads giving the desired impression of the moment: vulnerability. A child's—

There was a sudden, abrupt hush in the room and Promise looked to the rear.

"Oh my God . . .''

Aubry stood, stripped to the waist, wearing gray tights that had been stitched together roughly. They threatened to pull apart at the seams. His body, massively muscled, was certainly larger and more spectacularly proportioned than any other body in the encampment. The stitches were ragged X's, but still, the tights fit.

Head down modestly, Aubry walked the center aisle to
the middle of the room. The three girls in the front stared,
then tittered. Then, bless them, they made a place for him
between them, and joined hands.

What was he . . . ?

They began to move. Aubry moved more lightly than
the girls, despite the grotesque inequity of weight. There
was grace, but no elegance in his movement, only leashed
power.

Promise's heart went out to him. She could see the
concentration on his face, in his eyes. Aubry fought for
control, fought for both their lives.

There were titters of laughter in the room, and then an
unrestrained guffaw.

But the girls somehow managed to keep their poise.
They allowed Aubry to be one of them, and the four of them
tried to flow together. Their backs were more flexible than
his, but his legs split as wide. His pirouettes, clumsy
though they might have been, were perfectly balanced.

And slowly, the tenor in the room changed. His body
was soaked in sweat. The catcalls increased. Dasha stood
and called: "This is a mockery! Get him off the stage."

Aubry turned, and looked out at them, and his eyes
were vast and dark. He didn't have even a grain of resistance left in him. He just shrugged and began to step
down.

Jenna leapt to her feet. "The hell you say! This man is
trying. And he deserves your respect if not your admiration. He has his heart open. He is willing to be vulnerable,
and all you're doing is kicking him where he's open. Is
that what we are? Is that it?"

There was a grumble of protest, but Glenda Wright's
stolid, massive figure joined Jenna's slight one. Her massive forearms were folded, and her eyes narrowed. The
room quieted swiftly.

Aubry joined hands with the girls again. They began to
move, and this time the flow was a little more relaxed—he
wasn't trying so very hard.

And the catcalls became clapping, tentative at first, then
spreading through the room like a joyous infection. Here

was this great, hulking brute of a man spinning on his toes, flexing and rolling his hard, gleaming stomach muscles in rhythm to the music. Promise felt some of the ice around her heart begin to melt. It was possible. It was just possible.

And she turned. In the back of the hall, a lone woman stood. And as she turned, the entire gathering turned, and stood to face Ariane. Ariane said nothing, just watched Aubry on the stage, and then turned to look at Promise.

Please. Please . . .

Ariane nodded her head slightly, and the room exploded into cheers.

It was at that moment that the alarm klaxons rang.

CHAPTER SIXTEEN

Fire

Ephesus was in an uproar. Aubry stood in the middle of the oval, still dressed in his tights. Cars and aircars, motorbikes and teams of firefighters on foot, weaved around him in controlled chaos. Children in endless streams ran to safety, herded by nursemaids. He felt lost. This was not his place, not his world, but it was a fight. He wanted in.

Promise rushed past him without a word. She and five other women entered a long, low sheet-metal shed. She emerged moments later wearing hip boots and carrying a shovel. They headed directly toward one of the reconditioned school buses pulling smoothly into the oval.

He snatched at her arm. "I'll grab a shovel or something and come with you—"

She took his face firmly in her hands. "No. I know exactly what to do, and where I'm going. Stay here. Go to Firewatch Central, in the communications building, and get an assignment." His face must have been a holoboard, because Promise's attitude suddenly changed. "This isn't a put-down, baby. It's the way things have to be."

The bus door hissed shut behind her, and it lurched into motion, heading out toward Marjo Valley.

Aubry ran west across the camp and just missed colliding with two women who scurried out of the communications building. They barely noticed him.

The building held more electronic apparatus than the rest of the camp combined. The first floor was bisected by an immense map which tilted back at forty-five degrees to the floor. At present one triangular patch was alight with red, spreading out to black.

He stepped through the door, unnoticed by any of the women in the room as they concentrated on the sights and sounds before them.

"We have identified the fire area. South of Trask River, north of Marjo Valley. Satellite confirmation coming through from Northwest Digital. Please stand by . . ."

"—icopters? This is area 1402, Northwest, awaiting confirmation of availability. This is an urgent situation. We have two fires in process. We are—"

Jenna met Aubry at the door. "Aubry. Bad timing. You'll have to leave."

"There has to be something that I can do. I can't just stand here and watch everything happen. It's not my nature."

"We don't have time to argue. Look at the map. The way the fire is circling Marjo, it looks like arson. The best thing for you is to stay here. We'll need help with burn and smoke inhalation cases. If I have time, I'll find a better position for you—*it won't be make-work,* but I don't have time to argue with you. Can you understand that?"

"Not much choice, is there?"

A call from the other side of the room. "Jenna . . . we have the weather prediction coming in now. We've got no rain fronts in sight, but no high winds either. No help or hurt. It looks like we're in this alone."

"All right. Let's set up a backburn here along Flint Ridge. Fire's burning south here? OK. Get a crew in. Chop back the undergrowth, burn it here, *up* the ridge. When the fire gets to the other side, it won't—shouldn't— have anything to eat. I want security checks run on any aircraft in the area. See if there's been any unusual activity. Copters and hovercraft would be the worst. Ground vehicles have to worry about being caught by the fire. They'll be a lot more cautious—"

Aubry backed out of the room. He could see that he wasn't needed there, but still itched for action. He sat on the porch outside, watching a thin plume of smoke curling up in the distance. Out there, death was cooking, and he felt awesomely impotent and vulnerable. *What could he do?*

Nothing, until the situation had been judged, the forces organized. Until then, he had to sit back and do what he was told.

It galled him, that was all.

A woman's solitary figure moved across the oval, stopped in the middle. The camp was almost deserted. A final truck raced by her, leaving a trail of settling dust. It was Ariane who stood there, shoulders sloped as she watched the destruction of her dream.

He walked up behind her softly.

"Ariane . . . ?"

She turned, and he saw tears in her eyes. For a moment—but only for a moment—there was tremendous vulnerability in that expression. Then it hardened. "All for nothing," she said.

"What are you talking about? It won't be so bad. You seem damned organized."

"You don't understand. How could someone like you ever understand?"

She turned and walked toward the Bioworks building. Before she reached it an explosion shook the camp's southern end. The library gouted fire from its shattered roof. Aubry curled on the ground as wood splinters, mixed with smoke and soot, rained from the sky.

"Damn!" He rolled to his feet and sprinted toward the building. "What's happening here?"

As women ran from Communications/Firewatch, Aubry sank back into the shadows. What he was supposed to do was run toward the fire. What he was supposed to do was try to save people, try to save buildings. What no one would expect him to do was sit back and observe.

Where was the enemy . . . ?

There was a muffled *whumpf,* and a soft whistling sound. Another building roared with flame.

Rocket attack! Who in the hell would hate these women enough for that? To attack a woodland area with incendiary rockets was insane unless . . .

Distraction.

He backed out of the camp, scrambled back up into the woods, and watched. The entire scene was a madhouse now. Fires raged at two corners of the camp. Every available pair of hands was bent to extinguishing them. All right. The enemy has pulled attention away from the center. That had to be the true target.

He slipped back into camp, through the shadows, as much a part of the night as the moon.

Ariane. Bioworks. *All for nothing . . .*

She was the target, and she knew it.

Why? Why would anyone want to kill her?

Aubry crept into the Bioworks building, hunkered down in a shadow, tried to absorb the size and shape of the structure, find its relationship to his body, until he *felt* it down to its foundations.

Vibration. It was an overwhelming part of the night. The sound of traffic outside, of voices. And then of another explosion next door to Bioworks. A painfully bright surge of yellow light flooded through the windows. *Administration!*

And *there*, of a window being broken in the back of Bioworks.

The power went out in the building.

Killing time.

Aubry's eyes searched the halls, looking for a weapon. He found nothing. Very well. Until he could kill the first assailant, it would be empty hands only.

On the balls of his feet, Aubry moved through the darkened halls. Outside, the fires raged but Aubry's attention was on the blaze within him, realizing that he felt at peace for the first time since aiding the NewMen in Los Angeles. This was his world. It wasn't a place. It wasn't a person, it was a feeling, a particularly nasty void between ethic and efficiency. A place where violence lived like a hungry, red-eyed predator. Here, a man like Aubry Knight found his balance in a universe that didn't, couldn't, care about the lives of individual people. Only people could care about people. Ariane could think what she wanted of him. He wouldn't allow her to die.

Freeze.

Shape at the end of the hall. Aubry faded into the wall,

aided by the natural darkness of his skin, and his affinity for the shadows.

The man walked right to him, was almost on top of him before he knew that Aubry was there.

The edge of Aubry's foot speared out, cracking the knee. Before the man had time to use the long-barreled handgun, Aubry's arm was around his neck. The gun discharged, too near Aubry's eyes, and the barrel flash shocked the world into a blur of reds and blacks. Aubry wrenched sharply, and the body slithered to the floor.

He felt rather than heard the footsteps on the floor behind him.

Aubry dove and rolled, tearing the gun from the dead man's hands as he did. His hand slid over the weapon as he bounced toward safety. A silenced automatic pistol. Perfect for assassin's work.

Slugs chewed wedges from the floor. Aubry skittered sideways. Even through his clouded vision, he saw the laser sighting dot slide across his chest and off his shoulder. A wild surge of adrenaline twisted him out of line, and slugs tore up the wall. All the killer needed to do was keep the trigger depressed, and Aubry would have been dead.

He dove into a side room, checked the door connecting it with the next chamber, and slammed the flat of his foot against the door, finding the lock on the second thrust. It shattered, and he rolled through as bullets spattered around the room behind him. Without stopping, he hit the hall door, bursting out and into the hall, firing blindly. His shoulder and the door hit two people on the other side.

One went down instantly. Eyes tearing, Aubry ripped the man's throat out on the way back to his feet.

The second was smaller. Much smaller. Lither. Aubry wiped frantically at his eyes, doubting what his blurred sight told him: the tiny figure had rebounded like a rubber ball, snapping back to guard and attack faster than anything human could possibly move.

In the instant it took him to adjust his mind to the shock, a foot arced and hit his gun hand with a move that was timed to perfection. His arm went dead.

Aubry was ready for the second kick: heelkick/round

kick. That was the natural path of hip torque. That was the direction of momentum, and the only option, given that there was so very much follow-through left from the first technique. Without benefit of sight or conscious command, Aubry's body set him up for the counter, a whiplash block against a smaller opponent, followed by a crushing punch to the midsection.

But the arcing follow-up never came. He couldn't see, and everything was happening too fast. His opponent folded into a smaller target, jackknifed. The kick speared out directly, striking Aubry in the ribs with a sharp exhalation that was perfectly timed with the extension of the leg.

The blow missed his solar plexus by a fraction of an inch. Aubry rolled, mind numbed with shock. What in the hell was he fighting? All he had felt was *bone* and *movement*. It was the most perfectly executed technique he had ever experienced.

As fast as the kick had been launched, it was retracted twice as swiftly. Aubry's flashing hands found nothing to grasp.

He bounded off the wall, managed to get his chin down before a kick intended for his throat smashed into his jaw. Lights exploded behind his eyes.

But this time he caught the leg as it slithered away. Again, he was shocked again at its lightness. Was he fighting a woman? The leg was smaller and thinner than Jenna's—

A child?

He froze, and the moment was gone.

He grunted as his attacker's body curled in midair, supported by his own grip. The other foot hammered into his chest. It felt like the blow of a sledgehammer, and only Aubry's frantic torquing of the leg saved his life. Landed cleanly, that blow would have killed anything human.

Aubry staggered back into the wall, tasting blood. Shocked beyond words. Helpless. For two precious seconds he could do nothing but roil in the pain, struggling to find a breath.

He heard the sound of feet retreating through the darkness. Light feet. A small woman. A child . . .

Dear God. Was it even *human?*

Aubry stumbled to his feet, and spit salt blood. He heard a scream upstairs, and forgot all of his considerations.

Ariane! He took the stairs three at a time. A man-sized blur at the top of the stairs swung at him with a rifle butt. Aubry didn't even pause, just went through him, went under him in a response that Jenna had used. The attacker wheeled over his shoulder and sailed down the stairs, not making contact with a single one before striking the bottom with a crunch.

Bullets spattered against the wall. He felt a smashing pain in his right shoulder as he was grazed. He hit the ground and spun back down the stairs, behind the protection of the wall.

There was another scream, and then the sound of glass breaking on the far end. Smoke. And then quiet.

Aubry dragged the corpse back up the stairs, ignoring the pain in his shoulder. He heaved it up over the railing.

Nothing. He took the chance, dashed up, and smashed into the door on the far side of the hall. Nothing.

Aubry crept out into the hall, then staggered, choking back a throatful of vomit. Shattered glass was everywhere, and mixed in with the slivers were dozens of slippery pink fetuses. Some of them still moved sluggishly in a bloody syrup.

His eyes burned, and he wiped at them savagely. Something within him wanted to collapse and grieve, but he had to move, had to keep going while he could.

Three of the women were dead, their bodies twisted and broken. They lay with arms outstretched, as if trying to salvage their nonborn children. The room spun, and Aubry grabbed a bench, steadying himself.

He moved like an automaton, struggling to remember the business at hand.

Ariane. Where . . .

He heard a moan from behind a wall stitched with bullet holes. He thumped the wall with one fist, heard the hollow reply. A bolt-hole: one that hadn't entirely worked. Ignoring the pain in his shoulder, Aubry tore the leg off a table. With an exhalation of "*hyahh!*" he drove it end-on into the wall, levering and pulling until the edge of the door began to crack. The table leg began to bend with the strain. Aubry set his fingers into the crack, braced his feet against the wall, and pulled with all of the enormous strength of his upper and lower back. The steel bolts groaned, and one of the hinges popped. Panting, Aubry crawled back down, and wedged the bar down farther into the crack, and pulled with the improved leverage. The remaining hinge popped.

Ariane cowered there, crumpled into a corner. Blood leaked from her chest, and her face was ravaged with pain. She scrabbled at the floor, trying to pull farther away, to back into the wall. One hand lifted feebly, trying to ward him off.

Sickened, he understood: she thought that he was one of the assassins.

It had to be the smoke in the air, but tears streamed freely down his cheeks as he bent to lift her. She collapsed into his chest, mumbling, "Jenna. My baby. Get Jenna. . . ."

And he nodded.

Bioworks was blazing by the time he got Ariane from the building. Their shadows were flickering ghosts framed by the orange light. Aubry turned, staring back into the inferno as two women eased Ariane from his arms, their eyes shining with an impossible mixture of gratitude and hatred. The entire camp was shattered, burning, and a half-dozen fires smoldered in the forest itself.

"Where's Jenna?" he asked finally. He was afraid to close his eyes, even for a moment. When he did, the pink shellfish forms of the dying fetuses crawled in the darkness.

"Out in Marjo. That's the worst. They're trying to draw a line there."

The shoulder burned like hell, but he couldn't rest. Not yet. "Then that's where I'm going."

CHAPTER SEVENTEEN

Fire Flight

Northeast of Ephesus, across Trask River on a dirt road sheltered by a stand of trees, the black disk of a hovercraft hunched low on the ground. No lights issued from it, and no sound, but it hummed with activity.

A motorcycle pulled up, its front wheel juddering in shallow ruts. It slid to a halt. The messenger hopped off, touched his thumb to a telecast card on his chest, and stood very still.

The air shimmered, and an armored guard appeared from behind his optical shield. The guard checked the messenger again, then waved the man inside.

The craft was a honeycomb of narrow passages. The messenger took a left-branching corridor to a tiny room made smaller by its profusion of monitoring equipment. He took off his helmet.

At the side console, a chair pivoted. Marcel Killinger's gleaming metal jaw inched out from the padded leather, grinning without humor. "Where are the others?"

"Distributing jelbombs, except for three noncoms."

"And . . . ?"

"Medusas 2, 7, and 12 performed kills, but broke emotionally. Just went crazy. I had to terminate them."

"The bodies?"

"Cremated. That's the bad news. The good news is that Medusa-16 was damaged, but performed specplus."

"What—" The human tissue in Killinger's face twisted with savage pleasure. "Play the memory."

"Yes, sir." The messenger doffed his helmet. Killinger

removed a small cartridge from the side pocket, and slipped it into a playback slot in the blinking console.

Killinger folded his fingers together, and settled back to watch. *"Ephesus."* He hissed the word nastily. "Effie bitches." The holostage above the console rippled and flared with color. They watched as the camp's calm dissolved into chaos, as the women and men streamed out from their homes like ants from a shattered nest. They swarmed to their vehicles, to the fire stations in the forests.

And *there* . . .

"Freeze. God damn!" There was no mistaking the enormous figure caught in midstride on the oval. It was Knight. Aubry Knight. Raw animal hatred radiated from the Merc leader, and suddenly the messenger wanted to be somewhere else. Anywhere but close enough to be a potential target for Killinger's frustration.

"Computer." Killinger said it in a flat, ugly trisyllable. "Probability that woman Promise is an Effie."

A string of variables ran across the screen.

—*Coordination +22, Ferris scale.*

—*Given highest rating in manipulation of Plastiskin. Abnormal level of autonomic control.*

—*57% chance birth certificate falsified by former pimp Jamie Parks in Las Vegas.*

—*First 100% verifiable appearance Las Vegas 2016, in company of Jamie Parks. Travel itinerary of Jamie Parks included Oregon within 18 months of first appearance of Promise.*

Probability: 87%.

Killinger laughed coarsely, and the tension dissolved. The elephant stepped off the messenger's chest.

"Son of a bitch." Killinger shook his head ruefully. "It was there right in front of us all the time. All we had to do was ask the right questions. Computer: Promise surname?"

Cotonou. Used once, motel credit receipt, 2016. No other recorded usage.

Killinger switched modes, and followed the tape image as the assassin entered the main biofacility. The bitches had been taken totally unawares, bullets riddling their bodies before the threat fully registered.

"Glorious kill," he whispered. The woman Ariane was nowhere to be seen, although she was spotted climbing the stairs to the second level. "Where? Where. . . ?"

The Medusas were moving through the shadows, childish, somber figures carrying scaled-down machine pistols. Then they broke into the laboratory, the security women froze for an irretrievable second, and the Medusas triggered their weapons. Lead sprayed in a lethal web, smashing into bodies, shattering glass. Blood and fluid splashed explosively around the room. The bodies danced, smashed backward into the shelves and counters, slid twitching to the floor. And were still.

The Medusas paused. Fetuses slid out of their broken cases, slid down the walls and across the floor, almost to one of their feet.

Medusa-12 bent, and picked one of the fetuses up, its tiny hands wiggling, mouth opening and closing spastically.

Suddenly 12 screamed, hurling the slippery thing at the wall where it spattered in a starburst. 12 screamed and screamed, finger pressing the trigger of its machine gun, and then—

The tape went black.

"The cameraman was accidentally shot here. This is where we terminated the Medusas."

Killinger nodded. "All right. More." The images resumed.

Sounds of crashing, and more gunshots. A frantic turn of the head, and the first glimpse of Aubry Knight.

Killinger froze the image as Knight bounded up the stairs. "Damn, the man *floats* when he moves." There was both hatred and grudging admiration in his words.

"Medusa-16, you said?"

"Injured, not badly. But injured this man as well, in a one-on-one. We salvaged tape from his helmet."

Killinger seemed immensely pleased. "Yes. This is good. Very good. We lost three, but we only need three killers. 16 passes. Computer, note: rest and healing for 16 in Los Angeles. He and the others have an appointment next week. Then, return him to the Nation for final evaluation. Register that 16 has passed the very highest graded coordination test. If the other scores match, give 16 final approval for Perseus.''

He swung around in his chair. "Good. Primary is accomplished. We still have the opportunity to accomplish the secondary mission. Do we have a tracer on Knight?''

"He's headed toward Trask River. That's for sure.''

Killinger stared at the computer input again, finding his strange harmony with it. A three-dimensional grid of Marjo Valley appeared. Glowing red patches represented the fires burning out of control. "I want you to look at this. Tracking says that they're fighting down in the valley, and fighting too damn well. County fire equipment and manpower are controlling the outer edges. The women are building a firebreak along Flint Ridge. Here, where the logging winch operates. They have a lot of expensive machinery, and they're trying to save it. So if we move in behind them *here*, and firebomb the road and close the gap, the wind will do the rest. They'll be trapped. It will be an hour before the state forces get the go-ahead from federal to expend funds on a fire on private land. More foot dragging as they debate the Effie question. State will expend most of its effort to make sure that the fire doesn't spread to the rest of Tillamook nation. I think we can get the whole clitsucking lot of 'em.''

Killinger pulled the video disk from its slot, and crushed it with one hand's slow and steady pressure. His human skin, curling around the unmoving metal of his jaw, smiled beatifically. "Faggotry must be contagious. I wonder why he was wearing a tutu?''

The bus lurched as it followed the road. The air stank of smoke, although Aubry couldn't see any flame yet. It was almost midnight. He could see no smoke in the sky, but no clouds, either. Women and men lined the roads, resting aching arms for a few moments before going back up to Flint Ridge to continue chopping the firebreak. The bus was filled with replacement firefighters, recruited from outlying allied women's groups. Every able body was needed. Only three hours after the initial alarm, yet the situation was critical.

A whining sound above him made him look up. The winch was still in operation. The great slab of a cedar log dangled overhead, buoyed by the balloon, creaking and jostling as it headed out of the valley. The Ephesians were still moving a last few logs out of the fire's path. It was coming their way, and it was coming fast.

The bus screeched to a halt, and the firefighters spilled out. Aubry hit the ground running, and yelled his question to the first group of people he reached. "Where's Jenna?"

"Top of the hill," a short balding man in overalls panted, pointed. "Working a strip there. Can't fight the fire on the far side: heat rises. Hell to pay if it rips past the crest, though."

He barely heard the rest of it. He ignored the pain in his shoulder and began to run. He followed the paved road at first, then left it and scrambled up through the brush toward the top of the hill. He was glad he'd taken the precious moments necessary to pull his denims over the leotards: the underbrush would have cut his legs to pieces. Finally, he saw the dirty, weary, soot- and dirt-stained figures trudging back down the hill. On the north side there was smoke and the glow of something that would eat them alive without pausing to either mourn or gloat.

Above the ridge, an Ephesian transport copter hovered, dumping liquid that burst into foam on contact with the heat. It gave off a horrible, choking stench.

Up ahead he saw Jenna's wiry body as she worked a teardrop-shaped chain saw, clearing brush. She was greased with sweat, her dungarees blotched in patches as she worked the saw.

She turned and looked, finally focusing on him. "Aubry. Were you assigned here?"

"I'm supposed to bring you back. Ariane was shot."

She killed the saw. "What!?"

"She's dying." He shrugged helplessly. "She may be dead by now."

Jenna's eyes glowed. The fire beyond the ridge was cooler, less dangerous than that which Jenna held in check. "She was the target. And the lab." She whipped her head up toward the hissing wall of stinking smoke. "No time for that now. And no time to get back. If that fire breaks the ridge, we'll be in real trouble.''

"Where's Promise?"

She pointed east. "Last time I saw her. Aubry—we don't have time for play. If you really want to help, this is the time.''

He nodded silently.

Aubry ran through the underbrush, through the tangle. Branches whipped his face, blinding him, cutting his skin. He spotted Promise on the other side of a rise, with Glenda Wright and a group of six women and one man working to clear a tangle of underbrush.

"Promise!"

Confusion and relief mingled on her face. "Aubry. We could use you.''

"Ariane is dying. She needs you there.''

Promise leaned onto her shovel as if it were a crutch, silent, barely seeming to breathe. "She needs me HERE.'' She finally sighed. "If she dies, she dies. She'd want us to save the valley. I can't go anywhere.''

The wind shifted south, and Aubry was suddenly choked by the stench of fire foam from the far side of the ridge.

"Shit.'' Without another word to her he fought his way up the quarter mile to the top of the ridge. Much of it was already stripped and backburned. Chain saws and mini-torches whirred and flared around him as the teams fought their desperate battle.

Aubry reached the top and looked down, appalled.

Below, the entire valley was burning. How could anything so massive happen so quickly?

The brush smoldered with small fires. On the valley floor, trees writhed and died in flame. An Ephesian hovercraft dove into the smoke, dumping and spraying its stinking cargo. Where the fluid touched the flame, the flame died, and Aubry was heartened. But still, an ocean of jellied fire devoured the brush, seemingly more than human agency could quench. Or survive.

What kind of monsters . . . ?

And that fire galloped toward them despite all that the

firefighters could do. The mass of hot air licked at his skin, burning like an acid wind.

He slid back down the hill to Promise. "What can I do?"

She found a shovel for him. "Dig. Here—there. If this brush catches fire, burning chunks will fall downhill, igniting the lower brush as it falls. Fire has all the best of it: hot air on the way up, gravity assist on the way down."

Aubry glanced at his watch. "We should have help here within the hour."

"We have to do something *now*."

"Got it. I—"

There was a scream from below them. Aubry turned in time to see the black nightwing of a hovercraft float up over the south ridge of Marjo Valley.

Promise shaded her eyes. "That's . . . not one of ours. State?"

"Damned if I know . . ." *But I don't think so . . .*

That doubt turned into horrified certainty. A smaller Ephesian craft glided across the sky as if to greet its new sister. A line of light leapt from the belly of the larger craft, connecting the two craft like a glowing cable. The Ephesian ship exploded.

The rolling thunder slowly died away. Chunks of flaming wreckage tumbled from the sky, each piece starting new fires when it hit the earth.

The black wedge of the enemy hovercraft hung above the ridge, as if scanning the devastation. Silver ovals fell from its belly, stitching bright death across the horizon.

Promise was the first to recover from the shock. "*Oh my God.*"

Glenda dropped her shovel. "That was the road."

Numbed for a moment, unable to move, Aubry watched the wall of fire climb, crawl across the highway. Watched their exit from the valley churn with flames.

The hovercraft swooped back once, emptying its loads of death into the valley. Flame arced up as it sealed the dirt road leading up to the mill.

The hovercraft tilted its wings sardonically, and then disappeared over the edge of the valley.

Jenna stood in the middle of a group of women, their grimy faces streaked with sweat and tears. "What in the hell is there to do now?"

"Die," Glenda whispered.

"To hell with that," Jenna said sharply. "We can get the buses out. There's a logger's road that will take us out east. We can get through there—there shouldn't be a real problem about it. We have to move *now*, though."

She opened the communications pack at her belt and brought the handset tight to her mouth. "Fall back. Fall back IMMEDIATELY. Emergency. All normal exit routes have been sealed. Fall back."

Exhausted women and men began to materialize from the surrounding brush, tumbling down toward the floor of the valley. They piled onto the ancient, yellow vehicles.

Jenna spread a map on the ground, and Aubry crouched next to her to read it. "All right. We have fire blocking us here and here . . . but it should be possible to get out near the mill road."

"And if not?"

"I hope you brought popcorn. Let's go."

There were only three buses in the valley, and a small Nigerian Sokoto compact with a square funnel for a nose. Promise, Aubry, and Jenna waited until the three larger vehicles were crammed to full, then Jenna nudged them. "Come on. We'll take the car." Aubry squeezed in last, watching the thickening smoke nervously.

Jenna cranked the engine. The Sokoto lurched on its way, two lengths behind the rattling buses.

The road was abysmally bad, and the Sokoto's shocks seemed primeval. The wheeled box shimmied from side to side, and Aubry fully expected to feel the undercarriage drop out at any moment.

Fire erupted above them on the ridge, smoke curling up, sparks and ash spiraling into the sky.

Timing. Timing was everything. Could they . . .

They creaked past the mill. The pass ahead was shot through with smoke and ash. The wooden bridge was barely visible. The front bus stopped just before it reached the first planks.

Jenna barked into her handset. "Get going! The bridge will still hold you. Just *move!*" The bus began to roll again. The bridge creaked plaintively beneath it.

Aubry watched the bus nervously. "Isn't there another way?"

"None. This is the last road out. It's this or nothing."

The smoke from the surrounding brush was thicker now, and the second bus virtually vanished into it. Jenna's phone crackled. "This is murder," a male voice said, fighting hard to remain calm. "Send that last bus through *fast*. I don't know how long it's going to last."

"You heard them." Jenna's hands were slick on the Sokoto's stick shift, rubbed its knob nervously. The last bus began to crawl across the bridge. Smoke gushed up through the planks now, and as the bus reached the far side, a wheel smashed through the weakened wood. The rear axle sagged. Promise cursed between clenched teeth.

With a mighty effort, the ancient behemoth chewed its way free, crawled up onto the far bank as smoke and flame swallowed the bridge behind them.

"Damn!" Aubry jerked the Sokoto's door open, and jumped out. The bridge crawled with flame now. The heat drove them back.

"We're going to die. . . ." Jenna murmured.

Aubry put his hands over his ears, trying to block out the sounds, trying to think, drawing a blank. Then he looked up and saw Promise. Her eyes were locked on the mill, and the winch, and . . .

The hoist balloon. It bobbled at the end of its tether, straining toward the sky.

For a moment he didn't understand, then he cursed himself for not thinking of it first. He grabbed her and spun her around, kissing her. "Listen, Jenna. I'm going up to get the balloon."

"What . . ."

"Come on!"

He spun and began to sprint up the hill. Jenna caught up with him when he paused to catch his breath.

"All right—how do we do this?"

He traced lines and angles with his finger. "We have to

get into the mill, and get the balloon to drop its cable. Then we can attach it to the car, and cut the ballast. What have we got to cut a chain?"

"Chain saw do it?"

"Might, if the teeth are tempered."

"There's one in the station."

"Good enough."

He started back up the hill. Breath whistled in his lungs as he ran, and he paced himself. This was too damned urgent to let himself burn out before the job was finished.

The mill, deserted now, yielded to the driving force of his heel. The power was still on. "Where's the equipment shed?" Jeanna was right behind him. "Left side. Should be open."

"How do you disengage the balloon? Unfasten the hoist?"

"I can do some of that from here—better still, I can loosen the cable from here, drop it to the ground."

"Then do it for God's sake. We're running out of time."

The lights went on briefly, flickered, then strengthened again as the auxiliaries cut in. The gears began to grind, and fed more cable into the loop. Aubry watched as the hoist wire drooped toward the ground.

He wrenched a fire axe from the wall, smashed it into the lock on the equipment shed. Three blows and the door shattered on its hinges, swinging free. He snatched the red, teardrop shape of the chain saw.

Jenna yelled approval. "Good going. We may have to cut it free. We're running out of time."

The huge balloon, still weighted by logs and ballast, began to sink toward the ground. There was a triumphant yell from below as Promise grasped the tether.

"Let's go."

The fire was closer now. The entire ridge of the valley was ringed with smoke, and flaming debris plunged down through the underbrush.

Aubry was the first to the Sokoto. He backed up until the tether chain scratched its roof, then yelled, "Let's have it!" Promise fed it to him, and they ran it through the open windows and back up to the top. He knotted the chain about itself as best he could, and checked it.

"This will have to do."

The ballast line was stretched tight, attached to its nested rings of iron counterweights. He examined the chain, and grimaced. "We'll ruin the saw, but let's do it."

Jenna started the saw, and touched the burring teeth to the cable. Sparks flooded away from the cutting edge in a torrent.

Sitting atop the roof, Aubry scanned Flint Ridge in uneasy fascination. The fire was climbing down off the ridge, barely slowed by the firebreak.

The woven steel strands began to pop, twisting away from each other, *spanging* with tension. Aubry screamed: "Get in there!"

The cable was straining now, and Aubry jumped down from the roof, spun Promise around and swept her into the car.

She looked up at him with eyes that were wide and loving. "Whatever else has happened between us, Aubry . . ."

"Save it for later. We're winning this one."

The saw roared, and teeth flew, one of them scraping Aubry's arm. It ached, he ached everywhere. The air was hot now, and thick with smoke. The cable *spanged* again as another strand broke. Jenna said "that's it" and threw the saw down, climbing into the car. Aubry waiting outside. The last few strands, stretched impossibly taut between the car, the balloon, and the ballast, were still holding.

Aubry started the saw up again, leaning into the effort as the dull, broken teeth battled with the last strand of cable. The saw chain broke.

"Damn—"

And then the cable popped, and the car jerked into the air. Aubry grinned and leapt after the frayed end. His sweaty palms slipped the first time, then found purchase as he began to climb.

Hand over hand he climbed up, until he reached a window and Promise helped him in.

The air from the forest fire buffeted them as they rose.

The circle of flame surrounding Marjo Valley crawled down the mountainside, but they were no longer its targets.

"I still can't believe it," Promise murmured.

"The only way to fly." They were above the flames now, and the gusts of wind shook them more violently.

But still the Sokoto rose, buoyed by the swelling balloon, its yellow expanse pushed onward and upward by the mass of heated air.

Smoke boiled around them, and for a full minute there was nothing to breathe. Promise clawed at her throat for air, then collapsed against him. Jenna sweltered on the floor of the car.

Christ. Air. Air. They were too low. They were too high. In another moment the balloon was going to burst, sending them hurtling to their deaths, or they would suffocate. Air. More air, please—

Then they were through the smoke, and drifting south toward the camp.

Aubry sobbed for breath, and shook his head. He didn't ever want to come that close again.

He pulled a knife from Jenna's belt, and stuck it in his own. Checking his grip carefully, he climbed out of the window, and grabbed the cable to keep from slipping. The instant he clambered up the line, the balloon shifted and he almost fell, sliding down until his back thumped into the top of the Sokoto.

He looked down from the top of the car, and his stomach soured. They had to be sixteen hundred feet above the ground, and still climbing.

He gripped the cable, and climbed. His shoulder ached, and he wasn't sure how long he could climb before the abused muscles gave out.

Hand over hand the last few feet, hanging on, he pulled the knife from his belt, and slit the underside of the bag.

The gas *whooshed* out, and again the entire jury-rigged structure lurched. He lost one hand's hold, his entire weight dangling by a grip that grew feebler by the moment. He reached back and found the cable, put his weight on it, gritted his teeth as the car slowly began to drop.

The pain raced up his arm, and he hissed, cursing to

himself. It hurt. God, it hurt so much. Vision swam away into a line of thin white dots.

Then there was another jolt, and he fell. His back hit the roof of the car, and then rolled over. He reached out for a handhold. Something. Anything. There was no purchase. Arms reached out from within the car, grabbing. His shirt tore and stretched with the holds.

His senses swam. The ground was looming up, a slow-motion tumble. There were people down there, firefighters shouting and pointing. Now they were fifty feet below, and now thirty, and now—

The cloth of his shirt ripped. His fingernails clawed into the paint as he slid, and then he fell. . . .

CHAPTER EIGHTEEN

An Ending

Saturday, June 3

Promise stood at the edge of Ariane Cotonou's bed, senses blinded with pain and confusion. It felt so unnecessarily cruel to have waited all of this time, and come all this distance, merely to stand and watch her mother die.

Pale plastic tubes led from Ariane's nose and arms. Gleaming glass-walled, chrome-plated machines at the edge of the bed kept silent deathwatch, emotionlessly measuring each drop of life as it flowed from her body.

Three doctors were at the bedside, but they no longer desperately busied themselves. It was too late for that now. Now it was a matter of comforting, keeping Ariane as comfortable as possible. Ariane had aged horribly in the past three days. Her skin seemed to absorb the room's dim light only to throw it back hollowly, more reminiscent of something dredged from the bottom of the sea than a human being.

Promise was utterly exhausted. She needed sleep, rest, needed to close her eyes or just crawl off and die. That simply wasn't an option. She heard the growl of Scavenger machinery outside, and faintly the bark of Aubry's voice as he coordinated the engineering and demolition teams.

From the hospital window she could see the devastation— it would take years to rebuild, but at least the process had begun. Makeshift kitchens had been set up in the undamaged shelters, and the wounded and exhausted had been cared for.

Ephesus was filled with Scavengers—workers, medical personnel, and children, hundreds of children who were now screaming and running through the ash-strewn streets, playing makeshift games of pursuit and evasion with their new friends.

Trees still smoldered north of Ephesus, but Oregon state units were on the line now. They were fully patched into the Tillamook network, the most efficient emergency firefighting force in the Northwest. The gross danger had receded, revealing more intimate terrors in its wake.

Jenna sat at the edge of the bed, holding Ariane's hand. She kissed it gently as the old woman shuddered. Ancient lips breathed a single, indistinguishable word.

Jenna leaned closer. "Mother?"

"Doctors," she said. "Have them . . . leave."

Jenna stood. "Please," she said to the white-cloaked women. "She wants to speak with us alone."

There was no disagreement, no argument. Without a word, they filed out.

Promise and Jenna sat alone in the room. The wind riffled the curtains gently. It was near dawn now. The sun was close beneath the horizon. The air still stank of smoke.

Ariane opened her eyes, tried to focus them on the window. The curtains whispered to her. "I . . . have sinned."

"We've all sinned." Promise held her mother's hand desperately tight. *Mother. I don't even know you, and now it's too late.*

"No . . . don't understand. Listen. You have to . . . listen. I controlled everything. Everything. I . . ."

"Rest. Please." Jenna's voice was frantic.

"Too late for rest. Have to talk now, and . . ." She panted for breath. "Thousands of them, all dead. God, the lies. The clinics. Oh, God, it hurts."

"I'll have them add a little more painkiller."

"No." She gripped Promise's wrist with sudden, savage strength. "Must listen. And learn. No time. No time. McMartin. Oh, bastard. Freak bastard. I helped him."

"Helped him what?"

Ariane didn't seem to hear. "Feds tried to take our land. McMartin made deal—"

"Mother, you need to rest."

"Listen to me." Her eyes blazed. "The fetal storage clinics. It's a lie. It costs too much to maintain the fetuses. They don't care about reviving them."

Jenna's face darkened. "Then what are they . . . ?"

"Thousands and thousands of babies . . ." She began to cry now, her chest heaving with the effort. "I knew. I knew. I sold our babies to keep Ephesus alive." Her voice broke into sobs.

Jenna soothed her brow. "They what?"

"They stole . . . oh, they . . ." She coughed again, and this time blood was on her lips. "I don't care. They can kill the bastard."

"Kill who? McMartin?"

"DeLacourte. Kill him. Before it's too late. Only three months. I wouldn't be a part. That's why. That's why . . ."

"Mother?" Sudden, nauseating suspicion bubbled up into Promise's mind. Something cold and sharp stabbed into her guts, made her abdomen feel leaden and numb. "Who stole babies?"

"McMartin. Used the Ortegas. Used everything, everybody. I know. I know. Trying to live forever. Selling our babies . . ."

She coughed again, and this time the machines at her bedside screamed shrilly, and the monitors peaked with jagged spikes. "Ahhhh . . ."

Her eyes wobbled wildly, and she sobbed for breath, and her breathing grew quiet.

"She's exhausted. Let her sleep awhile." Jenna pulled the sheet up closer to Ariane's chin. She looked dead already.

Jenna and Promise looked at each other. Promise was reeling against the wall.

They steal babies . . .

"Stole fetu—"

The Ortegas . . .

You lost your baby.

Promise's mind whirled madly. The images came in an avalanche now. At first she fought for control, then gave up. All thought and sensation dissolved into a gray wall.

When her vision cleared, Jenna was standing over her. "Are you all right?"

"Yes." A gust of adrenaline cleared the gray mists, and once again the images danced. "Yes I am. I have to be."

"Do you want to go lay down?"

"No . . . I'll just wait here." She tried to smile. "We'll just wait here for a while, with our mother."

Jenna took her hand, and squeezed it once, briefly. "I'm sorry it took this, Promise."

Her temples throbbed as she descended the stairs. *I know now. I'm sure. It has to be true.*

Aubry waited for her in the lobby. He leaned against the wall, dark circles ringing his eyes, his body heavy with fatigue. He hadn't slept eight full hours in the past three days. Only his indomitable drive and phenomenal physical conditioning had kept him on his feet. His right arm was in a compact sling, and his skin seemed a little pale, but his facial lines were tight and ugly. They softened only marginally at the sight of Promise.

"Is it over?"

She nodded. "She just stopped breathing. Nothing fancy. I was holding her hand, and she just sort of relaxed."

"I'm sorry."

Promise took his arm. His skin was hot. "Aubry . . . It sounds crazy, I know it, but our child is alive."

His dark broad face twisted with shock. *"What?"*

"Listen to me—"

"Did Ariane tell you that?"

"No . . . but she told me that somebody named McMartin—"

"Him again? Who *is* this bastard?"

"—was involved in stealing fetuses from their mothers' wombs. Ariane was tied up in it somehow. I don't know how. She said that the Ortegas were involved."

"The Ortegas are involved in anything that makes a dollar."

"But don't you see? It was an Ortega doctor who examined me. I was unconscious for hours. They stole our baby!"

His mouth was still hard, and she realized that her words hadn't reached him. His eyes were swollen with his own pain and exhaustion. "I saw things here," he said, voice low. "I saw thirty years of work destroyed for nothing. I saw unborn children dying for nothing. I saw innocent people slaughtered. I almost died yesterday. I have to find out how, and why."

"What are you talking about?"

"I was attacked by someone during the fire. He almost beat me. I've never seen anything that fights like that. I have to know. I have to find him."

"Why . . . ?"

"Because . . . ." The pain in his eyes was mixed with something else. Hope. "What happened here was bad—worse than anything I ever did. And it's linked into something bigger. Something more evil than anything I ever was. It's my way out, Promise. I'm going after it."

Promise began to shake uncontrollably. "Aubry, our *child*—"

"Is *dead*, Promise."

"You're willing to just leave it at that?"

"I have to go on living. Without you, if I have to."

"I see." She stepped back away from him. "I love you, Aubry . . . but I have to find my child."

Aubry squeezed his eyes shut. "I don't know if I love you. I don't know if I ever did. That damned drug has twisted everything inside out."

"You won't help me?"

"Not until I know the truth. You won't come with me?"

"Not until *I* know the truth."

Aubry nodded. "All right then." He took her face in both hands, and tried to kiss her, but she pulled away.

"Just go," she said. "Just go, damn you."

He nodded, and a mantle of ice seemed to fall over him. "You can have the car. I'll take some Scavenger wheels."

He turned and walked away.

"Aubry!" she called. "Where are you going?"

"San Diego," he said. "The NewMan encampment. I want to find Bloodeagle. He owes me. He'll know, if anyone does. Promise—"

"Yes?"

"If it means anything to you—there's never been anyone but you. Not in my whole life. And maybe that's the problem."

Then he pushed through the door. The hinges squeaked a few times, then came to rest.

All at once, the weight of the last seventy-two hours fell on her like an avalanche. She collapsed against the wall, tears streaming down her cheeks.

Her mother. Her child. The only man she'd ever loved. *Goddess. How much? How much do I have to lose?*

CHAPTER NINETEEN

Moonman

Friday, June 9

Marina Batiste drove her groundcar through the outskirts of the modular park.

The chunks of houses were arranged almost haphaz-
ardly: these were pieces that had been auctioned at tossdown
prices, and never reassembled into completely designed
homes. Instead, they were hauled to one of the modular
trailer parks across the country, and set up in some sort of
a living arrangement.

From any distance the park looked like a wrecking yard.

One had to look much more closely to see that there was
a sense of order in the arrangement of the dwellings. From
inside them the eyes of children studied her. She waved
back, and the small, dirty faces grinned at her, giggling.

The park, ten miles south of Bismarck, North Dakota,
was special to her. She had been here twice before, and
knew its most celebrated resident, a man whom few of the
inhabitants had ever met. Some of them might have heard
of him, or read of him in the papers.

She pulled her car up to one of the jumbled heaps of
steel and plastic boxes. Try as she might, Marina couldn't
escape the feeling that she was in a gigantic playpen, with
construction blocks tumbled this way and that by the hand
of a godlike infant.

She wiped her forehead as she pulled into the shadow of
a box. The heat was almost unbearable.

A tarnished steel grille was set askew in the gap be-

tween two immense blocks of molded plastic. She pushed
a button at the front gate, waiting for almost a full minute
before the buzzer rang in answer.

"I am sorry," an androgynously synthesized voice said
solicitously. "No one is home at the moment. If you
would care—?"

"Jeffry?"

"—to leave a message, wait—"

"It's Marina."

"Oh." This voice was human, and high, and suspicious. There was a pause, and the sound of rustling. "All
right. Come on in."

The lock buzzed and clicked, and Marina entered. The
entire yard was filled with old packing crates and cartons,
and pieces of electronic apparatus. She picked her way
through a forest of obsolete gear, and stood at last in front
of the door. With the delicate hum of a servo, it opened.

A slender, spidery metal figure met her there. It was
attached to a rail that ran along the wall and back up into
the living quarters. The robot had vast faceted eyes, and golden
skin that looked spray-painted on. "And you are alone?"

"Always, Jeffry. I wouldn't try to hurt you."

"You'd better not," the robot warned. "I'll tie your
IRS records together with the national debt. Don't screw
with me, lady."

"I just want to talk with you. You owe me one, Jeffry,
and you know that's the truth."

"You got your story."

"You wouldn't believe how much heat I took for not
giving you up."

Disorientingly, the robot snickered and rolled its eyes at her.

"Come on," she coaxed. "Let's talk."

The robot revolved on its axis and glided back up to the
main floor, with Marina just behind it.

The place was just as she had remembered it from
eighteen months before: an absolute shambles, every inch
crammed with boxes and books and files. Laser chips,
bubble packs, and even a few ancient read/write CDs
were scattered around the room.

The robot torso rode a rail around the wall, came to a

branching post and hooked itself into a guide iron in the ceiling. "Follow me, please."

She did, walking past a stack of boxes and only then hearing the *snick* of an automatic being primed.

She turned and smiled, as calmly as she could.

Jeffry Barathy weighed perhaps ninety pounds, but would have weighed more if he'd had legs. She guessed that he was somewhere in his forties, but his total lack of facial hair or even the most minute crow's feet made it difficult to determine his exact age.

There was something almost comical about the crop of raggedly chopped mohawk hair, as if he were a throwback to another era completely.

But there was nothing at all comical about the little floatcar he'd rigged his torso into, or the elaborate track system that guided it around the apartment. And even less about the gun pointed directly between her eyes. "You come in here, no call, no parlay . . . who do you think you're screwing with?"

"You know I'm not wired, Jeffry."

"Damn straight you ain't wired. Scanned you three times already. Didn't know that, did you? Taught me that in Chad. Cost me my legs. The more expensive a lesson is, the better you remember it."

"I could have guessed. I know you're not a fool. You also know you can trust me. May I sit down?"

The little man scratched at his nonexistent beard. "Sure. Sure. You go ahead."

He put the gun down, but he pivoted the rim of his floatcar to watch her even more carefully now. "So it's payday, is it? I knew that you weren't going to let me alone. What do you want?"

"What do you think?"

His eyes narrowed craftily. "Want me to have you declared dead? Screws up the IRS to no end. I could transfer money to your account . . . no, that's not what you want. I don't know. I don't . . ."

She scanned the room. Everything had more dust on it than she remembered. "Haven't heard much from you for a while, Jeffry. What's the problem?"

His narrow face tightened. "You know what it is. It's that shitferbrains DeLacourte. One time. One time I bust in on his broadcast. Twelve seconds of heavy breathin'."

The laughter bubbled up from deep inside her. "It was his monthly lecture on venal sin, as I recall."

"I thought I raised the entertainment value."

"About eighty million people around the world saw that one, Jeffry. It cost you, didn't it?"

"Yeah. Damn good thing I had relays and redundant remotes and cutoffs all down the line. They came after me. God did they come after me." He looked up at her, and managed a smile. "But then, you know about that, don't you."

Marina closed her eyes for a moment, remembering the long trail she had walked to find the elusive "Moonman." She had used up more favors than she liked to remember, but at the tail end, she had her award-winning exclusive. Not to mention taps and traces on her credit, telephone, infax, and car guidance systems. "So he shut you down. How would you like a chance to get even?"

His eyes narrowed. "I'll get freakin' even. Count on it. I've still got my remotes. I can break into every network transmission in the continental United States."

"For about twelve seconds. They'll catch you this time."

"So I'll flame out. One more headline, and then down the hole. They owe me something. *They owe me*. I didn't volunteer for the PanAfrican thing—"

"I know," she said quietly.

"—they *drafted* me. I did my freakin' duty, tried to chop Swarna back. *They* screwed up. Like Harris screwed up two years ago when they tried to off that black son of a bitch." He grinned crookedly. "Hell. Most of my buddies are dead, or on the dole. But me, communications is communications. I merely shifted my venue."

"Do you want to get back some, without any risk? Do you want another shot at the Prophet?"

"What are you talking about?"

"I don't want you to interfere with transmissions. I just want information, if you can get it. And correlations, if you can generate them."

Jeffry didn't move a twitch, but a computer screen behind him popped into life. "What kind of information?"

"DeLacourte is suppressing data on Gorgon—"

"The fairies who blew the Swarna hit?"

Marina glared at him. "Think what you want, Jeffry, but don't talk like that around me." He hunched his shoulders apologetically, and she continued. "I want to know what else he's doing. His support base has been growing too damned quickly. I want to know what's going on."

"Can do."

"Good. I want you to generate a report for me, showing me who's tied in with him, and how fast it's grown. Start running correlations. Find me the unusual. Find me something I can stick my nose into. Find me what Sterling DeLacourte doesn't want found."

North Dakota is whiplashed daily by an extraordinary cross section of telecasts. Radio and commercial Omnivision, government scans, confidential economic bulletins to the trade centers, the entire spectrum of satellite broadcasts. Better than ninety percent of it is scrambled or encrypted.

Jeffry Barathy went to work sorting, deciphering, organizing. Slowly, the information began to come through.

Using cut-outs furnished by friends in academia, he routed information on DeLacourte in, running it past screens, through filters, looking for the extraordinary. Statistics on advertising expenditures supposedly intended for a Pol Ec class at the University of Hawaii were rerouted to North Dakota. Corporate structural data requested by the business law computer owned by NYU went to North Dakota.

Marina watched, and watched. Endless parades of statistics, many of them available to anyone with a library card or a long-standing newsfax subscription.

She moved into the trailer with Jeffry, sleeping and eating, and cleaning out a tiny corner of the house. It seemed that he had glued the rec room of a modular house onto a fancy bathroom and a library. The stairway led up and then twisted sideways like something out of an Escher painting, rails for his robot and floatcar twisting along the floors like mating snakes.

The days passed. Between other, legitimate, research projects, Jeffry sandwiched in a series of rather odd requests. Most of them probably slipped right past the awareness of the operators on the other end.

How many? How long? How much?

Paper and plastic strips reeled from the printers. The screens were crowded with data, and Jeffry worked on and on, without sleep, until sixty hours later, Marina found him leaning over, head down on one of the computer panels, sound asleep as the printer next to his ear churned silently.

She guided his floatcar to his bedroom and sighed. What a mess. She peeled a dozen layers of junk away, and when there was an area flat enough to lie on, she lifted him from the car and nested him down.

For a minute she just looked at him. He looked so young, so untroubled.

She lay down next to him and cradled one arm around him protectively, and quickly fell asleep.

"Clean. The man is clean." She sighed at last, feeling beaten. "Look. Some of his people do stupid things, violent things—but he's not responsible for them. There are always radicals on the fringe of any movement."

Jeffry, eyes dark-circled even after twelve hours of sleep, sipped at a cup of Marina's coffee. He scanned the list of supporters. "Look at this. Over the last eighteen months, he's gotten additional political support from all over the country. There are no irregularities in property holdings, bank records, anything that I can find. There doesn't seem to be any bribery. He could be providing kinky sex, but today, all you have to do for that is pick up the comm line. It would have to be something else."

Images flashed on the screen. Smiling, gray-haired Senator Grossman.

Steel industrialist W. P. Wekes, shown shaking hands with the president of International 105 labor union as they agreed to throw their combined weight behind DeLacourte.

"And they've got considerable weight, too. Both of them look as if they've enjoyed the good life for a long time."

A second picture of them a year later at another rally . . .

Marina squinted. "Would you go back to the last picture? Put them out side by side."

She looked at both of them. In the first picture, they looked like two powerful, dangerous old bulls calling a truce. But there was something about the second picture. What was it? The weight was almost the same. The color of the hair was the same. But . . .

"They don't look quite as old to me. They look like they're in better physical condition or something."

"Joined a gym."

"Must be a good one. Neither of 'em are spring chickens."

Jeffry sat back in his car. "Just a second." He thought about it for a moment, then his eyes traced designs on the screen. Sensors picked up the eye movements and the blinks, coordinated them quickly, and spat out columns of data.

"Twenty-eight radical switches in the past eighteen months, all of them moving more and more behind DeLacourte. Look at this. They're all over sixty years old."

"So he appeals to the older, conservative type. I can buy that."

"No . . . these are radical switches. Let's take a look at DuPrene. He was scheduled for some kind of surgery— canceled. Let's see his hospital records." The screen blanked for a minute, and a "classified" sign popped up.

"Well, yippie shit. Let's try it another route. I have a commission to study routing for medical emergencies in Kentucky. All right . . . Let's ask the University of Oklahoma Medical School to help us by feeding stats on the number of surgeries performed for men of DuPrene's physical profile. We'll get an abstract on him, without the program knowing it's violating its security codes." He looked up at her and grinned impishly. "Damn, these things are dumb sometimes."

There was a whirr of images on the screen, and then it cleared. "Hmm . . . look at the test results. Man is exhibiting signs of . . . well, shit. What can you call it except rejuvenation?"

"What?"

"Rejuvenation. All functions are closer to normal after the surgery canceled. I don't know what to make of it."

"Anything unusual? Traces of any unusual chemicals?"

"Not really. Ah . . . we have a blood test here. Total cholesterol, HDL cholesterol, uric acid, triglycerides. A physician's note that all values are closer to those you'd expect from a teenager than a sixty-year-old man. Cholesterol below one-twenty, uric acid three point six. Healthy dude."

"Anything else?"

"Well, another note—there are high levels of something called 2,3 DEA."

"What's that?"

"Damned if I know. Whatever that is. Can research it for you. Hold on." Jeffry's fingers and eyes moved. The screen clouded and cleared again. "Here it is. 2,3 diethylandroeternalone. It's an androgenic steroid, present in human blood. Levels of DEA are high in fetuses, decline to almost nothing after birth, pop up again in puberty. Decline drastically in old age. There is speculation that it could be a longevity treatment, but it's like insanely expensive to synthesize. Lots of footnotes. Want me to follow up?"

"Not now. What else do you have?"

Jeffry played with the console. In quick succession, three video images of DeLacourte appeared.

"I've got something else here. How long has it been since DeLacourte has appeared in public?"

"Almost two years. Why?"

"Take a close look at these pictures. This one"—he pointed at the image on the extreme left—"was the last one taken by an independent photographer, a little more than twenty-six months ago. Notice anything about these more recent freezes?"

Marina studied them. "I . . . well, he looks younger too."

"I'm not sure why that bothers me. How long have you worked for this geek?"

"Three years. First met with him two years ago. Does that mean something?"

"I don't know, lady. I really don't."

Marina sat back and closed her eyes. "Neither do I, Jeffry. But I'm going to find out."

CHAPTER TWENTY

Wu

Sunday, June 11

Outside, the cyclic rhythm of the city's sound and light was a constant, seething thing. But here, eighty floors up in the penthouse suite of the Ortega Towers, Promise might have been in another world.

The visual screens worked better than the sonic baffles. Standing almost to the edge of the terrace, and looking out, she could see nothing but a gentle, snow-covered landscape. It was dappled with trees and, in the distance, restful, broken arcs of mountain.

She could stay here. She could just remain here, and live out the rest of her life. For a moment she was lost in the holofantasy. Then it was gone, gone with the touch of feet on the carpeting behind her, gone as she turned to face the man whose feet made the impressions.

Wu.

The man looked exactly the same as when she had last seen him, on Terra Buena, after her operation. He had been in the hospital with her, nursing injuries in the aftermath of an incredible battle with Aubry.

Wu was exactly five and a half feet tall, and as thin as a skeleton. His eyes were frighteningly direct. He wore a purple silk robe that disguised his cadaverousness, but she remembered him in the bed next to hers, an enormous bruise coloring the side of his face. A bruise that shrank daily, as if there were some healing factor within Wu that radiated abnormal vitality.

The man was an enemy—the West Coast head of the most powerful criminal organization in the Western world. But there had been a truce for the last three years, and Wu had done nothing to exact vengeance, or to expose Aubry's identity.

Perhaps . . . just perhaps there was hope.

He held out his hand to her. "Promise. Time has passed. You are, as always, radiant."

She smiled. "I must tell you that I am surprised at the pleasure I feel in seeing you."

"We were not enemies," he said. He clapped once, and a servant appeared. "Will you join me in tea?"

"Certainly."

He led her to the garden, and sat with a folding, spiraling motion. The illusion was complete here. The outside sounds receded, and the walls themselves were utterly invisible. They could have been in the middle of a jungle, in the midst of a vast garden that stretched away into the distance.

"This is very nice."

"It is a quieting environment. I come here to think. To relax. Relaxation is a prize beyond measure."

"I can understand. Your responsibilities."

He smiled then, just a shadow of one, and Promise answered it with a sliver of her own. "I have to admit that I am surprised to see you back in the city. I heard that you and Aubry had found it . . . expedient to leave town." He shook his head. "That one. He is . . . amazing. He has never received proper training, but his natural skills, and the skills from that—what is it called? Nullboxing?—are almost beyond belief. When I think what might have been done with a proper teacher . . ." He shook his head.

"We had been forced to leave the city. I am back because I am deeply disturbed."

Wu inclined his head thoughtfully. "Some might expect me to have great animosity toward you. It is because of your man that my neck spent three months in a cast. But it is also due to your husband that I am the sole director of West Coast operations."

Promise felt uncomfortable, shifted in her seat. "I heard

that Marguerite died soon after we left. She never came out of her coma.''

Wu's green eyes closed gently. ''No. She just slipped away.'' He looked at Promise, and there was some emotion there that she couldn't quite label. ''Not a bad death, as they go. I doubt if mine will be so . . . peaceful.''

''And Tomaso?''

''Insane. Alive. He is in Europe, in a clinic. He has yet to remember his name. In any case, he was purely an organizational man. There was no talent for the human factor. Enough of that. Due to the Family's involvement with you, my fortunes have increased dramatically. I have to admit that I am also interested in renewing contact with Aubry.'' A girl brought tea. Wu sipped, watching Promise over the lip of the steaming cup.

''I . . . can't promise you that possibility.''

''Oh? Why?''

''Aubry and I aren't together now.''

''I see. Well. It may be that I can help you. What does it concern?''

''Does the Ortega Family traffic in human fetuses?''

Wu froze, his green eyes suddenly even darker and more piercing. He stood, and clasped his hands behind his back, looking out at the holo wall. At last he turned to face her.

''You have asked a question that I should not answer. The fact that you came to me to ask would be reason enough for a more prudent man to terminate you.''

Promise took a cautious sip. ''Then you've given me part of my answer.''

''I must think upon this. Before making a decision, I must ask you why you ask this.''

''Don't you know?''

He turned. His eyes were piercing. ''No.''

''I'm talking about Terra Buena,'' she said. ''I was told that I lost my baby. I spontaneously aborted while unconscious. I have to know if that was true, or if . . .''

Wu's face hardened. ''I see.'' He thumbed the control in his pocket, and the wall of images changed, became a rolling, powerful wall of water, the walls of a tidal wave, a rolling tsunami that challenged her powers of perception. How to remain calm if such a power came for her?

"I believe that there are certain things in this world that are beyond the efforts of man to stop or limit, or even influence. There is a possibility that what you say is correct. If it is, then by all that is right, you should find out. Certainly I would not live without knowing. I have no children. After infection with Cyloxibin I dare not make the attempt—I have no wish to give life to a freak."

"You will help me?" She could hardly believe her ears.

"You realize that some of the operations are legal."

"I know. As an alternative to abortion. My . . . mother helped originate the technology."

Wu raised an eyebrow. "Yes? McMartin Cryogenics maintains a facility in Los Angeles. Then there's Xenon in Atlanta, and IUH in Pittsburgh. But my specialty was . . . import and distribution, until Cyloxibin hit the market. Now, there is more profit in other black market products, and gambling."

"I don't understand. Why is that?"

Wu's laughter was sharply musical. "Cyloxibin addiction drives all other chemical substances out of the system. When it eventually fades, desires for any drug, including alcohol, are minimized. Whatever curses it may carry, it brings one gift, as well."

"You said that you might be able to help me."

"Yes." He sat down again. "You know enough to hurt me, and you have never spoken."

"And you knew enough about Aubry to hurt him."

"There was no profit in it. None at all. And in this world, there is no need to destroy potential allies."

"Allies?"

"There are other enemies on the horizon. There is this man, DeLacourte. He frightens me. It is said that there are only three kinds of men in the world. One says openly that he is out to take what is yours. This is the easiest kind of man to deal with—he is a businessman, and you can deal with him frontally. The second kind says that he is concerned with your best interests, but he is lying, and knows that he is lying. This man is a thief, and he can also be dealt with easily. But the most dangerous kind of man is the one who says that he is only interested in your welfare, *believes* that he is interested in your welfare, but somehow ends up taking what is yours. This man is the worst.''

''Why?''

''Tomás de Torquemada was such a man. He believed that torturing you to death was for your own benefit. Men of good will will follow such a man. Movements grow up around him. Adolf Hitler was undoubtedly such a man—he believed that what he was doing was ultimately for the good of the world. They are infinitely dangerous.

''Sterling DeLacourte . . . disturbs me.''

''He frightens you?''

Wu smiled secretly. ''It is not a subject for discussion.'' He shook his head, and appeared eager to move to a new subject.

''I don't have very much for you. But I have something. The doctor who worked on your case in Terra Buena also worked with the fetal operation until two years ago. I know this. It is therefore entirely possible that he might have done something while you were unconscious. His personal effects may be found. His contacts, friends, and relations interviewed.''

''I don't understand . . . is he dead?''

''He might as well be.''

''Why?''

''Thai-VI.''

Promise covered her mouth with her hand. Thai-VI, the terrible venereal leprosy which had ravaged hundreds of thousands of victims before the Containment Act of '23.

She felt sick. It was better for him if he were dead.

''Where is he?''

''The Hoopa camp, I believe. His name is Allred. Doctor Gerold Allred. There may be answers there for you . . . if you have the stomach to retrieve them.''

''It's my baby,'' she whispered. ''I don't have any choice.''

Wu nodded approval. ''Very well,'' he said. ''Then I will help you get in.''

"Why? Why do you do this for us . . ." She caught herself, looked down at her hands. "For me?"

"I like to play games," he said. "You and Aubry Knight are disruptive influences. I want to see what will happen. It is not my game I introduce you into. I ask you . . . where is Aubry now?"

She closed her eyes. "I'm not sure. I think that he's following his own leads. There was a man. Someone who hurt him in a fight. He has to find this person."

Wu nodded his understanding. "For a man like Aubry Knight, it would be almost impossible not to. Very well—I will help you. I ask you one favor."

"Anything."

"Tell me . . . how this thing develops. I am· interested." Wu drew himself up. "Promise. I must leave you now. Call me tomorrow, and I will have your information. Good luck to you in your hunting." He walked her to the tubular elevator shafts. She stepped in, and watched Wu as his body seemed to rise. Inside the tube, she felt no movement at all.

CHAPTER TWENTY-ONE

Bordertown

Monday, June 12

Traffic was snarled in downtown San Diego. Wherever Aubry turned his head, the view was clotted with humanity. Even now, in the midst of the Recovery, San Diego was still a favorite jumping-off point for American migrant laborers seeking work in Mexico. He could see the battered trucks filled with overalled workers hoping to get across the border, could read the tired faces on the street corners, could watch the electronic signs which flashed the relative strength of the dollar and the peso. From this, the Mexican government would decide how many Americans to allow across the borders to jobs in the Mexican oil fields.

The great desalinization plants north of Mazatlán and on the Gulf of Mexico had begun flowering Mexico's deserts, and there was work there for the lucky gringo with the grease to get across the border.

There were jobs in Los Angeles now, Aubry thought, allowing a bit of satisfaction to bubble up. He had been responsible for some of that. But now there was no satisfaction. Now he allowed himself to slide through a seething ocean of humanity, hunched over, smelling them, seeing them, feeling them, but not really letting them into his world.

He prowled past a Golden Arches, contemplated a McSushi and fries. He chose an El Pollo Muerto nestled under a smiling poster of President Roland Harris, wire-rims twinkling with sincerity as he reminded one and all that *this is* your *country*.

He ordered a slab of immolated chicken. As he waited

he scanned the room. It was full of men who were full of
beer, watching the stage at the front of the room, where a
girl who looked about twelve sat in the sawdust, strum-
ming a guitar and singing in a voice that was far too old
and experienced for her years. Her eyes were wide and sad
with wonder as her song told them how she had been
hungry, and frightened, and ultimately saved from a life in
the streets by the kindness of them.

"*I was saaaved . . .*" she sang, without a knowing wink. The room rocked with cheers, and bids for
the evening's favors.

Aubry felt sick, and left the restaurant, carrying his
steaming chicken with him. He chewed each rubbery mouthful carefully as he wove through the crowd.

He scanned, watching, watching for the head that seemed
to rise higher than the surrounding heads. For the voice
that struck a nerve, for the hunt, the sign.

He pulled his thin coat around him, not too tightly. Any tight
clothing would betray the dimensions of his body. Loose as it
was, he might have been mistaken for a barrel of a man, perhaps one somewhat overweight, not the two hundred and thirty
pounds of muscle and bone that damned near screamed for
attention.

But who were they? There were so many. . . .

A man strode the periphery of the crowd, and Aubry's
eyes went to him instantly.

He knew the face. It was strong, and unsmiling, and held
a kind of casual strength that Aubry empathized with instantly.
The man stood a head above the crowd. Some looked at him
admiringly as he passed. Others spit on the sidewalk. He
passed by, without the slightest recognition of insult.

Aubry fell into line behind him, following.

The man walked down two streets, and then turned into
a narrow building. Another of the enormous men was
standing at the front door. He carried a sidearm, a Walther
automatic pistol. God in heaven, how much grease had
been used up to get a pistol license for a NewMan, for
Christ's sake? They had enough trouble with just their
hands swinging at the ends of their arms, let alone a gun.

Aubry walked up to the front door. The man at the door

studied him. For a moment, an automatic smile of welcome came to his face. Then it cooled.

"I don't know you," he said. "You don't have any business here, human."

"Ask Bloodeagle about that. Tell him Warrick is here to see him." Aubry buried his hands deeply into his pockets. He hated standing out there, exposed and vulnerable. He could almost feel the crosshairs centered on his forehead.

The man on the front door had an amazingly, unnaturally broad face, as if the hormones which reinitiated growth had misfired on him. This one had to be a result of some of the forbidden hormones, drugs that were illegal in almost every nation in the world, despite a thriving underground market for them. Everyone involved in sports medicine knew that after the age of twenty-two or so it was impossible to get any further growth from the human skeletal system: the bones had capped.

But there were always people who tried anyway. Even if the result was the abomination before him, a grotesque misshapen lump of a man. An apparently clear mind stared out from the face of a monster, a mind which knew that its body had gone haywire, knew that its bones were thickening and the muscles growing even now. And that there was nothing to be done for it. He had made his choice.

The NewMan turned, and one great misshapen hand took the intercom phone from its hook. He spoke into it softly for a few seconds, then turned back to Aubry.

His eyes were piglike and suspicious. "All right. He says to come in."

The door swung open.

Something inside Aubry relaxed. Many of the people in the inner room were normal-sized human males, but a few—and they were clearly a breed apart—were Aubry's size and even larger, immense men, men who moved as if their bodies were driven by oiled cables rather than muscle. They turned when Aubry entered, and gave him a nod of recognition. He was among his own, accepted instantly, the flares of interest automatic but unintrusive.

Miles came down the stairs from the upper floor, and he held his hand out, his smile wide and genuine. "Warrick! It's good to see you. Where is Promise?"

"Up in Oregon, as far as I know. I have some business to attend to. And Miles—Warrick isn't my real name."

Possibilities ran through Miles's mind like lightning crackling in a cloud. "I see. Would you come to my office, where we can talk for a while? Privately?"

"That's exactly what I'd like."

Several of the men in the room grinned at Miles as he led Aubry upstairs, and a couple of inquisitive eyebrows were raised. Miles winked back, and Aubry gritted his teeth, trying not to pay attention.

Miles sat back in his office chair, settling his enormous frame comfortably, and pausing before asking the obvious question. "Well . . . what *is* your real name?"

"Knight. Aubry Knight."

The NewMan nodded. "I won't ask for explanations. This is the safest house on the West Coast, Aubry. There's the New York Commune, of course, and then Monument Valley."

"Has there been any grief in Arizona?"

"Not yet. Not that I've heard." Miles watched him closely, and Aubry drew up slightly in his seat, very conscious of Miles's eyes on him, and wondered why he felt so self-conscious. "Now then. What exactly is the problem?"

"If anyone would know of a group of mercenaries using unusual physical skills, I figured that it would be your people."

"Unusual skills? What exactly do you mean?"

"I mean that I ran into a man who wasn't half my weight who nearly killed me. I'm telling you that he didn't move like anything that I've ever seen . . . except that he was fast. God-awful fast."

"You say that he was small?"

"Four and a half feet tall."

Miles sat back, and thought.

"It was almost . . ."

"Almost what?"

"As if I was fighting a woman. Just a feeling. It's not easy for me to talk about this."

"Why not?"

"There was something *wrong*."

"Wrong how? What did you feel?"

"I can't explain it, Miles. It was gut-level. It felt terrible." Aubry gestured vaguely. "Empty."

Miles's voice became distant. "You say that it might have been a woman?"

"Might. I don't think so. Didn't have much time to think—I was fighting for my *life*."

"I see." Miles templed his fingers. "I owe you more than I can ever pay, Aubry. Even counting that, I just can't tell you everything you need to know."

"You know what is happening?"

Miles nodded slowly.

"Then tell me, man. Don't leave me hanging."

"I can't. But people owe me favors. Maybe we can talk to them. Would you be willing to try?"

"Hell yes. Who, and where?"

"His name is Quint."

"Head of the Gorgons?"

"Yes. And we have a project . . . one which involves hermaphrodism. I don't know how far it's gone. We have to go to Monument Valley, in Arizona. There may be some answers there."

Aubry stood, paced across the room. He peered out through the window. Outside the window, across the courtyard, was a flickering billboard, the picture of DeLacourte smiling at them. The man gave him the creeps.

Across the street was a board carrying the bland, paternalistic face of President Roland Harris. He had a very rectangular face, and honest, direct eyes. As Aubry watched, the image faded and shifted, alternating with a flag at full mast.

"This is something big, isn't it?"

"Bigger than you think. Otherwise I'd tell you, Aubry."

All right, Aubry thought. *There were people milling about down there in the street. How many of them had ever had their lives torn into fragments as he had? How many of them had any conception of what could happen to a man on his way to the grave?*

"All right. I'll go. I don't have much choice."

"None of us do, Aubry."

"It's that big?"

"It's bigger," Miles said.

CHAPTER TWENTY-TWO

Spiders

Wednesday, June 14

Courtney, the man from the service station, had been mistaken. The Hoopa Spider detention center's stench was not that of human corruption. It was a no-smell, the smell of chemical pots with their solid chemical deodorizers, an olfactory anesthetic that numbed the senses so strongly that it became a stench of its own.

"Concertina fence," Promise said into her radio as her skimmer coasted in to a landing. "It looks like the old days, back in the Maze. I hate it already."

"Save the hate until it has a direction, lady. We may need it yet." Leo's voice was pinched by tension and distance: he was ten miles away, outside the radius of Hoopa's security perimeter.

Rows of barbed wire stretched for miles, disappearing into the trees in either direction. Within the tangles smoldered the chemical pots, a tender mercy to passing noses.

And within . . .

The tiny bungalow on the outskirts of the camp was very clean, very neat, almost neurotically well kept. The four men who waited within were playing cards as they sat around a simple wood-burning stove. They looked at Promise as she entered as if she were something that had tumbled out of Santa's sack.

"Excuse me," Promise said carefully. "I'm looking for Templeton."

The biggest of the men stood, and he looked at Promise

in a manner that left nothing to the imagination. His eyes weighed and measured each curve. "What can we do for you?"

"I talked with a man named Templeton. I talked to him on the line. He told me—"

"He's in Washington, lady. That's a long way from here."

"Smells a lot better," one of the others said, and laughed.

"You got business, you talk to Jonsie. You tell me what you're selling, I'll tell you if we're buying."

The wind shifted suddenly, horribly, and the stench hit her like a basket of dead maggots. She suddenly buckled at the knees, and had to grasp a chair. She squeezed her eyes shut, struggling to regain her poise.

The big man laughed nastily. "It gets kind of bad here sometimes, sugar. Them that does the Lord's work sometimes got to wrestle with demons."

"Templeton . . ." she began weakly. "I just want to go in. I just want to talk with one of the inmates."

Jonsie pulled back. "What business do you have with this scum?"

When she managed to speak, her voice was too husky by half. "What in the hell are you talking about?"

He jerked a horny thumb in the direction of the camp. The wind had died down or changed, thank God, and the air no longer swam with corruption.

"Them. Sinners every one. Don't you listen to DeLacourte's America Hour? Every one convicted of secret sins by the disease in his blood. God's judgment is swift, and final."

The other men in the room grunted their assent.

Promise shook her head clear, and fought to keep the disdain from her voice. "That's . . . just not true. You can catch Thai-VI by being raped. Or buying black market blood . . ."

"A crime," Jonsie said dogmatically.

She spread her hands reasonably. "But not a sin."

"Ain't no difference, lady. You commit a crime, you weaken the mother country. You weaken the country, you wreck the 'Thin Line,' you're risking millions of lives. That's what got us into this in the first place.''

''That's just not true.'' Promise pulled a handkerchief from her pocket and held it tightly over her nose. ''We ran short on water. California got hit with the largest earthquake in its history. The entire Pan-Latin Federation defaulted on half a trillion dollars' worth of loans.''

''The Judgment was God's,'' one of the other men at the table said, rising. Subtly, she had been hemmed in. Suddenly there was an image in her mind, a terrible, cyclical one. She was a prisoner. These men were prisoners as much as the poor creatures on the other side of the wire. Only they were trapped by the economics of their jobs, and the unbreakable strands of their simplistic belief structures, reinforced by that champion of the people, Sterling DeLacourte.

''Templeton ain't here. He keeps himself at a nice, safe distance.'' Someone behind Jonsie laughed. ''What's the matter—ain't we good enough for you to talk to? We can help you—we're God's people too.''

Jonsie came closer. There was something smoky and nauseatingly strong on his breath. ''So, you gotta deal with us. Now, you need a favor, you should offer something in return.''

The door clicked shut behind her.

Aubry . . .

She shut the image from her mind.

Jenna.

She knew what was about to happen, and for a moment she resigned herself. Then another thought, one in Jenna's voice, spoke to her. A voice stronger than her fear. *No. Never again. No one uses you. Not ever again.*

''All right,'' she said huskily. Automatically her body posture changed, and the old tricks came to her. The eyes, the shoulders, the subtle play of the hands. All of the skills that she had used in years past came to her, and the men in the room were taken utterly aback. ''Let's do it. Don't worry. You don't need to protect yourselves.'' She lowered her voice further, eager now. ''Come on. I'm ready for you.''

Jonsie narrowed his eyes. "I, uh . . . I think I wanna wear something."

"What are you worried about? I'm clean. You first." She stepped forward, took a strong grip on his wrist. Jonsie tore his arm away, and backed up.

"Just wait a goddamn minute. Shit, what is it with you?"

"Nothing. I just want you—*all* of you."

The four men exchanged uneasy glances. "Just . . . what the hell do you have, lady?"

"Nothing," she said too rapidly. "The spectrograph said I was clean." She smiled. "I tried two of 'em. They *both* said I was clean. Damn machines are more accurate anyway. Come *on*." She was urgent now.

"Keep *away* from me," Jonsie said. He snatched his gun from its holster. "I get it now. God *damn*, I nearly fell for it. Shit. When are they coming for you? Next week? Next month? You wanted to play a little Thai-VI tag along the way. Robbie—" he said to one of the other men, without turning his head. "Get this bitch in there with the rest of the freaks."

You can't get Thai-VI from just breathing the air. There needs to be sexual contact, or exchange of body fluids.

She had heard that over and over again, but now, actually beyond the camp's gate, it was difficult to remember.

From the first step she took into the area, she felt as if she were walking into alien turf. The trees looked somehow stunted, unhealthy, as if the stench were seeping into the bark, soaking up through the roots. She took one of the dented bicycles leaning in a row against the rear of the infiltration gate and peddled it out down a twisting dirt road. She didn't think that motor craft ever traversed it. There was too much dust here, the rains had smoothed the ruts too often. No, more likely food and what medical supplies the Spiders were allotted were dropped from above. Aside from that, they were probably left on their own.

She checked her pack. A few food bars, a flashlight, a set of paper clothing. "For after you start to ooze."

Nice man. In the seam of her pants was sewn a slender

transmission beacon. It was her only hope, and she prayed that it would operate when the time came.

A large, gnarled tree marked with yellow paint loomed up on her left. She stopped the bike, and lowered the kickstand.

There were furtive movements behind the trees, as if the very sound of her bicycle were sufficient to disturb the peace that the Spiders had found with each other, here in the concealing darkness.

She shone her flashlight out into the night, and saw nothing, just the yellow marker that would guide her deeper into the camp. Promise drew the slender shock prod that the gate men had given her. Small enough protection from the advanced cases, but it was something.

The ground beneath her feet was carpeted with rotting vegetation. Her clothes clung to her body, and her breath whistled in her ears as she sucked sour, rotten air.

Be with me, Aubry, she said silently, and instantly felt hideously alone. He should have been with her. This was their job, together.

But Aubry didn't believe, and Aubry had another quest.

And she had to resign herself to the fact that Aubry might never cross her path again.

The grief that coursed through her was savage and consuming, but she controlled it within seconds. This was not the time. Perhaps there was no time, would never be a time.

And in that case her mission here was even more important. If that child was the only piece of Aubry that she would ever have . . .

Now her thoughts came back to the present with jarring suddenness. Something moved out beyond the branches.

At first she would have thought it impossible to believe that the shape was human. The body had grown so corrupt that the poor creature seemed to have almost melted into the earth itself. She stifled her nausea, and played her light over the corpse.

It almost glowed in the dim light. The hair was gone, all gone, the flesh of the head seemed to have flowed, melted almost, into a thickened mass of swollen, running flesh.

The maggots swarmed at it. The smell was something beyond hideous.

"He's dead," a voice sniffed. She pivoted, trying to find the speaker with her light.

"Is someone out there?"

"He's dead, he's dead, he's dead. . . ."

There was still no one standing there, but Promise searched anyway, and finally caught a small, hunched figure huddled against a tree.

"Please—don't be afraid. I need help."

"He's dead. We're all dead," the little Spider said.

Promise came closer. The figure huddled against the tree, cowering. Then, without any warning, it flew at her, screaming: "It's *your* fault, it's—"

Promise sidestepped, just brushed the creature with the tip of the shock prod. It responded as if all of its nerves had been linked together into a single massive ganglia, and then struck by lightning.

It flew backward into the tree, eyes wide, bony fingers wide, the impact shattering its arm with an audible crack.

It slid to the ground, whimpering, breath rasping in its throat. Emboldened, Promise took another step closer, and played her light over it.

It was a woman. Once, she must have been as tall as Promise. The disease had whittled her down, bowed her. She could scarcely have weighed eighty pounds, and her ribs were more prominent than her breasts. Her face was crisscrossed with the remnant of the crouching spider, tattooed in blacks and bloody reds across her face. It screamed to all that she was a pariah, a thing of death and disease.

"Don't . . . don't hurt. Please . . . sorry. Oh, God, so sorry . . ."

Promise squashed down the disgust, the pity, everything but a grim resolve to see this through.

"I'm going to hurt you," she said. "I know how vulnerable you are to pain. Your nervous system feels little else right now. And I'll stun you until you think the devil is chewing your tail. I swear it."

"What do you want?"

"I want a man named Allred. Do you know him?"

"Thousands here. How I supposed to know . . ." The creature screwed her face up in sudden grief. She stared at the dead, rotting thing stretched under the sky. "He's dead. Too weak to bury. Others don't help. You help? Please?"

"That's not in the deal. You help me first, then we'll talk about it. You're going to help me find Allred. He was a doctor."

"Doctor . . ." The creature scratched at her dead eye. The one good one batted a few times, then focused. "Oh. Oh. I think I know. Doctor. Camp doctor. Yes. You follow."

"You try anything and I'll fry you."

Promise followed the misshapen creature back through the trees, and now other figures began to emerge.

They slouched back in the shadows, keeping their distance, and she brandished the stunner at them, feeling like a dreadful pied piper.

The shambling, shuffling shapes followed her. One more emerged from the pack and ran at her. The others suddenly clamored, hooting. If Promise could be dragged down . . .

But their coordination was gone, destroyed by the same disease that ravaged their flesh.

Promise had coordination. She had that, and, buried deep within her memory, the lessons of Durga.

Promise slid to the side, and went under the grasping arms, whipping the stunner at its face as she slid through.

It howled in agony, clutching at its ruined face with hands that were little more than wet claws. At a sound behind her, Promise dropped. A moss-crusted two-by-four swung harmlessly over her head, smashing into the face of another Spider. She rose, and skated back on the balls of her feet, shocked by the speed and fluidity of her reaction. *Durga.*

"Well? Anyone else?" She struggled to keep the fear from her voice. "Who's next. You? You?" She pointed with the shock prod and now they knew, and kept their distance. They ringed her like creatures of another, darker, world.

She was heaving for breath, as much from adrenal rush as fatigue. *O Goddess. Not much more strength. Please. Help me.*

Hundreds of the spider tattoos stared at her, bunching in a colony.

"You! All of you. I'm not your enemy. Many of you received medicine from the Scavengers. My man and I ran the Scavengers. I come in peace. I just want to talk to your doctor, Allred."

One of the Spiders hobbled forward, and another one shook its head—Promise couldn't tell if it was a man or woman—and barred the first's path.

The crowd broke, made way for a skeleton of a man with bright, bright eyes, and a livid black widow spider emblazoned on his face. "I'm Allred." He looked at her as if she were the anomaly, she the creature of myth. He suddenly drew himself up, shocked. "Oh, God. I know you. I know you. Please. Come with me."

Allred's shack was one of a hundred in a clutch. There were seven other Spiders in the room. They sat around a small stove, no different from the wood-burning stove that their guardians had crouched around on the outskirts of the camp.

"Do you know why I'm here?"

Allred stared at her. There was something cooking in a brazier in the center of the room, but the air was already crowded with Thai-VI stench, and Promise couldn't smell it. The men in the room seemed hungry. It was in their eyes, in their body language.

"The disease," Allred said as if addressing a group of interns, "depresses the appetite centers in the human brain. We starve ourselves to death. We can't keep much food down. Vitamin injections help. We can keep water down. Not much else. . . . We like to smell though."

He sat, scrunched up like an accordion. He turned to face her. "Yes. I know why you're here. I don't know how you found out."

"Wu."

"Wu!" He laughed bitterly. "Don't trust him. He's the

reason I'm here, you know. He found out I'd developed an alliance with . . . some others. It just wasn't allowed. This is my punishment. He . . . found a man to infect me. He found out, he found me . . ." Allred buried his face in his hand, and sobbed.

"Dr. Allred. Listen. I have to know." Promise leaned forward. "Terra Buena. I had a miscarriage."

"No you didn't," he said as softly as a whisper. His ruined face was streaked with tears. "I stole your fetus. There's no reason not to tell the truth. Damn McMar . . . damn the whole thing. Oh, God, why did I ever—"

"Yes, damn you. How could you do it? Why did you do it? Why me?"

"How could you know? I knew that . . . certain fetal abnormalities were sought by a buyer." He pressed his hands to his forehead, as if trying to squeeze the memories from his mind like paste from a tube. "Hermaphrodism. Twenty thousand dollars for a healthy hermaphrodite fetus."

"But why?"

"I don't know. But I scanned you, and your child, and found that your unborn child was a true hermaphrodite. I didn't know then that it was because of the Cyloxibin—the bottom fell out of the market a year later. I had you under anesthesia, and when I knew I wouldn't be interrupted for two hours, I removed the fetus and put it on life support."

"You mean froze it?"

He laughed, more nastily than the first time. "Hell, no. I wanted it to stay alive."

"What are you saying? There are fetal storage facilities across the country . . ."

Allred just grinned toothlessly. "That's all I'm saying."

"Where did you send it?" she whispered.

"No," he said bluntly. "I admit to my guilt, but I won't say anything more. I want what life is left to me."

She raised the stinger, and then dropped it.

"Don't you have any children? Anything that you love? Don't you know what I'm feeling? You have to help me."

The man's ravaged face softened. "Once . . . a long time ago, I saw my lover dance. She was magnificent. She was a Plastiskin. Whole-body. She could make her body float, fly. She could chameleon. I remember. I . . . would you show me? Just once, would you show me?"

Promise stood, and looked down on him, feeling nothing but pity. There was no way that she could feel the naked loathing that had been so strong within her only moments before.

She moved her hips from side to side, moving to the music in her mind. She relaxed her guard, relaxed the automatic neural blocks that kept the natural color on the left side of her body. . . .

The men in the room gasped. The women, breasts and hips ravaged into asexuality by the disease, looked at her with a naked longing that was even more intense.

Then the light blazed out, and she faceted herself, turned herself into a jewel with concentration so intense that every centimeter of her body had its own sharply defined arc and color differential. The light flew up to the ceiling and for a moment the drab walls of the cabin housed a fantasy ballroom, something from another place and time.

Then she sat down again.

Tears were streaming from Allred's eyes. "Yes, yes, remember. I remember now."

She reached out with her hands, and took his. His flesh felt sticky and brittle. "Please. Please help me."

He wept openly. "No one . . . has touched me for two years. Aren't you afraid?"

"Aren't we all?"

He swallowed hard. "All right. You deserve that much. The fetus was shipped to Arizona. To the NewMan encampment. Find something called Medusa. That's all I know. All I can tell you."

Promise stood near the electrified fence, reached through the fabric of her pants, and hit the tracer. A radio beam screamed out into the night, and ninety seconds later, a hovercraft appeared. A circle of blazing light splashed down.

Promise ran to the center of the circle. A stream of yellow disinfectant foam played over her, and she gasped as it stung her eyes, but still rotated slowly, with her arms up. A rope ladder lowered to her, and she climbed up into the craft.

"Well?" Leo asked as he pulled Promise up. "Move it. The alarms are up. They'll try to burn us down, but I'm flying low."

The craft took off. Promise watched the screens as two patrol vehicles flew in to check the security breach. Leo's smooth hands on the controls whisked them away before the security vehicles arrived.

"Well?"

"I know where my child is," Promise said, and an enormous load seemed to lift from her shoulders with the words.

Leo nodded, thin face feral. "Then let's go get her."

CHAPTER TWENTY-THREE

One Nation Under God

Monday, June 19

Marcel Killinger stood in the security booth at the very rear of the Los Angeles Sports Arena, looking down over the thousands of cheering spectators who waited for the stage in the front of the arena to clear. This was the third in a series of six talks, a media blitz building the way for victory in July.

As in other arenas around the country, the rally would be piped via satellite. As had been his habit for more than two years now, Sterling DeLacourte would appear only by hologram.

On triple Omnivision flatscreens, Killinger scanned the parking lots outside. The fire department hosed the remains of three burning cars from the pavement. Bomb threats. More of them, and these had not been bluffs. The tension, the current, was mounting, the stakes rising.

That was the way that it had to be.

The room lights dimmed, and the crowd roared as a local politico took the stand. The man looked like a flesh-colored frog, all wide lips and hairless pate.

"We know why we are here today," he began. "In a month, the Democratic National Convention comes to Los Angeles. We are here to send a signal to the highest levels of our government. We know the man we want sent to Washington, DON'T WE!! We know the one man who can clean the corruption from our streets, who can set this great country back on the path of righteousness.

"Look at the cities! They are burning, they are roiling with hatred and intrigue. Look at the spending power that our parents enjoyed. Look at the relations with our neighbors who used to respect us.

"Today, we come to listen to a man who understands wealth—and has built a billion-dollar empire with his own sweat. Who understands communication, and is praised the world over for his unification of a thousand international cable links in the largest global network the world has ever known. We come to pay honor to a man who is a man of faith, who preaches the simple truth, because that is the only way that he understands. The man who helped guide the nation into a sane policy dealing with the filth who carry Thai-VI through our streets.

"Ladies and gentlemen, I give you the next President of the United States, Sterling DeLacourte!"

Killinger glanced to the left, where Nozawa, their communications tech, worked carefully, smoothly, coordinating the image of a man thousands of miles away with the stage before them. Everyone in the audience knew that DeLacourte's presence was holographic. They accepted it. But there was magic here, something that touched the hindbrain. He was almost a creature of myth, a man apart, above the masses. More than a leader. More than a king. A god, perhaps.

The image strobed as it took the stage, and Nozawa spoke softly to his console at the same time his fingers flew over the keyboards.

The distant scream of the fire trucks, the violence that stirred in the streets outside the doors of the sports arena, seemed only to emphasize the calm presence of the man on the dais.

"I come to you to speak of my wife Gretchen, and my precious son Conley. We have heard the other candidates speak of great issues, of the sweep of history, and the marching of vast armies. But we cannot, must not, forget that in the final analysis, all that has meaning—all that has *ever* had meaning—is the family. This country wasn't built for the politicians. Wasn't built by the armies. It was built by and for the families who crossed the plains, forded the rivers, cleared the land, and built cities that touch the clouds! For and with our *families* we clawed a place for ourselves in hostile land, for the possibility of building something for our children, and our wives or husbands.''

Nozawa whispered, ''Bring in Mrs. DeLacourte. On two—''

''And now, my wife—'' and Gretchen DeLacourte appeared, an enormous magnification above her husband's smaller figure. She bowed her head as if embarrassed, but still her great beauty spoke to them from the projections.

''And my son—'' Conley appeared like a cherub, silver-gilt and freckled, the magnification shimmering above DeLacourte's head. Every freckle was as large as a base-ball. ''My son cannot walk the streets of our great cities without fearing for his life. And this is the result of a hundred years of permissive government, when the 'rights of the individual' were ceded to be greater than the rights of the society as a whole. As a result, we have no free-doms, none at all, save the freedom to choose the manner of our death.

''Will it be pestilence? Then look no further than the dreaded disease Thai-VI, which is presently responsible for thirty-five thousand deaths every year. Will it be war? Look no further than the strife in Africa, which threatens to boil over into the bloodiest conflict in the history of mankind. Will it be pollution, and the death of the sacred environment that God gave us? Then note the death of our oceans. Since the year 2000, only twenty-eight years ago, over twelve thousand species of fish and mammals have become extinct.

''We are a dying planet, a dying culture—unless we make a decision *now*. It is not too late, unless courage has failed us!''

Nozawa turned off the sound in the booth. He pulled a cigarette out of his pocket, tamped it, and groped for a lighter.

Killinger extended a match. ''What do you think?''

''It's all in the perspective. DeLacourte in the center, wife and child in magnification to either side. The implication is obvious. We can juggle his image, make him a click or two larger when he's making a point.''

"You're just saying what you can do. Not what you think."

"What do I think?" Nozawa's creased, brown face was contemplative as he blew a smoke ring toward the ceiling. "I think that it's time I moved my family out of the country. I think we're headed down the tubes. But I'm happy to take your money. Anytime."

In spite of himself, Killinger grinned. "Cynical bastard, aren't you?"

"Every man is a mirror," Nozawa said flatly. "We all reflect what we see."

"You understand that this is an informal meeting, Mr. DeLacourte. We are not a committee," Valdez said heavily. "We have no power to approve or disapprove. We merely felt a direct meeting might well be useful in . . . clarifying the situation as it presently exists."

"Situation, Senator?"

Michael Valdez, the senator from Colorado, sat across from Sterling DeLacourte. Once, he must have been a fine figure of a man. Now, he was fleshy and somehow simultaneously cadaverous. A jarring combination of features, to be sure, but there it was.

His skin was olive, Hispanic mixed with something . . . Irish perhaps, judging by the shape of the face and the deep lines around his eyes. Once, those eyes had looked out on the world and laughed. Now little they saw brought mirth. Now, they were bloodshot and tired, as if they had seen too much for too long.

"Situation, Mr. DeLacourte." The brown man's thick fingers played on a console, and suddenly the room was filled with rioters.

"Atlanta. Des Moines. El Dorado—remember the lynchings in Arkansas? Sacramento, Albuquerque. All of these cities have experienced violence that has been linked with your name or your cause."

The other men in the room were still quiet. DeLacourte sat back in his chair, biding his time. They were old men.

His men. All he had to do was save them. There was nothing immoral in that—these were America's elder statesmen. Good Christians, good Americans all of them. And their health was deteriorating. Their time of service coming to an end. It was his duty to help them.

As it would be theirs to help him. He smiled a secret smile, a smile hidden by the darkness. How neatly things came together, when God was on your side.

"I did not direct these actions, nor do I condone them. But I do understand them, gentlemen."

Avery inclined his head from the shadows. "Could you explain that comment, sir?"

The holocamera in the ceiling adjusted its depth of field, and pushed in on DeLacourte. In a hundred auditoriums across the country, audiences leaned forward in their seats to hear the words, see the image of the man who asked for their funds, their support, their votes.

"Certainly, Senator. Our country has been torn by civil unrest and economic and environmental catastrophe. Only an atheist would reject the possibility that these things may be the response of a wrathful God, a just and angry God who has sickened of the filth we have tolerated in our midst. Drug addiction rampant in the streets, with a raft of drugs that duplicate the effects of heroin or cocaine or grubs, but are legal. A molecule of difference paralyzes our police. Prostitution is legal in four states, with men and women flagrantly selling their bodies in the streets.

"And most terribly, the specter of sodomy has darkened the sun. We have communities of homosexuals actually campaigning for the right to *breed*. Do you realize what an abomination this is? These acts of violence that so rightly disturb you—they would be committed if I had never been born. They are merely the only reasonable response to an intolerable situation."

"I see," Valdez said. "There is nothing of condemnation in your words, Mr. DeLacourte."

And in sixty million homes, DeLacourte's image flowed

down through the cables, in from the satellite dishes. Every major news service in the country recorded his words. And the following day, they would dissect and deliberate the impact on every level of the political game save the one that DeLacourte himself played upon.

DeLacourte's answering laughter was low and musical. "That is because, while I deplore their actions, I applaud their sentiments. Indeed, something must be done. The nation has become such a web of fear and legal red tape that nothing can be accomplished within the lifetime of a single citizen. Everything must be accomplished through generations of effort. I propose to cut through that. I can tell you that what America needs is a philosopher-king. We cannot have that—the Constitution is too strong. But I tell you that 'one nation united under God' will move as with a single purpose to right the wrongs of the past."

Avery squirmed in his seat. "It sounds as if you are suggesting a theocracy, Mr. DeLacourte."

" 'One nation under God.' Isn't that what we promised our children? And what have we done with that promise? Can our children walk the streets without fear of molestation? Have we brought peace between the races? Has the Christian brotherhood we speak of on Sabbath ever appeared in our weekdays? I think not. We have always prattled about America being a 'Christian nation' but because of our concern with the separation of Church and State we have never allowed the concept to actually take root. We've tried everything else. Why not return to the faith of our fathers, and try that. Four years. Would that be too much to ask?"

"And in those four years?"

DeLacourte shifted in his seat, seemed to swell with the magnitude of his words. "I will abolish the drug trade. The death penalty will be applied swiftly and ruthlessly against those found poisoning our children. I propose open season on organized crime. For years we have known exactly who the men and women were who have made a mockery of our legal system. I propose publishing their names on the front page of every newspaper in the country, and assuring our Citizens' Action Committees that the legal protection which had enfolded this filth in the past has now expanded to make the law what it was ever meant to be—an instrument of the public will.''

Valdez inhaled sharply. ''You're suggesting vigilantism?''

''Unlike my political adversaries, I will speak the truth. It is the only tool that I have. We are losing this country. We are losing the battle. The righteous citizens of this country are already running wild in the streets. Without direction, all of them become hunted criminals. We haven't a fraction of the police or jails to control or contain this force—why not use that force, then, instead of opposing it?''

''Aren't you afraid of assassination? You would be placing yourself in the most controversial position of any president in American history.''

''You can kill me, but you can't kill an idea. It is time for Americans to take back their country. I can't put it more simply and directly than that.''

Avery thrummed his fingers on the desk before him. ''It . . . is difficult to fault your basic beliefs, sir. But I cannot imagine you winning more than a pittance of the vote. It would take a miracle. . . .''

''But I believe in miracles,'' DeLacourte said quietly. ''And now, the meeting is, I believe, over. I asked for an hour of your time. I have no intention of imposing further. Thank you very much.''

Killinger smiled, and punched a seat number into the video computer. The camera panned and zoomed in on a man seated next to a young boy. Or perhaps it was a girl. It was hard to tell. The child's features were so androgynous. The child's skin was dark, the features very fine. The eyes were hazel brown, and intensely direct, as if drinking in every word, every syllable, every sound from the man in the front of the auditorium, the man who spoke so loudly, and to such effect that the entire crowd seemed to sway and heave with each word, each rolling phrase, each new gesture.

The child watched. Killinger punched in another seat

coordinate, and there was another man, and another child. No more than thirteen years old, this one was pale-skinned, and just as disturbingly androgynous. The eyes were wide and piercing and guileless. The child sat very straight in the chair, and hung onto every word.

And another . . .

And another.

And finally Killinger sat back.

It was good, all of this. The children were real, and it might work. They could kill, as Medusa-16 had proven. They could follow orders, and be accepted as normal human children.

They were ready.

The intense overhead lights dimmed, and everyone in the room emitted a sigh of relief.

Jack Hands moved in from the side of the room. "And once again, thank you, gentlemen. I hope that it has been an interesting experience for you."

"Thank Senator Avery," the senator from Colorado said. "He was primarily responsible."

"I intend to."

Four men filed out of the room, leaving Valdez and Avery behind. Avery sat on the other side of the table, a lean gray man with dark, intelligent eyes.

Valdez's breath was a heavy rasp. *A good man,* DeLacourte thought. *But unwell. Grown old and sick in service to America. If I can use the lowest to aid the highest, so be it.*

"He did his part, Sterling," Avery said calmly. His dark eyes glittered.

Now, with the holocameras shut down, Tyler-Watt seemed to collapse. "I can't promise you their minds, but I brought you their bodies."

"Indeed you did, my friend. And I intend to keep my bargain."

DeLacourte walked to the side of the room and ran his fingers along a strip on the wall. A beam of light shone out at eye level, instantly analyzing his retinal structure. He blinked a special coded sequence. Another sequence would have flooded the room with anesthetic gas and alerted a squad of guards.

A seam split in the wall, exposing a heavy steel safe door. The door was chill to the touch, but swung open. Beyond was a refrigerator, and several vials, faintly greenish in the light.

Avery sighed audibly.

DeLacourte attached one of the vials to a feeder device, and charged it. Fluid drained into the vial.

Valdez shifted uncomfortably, anxiously. "Is that . . . is that for me?"

"No, Senator." DeLacourte carried the green vial over to Avery and said, "Open." Avery unbuttoned his vest, then his shirt. Two thin white lines of scar tissue formed a cross on his shoulder, a tiny nylon nipple protruding in the center. DeLacourte slipped a needle into the nipple, and injected a carefully measured dosage. "Your reservoir is charged for another month. For one month it will administer twenty-five micrograms of DEA per hour. After I am elected, you will receive one dose per month as long as I remain in office, and you continue to support my policies." DeLacourte smiled, and slapped Avery's shoulder. "Hell, there isn't even a need to say that. We're all friends here."

Avery nodded, his finger rubbing the nipple self-consciously before buttoning the shirt back up.

"You find me the men I can trust. The ones who love this country. The ones who love their God. And I can save them, too. Find the ones who have lived long enough to see the cycles, the ones who are afraid for the land they love. Bring them to me. I will take their fear, and give them new life."

The color was already returning to Avery's face, and he was breathing more calmly. A sweat flush broke out on his forehead, and he mopped it with a large red handkerchief. "Yes. Yes, I will."

"Mr. Valdez." DeLacourte turned to the other man. "In one month, your influence, your votes, will be critical. I give you a gift, in acknowledgment of the services you have provided our nation."

DeLacourte took a small plastic tab and stripped the backing away. In the middle of an adhesive pad was an eyelash-thick needle. "Take off your shirt, and raise your arm."

Shaking, Valdez did as requested. The flesh on his upper body sagged as if he had slipped into the wrong man's skin that morning. "I have heard of this . . . chemical. I am not a rich man, but I have wealthy friends. They tell me. They say that for a million dollars a year, I can stay young. Is this true?"

DeLacourte smiled, and slipped the tab into place. Valdez started for a moment, and then relaxed. The tab, pale for the first few seconds, slowly took on Valdez's skin tones. Within a minute, it was all but invisible.

"You'll feel the effects in a week. This tab will last for ten days. You'll want to visit me again."

"What of . . ." Valdez groped for words. "My wife and I. I . . . haven't been a man for six years."

"Believe in miracles," DeLacourte said quietly. "I do."

Medusa-16 sat very quietly as the crowd filed out around him. His eyes were, as Killinger had noted, hazel brown, with a slight Asian cast to them. They blinked infrequently, never looked away, and were most unsettlingly direct.

Medusa-16 could smile, when necessary, and could laugh, and cry, or any of another hundred programmed emotional responses. His true emotions were buried far, far below the surface, however.

This was his first experience with so large a group. There were thousands and thousands of people here, and although he had received image inputs of crowds far larger than the present group, there was a difference. The smells. The touches. Strangeness. It would be good to return to the Nation for final programming.

He felt the chemical responses to the changes, and knew that this was extraordinary. This was what he would have considered, in a target, to be an "emotional response."

Curiosity. That had been programmed. That was a good

feeling, within limits. He wondered how many of his siblings felt the same. Or was he alone, even in this?

There had been, in fact, only one time when he had felt this way. It had been in Oregon, during the obedience test. His body still ached from the memory, despite the hormonal nutrient baths.

The Man had been different. He had not responded as Medusa-16's trainers had responded. Not as strong or quick as Quint, but there had been something extraordinary about the encounter, and in a secret part of Medusa-16's mind, he was glad that the encounter had not been terminal. He . . . wanted to meet that one again.

Why? That question wouldn't form. So many wouldn't. He knew that an abyss gaped for those who asked the wrong questions.

So Medusa-16 concentrated on DeLacourte again. Watched the man's movement, his facial expressions.

Listened to his speech patterns.

DeLacourte was important.

DeLacourte was Target.

It was bad to be programmed, and prepared, and trained to perform a function at a very high level of efficiency, and never fulfill that function.

Fulfilling one's function was good. Quint said so.

It would be good to kill.

CHAPTER TWENTY-FOUR

NewMan Nations

> Now I walk with Talking God
> With Goodness and Beauty in all things
> around me I see.
> With Goodness and Beauty I follow
> Immortality.
> Thus being, I go . . .

> —Navajo *Song of the Talking God*

Wednesday, June 21

The ground beneath them opened like a raw, ancient wound. It was discolored and ragged and the plane's shadow dove and skipped around the slashed rock like a dark fish diving through a coral reef.

The plane itself was an ultralight structure, barely more than a synthetic skin strung over a framework of hollow tubes. The engine driving the single prop was a miracle of efficiency, smaller than the typical twentieth-century auto engine. It purred along without complaint, carrying Aubry Knight and Miles Bloodeagle farther north into Arizona with each passing minute.

Miles swept down lower, giving Aubry a better look at the Grand Canyon. "Never seen it before?"

"Just pictures."

"Nothing like it. When I was a kid, I used to crawl

around in the gorge, camp there overnight. Just crunch up into the rocks, and listen to the wind come whistling through the gorge. It was a way of purifying myself. It was a clean time.''

''Never been anything . . .'' Aubry paused, considering. ''I like to climb buildings,'' he said in a surprisingly small voice.

The color of the sand beneath them began to change as they crested the far side of the gorge. Less reddish now, and then more golden, as if with vast brush strokes laid down from a titan's paintbox. The colors mingled and ran together, and were wholly beautiful.

''We're about ten minutes away now,'' Miles said. The silver wings of their aircraft glinted in the sunlight so that even through the tinted sunscreen Aubry had to shield his eyes.

Aubry listened to the slow and steady roar of his breathing. Unbidden, Promise's image rose into his mind.

Where was she? How was she? And could she ever understand, or forgive him, for doing what it was that he had to do?

Perhaps not. But it was what was right for him, nevertheless. When it was over, perhaps they could be together again. . . .

A flash of panic coursed through him at the thought that they might not be able to be together. She seemed a natural extension of him. . . .

But that was *wrong*. As much as he hated the thought, in that, DeLacourte's holo ravings were quite right. For a chemical to create that bond was unholy. It could blind you, bond you to a monster. Where you had no choice in the matter, there was nothing good, could be nothing good.

No real understanding, no real feelings. Only an unholy chemical substitute. He had to break those bonds, or he could never be free.

He *had* to break them—any way that he could.

There was a starburst-shaped network of buildings stretched out on the desert beneath him, near the edge of a range of mountains.

''The Nation?''

''That's it.'' The light through the window seemed to

split as Miles wheeled the plane around, putting one-half of his face almost violently in sun, the other deep in shadow. In some ways the layout seemed like an army camp, with rows and rows of barrack buildings at the southernmost edge, and other structures spiderwebbed out in a fan. It was actually a decent-sized city, covering about three square kilometers.

Land was irrigated down there, and some sort of farming was going on.

"There are communal farms, but the cost of irrigation is very high. There are a few mineral subleases operated on a time-sharing basis, profits split with the Navajos. We have virtual autonomy from outside jurisdiction."

"The Indian Lands Independence Act?"

"Yeah. 2010 was a very good year."

"But that was just an excuse to sell off more of your land, wasn't it? That's how the Spider camp at Hoopa got started."

"True. The upshot was that the Navajos won total control of the land they had left. Leasing it to the NewMen was a brilliant piece of nose-thumbing. A lot of the inhabitants earn their money in the outside world six months of the year, and then retreat here to be free."

"What about the permanent residents?"

"Mostly hardcore NewMen. Not many of them—the physical requirements are too high. Those who aren't do everything you can think of—curiously, there are a lot of architects and chemical engineers. Disproportionate to the general population. Aside from those groups, there are doctors, and lawyers, and teachers—well, not so many public schoolteachers. There's been a lot of pressure on."

"Many straight men?"

Miles laughed. "Some of them think they are, at first."

"Ha ha. Let me get this straight . . . ah, let me be sure I understand you. You and I are supposed to be lovers."

"And you want into the NewMen. I think that you'd have no trouble passing the tests. They'll want you. Show you around. That will give you a lot more freedom than most of the new prospects ever get—remember. They've got a lot to be paranoid about since Ephesus."

"Got you."

The plane circled in for a landing on a wide, paved runway, and Aubry gritted his teeth. He preferred floaters, but in a pinch was willing to take whatever he could get.

"Remember," Miles said quickly, "I can't guarantee you'll find what you're looking for here. But what you experienced sounds like a project I heard of once. And if it has anything to do with combat, you'll find information on it here."

The glider bumped down, rolled to a stop. "But do not—do not allow anyone to suspect that you are an outside agent. Don't let them know that you are looking for something in particular. It could cost us both our lives."

"Miles—I really appreciate this. I don't know—"

Bloodeagle touched his forearm. "I told you that you'd need a friend one day. I meant what I said."

The outer hatch of the plane opened. The young man standing there was all blinding yellow hair and white smile. "Miles! Good to see you! Long time. How are things in Diego?"

"Most of the straights are so busy buzzing the border that they leave us alone. Hell, they've even recruited us to help their cocaine patrols."

"That's a switch." The young man at the door was of average height, with premature crow's feet at the corners of his eyes, skin leathery from long exposure to desert sun. "Hi! I'm Kevin."

"Aubry." Their palms met, and Kevin gave it a good hard shake.

He glanced from Bloodeagle to Aubry, and shook his head admiringly. "So you're the friend Miles called about. He's always had great taste."

Aubry tried not to roll his eyes. "Uh—thanks."

He turned, and whispered through gritted teeth. "I don't know how much of this I can take."

"You'll survive. If not, we'll bury you with honors."

"Face up, I hope."

"Nasty, nasty."

Aubry pulled his duffel sack out of the back of the

plane, and threw it into the waiting Jeep. The ground was baking hot, the sun still high. In the distance, a row of adobe-brown buildings shimmered in a heat mirage.

Aubry swung into the car. "I've never been here before. What can you tell me about operations, Kev?"

"Well—you might want to go out for Gorgon—jeeze, you're a big one. Hey, Miles, just how big is he?"

"You'll never know."

"Hah. You wait. Anyway, NewMen and the Gorgons on one hand, and the rest of us on the other. Both groups interface at the tribal council."

"Navajo?"

"No—the Navajos just lease us the land. There are a few Indians—like Miles—but mostly they leave us alone. The council calls itself a tribal largely as a joke."

"Who's on this council?"

"It rotates."

The Jeep moved out, heading across the cracked flats toward the buildings wavering in the heat mirage. Now Aubry could make out more figures, and hear the sound of machinery. There was construction going on around them. Buildings were being erected, and one being torn down. There was a helicopter overhead, carrying a girder, and men beneath it riveting and gluing and searing steel beams into place.

There were hundreds of men on the jobs, in the streets, many of them stripped to the waist in the sunlight.

Aubry had never seen such a mass of healthy male bodies in all his life! They seemed spectacularly healthy, and as they drove between the buildings, there was a part of him that understood the camaraderie, yearned for it. He shut that part down with brutal speed.

The Jeep pulled into a two-story textured clay ranch building labeled ADMINISTRATION.

"Register here," Kevin said. He grinned at Aubry openly, admiring the swell of his chest. "Well, I hope I'll see you later."

"I'm sure."

Aubry pulled his sack out of the Jeep, and over one shoulder. As tall as he was, he still felt lost in the crowd.

A group of men came down the way, all of them over six feet in height. They laughed easily, holding hands, arms about each other's waists.

Aubry gritted his teeth.

Oh, God—

Miles laughed at him. "You're a man, you can take it."

"Right."

"Walk this way."

"If I could walk that way, I wouldn't need the talcum."

"Hah hah."

Aubry stood on the lip of his balcony, looking out over the camp, out over the hundreds of small and large buildings that made up the Monument Valley colony. His primary impression was *noise*. There was continuous sound, continuous movement, almost as if silence was to be dreaded.

Everywhere in the streets below him, men walked together, moved together, their arms around each other as if to disguise the Siamese-twin flesh bridges joining them at the hip.

Something in Aubry was torn in three different directions at the same moment—faint revulsion, amusement, and something else that he didn't want to identify.

"Where do we start?" Bloodeagle said.

Miles sat on the edge of the bed. Of course, there was only one bed. Anything else would engender suspicion. Aubry sighed. The floor looked hard.

"We start by understanding each other—"

Miles laughed. "You know something, Aubry? You're not as tough as you think you are. I'm not going to rape you. We can hang a sheet over a clothesline if that would make you feel more comfortable."

Aubry plopped down into a chair, miserable. "I . . . don't want to offend you. Right now, you're the only friend that I have."

"Then let's leave it at that."

Aubry sat, silent for a long while, fingers templed. "How do I get to this Quint?"

"I've arranged an interview this afternoon. Remember,

though—you're playing with fire. If they had anything to do with the raid on Ephesus, and you ask the wrong questions, you're dead.''

"It wasn't Gorgon, that I'm pretty sure of. Hell, I went right *through* three of those men. One of the fighters, just one, was freak fast. Impossible reflexes. Small—under eighty pounds. It doesn't quite sound human to me. I've heard rumors—how much of Gorgon is natural, and how much is accelerated? Mechanical?''

"Probably no more than a lot of professional athletes.''

"Which is to say, a hell of a lot.''

"What you need is the tactical resource computer system, or the people familiar with it. If anything can analyze the patterns of attack and defense, or identify any weapons used, that would be it. But once again: if Gorgon was involved, and they consider you an enemy, you're dead. Quint and Ibumi . . .'' He shook his head. "They can't be reasoned with, Aubry. They can't be stopped.''

Firedance Plaza was busy, the painting and drilling and carrying making the quad look like an ant colony struggling to repair its nest.

Activity. Activity. The feminist colony of Ephesus seemed less frantic but accomplished as much.

A statue was erected in the central plaza, of a slender, graceful youth draped in a robe that fell open almost to the crotch. His eyes gazed on some distant point. His arm was outstretched, lips slightly parted as if caught in the moment before pronouncing sentence, or reciting a couplet.

It wasn't beautiful, as Aubry understood beauty. But it was strong, and, in its way, powerful. It spoke to a part of him that was direct, and pure. The outstretched hand might have touched his brow.

Miles touched his shoulder. "It has that influence on a lot of people. The artist donated it. Like I said—most of the land here is owned in rotation. People pay in different ways.''

"How am I supposed to pay?''

"However you can.''

The interior of administration was quieter, but richly

paneled, almost lavishly, and the same earth colors of brown and gold predominated.

The visual line of the hall was punctuated with paintings and busts. All were of men: men thinking, men studying, men speaking intently. Aubry didn't really notice them at first. What was far more obvious to him were the vibrant bodies passing him in the halls, surrounding him, and lounging in the foyers.

These were *men!* They were as tall as he, as firm-bodied. They watched him with cautious appraisal. They lounged around waiting for appointments with doctors and strategists, and men who understood the dark mysteries of their craft.

NewMen. Perhaps even Gorgons.

Miles paused outside a door, and turned to Aubry. "You wait here. I'll get you in as soon as I can."

Aubry nodded, and found a chair in the foyer. He sat quietly, listening, observing. After the first flutter of interest in him, there was an almost palpable retraction of feelers. What he was, he was, and there was no overt prying.

After a few minutes, the door to the inner office opened again, and Miles exited. "All right."

Aubry rolled his newsfax into a tube, straightened it out again, and then smoothed it down atop a pile of magazines.

The office within was extremely spare, almost Spartan in its simplicity. A young man worked at the speech-sensitive console of a computer. He enunciated clearly, occasionally correcting with a blur of flying fingers at the keyboard.

He sat bolt upright as Aubry entered the room. "Right this way, please." The young man was thin, and of average height: he looked like a midget in these surroundings. Clearly, he was overwhelmed by hero worship. He worked with NewMen! More, he was privy to the offices of the dreaded Gorgon itself!

When he stood, Aubry was startled to note the maternity robes, and the obvious swell at the belly. The young man noted Aubry's stare.

"Oh . . . people take some time to get used to it. I'm still not totally used to the idea myself."

"Ah . . . when's the happy day?"

"November. The artificial womb is a pain, but it's balanced like the real thing, and I don't have to worry about natural childbirth."

"I guess not."

Aubry was still staring as Bloodeagle hustled him past a closed, bolted door to one labeled OFFICE OF NEWMAN ADMISSIONS.

The man behind the desk was extraordinarily broad across the shoulders, but seemed heavy, as if the concerns of the entire camp weighed upon him. His left eye seemed dull, lifeless.

He stood for Aubry, extending his hand. "Winters," he said. "You might call me the mayor of this marginally controlled chaos. Please sit." Aubry did, and the door was closed behind him.

"Of course, I've heard about what you did for our people in Los Angeles. We're very grateful. If there's anything that I can do for you . . ."

Aubry was silent for a moment, then threw caution to the winds. "There *is* something. Something very specific. I was in Ephesus when it was blitzed—"

"*What—?*"

Aubry nodded soberly. "It wasn't pretty."

Winters turned back to the window. "I hope you don't think we had anything to do with it. We didn't. You have to believe that."

"I do," he said bluntly. "But I want to find the men who set it up."

"Vengeance?"

"Yeah. That, and something else. Something happened during that attack. I was shot at, nearly burned and blown up and suffocated. Fine. But something happened that shouldn't have. There was a fighter. Barely five feet tall. Moved faster than anything human, stronger than anything that size has a right to be. I know that if the answers can be found anywhere, they'll be found here."

Winters glared at him, and once again, Aubry couldn't shake the impression that one of his eyes was dead.

"The training programs relating to combat are exclusively for the NewMen, and the forces of Gorgon. Quint is insane for physical combat. Insane." Winters shook his head. "The shortest Gorgon is Alfred Eubanks, at five feet ten."

"I didn't say that you trained him. Grapevine says that Gorgon knows more about combat than any group in the world. Somewhere in this camp, there has to be someone who can give me a lead."

"Were there . . . bodies left behind?"

"Three. Normal human size. On the record as mercenary soldiers, seen action in a half-dozen theaters. Anyone could have hired them. Dead end."

"They were very thorough."

Winters stood, and looked out across the camp, his fingers laced behind his back. "These are . . . bad times, Mr. Knight. As you yourself know. We are under many pressures. I wish I could help you, but I cannot."

"Then find me someone who can."

"I'm sorry."

Aubry looked over to Miles, who shook his head.

"All right, then," Aubry said. "Let's talk about another rumor. I've heard tell that a man can get a new start in the NewMen. That if he's willing to go through the operations and procedures, that he can put his past identity behind him."

"That was . . . sometimes possible in the past. Understand, Mr. Knight, that you are . . . somewhat notorious."

"Only in California."

"I'm sorry. We can't take the risk."

Aubry stood, and his face was twisted with fury. "What in the hell are you talking about? I risked my *life* for you people. The reason that I'm *notorious* is that I came out and saved Bloodeagle and his group from being killed by the same bastards that are after me now. After *you* now. And just maybe did the damage up in Ephesus and tried to blame it on you. All I'm asking for is sanctuary. If that's too much to ask, then I made a big mistake, didn't I?"

Winters paced again, face troubled. "You're right, of course. You are our guest. We will do everything possible to make you comfortable, and give you what aid we can. I tell you though, Mr. Knight—"

"Aubry."

"Mr. Knight. You will get no satisfaction asking questions about the 'small figure' you claim you saw."

"If it was an illusion, it left some hellacious bruises."

"There is a reality that I had to deal with, as the NewMan Nation became stronger," Winters said, his voice was sad and rather flat. "As we grew, we became a symbol, and drew people to us from all over the country, until we became a force in Arizona. With power comes politics. I give you my word, Mr. Knight. None of our people were involved in the Ephesus affair."

"You're—"

Miles reached over and grasped Aubry's hand. "Thank you, Joseph. That will be enough for now."

"You are . . . welcome to our camp," Winters said. His eyes were narrowed.

Aubry rose, nodded. "When will I be contacted? What are the tests?"

"Soon. For now, enjoy yourself. Enjoy the hospitality of the camp."

They were halfway down the stairs before either of them spoke again. Miles broke the silence. "Winters is at the top of the political structure."

"Then he's in charge?"

"No. Not exactly. Gorgon pulls a lot of weight."

"How do I meet them?"

"Hard, Aubry. Not easy at all. They have a favorite bar, but it's private."

"Can you get me in?"

Miles shook his head. "Not really. I can show you where it is. From then on, it's up to you."

"Got it."

Aubry shook Miles's hand outside the Golden Bough and clapped him on the back. "I need a chance to move around here, to get a feel for the place. Do you think it's all right?''

"No problem. I have business to take care of. I'll keep my ears open. If I hear anything . . ."

"I know."

Aubry moved off through the streets. The farther he wandered from the industrial section, the more frankly sensual the designs and decorations became.

The doorways and stenciled windows, the endless images of men embracing, were almost overwhelming.

The main boulevard branched into dozens of side streets, many of them lined with apartments. It was interesting: the layout was more crowded, more cluttered, less territorial than that of the women's encampment. The men here were dressed with the very flash that Ephesus seemed to have disavowed. They were bedecked in colored silks and hand-carved leathers, and carried themselves like peacocks.

There was more laughing and singing and general cama-raderie than he had ever experienced. To either side, bars and taverns called to him, their music playing a raucous, gut-pounding beat. They smelled of sweat. As the evening wore on, and he made his circuit of the camp, he became more and more aware of his own difficulty in dealing with the very level of intensity.

There were almost no women in the camp. The ones he did see were sad and scrawny, or pathetically overweight. Not one seemed even as healthy in mind and body as the men in Ephesus, and none of those had been prizes.

He felt awesomely, achingly lonely. There seemed no place that he felt comfortable sitting and thinking. He felt like a shark. That he had to keep moving, moving, or be swallowed by mysteries that he barely understood.

Where is Promise? Now?

He didn't know, and wanted to so badly that it hurt. He sat on a bench across the street from a bar called The Pitstop. He watched the men drifting in together, and listened to the laughter, and the music, felt a clinching sensation in his chest.

Then he noticed the figure watching him. The man was average-sized, and slender. Bundled in a windbreaker and slacks, it was difficult to make out any physical characteristics, but there was something disturbing about the way that he moved. Aubry felt himself pulled, and the pull was almost more than he could stand. The man entered The Pitstop.

Aubry watched the door for a long moment, then squeezed his eyes shut and walked, then began to run, back to his room.

Miles was waiting. Aubry closed the door behind him, and walked around the bed to the plush chair by the window.

"What did you find?" Miles asked.

"Just . . . checked things out. The lay of the land. Found out that the lay of the land was me."

"You are quite a hunk."

Aubry squeezed his eyes shut. "Miles. I'm flattered. I'm also trying to figure out things I've never even thought about. So do me a favor and don't start with me, all right?"

Miles grinned at him. "Well, I've got the clothesline, if you need it."

"No. I'll . . . just sleep right here, if that's all right."

Miles sobered. "Aubry, that's ridiculous and you know it."

"Just . . . let me be ridiculous tonight then. OK?"

Miles nodded and turned over. Suddenly his voice rose again. "Oh—by the way, did get one thing for you. A name. 'Medusa.' "

"Lady with the snakes?"

"I don't know what it means."

Miles rolled back over, and was almost immediately asleep. Aubry was awake much later. He stared at the ceiling, and listened to the distant, potent roll of the music, and the sound of his own breathing thundering in his chest.

Miles awakened suddenly. The darkness was enveloping, but he heard the sound again: a soft, urgent cry, like a child tossing in nightmare.

The words "walls" and "dark" and a muted scream were all that he could make out. Miles rolled out of bed.

Aubry lay curled onto his side on the lounge chair. He shook uncontrollably, the sweat beading on his forehead like raindrops on oilskin.

Miles wanted to touch, to hold or comfort, but there was nothing he could do that Aubry would not misinterpret. There was no way to reach him that would not damage. The walls were too high, the darkness too deep.

Miles pulled a light blanket from a cabinet on the wall, and spread it out over Aubry, tucking it gently under his friend's chin.

It wasn't much, but it would have to be enough.

CHAPTER TWENTY-FIVE

Deliverance

Monday, June 26

"Lord, let our bodies and minds be equal to the tasks ahead of us this day, and every day. Lift us up into the heights. Let pain, let defeat, let disappointment but drive us on, and yet on, toward perfection. Let our minds and bodies be temples unto your spirit. Let it be thus now and evermore, Amen."

Aubry looked out across the amphitheater, and felt the words in his bones. There were only one or two women to be seen in the entire theater. There certainly would have been more if this had been merely a gathering of male gays. There would have been sisters, mothers, and the inevitable "fag hags."

But, and he had to remind himself, this wasn't merely a gathering of the homosexual elite, those who could afford the time to support a leisure environment that affected the politics of a state.

It was a subset of that group, those who believed in a hyper-male ideal. And as an intensification of that ideal the NewMen, who grew out of the hormonally altered athletes of the eighties, were the children of parents obsessed with performance. Inevitably, when it became known in the nineties that genetic modification of fetuses could create a hyper-athlete, some parents selected the option. Call them frustrated athletes, call them unfeeling monsters willing to create pariahs in the service of an illusory ideal, the NewMen were a reality, and an extraordinary number of the experiments, male and female, had chosen homosexuality as their life-style. In Arizona, the NewMen gathered. The female "hyper-women" had never banded together to become a force.

A very few hyper-hyper heterosexual relationships had been formed. Fewer lasted. None bred true.

Aubry looked around, noting the endless rows of suntanned bodies. Some, but not many, were overweight. Some, but not many, were unpleasantly thin. The Nation's emphasis on male beauty put the plain or unconditioned at a prohibitive disadvantage.

There were a few bulky figures, the men carrying the artificial wombs. Their faces were serene and calm, and they smiled sweetly.

The meeting broke up, and the men began to stream away to their jobs, their commitments, their various pleasures, leaving Aubry with a few dozen men in the meeting hall.

The central icon at the front of the hall was not the traditional crucifix, a symbol of suffering, death, and guilt as much as redemption and rebirth. In its place stood the stone image of a beautiful Christ, a smooth-muscled God whose wrath would have been awesome to witness.

Aubry walked down the center aisle toward the statue, and gazed up at it. It dwarfed him, and looked down on him with a faint smile curling those alabaster lips. Aubry felt lost.

In the week that he had been in the camp, he had seen nothing that would help him, had grown only more and more disturbed by the emotional tone. Things were happening here. Something important, but he couldn't grasp it. Couldn't grasp *them*. Perhaps the growing unease that he felt was related more to what was happening inside him than what was happening outside.

To understand, one must go to the heart.

But he *couldn't*. Not here. He was . . . troubled.

Aubry looked back up into the clearing rows, and once again he saw the figure that had eluded him earlier. It drifted like a shadow, wearing a cloak that disguised the figure somewhat. It stopped and talked to someone else in the stands.

Aubry felt himself pulled, and gripped the edge of the granite block on which the statue rested.

Why was everything so out of control, unraveling more swiftly all the time? There didn't seem to be any answers in the realms where he ordinarily looked for answers. It was terrifying, and he had to go forward, couldn't go back.

Bloodeagle had given him his space in the room, and the space between them yawned like the Grand Canyon. Too wide. Impossibly wide.

He wanted . . .

He wanted to *touch* someone.

He bowed his head. What was happening to him?

He heard footsteps behind him, and the sound of robes swirling in the faint wind, and he held his breath. It wasn't fair. It wasn't.

Promise, damn it, where are you when . . .

He turned, hands still gripping the block behind him, and stood very still.

The hair was cut very short, the eyes golden, the lips full and now drawn tight, curled down at the corner with a question.

Feminine. Too damned feminine. *And he felt his body cry out, and he was ashamed.*

Then the figure spoke. "Your name is Aubry Knight."

Aubry swallowed, hard. The voice. It could have been a woman's voice—low, powerful, intelligent. The lips could have been a woman's lips, full, and moist now. Aubry felt his body respond. His shame deepened.

He nodded his head without speaking.

"My name is Marina. I think that you want to talk to me."

The noise in the bar was intense, but if they hunched together and spoke in normal tones, they could hear quite well.

"I recognized you. You're lucky nobody's turned you in." She smiled like a circling shark.

Aubry peered down into his glass. "I didn't think that those broadcasts were being seen outside of California."

"They aren't—but I've researched everything that influences or has influenced DeLacourte in the past few years, and your picture came up. And then your name in camp. Among the Gorgons."

"Gorgons? You've talked with them?"

"A little."

"How the hell—I haven't been able to get in to see Ibumi or anyone. How did you—"

"You mean, as a woman?"

"That's exactly what I mean."

"I usually get what I want."

Aubry took another drink, watching the male dancers in the front of the room. Suddenly the gyrations and contortions seemed almost humorous, and nothing like the threat they had seemed just hours before. He watched Marina over the rim of his glass, and the slow fire of his anger seeped into his veins like lava.

"I have other connections with them. The full name is Batiste. Marina Batiste. I was a newswoman working with TriNet."

"Past tense?" The curves under her jacket were still boyish, but it was easier now to see the woman beneath the thin disguise. "You don't really think that you can pass as a man, do you?"

"I'm not trying to. There are women in the camp. I got in through my connections with Gorgon, but I can move more freely if I'm not stared at quite so much."

"Just what do you want from me?"

"Something very odd happened a month ago. I was sent on a news story, to cover Gorgon's activities. I actually got footage of them making the rescue in Nigeria. You must have heard of it. DeLacourte won't run it."

"Why? It make Gorgon look too good?"

"Exactly. Now, everyone knows the antipathy that DeLacourte has for Gorgon. What you may not know is that Gorgon hates DeLacourte just as much. DeLacourte probably leaked the Swarna assassination to the press."

"So there really *was* a hit scheduled?"

"You bet your ass." She dropped her voice until it was barely audible above the music. "Harris OK'd it right after entering office. Full approval. If it hadn't been for the leak, Gorgon would have blown Swarna's head off: the plan was good. Officially nothing ever happened, but Harris knows, and Swarna knows. He lost his brother Kibu. Blown to bits. Not enough left to bury. Swarna's been quoted as saying he'll kill Harris *and* Gorgon.''

She took a pull of her beer. ''Anyway . . . I'm going to be making a documentary on Gorgon, to be released to the general public. We have this group of heroes in the midst of one of the most hated and misunderstood minorities in the country. I think that that is a story worth telling. Don't you?''

''Yes. Now—why are you talking to *me* about it?''

''I want to know what your connection is. You helped them in Los Angeles. There wasn't a lot about it above-ground in the media, but the name Aubry Knight has turned up in closed sessions.''

''Why would you remember it?''

''Well, not that many men go up for Nullboxing. Then, not many Nullboxers get framed for murder.''

Aubry felt himself tense. ''Framed . . .''

''Shit. Didn't you know that there's a rumor that Luis Ortega had a tape of the entire frame-up? Showed it to his guests at night. You were had, my friend.''

Aubry sat bolt upright in his chair, and suddenly he wasn't in the bar anymore. He was in Luis Ortega's study, and Promise was there, and Luis was stark naked, vulnerable, frightened. And Promise triggered a tape, a tape of the night on the beach when Maxine betrayed him, and his entire life crumbled like a shattered stained-glass window.

The tape! How could he have forgotten it all of this time? Could it clear him? Lord—could it? If it did . . . if it was possible . . . then . . .

And Maxine. There was a time when the only thing that had kept him alive and sane was the hope that one day, somehow, he could kill that lying, manipulative bitch. Feel her neck between his hands, and squeeze, and twist . . .

He jerked his mind from that track. ''The tape. Where is it now? Do you know?''

''After Tomaso Ortega disappeared, the West Coast

Family was a shambles. Records were burned, destroyed, before tax and drug enforcement agents could seize them. There went the tape.''

Aubry lowered his eyes again. Damn it. Damn him for daring to hope, even for a moment . . .

She reached across the table, tapping his knuckle with one fingernail. ''You are a part of it somehow. You help me, and maybe I can help you.''

''And if I don't?''

''There's a line from an old movie. Something about a coward hiding in the middle of a battlefield.'' He didn't answer, and she changed her tone. ''I'm sorry. That was uncalled for. Somehow I just don't get the feeling that you're hiding. I think you're looking for something. Let's join forces.'' She smiled with heartrending sincerity.

His voice lowered. ''I don't know. I really don't.'' He sat there in the bar for a few minutes, listening to his own heartbeat, and then turned back to Marina. For an instant, her face was paler, fringed with brown hair, and he was confused: Why did Maxine's voice sound different? Why was her face . . . ?

He shook his head, and the vision cleared. ''We need to talk. But not here. Do you have a place?''

Her grin said *checkmate*. ''Come on. We do need to talk.''

He followed her through the twisting alleys of the Nation, and eventually they reached an apartment building. Odd, synthesized music blared from one of the windows, and the silhouettes of two men dancing were painted on the shade like a writhing cardboard cut-out.

Again, he felt the panic, and the retreat from reality. Marina, moving in front of him on the stairs, was more and more of an anchor, something that he could cling to in the midst of the unreality that swirled around and around in his head.

She unlocked the door to her room. Within, it was surprisingly quiet, and very clean. There were two chairs, and a table, and a single bed by the window.

He turned, the blood thundering in his ears.

Marina sat, slender legs crossed neatly, lighting another cigarette.

The room seemed to be spinning. "Why are we here?" he asked thickly.

She cocked her head sideways, lips curved in an inquisitive smile. "We can help each other."

It was Maxine's face staring at him, lips curved sweetly, saying, *Your life is headed for big changes, lover.*

"You keep saying that. I'm a story to you. What the hell do you think you can do for me?"

If he stayed where he was much longer, he was going to lose control. Aubry spun and went for the door. "This isn't going to work."

She crossed the room and grabbed his hand. "Wait a minute . . ."

He looked down at Marina's hand, and then into Maxine's face, and for a moment the tableau was frozen. Then he spun her around and crushed her to him.

"No—"

"What kind of story are you looking for?"

"Let me go—"

He pressed her back into the bed, their faces only inches apart. "You like danger, don't you? You like to get close to the fire? Try this."

His fingers were at her dress, forcing their way under her buttons, ripping away the threads.

"Don't—" Their eyes locked, and he didn't see her, saw only himself. Ruined and dead, nose and lips and cheeks shorn away to reveal his true face. The face of Aubry Knight, the child of war, a cold and voracious infant he embraced with all his heart.

CHAPTER TWENTY-SIX

Medusa's Children

Tuesday, June 27

Aubry woke up slowly, unsure of who or where or when he was. He could feel the pressure of his body against the sheets, could hear his breathing, smell his dried sweat.

Beyond that, it was a blur, one that resolved slowly, coming into focus . . .

He jerked upright, stifling a scream as the memories became vivid.

Next to him, the sheets were crumpled, and there was a hollow where a body might have lain for hours in exhaustion or slumber.

He heard a *click*, and finally focused on the far side of the room. Marina sat there, a cigarette in one hand, a .25 caliber automatic pistol in the other. An ugly bruise purpled the left side of her face.

He looked down the bore for long heartbeats, then dropped his eyes. "You don't need that," he said dully.

"I sat here," she said. Her voice was shaking. She stopped, took a drag on her cigarette—by the sweet scent of it, he knew it was clove. "And I waited for you to wake up. And waited." She wiped a shaky hand across her eyes. "Damn you. I was going to wait until I could tell you what I think of you, and then blow your fucking heart out."

He thought of the things he could say, or do. For a brief

moment his mind flared with ideas: How to distract her? How best to move . . . ?

Then his survival computer shut down, dampened like a wet candle. "Go ahead," he said. "Do us both a favor."

She exhaled a long, nervous stream of smoke. "I might. I was going to."

"Christ, lady, what's stopping you? You want me to say I'm sorry? I am. Shit, I'm so goddamned sorry."

She paused, looking at him over the bore of the gun. "I watched you, while I was waiting. You kept talking about death."

He turned his face away, unable to look at her. "Death Valley. Prison."

"Something happened to you there?"

"Yes!" He screamed it at her. "Something goddamned well—" His head was spinning again, and suddenly his scream became inarticulate, and he was holding his head, howling as the walls closed in, and the bloody mouths screamed accusations.

He was back in the hole, chemicals seething in his bloodstream, the images of Nullboxing flashing on the screen before him, and it all joined together in a long, long scream for mercy.

When he came back, when the room stopped spinning for him, she stood over him, the pistol still in her hand, still pointed at him, but her finger was no longer tight on the trigger.

"Last night," she said. "You hit me, and you called me Maxine. Who was Maxine?"

He was still curled on his side, perspiration popping out over his body. "Maxine. Maxine Black. Luis . . . used her to set me up."

"Did you . . . love her?"

"Hell, what do I know? She was the kind . . . the kind of woman who could make you believe you did. God *damn* I was such a fool, such a fool." He managed to pull himself together, still heaving for breath, and sat upright. "I got no excuse, Marina. I just don't know anymore."

Marina plopped down in one of the chairs, and watched him. "They say you're this big-time killer. I don't know what you were, when you worked for the Ortegas, but last night you cried in your sleep.'' She looked down at the gun, and the barrel dropped. ''You used me. The woman you wanted to hurt wasn't here, and you used me instead. I can kill you, or maybe turn you in . . . but I don't know what I'd get from that. Rough justice, maybe.''

''What, then?''

She paused. ''Something's going on, Knight. DeLacourte's people have been heating up the action against the NewMen. Ephesus was attacked a month ago. DeLacourte suppressed tape of Gorgon effecting a miracle rescue. And then there's the Oath.''

''Oath?''

''It's said that Gorgon has sworn that if DeLacourte runs for office, they'll kill him.''

Aubry frowned, trying to get the gears in his head to turn. ''Do you believe that?''

Marina shrugged. ''There's a rumor that DeLacourte will throw his support to President Harris if Harris denounces the NewMen.''

''He wouldn't. Hell, Harris's support has been all that has kept this place going.''

''A rumor like that would raise a lot of hackles, though, wouldn't it.'' When he didn't reply, she went on. ''You were in Los Angeles. DeLacourte's people ran you out. You were in Ephesus during the fire. And now you're here. You're either a generator or a lightning rod, Knight. Whatever his story is, you're connected to too many pieces of it. I'm going to use you like you used me. You're looking for something. I can get information, so you need me. And if they manage to kill you, I'll be right there to get the story.'' She smiled coldly. ''You're in good hands.''

''Right.''

She nodded, and ground her cigarette out, compulsively lighting another.

''All right, lady. I owe you. I can't wiggle out of that. You say you can help me. All right—what do you know about the NewMen?''

She looked at him for a moment, then put her pistol away and drew her knees up to her chest, looking for all the world like a little girl. Her breasts were small beneath the robe, and supported by good muscle in the upper chest.

"The NewMen are trying to build a society totally separated from women. When they started, twenty years ago, it was an offshoot of the Cyber-Macho thing that grew out of the changes in professional football. Hell— artificial knees, spine braces, programmed reflexes, blood doping, steroids, hypothalamus implants—remember the acromegaly scandals? It all just got out of hand.

"People can get used to anything. Hell—the bodybuilder look was bizarre in the sixties, and almost the norm by the nineties. There was a group of men who felt that NewMen were the future. They loved it."

Aubry rose from the bed, went to stand by the window, away from the smoke. "It just gets weirder, doesn't it."

She nodded. "When the federal government began selling off Indian land back around 2010, the Navajos retaliated by leasing a parcel of their remaining land to the homosexual separatists known as NewMen. They took over the county, influenced state politics. With Arizona as a rallying point, the gay voting bloc was heard in national politics for the first time."

"I remember the first gay military divisions. Jesus, what a fuss."

"But performed superbly in Africa. Gorgon came out of that. Sort of an attempt to say that 'real men don't need women.' Judging by their battlefield records, they're right."

"And what are they up to now? Are they really making moves toward creation of this 'perfect man' thing?"

"Yes. I think that a lot of the action in Africa has been two-edged—they're hoping to get a tract of land out of it."

"If they can break Swarna?"

"If they can break Swarna."

"And what about that?"

"Aubry—you aren't thinking. They want the colony to be self-sustaining."

Aubry thought for a few minutes. "You mean kids?"

She nodded.

"I guess they can buy eggs, and freeze 'em. . . ."

She shook her head. "Haven't you guessed? Cyloxibin made it practical. Hermaphrodism. Fertile hermaphrodites of predominately male characteristics. Deadly warriors who can be hormonally stimulated to become child-bearing females. Project Medusa."

Aubry slammed his hand down on the sill. "It's real. I met one."

"You've seen a Medusa?"

He nodded. "It almost peeled me. It was in Oregon during the attack on Ephesus."

"*What?* Aubry—it *can't* be."

"Why not?"

"Because the whole project was just a dream five years ago. Their oldest Medusa has to be about four years old, Aubry. Were you attacked by a killer baby?"

"Shit." Aubry slammed his hand into the wall again, chipping plaster. "Are you sure? Damn. I thought . . ." The tension drained from him, and he wagged his head regretfully. "I guess I was just wrong. Oh, what the hell. I don't have an answer, but I think I know someone who will."

Miles sat quietly as Aubry and Marina spoke. His dark face was thoughtful, and he sighed when they were finished. "Yes, it might be like that. I don't know exactly what Gorgon's up to. I've been away too long."

"What if they'd been older, Aubry? What if you broke into the Bioworks security and saw the hermaphrodites? What difference would it make? What are you going to do? You never saw this one attacker's face. You couldn't identify him. If you could, what would you do, challenge him? Kill him?"

Aubry sat, head in his hands. "But someone attacked Ephesus. Killed people . . ."

"Why would we attack Ephesus?" Bloodeagle said, puzzled. "We have nothing against them."

Marina sat, scratching one fingernail at the tabletop. "Somebody is hiding behind all of this," she said. "Where is Gorgon getting the biotechnology to pull this off?

Ephesus? Then somebody is acting as intermediary—long-range transport. Who?''

"McMartin," Aubry said positively. "He's behind Killinger in Los Angeles. He's got the equipment. That bastard Killinger controls the manpower."

"Then McMartin and DeLacourte are in bed together. Why would they destroy Ephesus?"

Aubry shook his head. "They didn't. They were trying to kill one woman. Ariane Cotonou. Promise said that she developed a lot of the baby-freezing stuff."

"But we still don't know *why*."

Marina's face was blank. "DeLacourte. Harris. Ephesus. Gorgon. Swarna. They all tie together somehow, but how?"

"Somebody's covering their tracks, but what? Maybe that Oath about DeLacourte?"

"It would make sense—but why would this McMartin want to kill his boss?"

"Could be a hundred reasons. All of them good," Bloodeagle said.

"Well, shit," Marina said slowly. "It would make sense. Everybody hates DeLacourte. He's done everything he can to destroy the Nation. But assassination—"

Aubry caught one of her shoulders with a great hand. "It's just a bunch of guesses, lady. Before you fly off the handle, let's think about this, see what fits."

"Aubry—if it's murder, I can't sit still."

"Sure you can," Aubry said coldly. "You've got nothing now. You start talking about it, and you'll either hurt a lot of innocent people, or make them change their plans. They'll hit him later, that's all. Wait until we know something. Can prove something."

"And if they kill DeLacourte in the meantime?"

"Then you'll have the big scoop, lady. Isn't that what you want?"

Her eyes blazed at him. "I'll wait a week. Let's see. Bloodeagle," she said, voice turning businesslike. "Can you get me information on that cryobiology center of Gorgon? Any specs?"

"I can do what I can."

*   *   *

From the terrace of the room he shared with Marina, Aubry looked out at the Bioworks building. It was a quilted, stilted three-story dome, shining pale white in the afternoon sunlight. He had seen pictures of it: Scavenger contractors had installed some of the electrical wiring.

It made his head hurt to think of it. It didn't matter anyway. Whatever marginal involvement he had with the whole question would soon be academic, a thing of the past, an icicle's shadow.

It had taken fear, and rage, and death, and dishonor to tear asunder the bonds that had been melded with Promise. The one thing that he couldn't do was go back.

Marina sat in a corner of the room, dictating into her computer while it quietly spit out pages of thermoplas. She didn't talk to him unless there was a direct need, but there was a curious bond between them. Not hatred, not attraction, not quite mutual need. Maybe a mutual recognition of type.

Marina stopped typing for a minute, and looked at the ceiling. "Damn."

"No luck?"

"I'm just not getting anywhere. I sure think they're planning to kill DeLacourte, but I don't know where or when—*probably* before the Democratic National Convention."

She closed her eyes again, and he could almost hear the thoughts surging.

"How do you do that?" Aubry said, finally.

"Do what?"

"Put the pieces together. I watch you take facts, and stick them together with other facts."

"Sure. It's called thinking." She watched the hurt expression on his face. "You think, Aubry."

"Not like that. Promise. Promise can think like that."

Marina scratched her eyelids. "I just make . . . pictures, and compare them with other pictures, and see what fits. Don't you do that? When you fight, or something?"

He shook his head. "No. Everything's too fast for pictures. I get a feeling, and then I do something. That's all."

She looked at him curiously. "You're a kinesthetic. You live in your feelings. And you've shut so damned many of them away."

He felt awkward, almost embarrassed to ask the next question. "Is there any way . . . could I learn to do that? To think like that?"

There was a long pause, and she didn't answer. His ears burned. "I guess that was a stupid question."

"Not everybody thinks in words, Aubry. Or pictures. You must be a genius at what you do." A light went on in the back of her eyes, and then dimmed again as she sat, humming. "Let's say you were in a river. And there were currents coming from different directions . . ." She sighed. "No, that doesn't work. Shit."

She stood and began to pace the floor. "DeLacourte wants to be president. Harris wants to be president. McMartin wants DeLacourte to be president. Gorgon wants Harris to be president. But there was some kind of cooperation between Gorgon and McMartin at Ephesus. They should be blood enemies. . . ."

Aubry closed his eyes. "You know, when you're punching and kicking, you can look at the target. But when you're fighting say three people, you look at what *isn't* there. At the space between people."

"Negative space."

"Whatever. You've got all of these people, whose motivations should be obvious, and two groups of them did something that doesn't make sense. There's someone that isn't there. I can feel it." He smiled, for the first time in days. "I can't see him, but I can feel him."

"Swarna? He hates *everybody*."

"But everybody hates him, too. Nobody's going to take orders from him. Somebody else. Somebody close to the action."

"All right. Where do we go?"

"Back to Los Angeles," Aubry said. "I say I find this McMartin and screw it out of him."

She stopped, looked at Aubry quizzically. "You'll do it out of your obligation to me?"

"No. I'll let you tag along out of obligation. He killed good people, and almost crippled me. . . ."

And there are these dreams. Of pinkish slippery things crawling in glass. And they won't go away. Somebody has to pay for that.

She nodded. "All right. Let's go."

There was a knock at the door, and Aubry crossed the room to answer it.

"This'll be Bloodeagle. Hope he's got a route back to L.A. for me—"

Promise stood there, accompanied by Leo Baker. Baker peered around the room as if he expected to find someone hiding in the corner.

Behind them, Bloodeagle shook his head. "Sorry for the surprise, Aubry."

For a few seconds, Aubry chewed air, and then he managed to find a smile. "Well. It's that, all right." He stood there for another few seconds, just watching Promise, his mind refusing to function.

Her smile was tight. "Aubry—aren't you going to invite us in?"

"Yeah. Sure."

He stood back away from the door, and opened it wider. Marina smoothed her hair and came to stand next to Aubry. Promise stood an inch taller than Marina, but the reporter outweighed her by perhaps ten pounds.

Marina tried to smile. "So—you're Promise. I've heard about you."

"I wish I could say the same," Promise said. Her voice was husky with some suppressed emotion. Face neutral, she extended her hand and gave Marina's a brief, firm shake.

Promise folded her arms across her chest. "Aubry. I have to talk to you."

"Sit down?"

"Good to see you, Aubry," Leo said, pleasantly enough. He peered into Aubry's face, the flicker of a question in his eyes.

"Is there anyone else out there?"

"Jenna is in a small camp near the north lip of the

canyon. If anything comes of this, she'll be ready to move."

Aubry shook his head. "If anything comes of what? What is this about? Why are you here?"

"Aubry . . ." Promise folded her hands. "The NewMen think that we're here to negotiate a construction project. It's as simple as that. We underbid everyone else. They know our work is good, and so we were invited in to take a look and discuss things with Winters and Ibumi."

"Is he back?"

"In the morning. I . . . that's why we have to move quickly." She paused, and a silent communication flashed between her and Leo. "Aubry . . . I found the doctor who treated me on Ortega island."

Aubry's eyes narrowed. "Yes . . ."

"Aubry," she whispered. "He confessed. He stole our child."

"W–why? In the name of God, why?"

"Because our child was the first Cyloxibin baby. An hermaphrodite. They needed her for some kind of project here."

Bloodeagle paled. "Medusa."

Aubry stood, stalked to the window.

Marina came and sat across from Promise. Her eyes were alight. "Are you sure about this?"

"It was virtually a deathbed confession. The man had no reason to lie. Wu verified the possibility. Aubry—our child is *here*. No matter what you think of me, or what you intend concerning us"—and here she pointedly avoided Marina's eyes—"you can't turn your back on your child."

Aubry's head spun. Christ! *His child.* Was it possible? He didn't want to believe it, and yet . . .

"All right. What do we do?"

Miles was tense and nervous. "Whatever we do, we've got to move before Ibumi and the Gorgons show up— about six hours. We can't try anything with them in the camp. It would be too dangerous."

"Then we have to move now. Where are the children likely to be stored? Is there a nursery?"

"In Bioworks, Aubry."

"Where is it?" Leo crossed to the window.

"It's that one," Aubry pointed. "Sort of a dome on spider legs."

"All right. Leo. One of your teams was in there?"

"I wasn't with them."

"All right, but you oversee the work. Can we crack it? If we cracked it, would it do any good? Could we find what we're looking for?"

"We don't have much time to get in. No time for anything clever. I don't have the floor plans or drainage plans, so I can't promise anything if we try to get in from the bottom. I'd think it was pretty secure."

"But the whole camp is secure. What kind of risks are they worried about?"

"Sabotage. DeLacourte has been coming down pretty hard."

"We don't have time for anything clever. Shit!"

Aubry turned to Bloodeagle. "How well is it guarded?"

"You can't get in frontally," Miles said. His lean face was troubled. "Aubry—I don't give a damn about DeLacourte. I hope he burns. But your child—I owe you that."

"What are you saying?"

"I'm saying that I can get you in. It will finish me here, but I already owe you my life. If you swear to destroy nothing, and take only your own child, I'll help you. Is that fair?"

Promise took Aubry's hand, gripped it with fierce pressure. "Aubry—please. I have to know."

In Aubry's mind there were no pictures, there were feelings with labels. And the labels read Harris, and DeLacourte, and McMartin, and Gorgon, and Swarna. And the feeling swirled like the infinitely complex motions of combat. Once the question was posed, the combat computer seized the problem like a terrier snapping up a rat, and was worrying it, and worrying it. . . .

He *had* to know too.

"Bloodeagle, Miles. Identification San Diego Commune 556XY."

The guard at the door was relaxed. "Miles. Yeah. Heard about your rumble in L.A."

"Got pretty hairy. Listen. I need to check records. I've got an interview with Winters in the morning, and if I don't have my facts straight, I won't be able to get a breeding permit."

"Well . . ." The guard paused, thinking. "Not really supposed to without a specific pass, but I guess that would be all right."

The lucite door hissed open, and Bloodeagle strode in. "Thanks."

He headed for the elevator. Where was security? The cameras and sensors that watched the door were linked in somewhere. To main camp security, and to the security complex within Bioworks. He took the elevator up one floor, and stepped out, scanning the empty halls. Where was the directory? There, and the security section was listed in the basement. Back into the elevator again, and this time it slid him down to the basement.

The door hissed open. One man was at the center. He was pleasantly ugly but hard-muscled. "You're Bloodeagle, aren't you?"

Miles smiled, allowing his chest to swell slightly, meeting the man's eyes boldly, a slight smile curling his lips. "Haven't we met? I'm surprised. This camp is usually a small place."

"Yeah. What brings you here?" The man was relaxed. Miles's reputation was serving in good stead.

Miles came a little closer, bent over the man's shoulder as if peering at the bank of screens. The physical proximity was powerful, and they were both grinning, acknowledging the tug.

"One of the primaries in my commune is applying for Breeder. I have to discuss the results of the tests."

There was the proper screen, and Aubry was walking up to it now.

The man at the console opened his eyes at the sight of Aubry. "Well, hello . . . he's a *big* one, isn't he?" He grinned crookedly at Miles. "I've seen him around camp, but didn't know that he was yours. Well, he'll have to wait outside."

"I know." Miles smiled, and dug his thumbs into the man's carotid artery.

Aubry heard the door before he saw it. It hissed, and then trembled, and swung open. The guard at the front shook his head in shock, and then looked at Aubry, who stood by passively.

Aubry blew him a kiss. Confused more than ever now, the guard fought to get through to control for confirmation. The instant that his eyes were off the door, Aubry moved. His feet slammed into the plastic. With the security bolts disengaged, the door shivered and popped out of its lock.

The guard scrambled for his sidearm. Aubry got to him first. The man got off one shot, and Aubry swirled, diving to the side, catching his weight on bent arms, and handspringing back up, jackknifed, and brought both feet smashing into the man's chest. He fell backward and hit the ground. Aubry was on him in an instant. One swift palm-heel strike sent the guard into unconsciousness.

Aubry held the door while Promise, Marina, and Leo entered.

Miles came back up in the elevator. Hurriedly, he switched clothing with the downed man.

"This guy's a little smaller than you."

"So I'll pop a button. Won't be the first time. Get going. I don't know how long this can hold up."

Aubry clasped his friend's shoulder. "Miles—"

"You saved our lives. All of us. It's not too much, Aubry."

Aubry nodded, and hurried to the elevators. The four of them entered, and the doors shifted shut. "How long will he be able to hold those doors?"

"It's two in the morning. We're not likely to be interrupted until Ibumi returns. We should be all right."

The elevator stopped at the bottom, and the doors shifted open.

Aubry expected to see the kind of fetal storage facilities that were in Ephesus, and was confused. What there were, all around them, were rooms, booths, where seventeen young children reclined in sleep.

Each was on his separate couch, and each was hooked to a terminal. All appeared to be about thirteen years old.

Aubry walked among them, and felt his skin crawl. One of these children, or someone very much like them, had very nearly killed him outright, in fair combat.

How? Which one? It was impossible to say.

Leo was already at one of the computer consoles.

Promise wandered in the room. "Where are the infants?" she whispered. "I want my child."

"I'll find them," Leo said. Marina wandered through the room, taking photos. She seemed thoughtful.

"What date was the theft?" Leo asked.

"June, 2025."

"All right . . ." Leo typed for a minute. He paused, as lights crawled across the screen. Then he looked up, his face painted with shock. "You're not going to believe this—"

Marina cut in. "The child is in this room."

"What? How could that be? It just can't."

"It can, and it is." He hunched over the display board, shaking his head. "Look at this. Speculation on bone growth and problems with calcium and phosphorus transport. Eighteen-hour-a-day IV feeds." He scrolled the screen, whistling. "They had subcutaneously mounted monitors on the kids, and still lost fifty percent. Look at this projected growth chart—"

The graph climbed as steeply as a skyscraper. "A generation every five years? Domination of a plot of land the size of Zimbabwe in a single century? Don't you see?"

Marina sagged against the console. "Shit. It was right in front of me, Aubry. The NewMen want their own country. That's the dream. A chance to start over. It's what everybody is talking about, but they're going for it. A race of superhuman, hermaphroditic children who reach sexual maturity in four years? *You* think of the implications."

Leo tapped her arm. "I've got the number—"

"I don't need it," Aubry said.

Six of the children were dark-skinned, and Promise

gravitated immediately toward one of them. His face was slender, feminine, with delicate bones. Asleep, he was beautiful, and the sensors lightly attached to the sides of his head were grotesque additions. The label at the side of his bed read "Medusa-16."

"Here," Aubry whispered, and pulled the leads free.

Medusa-16's hazel-brown eyes flew open, and he *hissed*.

The child shot upright, his hands jabbing instantly at Promise's eyes as it awakened. Aubry moved faster, jerking her out of the way, interposing his own body.

Medusa-16 was still half asleep, and Aubry's hand tapped him along the edge of the jaw with concussive force. He fell back, unconscious.

"Tie his hands and feet."

"You didn't have to hit her so *hard*." Promise's eyes were scathing.

"Him. You weren't there. You don't know."

Miles got between them. "No time now for talk. We have to get going."

CHAPTER TWENTY-SEVEN

Challenge

Promise knelt next to Medusa-16 in the hovercraft, crying silently.

Was this pale, thin child her offspring? Gently, she unfastened 16's pants and underwear, and new tears came to her eyes as she inspected the dual sexual organs.

What had they done? What had *she* done? Medusa-16—

"No, I can't call her that," she said softly.

Aubry squeezed back between the rows of equipment. There was very little room for him: the craft was overburdened. The Scavenger engineer and Marina and Bloodeagle were unexpected passengers.

Below them, the night-dark Colorado River flashed by, a twisting black ribbon in the early morning.

"So," Aubry said finally. "What do we have here?"

Medusa-16's eyes flew open and he sat upright, pulling at the straps until they strained tight. The angelic child-face became that of a demon, spitting, hissing, biting at them. One strap popped, whipping up to lash Promise across the face.

Aubry held the child's shoulder down, and Promise refastened the straps.

The child turned and bit, savagely. Aubry roared. "*Will* you strap this kid down? Christ, but he's strong."

"See? I *told* you she's ours."

Aubry glared at her. He examined the bite ruefully, and bent to a first-aid kit to take care of it.

Medusa-16 looked at them. "What—do—you—want—with—me?"

"I'm your mother," Promise said quietly.

His face quieted, grew crafty. "You're lying."

"It's the truth," she repeated patiently.

Medusa-16 turned and looked at the man bandaging his arm. "If you are my parents, I hate you. You deserted me. Tried to kill me."

"I don't know who told you that, but it isn't true. You were stolen from my body three years ago, by a man named Allred. This is your father."

16's mouth narrowed. "Your skin is dark, like mine." He peered at Promise. "And you carry Eurasian blood, which would explain my trace of epicanthic fold. There is a remote chance that you speak the truth. It doesn't matter. Ibumi is the only parent I acknowledge. He will kill you with his hands. You are nothing." Medusa-16's eyes grew unfocused for a moment. "I know you. I almost killed you in Oregon." There was a new expression on the child's face, that of grudging respect. "You . . . are different from the others."

"My name's Aubry. Yours?"

"Medusa-16. After I finish . . ." The child stopped, as if halting in mid-thought. "I will win my name when I have proven myself."

Promise took one of Medusa-16's hands in her own. The pale, thin fingers locked on hers. "And now," the child hissed, "you will cut me free, or I will crush your hand into paste. Like this."

The small hands closed on hers. Agony flamed up her arm. *Her child was crushing her fingers! Oh, God—*

She closed her mind to the growing pain. "I . . . can't call . . . you Medusa-16. That's not the kind of name a mother . . ." She felt something give in her hand, and tasted blood in her mouth. ". . . calls her child."

Aubry started forward, and she shook her head in negation.

"I think I'll call you . . . Leslie." Her eyes locked with the child's in a deadly serious battle of wills.

The pressure stabilized. Then slackened.

The child looked at them, his hazel-brown eyes examining them. He looked at Aubry. "What do you want with me?"

With returning circulation, pain flooded into Promise's hand. "I *love* you. You're my child. What other reason do I need?"

Leslie pressed back into the cot. "Love? A word one person uses to enslave another."

Promise slowly pulled her hand up to her face and nursed it. It throbbed horribly.

"You are . . . brave," Leslie said. The hermaphrodite's voice grew questioning. "You want me to believe you would have born me into the world through your body?"

"Of course," she whispered.

"There is pain. There is risk."

"Nothing today, compared to what women have suffered throughout history."

"I . . . might be asked to bear children." Leslie looked down at his body, childish voice husky with excitement. "I have never talked with a woman about these things. I am sorry that you must die. There are things I could learn."

"I—"

"Aubry—" Jenna's voice was urgent. "We've got a bandit on the screen."

Aubry went forward to the cockpit. Through the windows to either side, Promise saw the walls of the canyon flashing by, and heard the hail. "Warning—this is the communications officer for Gorgon. We are tracking. You cannot escape. We warn you . . ."

"Do you see?" Leslie asked, eyes questioning. "I don't understand. You may be the source of my genetic material. I don't understand, but it may be. Perhaps I was stolen from you. Little else explains the current circumstances. More likely you are deluded. But you have to know that you couldn't get away. Why did you try?"

"I love you," Promise said. "I don't know what they're doing to you. My God. You're only three years old. I came expecting to find someone who could barely count to ten. And here you are—you have to be feeling things inside your body. Changes."

"Yes," Leslie admitted reluctantly.

"The changes get stronger. I don't have time. Oh, God,

there's no time at all. But I have to try. If I'm killed, Leslie. If I die—I don't know what these people want of you, but it can't be good. Not if they give you a number until you earn a name. I love you because I can't help it.''

"If you have no choice, how can that be real?"

"You sound just like your father. Feelings are real, Leslie. There's nothing realer than that. It's a lie to think that your intellect makes your decisions. Whatever you're doing, whatever you're going to do, you're doing it because you want the approval of the monsters who have programmed you.''

Leslie grinned at her nastily. "Not long now, it said.''

"Not long."

The skimmer jolted horribly. "Damper field!" Jenna screamed. "They have some sort of damper field.''

Marina groaned. "Of course they do! Hell, they used it in Nigeria last month. As soon as they get a clear shot they're going to bring us down.''

"Then I'm going down now.''

Jenna jolted the skimmer up over the lip of the canyon, streaking it toward a great tumbled tower of stone.

Aubry grabbed Jenna. "You've got to get out as soon as we touch down. Bloodeagle, Promise, Leo, and 16 they know about—they won't stop looking. But if you can get Marina to safety, she might be able to help.''

"I'm not leaving.''

"Dammit, Jenna, this isn't about pride. Someone's got to get to safety, and put this whole thing together.''

Jenna cursed vilely. She looked back at Promise.

Leslie looked at her with interest. "Jenna. Brood mother Ariane? Lot 17. Highly rated for personal arms. Highly rated personal combat. Formidable. Security chief, Ephesus.''

Promise's eyes were beseeching. "Get out, Jenna. Aubry's right.''

She brought the skimmer down to the ground, and bumped it once. Leo took the controls. "Marina. Come with me.''

The skimmer touched down for a moment, and the door swung open. Marina looked back at Aubry, face taut.

"Looks like you don't get to watch me die.''

"Maybe later." She looked as if she were on the verge of saying something more, and then changed her mind. She turned to Promise. "Good luck. Both of you."

And she was gone. Leo touched them off again, and the skimmer danced away as the black disk of a Gorgon ship loomed up behind them.

Aubry watched them on the screen. They were too damned fast, and too damned powerful.

"Up there." Bloodeagle pointed. "There's a ranger station ahead. If we can make it there—"

"Quint won't back off. He'll kill them all if he has to."

"Then—"

The lights in the skimmer went off. The jets died, the electronic servos and governors failed. The skimmer plunged toward the ground.

Promise threw her body over Leslie, her only thought, *Goddess, Goddess—I've killed my child—*

Three seconds before the skimmer would have hit, the power resumed, and Leo took enough control, wrenching at the controls, to guide them in to a landing.

"Out, out, everybody *out!*" Aubry screamed. He snatched up one of the rifles.

Bloodeagle grabbed his arm. "Forget it, Aubry. They've got enough firepower to turn this ship to slag. You're dead if you try to shoot."

"What then?"

"They might take a challenge. Ibumi is crazy for hand-to-hand combat."

For a moment Aubry's body was unnaturally tense. Then he relaxed, and even grinned. "All right then. I'll give him a show he won't believe."

The skimmer crashed in landing, and Promise fell away from Leslie. The child grinned up at her. "You are crying. You are weak, after all."

Promise bit her lip, and tried not to cry out loud. *Nothing. All for nothing . . .*

Aubry grabbed her from behind. "Come on. We need to get Leslie outside, where they can see him."

"Her," she said, sniffing back a tear.

"Oh, cut it out." Aubry turned to the child strapped to the table. "Boy, I hope you're mine. If you aren't, I'm sure in a lot of trouble for nothing."

"I hope you die well," Leslie said.

"Great."

Two of the Gorgon vehicles were saucer/skimmers, and the heat of their backwash blistered the ground. The others were helicopters, black against the morning sky, and hovering like bumblebees.

Bloodeagle, Promise, Aubry, and Leo stood in the clear, under the rise of rocks, as if in a natural amphitheater. Their weapons were stacked neatly on the ground. Next to them, strapped to the cot, was Leslie.

The lead saucer touched down with barely a whisper of sound.

The door slid open. Two men stood framed in the opening. They were of equal size, and both were gigantic. Aubry knew immediately that they were his height, if not a little taller. They walked down a gangplank as if joined at the hip, each carrying what looked like a combination automatic rifle and grenade launcher. One dropped to a knee, and swept the area, peering through a night scope.

A red dot slid across the ground, and one settled on each of the four adults, anchoring directly on the forehead.

Promise stood perfectly still. Sweat drooled down her face.

Leo's hands quivered, and Aubry's eyes flickered over to him. "Cool down."

"They're going to kill us?"

"Then they will. There's a chance if we don't panic."

"There's no chance . . . there's—"

Leo lost his nerve, bleated and bolted for the ship. He made it as far as the gangplank. One of the two leather-suited figures laughed, and raised his rifle.

What seemed like pulses of liquid light flamed from the barrel of the rifle, and the Ephesus skimmer was aflame instantly. Leo's scream was horrific. He staggered back out of the ship as it exploded behind him. Flaming plastic coated his body.

He was a charred mass of tissue before he hit the ground.

Leslie watched unemotionally. "A bad death," he said.

Promise choked back her anger and grief. The wrong move, the wrong twitch now would kill them all.

The two men came the rest of the way down the gang-plank, followed by five others, all of them wearing the identical leather garb and the black masks. They came up to stand only a few meters away from Aubry.

The one to the left hitched his faceplate up. Ibumi. His face looked as if it had taken the perfect meld of features from mixed parentage. One could see whatever one wanted in that face. Caucasian and Negro and Oriental, and odd bits of Indian and maybe Eskimo. There was infinite strength and intelligence. He looked like the ultimate distillation of humanity, and he was huge.

"You have not harmed the child. Good."

"Why would we want to?"

The man on the right lifted his faceplate. Aubry recognized him—Quint, with the face of a Jesus atop the body of a god. There was something utterly chilling about his eyes. They seemed dead, moving as if pulled by a string in the back of the sockets. They were shockingly blue. They examined Aubry as if dissecting an insect. "Your kind never needs reasons." He faced Bloodeagle. "You betrayed your own kind—for these?"

"He saved my entire cadre. I had to help him find his child."

Quint turned his head almost mechanically, nodding. Then his right arm blurred like an arrow released from the bow. It smashed against Bloodeagle's jaw with a sound like a bag of rocks hitting wet planks.

Miles hit the sand and twitched once.

"He tried to repay a debt of honor. He will be tried."

He stood before Aubry again. "You are Aubry Knight. I have heard of you."

A smaller man, the smallest Gorgon in the group, spoke loudly. "He killed Diego."

For the first time, something sparkled in the back of those dead eyes. "You killed Diego Mirabal in a fair fight? Impressive. I have seen Nullboxers. They can be—interesting. Limited, but interesting. You can die, or you can fight for your life.''

''And the woman, and Bloodeagle, and the child.''

''You, and the woman. Bloodeagle and the child are ours.''

Aubry looked over at Promise, who shook her head desperately. He swallowed hard.

''All right, Quint. Let's get it on.''

The eyes went dead again. ''I have no interest in killing you. I just want to watch. You will fight one of our combat men. Sawa!''

One of the helicopters landed, and the door opened. A stocky man in leathers jumped down, and Promise felt Aubry tense.

Leslie grinned. ''Sawa is not Quint, or Ibumi, but he is good. My 'father' wins his death.''

''You *want* him to die? Why?''

Leslie was silent.

Promise watched Aubry strip away his gear until he stood in dungarees and boots and torn sweatshirt. His muscles gleamed and rolled as he carefully stretched them, preparing for action.

Sawa was muscled like a gymnast, bulky without being tight. Promise felt her stomach sour.

Sawa turned to the man who stepped down from the helicopter with him, and they kissed wetly. He turned, grinning, and pulled a knife from his belt. Grinning, he tossed it to the ground.

Sawa balled his fists, and Promise could see that they were oversized, probably horned with calluses. Knees bent, Sawa inched forward until he was five feet from Aubry.

Suddenly he blurred, and his rear hand speared out in an incredibly quick traditional karate reverse punch.

Aubry leaned out of the way, and Sawa's follow-up punch grazed his head. Sawa's momentum carried him a step past Aubry. He pivoted, his breathing quick. He feinted with the front hand and lunged in again with the punch.

Aubry dropped to the ground with perfect timing and

speared the heel of his foot into Sawa's rib cage. The kick caught the Japanese solidly, and jolted him back into the air. The armor of muscle around the midsection was enough to absorb the shock, and the man grunted as he rolled to his feet.

Next to Promise, Leslie hissed, and slapped his bound hands against his leg.

The Japanese circled Aubry cautiously. The Nullboxer stood quietly watching.

Waiting for what? What was he doing?

Sawa feinted with his right front hand, then a left punch, and then followed through with a lashing right round kick. Aubry went under the kick, caught it, and twisted the knee savagely. Sawa howled in pain, tried to roll out but couldn't get free.

His other foot swept up, heel catching Aubry in the head, narrowly missing the temple. Aubry held onto that leg, rolling Sawa onto his back. He pivoted on his heel so that his back was to the prone man, yanked up and stomped back into the groin.

Sawa's scream was hideous. Leslie squealed with pleasure.

Ibumi smiled. "Most instructive. Again?"

Aubry glared at him.

"Morris."

Sawa's lover stepped forward and picked up the knife that Sawa had dropped. He was white, very pale, with a thin knife wound bisecting his face. He edged in, feinting with the blade.

Aubry backed up, took a step, and stumbled. Morris came in quickly, and Aubry scuttled back, crablike, then swept his feet around, clipping at Morris's ankles.

The man hopped back and Aubry lunged up to his feet like a coiled spring. Aubry feinted with his left—and threw a handful of sand with his right.

Morris blocked his eyes with his hand. As Aubry moved in, Morris's knife blade, spring-propelled, leapt out from the handle. Aubry spun sideways as the knife tore a shallow groove along the side of his neck.

He slapped his hand there, grimacing. Morris caught him in the chest with both feet.

The two men went down in a tangle, Aubry bleeding from the side of his neck. The Gorgon was riding Aubry in the dust, snaking his hands under Aubry's arms until the fingers linked behind the Nullboxer's head. A classic neck-breaking hold. Aubry linked his fingers together at his forehead and scissored his elbows back, pushed back with all of the immense power in his neck. Morris's face reddened as his grip broke.

Blood was drooling down Aubry's face now, smeared into the dirt and dust around him. Too much blood. Promise's heart trip-hammered. . . .

Aubry's head snapped back, missed contact. They were both standing now, and the Gorgon punched Aubry in the kidney. His knees buckled, and the full nelson went on again, Aubry's head bent inexorably toward his chest.

Desperately, Aubry stomped Morris on the instep, twice. He kicked back until he caught the knee, scraped savagely down the shin, and stomped the instep again. Morris roared with pain, and Aubry reached back, grabbed a double handful of hair, and dropped to one knee. Morris sailed over Aubry's shoulder. In midair Aubry torqued arms and shoulders somehow so that Morris's whole body whiplashed an instant before the back of his head hammered into the ground.

Morris's body arched, and his eyes rolled white, blood foaming from a bitten tongue. He spasmed uncontrollably, making thick-throated, inarticulate sounds. Two Gorgons hauled the dreadfully wounded man away.

Aubry stood uncertainly. His neck was bleeding profusely. Leslie watched him with huge eyes.

Quint looked at him and nodded. "You have earned your freedom. Take your woman and go. What a waste."

"I want Bloodeagle, and the child."

"They are ours."

"Then I challenge you for them."

Ibumi and Quint laughed uproariously. Once again the life flared in Quint's eyes, and then died. "You can barely stand. You amuse me. Come back to us after you've healed. The Gorgons need men like you.''

Blood coated Aubry's face, drooled from the side of his neck, but his eyes were blazing. ''God damn you!''

Aubry lunged at Quint, and caught the Gorgon leader. It was possible that nothing human could have evaded that first strike, so swift was it.

Ibumi was on Aubry in an instant. And now, Promise saw Aubry exert himself fully. He was *gone* from Ibumi's grip, and on Ibumi again. But the first moment of shock was over. The leader of Gorgon curled into a ball as Aubry was at him like a cat. Ibumi suddenly uncoiled, his elbow leading the way.

Aubry's head jolted back and Ibumi had him. Aubry went down as the two torqued him into a knot with little effort.

''This becomes more and more interesting,'' Quint said, breathing a little hard but smiling now, those awful, dead eyes totally alive. ''All of you are returning to the camp with me.''

CHAPTER TWENTY-EIGHT

Tribal Council

Wednesday, June 28

Aubry regained consciousness slowly. He could see a vaulted ceiling above him, sunlight canting in from angled windows. From the echoing voices, he knew that the room was large.

There were perhaps a dozen seats in front of him. Half of them were filled with black-suited Gorgons, and the other half, by Winters and his coterie.

No ordinary humans were there, it seemed. All of them were the enormous NewMen. He craned his head, but Bloodeagle was nowhere to be seen. Was he even alive? After that terrific clout to the head . . .

Aubry's hands were tied behind him. His neck wound had been bandaged. Whatever was to follow, it was clear that they didn't want him to bleed to death.

There were two daises in the front of the room. Winters stood at one of them, and Quint at the other. Behind and to the left of Quint stood Ibumi, watching the room like Quint's spare set of eyes.

Until that instant, Aubry hadn't fully appreciated the impact of Ibumi's personality.

The man was too large, taller than Aubry by almost three inches. Impossibly large, and his movements were inhumanly precise. For precious instants, Aubry was frozen in something close to terror.

He watched Quint again. For all of the man's imposing stature, something was wrong. There was a curious vacancy in Quint's eyes. He was like a man only partially alive.

The calm, admonitory voice of Winters snapped him from his trance.

"I'm telling you that this struggle can be resolved peacefully."

"You're dreaming." Quint slurred the words as a dreamer might. "We can stop this madness before it begins. Sterling DeLacourte cannot win the Democratic nomination, but he could split the party. My sources"—and here he glanced at Ibumi, who smiled and beamed at him with love and admiration—"tell me that the deal has been cut. That in exchange for DeLacourte's support, Harris is prepared to denounce us."

Ibumi spoke, and when he did, Quint paused to listen. "DeLacourte is a monster. We kill him now, or he kills us later. It is as simple as that. He has sworn it on public record!"

"The President—"

Quint cut Winters off. "Roland Harris is a good man, as straights go. But he's pure politics. He'd sell his soul for another four years in Washington."

He looked out at them. "You've all seen the plan. The circumstances are good. The arrangements are good, security excellent. I say that we go ahead."

"No!" Winters screamed. "That isn't what we are about. Not now. Not ever. We can't sink to their level."

"Your sack has dried, old man," Quint said, looking at him pityingly. "Where is the man who fought the United States Supreme Court to establish the Nation we love?"

"Right here, dammit. And I won't bow to your cheap theatrics."

"No?" Ibumi said, speaking for the first time. "Then will you remember your oath to uphold the security of our Nation at any cost? Blood, or love, or loss of life? Remember the oath, Winters?"

Winters seemed lost in a memory, trying to dredge back up some forgotten piece of himself. When he spoke again he *did* look old, and lost. ". . . Remember," he whispered.

"Then honor it!"

"I cannot sanction the killing of an American presidential candidate."

"Then step down and let younger men do this job for you."

Winters bowed his head. "I . . . cannot."

Quint screamed at him now, spit flying from his mouth, streaking the golden beard. "Then, by God, fight me! You are a NewMan! We have articles of personal combat. What in the hell—"

Winters shook his head. "Quint, this thing is wrong. It will destroy us—"

"It will save us!"

Ibumi said something in a foreign language, a sharp, nasty word filled with harsh consonant sounds, and Quint reacted instantly.

With a single flicker of movement, Quint drew and threw a knife. It flashed through the air between them and buried itself in Winters's throat before anyone could move.

Winters's hands flew to his throat. His wide, astonished eyes fixed on Quint as he gripped the hilt, and began to pull, blood gushing over his fingers.

Slowly, he slid to the floor.

The room exploded into pandemonium. As if he were a magician performing a card trick, Ibumi produced a machine pistol, and released its safety loudly.

"Silence!" the gigantic Gorgon screamed. "This was no treason. Winters refused to act. He refused to step down. This is war! DeLacourte must die!"

The two dozen Gorgons and NewMen, frozen in shock at the events, began to mutter.

"This is our land," Quint said. "We have been driven far enough, and I am ready to fight and die for what we have built. If there is anyone here who will confront me on the Articles of Combat, raise your voice."

Aubry struggled to his feet. "I'll take you, Quint—or maybe Ibumi. It's obvious who the real power is here. How long did it take you to screw your way up the ladder, Ibumi? Where are you from, anyway? Who are you really working for . . . ?"

"You aren't a NewMan," Ibumi said calmly. "Too bad. I would love the opportunity to pull your spine out."

"I'm as good as a NewMan, and you know it. Physically? I've taken your best. Ethics? If it weren't for me, every NewMan in Los Angeles would be dead. I have no love for DeLacourte. His people chased me, killed my friends, tried to kill me, and God dammit, I want my say!" His eyes narrowed. "I want my freedom, and the same for Promise, and our kid, and Miles Bloodeagle. And I'll do anything I have to do to earn it."

The other Gorgons conferred while Ibumi and Quint watched wordlessly. The small Gorgon spoke, with an accent that Aubry guessed to be something Middle Eastern. "This is our decision, Ibumi. Aubry Knight has earned the right to test—not for NewMan, he cannot. But presidential decree, which you swore to abide by, says that any American citizen may test for Gorgon."

Quint and Ibumi whispered briefly. Then Quint returned to the dais. "All right, that's true—but I choose the test."

Behind him, Ibumi smiled grimly.

"And if he passes, he may challenge you. And if he wins . . ." The small Gorgon shrugged, and Aubry thought he saw the hint of a smile.

"All right," Ibumi said. "Tomorrow. The Hell Run. Monument Valley."

Leslie lay in a state between wakefulness and sleep, drifting high in the stars.

The computer fed him information of the target, on the assignment.

But he asked the computer for information as well.

Where did the sperm and egg that created him originate?

The computer answered CLASSIFIED.

Leslie laughed. His mind reached out. Few of Leslie's skills manifested on the conscious level. There were simply many things that he could do, had been trained to do, bred to do, that were so thoroughly ingrained that they were as automatic as the thousands of tiny physical and mental adjustments an ordinary child makes when riding a bicycle or climbing a tree.

To Leslie, the barriers erected by the computer system were like physical things, the abstract electronic gates converted by tricks of programmed perception into walls lined with screaming jaws, and raging flaming rivers, and flower beds planted with rabid cobras. And one obstacle at a time, he met them, and conquered them, the twitching of his muscles, the hallucinogenic responses to phantasmal threats converted to their electronic analogues.

One after another, the barriers fell, and Leslie found himself in a shadow-world of pure information.

He took a moment to enjoy the satisfaction of a job well done, perhaps the only true pleasure in his short life, and then got down to business.

Interesting. So the man Aubry Knight and the woman who nursed him, Promise Cotonou, actually *were* his mother and father.

Did it make a difference? Of course not. His family was here. And they would be proud of him when he killed Sterling DeLacourte.

But something within Leslie warmed when he thought of his father, magnificent in the long shadows, fighting for a child he had never known.

Or his mother, throwing her body over Leslie as the crash became imminent.

Was this love?

It was something to think about.

After the assignment was over.

After DeLacourte was dead, and everything was right again.

CHAPTER TWENTY-NINE

Hell Run

Thursday, June 29

The sensors were small white circles glued into place at Aubry's forehead and spine. Fine wires transferred their messages in turn to the transmitter at his hip.

It was still dark out, and chilly. The sun was just beginning to rise out behind the buttes. Aubry knew that soon, too soon, its heat would wash across the valley, sparing nothing.

The delegation from Gorgon was there, and a selected group from the NewMen.

"This is the Hell Run," Quint said expressionlessly. He held a rock twice the size of a man's head cradled in his arms. "A ritual practiced by various Native American nations. Their young men would pledge to endure it, to retrieve an object, or to climb a mountain. It is a quest, of a kind. A quest for your personal vision."

"What are the sensors for?"

"They represent a modern refinement. Everyone has a different tolerance. With these monitors, we can check your heartbeat rate, your level of moisture loss. And we can be far more precise than they ever were. We know exactly what we want to test."

"And what is that?"

"You don't need to know. All you need to do is run."

He handed Aubry the stone. He hefted it, adjusted his muscles for the stress. He figured that it weighed about sixty pounds.

The cut in Aubry's neck still burned. His leg ached, and he felt rust in every joint.

But back at the camp were Promise and Leslie and Bloodeagle. And there was something else, something dreadful that had to be stopped.

"How will I know when it's over?" he asked.

"We'll alert you. Don't stop running. Stay with the pacer. Don't fall. Keep going."

He nodded without speaking. Aubry took another sip of water from the bottle at the starting line.

"One more thing," Quint said. Gently, he ran his fingers through Aubry's beard. "Take the rest of the water from the bottle—and hold it in your mouth. You have to spit it out at the end."

"Would you like me to carry you on my back?"

"You really are quite lovely, you know."

Aubry swallowed deeply, then took the next mouthful and held it. He'd hold it, all right. He wanted the pleasure of spitting it in this monkey's face.

He inhaled once, harshly, and then the pacer button in his ear beeped, and he set off at a steady jogging pace.

Ibumi clapped Quint on the shoulder. "Knight is a fine man. Too bad he ended up on the wrong side of this."

"We didn't deal the hand," Quint said dully. "We're just playing it out."

He touched a button in the top of the sensor, and a plastic card slid out. Quickly, surreptitiously, he slid in a second card. "Good-bye, Aubry," Ibumi murmured.

The sun was high now, and Aubry felt the first real stab of heat. The flat, spiny leaves of the cactus wavered in mirage, and the very rocks rippled in the searing breeze.

He sank to his knees, balancing the rock, and wiped his forehead with an elbow. He had to keep going. The perspiration from his forehead beaded on his hand, and he wanted to suck at it. Water. He craved water. But he couldn't even swallow what he had in his mouth. He let a trickle of it down his throat, and groaned with pleasure. He could make it, whatever they threw at him. He knew, in the bottom of his heart, that he was the best, the toughest, the strongest man in the world. And as long as he held that image in his mind—

The beeper trilled a warning at him. *All right! All right, already!*

He pushed himself back up, and started off again. The pacer's tone was relentless. A hundred and eighty beats to the minute. Ten thousand eight hundred steps per hour.

His arms were set in a curve, holding the rock. He studied it as he ran. It was grayish, with silver speckles. Almost perfectly round, and fit his arms perfectly.

It all seemed so pointless, though. He wasn't running anywhere. He wasn't running *from* anything. He was just running. On and on into the desert, until a noise in his ear told him to stop, and the black shapes of the hovercraft dropped from the sky to claim him.

He had to move.

There, in the distance, sat a horse and rider. Their centaur silhouette wavered in the morning heat. They shimmered and clarified, then disappeared again.

Maybe they were there. It was possible.

He shook his head. Sweat drooled down into his eyes, and for the first time he noticed that his arms were aching. He slammed down the pain barrier in his mind, and kept going.

He was the best.

The sun was a blinding yellow orb, slamming down on him, the day beginning to heat now. The shale beneath his feet was hard-packed, gave good support to his feet, and he could keep moving.

The best.

But, God, it was hot.

He could look up at the sun and see that it was after noon. The sweat had stopped drooling now. His skin was beginning to feel tacky and dry, and then hot. So hot. Everything was hot—the sand beneath his feet, in the sun overhead, the air he breathed, his skin. His blood boiled.

His arms! The rock, the damned rock that he carried in his arms felt as if it weighed a thousand pounds. It was pulling his shoulders out, twisting his back, setting his elbows aflame. The muscles knotted, trying to maintain tension. Twice his sweat-slimed hands almost opened, and twice he bore down, linked fingers beneath its prodigious weight and ran on.

The best, the best, the best—

Aubry sucked air through his nose, each lungful more scalding than the one before. His throat felt as if it had been napalmed.

He stumbled, and fell, smashing his face against the rock. He groaned in pain, and lost water from his mouth, choked trying to seal in the rest.

He wiped wetness from his nose, looked at the red smear on the back of his hand, momentarily wondering what it was.

Oh, yes. Blood.

Dazedly, he looked around—where was he? What was happening?

Run. Yes. He had to run. He forced himself back to his feet, felt the muscles in his back creak as he pulled the rock back up, and began again. He coughed, choking, lost a precious spoonful of water, almost spewed out what was left in a frantic attempt to breathe.

thebestthestrongestthebestthestrongesttheycan'tbreakme, can'tstopmenotevereverever

He was wobbling now. Everything around him was spinning, a kaleidoscope of browns and dull greens. And yellows.

And he ran. The air was too hot, every breath scalded his lungs, and he had to stop. Had to . . .

But couldn't.

There was something that he had to do. His head felt as if it was going to burst, throbbing and pounding at him now, and he felt himself slow . . .

No. thebestthebestthebest . . .

He trotted again, the sun pounding down on him. His arms felt swollen, numb but filled to bursting with blood.

God. Where was he? The beeper pulsed angrily at him.

Run. Run.

He began to move again, the sound of the pacer a constant, rhythmic buzz in his ear.

Keep moving. There was something—

(but he was beginning to forget what)

—that he had to do. Blood was drooling down from his
nose, and his neck wound again. The silica gel bandage
was working its way open, and blood was trickling, flowing now, pulsing warmly.

He sniffed, hard, swallowing blood and water, struggling for air. Aubry twisted his head to the side, managed
to rub some of the blood up onto his shoulder. He smeared
his face in it, rubbed its sticky thickness against his parched
lips.

The pulse beat in his ear, and he kept moving.

I'm the . . .

the . . .

He was suddenly confused, terribly confused. Who or
what was he? He was somehow up, outside of his body,
watching it running, staggering through the sand, trailing
droplets of blood like Hansel and Gretel's crumbs. Carrying that silly-assed rock, telling himself that he was uncon-
querable, and the toughest human being in the world, and
all of that other tired macho bullshit, when it was so
obvious that he was dying.

What difference did it make? Why had he clung to that
image for so long? How much energy had he wasted,
violence had he wreaked, loves had he lost, to preserve
that image? What had it cost? And could anything be
worth it?

There was a blurry sensation, and suddenly Aubry felt
his consciousness *peel away* from his body. Illusion, but a
fascinating one: outside of himself, floating up above his
head, watching his body staggering wildly now along the—

And trip. In the body again, sliding down the side of a
dune, exhausted, the world spinning. The beeper pulsed
on. Quicker now. Was that possible. No. Cheating.

He sobbed for breath. It wasn't fair, wasn't fair . . .

His strength, vaunted, inexhaustible, was draining away.
His image of self, sufficient for so long, was no longer
enough to keep him going. All right then. For Leslie and
Promise.

Where was the rock? He found it, and wrapped his

hands around it and wrenched, pulling himself from his feet, and the rest of the water sprayed from his mouth in a mist. He barely noticed.

Promise. How could he . . .

What?

Oh, yes. How could he do anything for her? He didn't love her. It was just the drug. Just Cyloxibin. He couldn't love her. Couldn't love anyone. Didn't need anyone.

Aubry wrenched himself to his feet, staggering now like a wind-up toy with a broken spring.

There. There was the separation again. There was him, his body . . .

And then, what was he? If he wasn't his body?

Who was he, if he wasn't his feelings, his sensations, his experience? He had no answer, and yet there was a part of him, unsuspected all of these years, which stood back from the agony, back from the torn body, which watched dispassionately.

Which urged onward without wanting victory. Which kept heart beating and lungs pumping without attachment to life. Which pushed his body to the limits of its tolerance without seeking death.

Apart from life, or death. Pain, or pleasure. Hope, or fear. Without denying any of them. A part of him which found a curious peace in the center of the storm.

No sound now. He watched his feet silently striking the earth, a hundred and eighty times a minute.

The path he ran had been run by innumerable feet before him. Did they have water? Drugs, perhaps? Were they bleeding from the neck, their joints aching from mortal combat?

He didn't know. The pain was part of his body, that wonderful, monstrous body, which had so eclipsed his mind, his feelings, his spirit. Had stolen his identity until he craved . . .

Its death.

With a burst of light, Aubry saw it, saw it so clearly that, staggering utterly exhausted through the sand, he *knew*.

Not "knew about." Knew. Saw his body for what it

was, a ridiculous meat puppet. An automaton fiercely defending its absurd attachment to life while simultaneously seeking death, thereby guaranteeing his eventual defeat.

No man escapes Death. So Death must not be the enemy. Life must not be the prize. It must be the gameboard, on which Death teaches its savage lessons. You could heed those lessons, or ignore them, but never evade them.

Death, then, was the ally. Not to be sought, but heeded. *Attachment to life* was the enemy.

He chuckled hysterically, silently, until tears began to roll down his cheeks, cooling them with their evaporation.

Something hard hit him on the knees.

Oh, yes. The ground.

Up! Up!

His body laughed at him. He pulled the body up, and it balanced unsteadily on its heels, then fell again.

Oh.

Well, if this was the place for dying, that wasn't so bad. He had finally learned the lesson he had ignored all his life.

And the lesson of the day, class—

(repeat after me—)

He felt himself drifting up farther from the body, could see it, curled small and almost insignificant on the sand. It was a nice body, he supposed, and bodies were good while you needed them, but he didn't need his anymore.

Oh. An image of Leslie, and of Promise, came to him. Promise. Still, here at the threshold of death, her image, the thought of her face, the remembrance of the silky depths of her body, came to him, made him weep with remembered pleasure.

Promise. Even here, his body wasted, she came to him. And at last he realized that what he felt for her was the realest thing that had ever existed in his world, and it was only his fear of deaths large and small that had made him such a fool.

He, and Leslie, were not creatures of Life. They were Death incarnate, and had known each other in that first instant. Father and Daughter/Son. Unholy trinity.

How simply, absurdly true.

It would have been a terrible thing to die a fool and a liar. Truth, at any cost, is worth the price.

Up. Get up now.

As if pulled by strings from above, as if a marionette with no life of its own, Aubry's body rose again, following the bidding of his mind.

It lurched on, in a bizarre parody of running now, past pain, skating along a razor edge between life and death. Eyes staring glassily, and legs twitching mechanically, even as the shadows descended from the sky, drumming the sand into a storm, and plucked him up.

Sound. Coolness. Slowly, the presence of faces, images. What . . . ?

He was in a room, and there was a respirator attached to his mouth, breathing for him. He coughed, hacked, thrashed, and tore the respirator out.

Where . . . ?

He sat up suddenly, and gentle hands pushed him back down.

"Rest, Aubry. You need rest. You almost died yesterday."

"Yesterday . . ."

Promise was over the bed, Bloodeagle beside her. His friend's face was a mass of bandages, and when he spoke, his voice was a whisper. "Quint sabotaged the monitor. We lost track of you—didn't know where you were when we found out that a false, prerecorded reading was coming through. You lost almost fifteen percent of your body fluid. I don't know how you kept going."

"I . . ." He could barely make the sounds. "I didn't. I died."

Promise squeezed his hand. "Aubry?"

There were no tears, but Aubry cried, great racking sobs that were mixed with laughter, powerful gusts that shook the bed.

"Miles . . ." Promise whispered, alarmed.

"He's not back with us yet," Bloodeagle said. "It will pass."

In a few minutes Aubry curled onto his side, and looked up at them, eyes wide and guileless.

"Leslie. Wh—" He stopped. A nurse offered him a bottle. Aubry pulled at the nipple like a nursing infant. "Where is Leslie?"

"Gone. All of the children gone. Quint and Ibumi have disappeared, with about sixteen of the Gorgons. That's half."

"Gone where . . . ?"

"Los Angeles."

Aubry tried to fight himself to a sitting position, but his strength failed him. "We've got to stop him . . ."

"How?" Promise asked bitterly. "If we admit what Quint was trying to do, Gorgon and the NewMen are finished. DeLacourte will see to that. Quint won't surrender without a fight. Leslie will die."

"All of that . . . to save that bastard's . . . life?"

Let him die. Let DeLacourte die . . .

The voice was seductive.

But it was the voice of his body, and not the voice of his spirit, and his body had died on the Hell Run.

It simply didn't matter what his body wanted. His body walked the path of Life, a path filled with fear, and would lie to him in its terror of the Void.

He had to walk the path of Death, without seeking Death. Death need not lie, would never deceive him. Death was Truth itself.

Death knew that love was the truest, sweetest comfort in a lonely world. Cyloxibin was a joke: mushrooms don't create love. They might, at the very most, open the loving heart.

Life might deny Death, but Death knew all Life's truths, and kept them holy.

Truth could not be spawned in lies and deceit.

The assassination had to be stopped.

Even if it cost the life of his only child.

CHAPTER THIRTY

Pleasure Dome

Sunday, July 2

The 12:07 tubeway into Los Angeles was four minutes early. It shushed in on magnetic rails, gliding through vacuum tunnels, finally sliding to a halt in Santa Monica, close enough to the ocean that Aubry could smell the salt as he emerged.

The crowd surrounded him, obscured him, gave him a welcome anonymity. He didn't touch Promise, hadn't for the last few minutes, although he had held her in the tube as it burrowed beneath the mountain, raced them toward the Pacific.

Even within their personal turmoil, there was comfort in knowing that they shared more than a common concern.

If they survived the next few days, they might, just might, have a life together.

The crowd parted for a moment, and Marina stood there, her face blank. She looked small to Aubry, and vulnerable, but with no acknowledgment of that vulnerability.

Aubry approached her, and her eyes blazed at him.

He stopped before he reached her. "Looks like you get another chance."

"To what?"

"Watch me die."

The shadow of a smile flickered across her face, quickly dampened. "Son of a bitch. I thought maybe I'd kill you as you came out, but I still need you. Something is cooking, of course there is. Tomorrow is the rally at the convention center. Democratic National Convention. DeLacourte is making a personal appearance. That happens slightly less frequently than a solar eclipse.''

Promise moved between them, taking Marina's arm. "Jenna is with the Scavengers. We have a vehicle waiting outside.''

Quietly, trying not to attract any attention, Aubry and Promise and Marina moved through the crowd up to Sixth Street. There, a floater waited for them, air cushion humming. Aubry held the door for Promise and Marina, then slid in beside the driver.

"Quarry,'' he said heavily. His lieutenant smiled tightly and headed them off through the traffic. "I hope that I didn't leave things in too much of a state.''

"Things can't be like they were. Maybe that's good— but it feels strange. They came and sorted through everything. Searched for you. We've lost use of a lot of the transport tunnel—the Los Angeles Transit System is starting up again in the central city.

"It was an excuse. They wanted it, they found it. I know what we own, and it's ours. We have the paperwork. I wish that things hadn't happened like this. . . .''

"But they did.''

"Aubry,'' Marina said. Her voice was tight and controlled. "What can you tell me now?''

"First—can you get into this convention thing?''

"I'll have to pull some strings, but yes.''

"Good. Listen to me. Sometime during the convention, Sterling DeLacourte is going to be assassinated. It's a rogue operation. Quint and Ibumi had a cadre within Gorgon. They were the ones running Medusa. They're going to use the kids somehow. Bloodeagle and the rest of the Gorgons are coming in today and tomorrow, in varied transit. We need to coordinate things carefully.''

"Aubry . . . we have to tell the authorities.''

"Just give me a chance to save my child,'' he said intensely. He gripped her arm with sudden, terrible strength. "DeLacourte has to be stopped, but we're still just guessing. Quint can destroy the evidence and get away free. If they corner him, the children will die. If they don't find out, the attempt goes on. If it fails, they die. If it succeeds, they probably die anyway. The only hope that I have is to find out where and when the attack is to take place, and try to throw the timetable off.''

He sank back into the seat and closed his eyes. Marina pulled her arm away from him, and her eyes locked with Promise's.

"Just give us a chance," she said, and there was a plea in that voice.

"A chance." She stared out of the window, watching the buildings glide past.

"You like dangerous stories," Aubry said matter-of-factly. "Well, welcome to hell, lady."

Marina opened her mouth to protest, then found it closing again without sound.

Monday, July 3

Televisions and tridees and Omnivision receptors had been moved into the Scavenger planning room, surrounding a model of the Los Angeles Convention Center.

Onto the model was projected a holographic overlay. It showed the skimmers and helicopters coming and going, the security vehicles everywhere.

Bloodeagle stood next to Aubry. "I don't know what Quint has planned." His voice was bitter. "He hasn't been the same since Ibumi became his lover."

A sudden thought occurred to him. "Is Ibumi an American citizen?"

"Two generations back."

"Shit. Go on."

"I can tell you that he has a dozen of those children, but only three have been fully tested. I swear to you—we didn't know about this."

Aubry nodded his head sullenly. "All right. DeLacourte arrives tomorrow. Why would Quint, or Ibumi, want to kill him at the convention? Why not in transit? Or on his home turf? Maybe I'm a fool, but it looks as though security will actually be *tighter* here."

"A greater coup if they pull it off," Promise suggested.

"True—but no one is going to want to take *credit* for this."

"Look, Aubry," Marina said. "We don't know what or how. We're going to make a terrible mistake if we do. Second-guessing Quint or Ibumi's motivations and trying to extrapolate actions from them is a losing position."

Aubry nodded, then slammed his hand down on the model, rattling the houses. "Dammit. There is still something missing in the picture. What about this McMartin?"

Bloodeagle lowered his voice. "Quint purchased his fetuses. I know that."

Marina sounded disgusted. "McMartin seems to be playing every end against the middle. He deals with the Mercs. He buys fetuses from Ephesus, and sells them to the NewMan Nation."

"And he probably helped transport the Children up to Ephesus," Jenna said bitterly. "He killed my mother."

"We've got to find this man. Have you ever met him?"

Bloodeagle shook his head, wincing.

"Almost no one has," Marina said. "He's supposed to be a freak, an utter grotesquerie. A sybarite. I've never gotten specifics on it. The very few people who have seen him never talk."

"Where does he live?"

"Long Beach industrial district, a penthouse atop McMartin Cryogenics. He never leaves."

"Let's have the display," he said brusquely. Long Beach came up on the table, and they scrolled through the neighborhoods until Marina pointed her finger. "There."

The building was fourteen stories, and topped with a glass dome over what appeared to be an indoor swimming pool.

Promise closed her eyes. " '*In Xanadu did Kubla Khan a stately pleasure dome decree . . .*' " She shook herself out of it. "Sorry."

"No problem." Aubry laughed. "What can we do? Can we get a skimmer or helicopter in there?"

"Not without the civil air authorities picking us up."

"The building?"

Quarry examined the specs as they floated in the air before them, in rows of glowing insects.

"Don't know, Aub. McMartin Cryo looks pretty damned secure."

"Shit. We have no time. From underneath?"

"Negative. Private sewer lines. Specs say full security. If you want to do a soft-shoe, you'll need experts. We don't have that kind of talent on tap."

"Miles?"

"We can do it, given the specs. And the time. Need a day for recon."

"We don't have that. These buildings to the sides. How tall are they?"

"Ten stories, five, and twelve."

And the last side?

"Vacant . . ." Quarry's fingers busied themselves at the console. "I think. Let me get an update. We haven't used this section in months—"

His face brightened. "We have a building going up. Twenty stories. Incomplete."

Bloodeagle stared from his one good eye. "That might work."

"Might?" Aubry asked. "It has to."

To turn on the elevators in the abandoned skeleton of the building was to invite disaster. Aubry and Bloodeagle, and two of the other Gorgons, climbed the structure. The cables ran from one floor to the next. Wearing thick gloves, Aubry climbed. He still felt weakened from his ordeal in the desert, but that was just his body.

He swung himself over to the edge to rest for a minute. Bloodeagle caught up with him. "Are you sure you're up to this?"

Aubry gritted his teeth and nodded, then rose. The pain in his shoulder and neck and side were still dull aches, but he floated above them, found in the climbing a rhythmic, healing satisfaction. Just grip with the hands, pull the legs up behind, and . . .

His lungs felt aflame. He wasn't completely healed, and if he wiped his hand across his forehead it came away sopping with sweat. He was running a temperature.

He had to keep going, and could. Not for himself. For Leslie.

The image was still bright in his mind. A burning building in Ephesus, and a tiny wraithlike figure moving like lightning. What a child! Son, daughter, both, neither, it hardly mattered. What mattered was that child needed him and, in a way that he barely understood, Aubry desperately needed that child.

The wind plucked at him, and as he looked down on the black, light-dotted street below him, he felt a moment's dizziness.

Bloodeagle came up behind him. From where they stood, Aubry could clearly see the greenish plastic dome of the hothouse. It was faceted like an emerald, and gleamed in the city light.

Bloodeagle unslung a harpoon rifle with an attached reel of kevlar filament. He aimed carefully.

"Here." He pointed. "Where in the structure do you want to land? You've got to land soft, then cut through the panels."

"Give me the middle. As close to the top as you can come." Bloodeagle nodded. He aimed carefully, and the rifle gave a slight *phut*. The reel began to hiss.

"Damn." He grimaced. "Let's try it again." He clipped the line free, and attached a new tip. "Here . . ."

Phut.

Bloodeagle spit on the beam beneath his feet, his hawk face alight with pleasure. "Hah. That's the one."

He clipped the line and tied it in a loop to the stanchion next to him, attached a lever and pulled, taking up the slack.

"You're sure this is strong enough?"

"Plenty strong. Take five times your weight. Test it."

Aubry did, put all of his weight on the line as Bloodeagle took a small hand pulley and clamped it over the line.

"All right. This is your hand brake. You can slow descent if you want, by tightening your grip."

"You're sure this will hold?"

"Do you want one of us to go first?"

"No. And if anything goes wrong, don't follow unless I signal."

"You've got it."

"I'd better."

Aubry checked his backpack with the saw and drill bits.

He needed to slide down that line, braking to almost a complete stop at the bottom. He tested the hand brake. It seemed simple, a clamp of metal and plastic and some kind of synthetic asbestos.

"All right," he said. He peered down the line. It curved away, disappearing in a slow arc toward the roof of the building below them.

Unaccountably nervous, he borrowed the rifle scope for a minute. The tip seemed firmly anchored.

He clinched the brake, testing it a final time, nodded to Bloodeagle. "See you in a few minutes," and stepped off the beam.

The world dropped out from underneath him, and his stomach leapt into his mouth. Then he calmed, found his spiritual center and, a moment later, his physical. The long descent became almost a lark, a pleasure.

He was dropping quickly now, and he tightened his pressure on the handle—

And nothing happened. "Shit!" he cursed to himself.

He was dropping along the line, accelerating, the wind whipping at his face as he slid. Greater pressure on the clamp brought no response. The glass dome loomed up quickly now, and he cursed, cursed the defective apparatus, cursed—

His feet hit the plastic. He felt the jolt up his entire body as he smashed through, losing his grip on the hoist, and chunks of the roof collapsed behind him.

Then, with an impact that shocked him into insensibility, he hit the water.

Aubry rolled, swallowing filthy water, struggling to regain his bearings. Where? What . . . ?

A pale white form rolled against him, and he pushed it away automatically. His eyes burned horribly. When he managed to focus them, he saw that it was a woman's body, her hair plastered against her forehead, her eyes open and staring. He thrust it away frantically, gasping for air. Where in the hell was he?

A high-pitched wailing sound filled his ears, a sound which rose higher and higher, only vaguely recognizable as a human voice.

He had to clear his head. Leslie . . .

The thought sent adrenaline pumping into exhausted muscles. *Leslie*.

The water was erupting around him, and through blurry vision he saw a vast white shape thrashing clumsily toward the far end of the pool.

McMartin! He must have damn near landed on top of the monster! Screaming inarticulately, McMartin fled toward the shallows. He struggled to haul his bulk up and out of the pool, to no avail.

Aubry leapt on his back, digging his thumbs into McMartin's ears, his fingers in the fat man's eyes. The screams grew intolerably sharp, and then broke into sobs.

Aubry released him and rolled over onto his back, coughing slimy water.

He had opened tears above McMartin's eyes. The fat man was blinking slowly, painfully, blinded.

"Who . . . who are you? What do you want?"

"The man who will kill you if he doesn't get the truth."

McMartin slid around the edges of the tank, blood drooling down his face. He was blinded in one eye.

"You set it up," Aubry said. "You set up the hit on Ephesus."

"You . . . you can't prove that."

"I don't want to prove anything. I'm not interested in taking you to court. We're holding court right now, and if I don't get answers from you, you're going to be dead."

"If I tell you anything I'm dead anyway. To hell with you."

Aubry heaved again, spitting glycerin water, when there was a whirring noise above him. Bloodeagle and one of the other Gorgons slid down the line after him. They peered down into the pool area, and Bloodeagle lowered himself to the deck.

With a rattling noise, a basket containing the terrified form of Jeffry Barathy trundled down, Jeffry screaming all the way. When he stopped, and was lowered down to Bloodeagle, Jeffry uncrossed his eyes and grinned. "*Damn.* That's the most fun I've had in *months*." He looked at McMartin. "Who is this toad?"

"Maybe nobody. Maybe the most dangerous man alive. Watch him. Jeffry, we have work."

*   *   *

Aubry stood in the lab, watching the playbacks.

"Christ," Jeffry said, shaking his head. "This asshole is dead tight with DeLacourte. Four of his transport vehicles were in Washington at the time of the Ephesus fire. He hit Ephesus, all right. And he supplied the fetuses to the New-Men, which means that he must be in on the DeLacourte hit."

"Why?"

He triggered another button, and regained the image of McMartin in the pool. Aubry took the microphone. "Why would you do it? It looks like this guy's your buddy."

McMartin glared at them balefully.

"Where are they? Where is Quint? For that matter, where is Killinger?"

McMartin said nothing.

"God. What is happening here?"

"I don't know," Bloodeagle said, "but we're running out of time. DeLacourte arrives in an hour and forty minutes."

In the pool, McMartin smiled tightly. "It's too late. You can't stop it, can you? You can't talk to the authorities, can you? You're dead, all of you."

Aubry punched the button, starting the pool drain. McMartin thrashed in alarm. "Are you sure you don't want to talk? We can wait."

Jeffry Barathy hummed to himself, fingers flying. "Nice system he has set up. Security isn't for shit, but—"

The panel behind Moonman exploded, and a second shot took him in the shoulder. He gasped, clasping the wound, and fell back.

Bloodeagle reacted before Aubry. "Mercs!"

He gestured quickly, and half of his men sped down the corridor. "You stay here with Barathy. See what he can get."

Aubry nodded curtly. The sound of rapid-fire explosions shook the computer room. The floor thundered, and it took a moment for the computer display to restabilize.

"I'm not finished here," Jeffry said between his teeth, fighting his way back to the console.

"Christ," Aubry said, peering into the wound. He stripped away the cloth protecting the shoulder, and grimaced at what he saw. Jeffry's eyes were fixed on the screen before him, in a video trance.

"We . . . let go of my arm."

"I've got to stop the bleeding." Jeffry looked down at the wound, and his mouth pursed in an O.

His left hand went to the keyboard and punched the function keys, throwing the mindlink parameters up to the screen.

Arrows flew, and in a few moments, he lifted the headband and attached the electrodes to his wrists and forehead, and the base of his skull.

The holo field in front of his face fluxed until it was virtually a mask, shielding his eyes. Information, coded to his brainwave patterns, flashed through the field in bits and bytes.

Aubry finished with the dressing. "Finished."

"Huh?"

"Never mind."

"I have . . . data feeds coming in. Medical. These are coded last week. Senator Thurmond. Rejuvenation treatments."

Jeffry's pudgy body stiffened. "Ephesus. Fetuses."

"I saw a vehicle collecting something from Ephesus. It seemed heavy and cold."

"Fetuses."

"There is . . ."

A grenade exploded in the passage outside the computer room, and for a minute Jeffry's eyes remained sealed, and his teeth clenched. Then he relaxed, as if giving up resistance to the computer input. "I can see it. Aubry—there's a pattern. Fetuses from Ephesus to the NewMen camp . . . McMartin and DeLacourte. McMartin to Killinger to . . . to Ibumi. I can see the lines. I can see them, but I don't understand . . ."

Jeffry suddenly convulsed, and tore the leads away from his forehead. "God *damn*! That is a serious trip. But it's all coming too fast."

Aubry looked at the band. "Let me." He placed it around his forehead, and Jeffry helped him place the leads in position. "Now just relax, Aubry. You'll get images, and sensations. It will adjust to your mental predicates. OK?"

Aubry slumped down on the floor, and had barely relaxed when a flood of images flowed into his mind. Places and people were pictures, and he was suddenly plunging through a twisting world of facts and feelings, and Aubry was overwhelmed, exulted with the flood of knowledge.

The facts and numbers and faces and images were like an infinitely branching network of tunnels, of waterways, and he controlled them with his mind, sweeping down at first one, and then the other, and another, exhilarated, drunken with information.

Why, why had he ever been afraid? Why had he held so strongly to his body, punished and stunted the growth of his mind?

All of the names and faces of the equations flared in his mind, and he chased them down all at the same time, in a bizarre variant of his ability to move his body in two directions at the same time. He laughed and laughed, names for all of the things that he had only had feelings for racing into his mind, and, and—

There was a flash of light, and Aubry *screamed*, the brightness searing away all images, all feelings, and leaving only pure, pure pain—

"Aubry?"

The voice was as distant as the stars.

Slowly Aubry rose from a world of light, readmitted darkness to his world, allowed images to form again.

Bloodeagle's face, lean, scarred, still bandaged, was above him.

Aubry reached out to him, and grabbed Bloodeagle roughly around the neck, crushed him to him. "Miles. Miles. God *damn*, man. I can't tell you what happened. What I saw."

Bloodeagle disengaged himself, peering into Aubry's eyes, somewhat embarrassed. "Aubry. We thought we'd lost you."

"No. No way. What happened?"

"They dumped the computer core. You were hooked into it with that damned learning device. Jeffry says it should have burned your goddamned brain out."

He shook his head. "No. But I saw some things, Miles. Learned some things . . ." He shook his head. "I'll tell you later." Aubry shakily pushed himself to his feet. "What's happened here?"

One of the Gorgons returned to the room, dragging two prisoners. "It was a small group, responding to what they thought was a medical distress signal from McMartin." He threw one of them to the ground. "Do you know this?"

Aubry stared into the face of Marcel Killinger, and he grinned. "Marcel. Well well. Long time no see. He belongs to McMartin."

"Then he's in on it too."

"Has to be."

Aubry slammed Killinger into the wall, felt his arms and elbow joints. "Cyborg. Left arm isn't real. Give me a climbing spike."

Bloodeagle handed it to Aubry. Aubry weighed it carefully in his hand, then slammed it down, into, and through the synthetic hand.

Pain sensors flared, and Killinger's body heaved with agony, white fluid oozing from the wound. "Hello, Marcel," Aubry said conversationally. "Understand you've been looking for me."

He took a second spike, and felt Killinger's legs, found the one he wanted, and rammed the spike down, pinning it to the ground. Killinger's body arched, and he screamed in a high, thin voice.

"You want to kill DeLacourte. Why?" Killinger spat at them.

"You don't understand. Maybe we're not interested in stopping you. Maybe we're on your side."

Killinger twisted, and writhed, right hand and left foot nailed to the ground.

"Well, we're out of artificial limbs now. I suppose we could start on the real ones."

"No," he said frantically. "I . . . DeLacourte was a joke. He was a powerful man who we could manipulate."

"How?"

"He's addicted to the rejuvenation process."

"Then how did you decide to kill him? Why?"

"He has a chance," Killinger said, his voice growing softer, as if with exhaustion. "He might make it to the White House." His eyes, mad with pain now, raced from one of them to the others, as if thinking at Mach speed. "He would have destroyed us. We have to destroy him first."

Bloodeagle slapped Killinger with brutal strength and speed. "Who is your contact in Gorgon?"

Aubry twisted the climbing spike. Killinger screamed, his body arching.

Jeffry turned and vomited.

"All right! All right! It's Ibumi! He's . . . he's from Cameroon. We set him up with a phony identity, got him into Gorgon, helped him control Quint with Cyloxibin and other mood drugs."

"Shit," Aubry said in disgust. "I should have known. This bastard worked for Wu. He'd know about that, and every other way to crack someone's head open."

Jeffry looked from one of them to the other. "Well, could Wu—"

Killinger exploded from the floor, the pins ripping from his hands. The point of his elbow smashed into Bloodeagle's forehead. A quarter second later he had his hands on the AT-14, and death was in the computer room.

Bloodeagle and Aubry had moved almost instantly. Aubry hit Jeffry at the waist, and knocked him behind the cage as the bullets tore through the paneling and into the wall behind. One of the Gorgons was cut in half by the hail of bullets. He screamed once, briefly, the sound mingled with an ugly burst of sound from the AT-14. Then there was silence.

Then another burst of sound as the computers were torn to pieces.

"To hell with you. To hell with all of you—"

Bloodeagle twisted the nose of a grenade and performed a perfect bankshot as Aubry screamed, "No—!"

It bounced off the wall, around the corner, and landed in Killinger's lap. Killinger had enough time to scream once before the explosion tore him apart.

Aubry rose, and forced himself to examine the room. It wasn't pleasant. In an enclosed area, a fragmentation grenade does ugly things to a human body.

Jeffry examined the bank of shattered electronics.

"We're not going to get any more information here."

They traveled the rest of the corridor, carrying Jeffry. They came to a bank of elevators. Keeping a careful watch, Bloodeagle triggered the elevator button, frowned when nothing happened. He ripped open the box and checked the data lines, and toyed with them for a few moments. The elevator began to hum.

"Come on." They piled in, and Aubry suddenly felt terribly uncomfortable.

There was something wrong here. . . .

The lift sank, and sank, and went down two levels. Then the gate opened again.

"Cryogenic storage." The hall was terribly silent, the vibration of the machines barely noticeable beneath their feet. Plastic cases surrounded them. Everywhere they looked were the storage facility for thousands and thousands of frozen fetuses.

"Can you get any information out of these?"

Jeffry shook his head. "The central processor is dead. These substations won't function without it . . ." He frowned. "Unless they have separate volatile memories. If there's a unit that has been used and not shut off, there might still be something in Vol that we could tap." They carried him down the line, peering into one after another. Most of the terminals were off, but at the far end, near a bank of tables, one was still on.

"Huh." Jeffry slipped the induction band around his forehead, and a tiny holographic data simulacrum blossomed in the air. He sank back into his trance, and began to manipulate the color and depth fields. "There's been work in here. I have the listings, but I can't tell you who, or why. I'm sorry."

He stripped the helmet off.

Aubry turned to Bloodeagle. "Leave two men with McMartin. And let's get out of here."

CHAPTER THIRTY-ONE

Independence Day

2:27 P.M. Tuesday, July 4

Marina's smile was pure artifice, something that she kept in place for fear that the alternative might be a kind of leering, synthetic grimace.

The Los Angeles Convention Center was packed, with the delegates and the nominees, the interested electorate and their assistants. And the press, oh yes, the press.

Because this was the time, this was the place. Within hours, a man would be nominated for the highest office in the land.

And somewhere in the crowd was a three-year-old assassin. Where—there? There was a child, a young child with a fresh face, who seemed blissfully unaware of its surroundings. Could that child . . . ? But it was overweight, *plump as a piglet*, her mother used to say. All of Project Medusa's spawn were incredibly fit.

So her eyes kept moving, and as she watched the events and the speeches, the pomp and ceremony, she began to feel cold, colder than she ever had in her life.

There was a tiny transceiver built into her recorder, and at a signal from her button, she would be capable of broadcasting her discovery to anyone listening. Aubry Knight and the Scavengers would be listening.

But so far there was nothing to be said. Nothing to be seen, and her fear expanded within her like a living thing.

She pushed her way through the crowd, listened to a thousand snatches of conversation. Her heart thundered in

her chest, the sound growing louder and louder, as if she
had no control over her own emotions, her own viscera.

Fiercely, she narrowed her concentration and brought
her self back to the moment. Where? Where was it . . . ?

The limousine cruised up the La Cienega Compway,
switching onto the Presidential Network, a constantly monitored electronic/optical hotline. There were three police
motorcycles accompanying the black car, and Jack Hands
let his hands slide lightly over the wheel.

He turned to the federal agent in the front seat next to
him, and smiled.

"I'm glad that you guys are here—I don't trust this city.
Too many whackos."

The Secret Service man smiled bleakly. "Nothing to
worry about." He turned his shoulder to Hands, and spoke
rapidly into a hand-held microphone. "Station One?"

"*Secure.*"

"Station Two?"

"*Secure. ETA, Jack?*"

"On sched, Winston. Station Three . . . ?"

In the back seat, Sterling DeLacourte sat with his wife
and son. He held their hands with intensity, and smiled.

Gretchen looked at him somewhat apprehensively. "Are
you all right, darling? You seem a bit peaked."

"No. This is just a moment that I have waited for for
more years than I can remember."

"And the President has agreed to meet you on the
platform?"

"To receive my blessing."

She moved in closer to him. "Does it hurt?"

"This is his last term. I can consolidate power today
that will snowball for the next four years. The long view,
Gretchen." He sighed, and rested one large hand on her
leg. When he spoke again, his voice was husky with
emotion. "They said that I haven't suffered enough."

"What?"

He didn't answer her. "The long view. Always take the
long view."

She leaned her head against his shoulder, and looked up at him, eyes wide.

"There's something wrong," she said at last. "You're hiding something from me. I know you. I've been married to you for twenty years. I know."

"Gretchen . . ." he began, and she shushed him.

"I also know that you're not going to tell me. I just want to look at you. Is it the death threats? Have you received more of them?"

DeLacourte stared straight ahead, his face immobile. Suddenly he hugged Conley to him, and his voice was husky. "I love you. Both of you, and I swear it. If anything happens . . . please, please try to understand. Sometimes a man makes the choices that he has to, rather than the ones he wants."

Conley hugged his father back, and then pulled back into the corner of the limo, watching and thinking and feeling, suddenly, unaccountably, frightened.

At Station Two, Winston Kyle Terrace snapped his communication into its folding position, and replaced it in the pocket of his dark blue blazer.

"Dull day," he said to his partner, a big New Mexican named Shelly Olajade. Nobody called Shelly "Shelly." It was "Mr. Olajade," or "Rocky," with "Rocky" recommended by nine out of ten orthodontists.

They were situated in the basement of the convention center, near a complex of freight elevators and ventilation ducts. Rocky sat quietly, his considerable bulk balanced on an improbably tiny folding chair. His police and executive band radio earphone was snugly in place, and his eyes scanned the flatscreen monitor giving them their view of the convention floor.

Winston paced. "Helluva duty we drew, Rocky. 'Important but Non-Critical.' "

Rocky's reply represented, Winston mused, the very height of his temporary partner's ratiocinative capacities. "LAPD ain't Secret Service." He picked something green from between his teeth with a fingernail. "Ya want glamour? Join the Feds."

Roughly translated this meant that all access to this area was sealed, and that the elevators themselves were rendered non-operational for the remainder of the day. There were no direct routes from here onto the convention floor. Metal detectors and magnetic field sensors were in place all over the building.

It was likely to be a dull day. . . .

Winston whipped his head around at the sound of approaching footsteps, and his hand immediately went inside his jacket.

"Chill, Winston." Rocky's voice snapped in command.

He narrowed his eyes in shocked surprise.

It was two children, a young boy and a young girl. Perhaps eight years old, and holding hands. Their faces were slender heart shapes, cheeks red with exertion, eyes wide with fear.

"Mister?" the girl said. Her voice was high and sweet. "Do you know how we can get out of here?"

Rocky pulled his bulk out of the chair a section at a time.

"How the . . . how did ya get here, kid?"

The boy spoke up. His speech had a kind of military school precision that mixed with the preadolescent softness made Winston smile. He must have sounded a hell of a lot like that, himself. "We were looking for the restroom, sir. I guess we got lost. There was a stairway, and a sort of garbage door thing. I crawled through and opened it from the other side. I thought we could get back to the convention."

"Shit," Rocky said, his shoulders relaxing. "Ain't that just like—"

The kids had walked closer, and one of them was crying, tiny jewellike teardrops glistening on a pink cheek. The little girl held out her hand to Rocky. With a craggy, fatherly smile, Rocky extended his own in return.

It was a minor relay, Gomez mused, but today was important. Even a secondary communications switchbox might be valuable. If the primaries failed, the backups had to switch online instantly, or the country would miss its minimum daily requirement of prime political bullshit. Thus deprived, the symptoms of feces deficiency would set in immediately: clear heads, clear eyes, and increased difficulty swallowing new tax increases.

Long before the patient became critical, Dr. Gomez was on the job. He wandered down the narrow corridors back to the core of the communications complex, turning sideways sometimes—his girth had expanded regrettably in the past eight years, although Maria did not seem to mind at all. In fact, he wondered if his ever more prominent profile actually comforted her. Her own outline had become more sundial than hourglass with each successive child.

Gomez stopped, eyes widening at the sight before him. The panels had been *dismantled*, and a device of some kind, a piece of electronic apparatus, added to the transformer. His hand went for the beeper in his pocket, but froze when he caught a glimpse of movement behind him.

A child. A slender, beautiful, smiling boy, his skin so smooth and beautiful that in the dim light it seemed translucent.

"Mister," the boy said, his voice soft, as soft as a baby's kiss. "Can you help me?"

"Station Three. Secure?"

There was a pause as tiny fingers wrested a transceiver from hands which strove, futilely, to fulfill duty even after death.

"Station Three. Do you copy?"

The slender, childish throat trembled, vocal cords making the adjustments necessary to produce the deeper, fuller sound of an adult male.

"We copy. What is your ETA?"

"On sched. Over."

"Over."

The conduits above the ceiling were impossibly small, inaccessible to anything much larger than a big rat. Leslie slowed his breathing to a crawl—the air was very bad here. He was surviving on bare spoonfuls of air. But his body was so firmly under his control that he barely noticed the discomfort.

Keeping his mind remote, he began the process of dislocating his joints. The pain was excruciating, had always been, but it was an invaluable skill when getting into places too small for anything human.

The ancient *ninjas* of Japan had perfected this art. From childhood they practiced manipulating their joints, stretching ligaments systematically, scientifically, until arms and legs could move from shoulder and hip joints, and the human body became phenomenally malleable.

The trick was keeping your mind away from your body when you did it. And Leslie was far away, lost in a puzzle that clouded his mind, and that was dangerous.

A puzzle. Who were Mother and Father? What difference does/did it make?

And had he been lied to? If Quint had lied . . .

Then what else might have been lies? How many other lies had been included in his training? What other lies . . .

In the darkness, Leslie crawled toward his goal.

Just ahead now. A mental map guided him as he squeezed through the last of the obstructions. His breathing changed, and over the next five minutes he performed the quasi-yogic movements that slipped his bones back into their proper places. There was no way to distract his mind during this part of it, and the pain was horrendous.

Clamp the mind down, with the skill that had never failed him. He knew. He had been taught. Still, tears ran down his cheeks, and he trembled. There was only the job. Only the task.

He should be able to seal away any doubt, any fears, any concerns other than the mission at hand.

But he couldn't. He couldn't forget Aubry Knight, the man who was his father. Who had *not* abandoned him. Had not deserted him. Had come for him, and refused to leave him even when his own life was at stake.

What had happened to him? What had happened to the man, Aubry Knight? The man who was a great fighter, even by the standards of Gorgon?

And what of the woman, Promise? What had happened

to her? And why did she weep? Ibumi said that tears were a sign of weakness. But was it weakness that motivated one human being to shield another with her body? Is that weakness? There were situations in which one might sacrifice his life for the good of the many. But one life for one? How did this make sense?

What was real? What was real?

The puzzle.

Why did Leslie have the awful feeling that the puzzle had to be solved now, right *now*, or it would never be, and the consequences might be . . .

Something dire. Death?

Or worse . . . ?

CHAPTER THIRTY-TWO

Logic Puzzle

3:39 P.M.

Wu bent gently at the waist as he poured tea for Aubry, Promise, and Jeffry Barathy. Aubry noted that although Wu's almond eyes never remained on him for more than a few seconds, they never strayed away for long, either.

"It has been a long time, Aubry," he said softly. "There are times when, at night, I rub ointment into my neck, and think of your name."

"I hope that your neck doesn't trouble you too much."

"You don't understand," Wu said, his green eyes glittering. "I admire you. With no traditional training, you have managed to overcome formidable barriers of perception. I doubt if there are a dozen men in the world who could have accomplished as much."

Aubry sipped at his tea. "I didn't come here to talk about Nullboxing," he said bluntly.

"Yes, I know."

"I came because you are the only person I know who might be able to put this whole thing together."

"And if this is true, why should I help you?"

Aubry took another sip, and then put the cup down. "Because, Wu—you are the missing piece in this puzzle."

Wu inclined his head politely. "Would you care to explain further?"

"Look at the pieces. Cyloxibin. A Thai-VI infected doctor who worked for the Ortegas. Killinger—who used to work for you, and ended up working for McMartin."

"A former employee is no interest of mine," Wu said mildly.

Aubry leaned forward. His mind was still swirling with the images and labels, all of them riding on flows of feelings. Never in his life had his mind felt so crisp and open.

"My own case is a perfect example, Wu. The Ortegas never let *anyone* go. But you kept a string on me. There's something big going on, and I can't quite smell it."

Wu sat down across from Aubry, his robes swirling like rose petals in a shallow wind.

"Perhaps you should tell me what you know. Then I will decide what to say. Is that fair?"

Aubry nodded. Promise leaned forward. "There are a number of facts, and none of them lead anywhere happy. One, Sterling DeLacourte is scheduled to die."

"There have been rumors of the 'Oath' for months," Wu said. "I wouldn't be surprised."

Moonman spoke quickly. "Did you know the tool that is intended as the instrument of assassination? Medusas. The hermaphroditic kids the NewMen have been raising for the last few years. They were reaped from the cryogenic child storage facilities created by Ariane Cotonou. Something about what they were doing with those children is part of this whole thing. That's why she had to die."

Wu's eyes narrowed. "I . . . have never considered it appropriate to use young children for a mission such as that."

"They are using them. Next, McMartin Cryogenics is involved. Why? They are linked with DeLacourte."

"Perhaps, just perhaps, they now consider DeLacourte to be more dangerous than they had originally thought."

"Yes. That was what we were told. It doesn't entirely ring true."

"Why not?"

"Because the President of the United States is always bound by the deals that he makes to get to his position. DeLacourte can't make any kinds of drastic changes, regardless of what he claims. The chief executive isn't an emperor."

"There are stories that DeLacourte had made deals with Harris."

Aubry laughed. "To denounce the NewMen? Why in

hell would McMartin care? He's the one who drove them out of L.A.''

Wu sat staring off into a far horizon, his lips pursed tightly. ''I'm not sure we can help each other, Aubry. I think that this interview has reached its conclusion, my dear young friend.''

''What?'' Promise half rose.

''I'm sorry—''

Aubry met Wu's eyes. ''No,'' he said. ''Not this time. No matter what happens to you, Wu, you seem to come out smelling sweet. Not this time. This is too large. It involves my child. And you tried to kill Promise.''

''Excuse me?''

''You set me up,'' Promise said. ''You said you'd clear the way for me into Hoopa, and the first thing they did was try to rape me. If I hadn't had a backup, I never would have gotten out alive.''

''I assure you—''

Aubry finally opened his eyes. ''Wu. There's a piece that's been missing here. Everyone's been trying to figure it out from the pieces. How about taking a look at the man? At *you*, Wu.''

''What exactly do you mean?''

''I mean that your specialty is drugs, so drugs figure in here somewhere. Somehow nasty.''

''Cyloxibin . . .'' Wu offered. His composure was slightly ruffled. Only slightly, though.

''Old hat,'' Jeffry said. ''But I know something that isn't. DEA.''

Wu stood slowly, turned like a petal spinning in the wind, and looked out over the city. ''2,3-diethylandroe-ternalone is very valuable, but almost impossible to synthesize.''

''You can extract it from fetal tissues, Wu.''

Promise looked at Moonman. ''What are you talking about?''

''Youth serum. About thirty makers and shakers swung over to DeLacourte's camp in the past year and a half. All over sixty. DEA. He hooked 'em.''

''Shit. And that's only the ones we know about,'' Promise said, alarm in her voice. "He could have more—a hell of a lot more support than anyone thinks."

Jeffry laughed. "If he has so damn much support, why would he be giving in? Why would he give . . . ?"

He and Aubry looked at each other at the same moment. "Unless . . ."

"Unless he isn't giving up." Aubry looked at Wu, whose back was still turned.

"Wu," he whispered. "You've got everyone running in circles. Everyone is killing everyone, and one thing that could make sense of the whole damn thing is if Harris is the real target."

"Why would the Gorgons kill their greatest supporter?"

Wu turned, and thought, and the silence was almost a tangible thing. "I have no involvement in this thing, of course. . . ."

"Of course," Aubry said. "But if my child dies, and I find out that you might have helped me save him, I swear to God you are dead. The Scavengers owe me, owe Promise. There will be no place to hide, Wu."

Wu paused, weighing alternatives, and finally exhaled harshly. "What I know changes nothing." He was still thinking at hyperspeed, and finally came to a decision. "Gorgon may not wish Harris's death, but there is someone else who does."

"Swarna."

"Ibumi."

"Holy God. How do we stop it?"

"You cannot," Wu said, almost sadly. "All of the pieces are in place. But perhaps what I have said will help you to save your child. The plan may work, it may not. A person who arranges such a thing has many, many layers between himself and the actions. Only a very few would know the actual plan. Harris will die. DeLacourte thinks that it will help his bid for the presidency."

"When?" Promise whispered.

"You must examine the convention schedule," Wu said thoughtfully, "and see when both DeLacourte and President Harris are scheduled to be in the same place at the same time. That will be the moment. That will be the place."

CHAPTER THIRTY-THREE

Death

The motorcade was moving down Jefferson Boulevard toward the convention center. Within the car, Gretchen DeLacourte watched her husband, and thought about things that she hadn't allowed herself to dwell upon in weeks past.

She reached across to take her son's hand, and she held it tightly. Her husband stared straight ahead, hardly blinking, a thin smile frozen to his face, a thin sheen of perspiration on his forehead.

The interior of the limo seemed very cold . . .

In the crawl space, Medusa-16, also known as Leslie, was contorted beyond normal human tolerance. There was barely room to move, barely air to breathe. He had slowed his respiration down to one per minute, and was in a state that was near coma, all systems on automatic. On the level of subconscious awareness, Leslie was thinking faster and harder than he ever had in his short life.

Information. All he had was information. Barely any impressions, barely any time to form opinions. Evidence suggested that a majority of human action and thought took place in the gray zones between absolutes, between certainties. Yet in his entire education, all that had ever been given to him were absolutes. The statistics, the facts, with the conclusions already neatly drawn.

His head hurt. There was so little time.

His parents had deserted him.

His parents had come for him.

Ordinary humans could not understand what the NewMan culture had to offer.

His father was the greatest fighter that Leslie had ever seen, except for Quint.

Women were weak and cowardly and manipulative.

His mother had cushioned him with her own body. . . .

The Gorgons were the only family he had. Quint the only human being he could trust.

Quint had *lied* to him. . . .

There was so much confusion, and so little time.

Aubry and Promise, Bloodeagle and the Gorgons, watched the convention on their Omnivision scans, and the silence was dreadful.

"We can't let him do it, Aubry," Bloodeagle said.

"Could Quint possibly know DeLacourte's true plans?"

Bloodeagle looked at Aubry with scorn. "I thought you understood us better than that. We might have planned to kill the man. There is no chance that Quint would plot against his own people. What could the straights possibly offer him? There is no place for him in the other world."

"All right. What is there for us to do?"

"We can't reach Quint. We can't warn the police."

"Yes we can," Bloodeagle said. "We have to. You're right, the children may die." Bloodeagle pulled himself to full height. "Aubry. I can't let the NewMan Nation be destroyed."

Aubry hung his head. "No . . ." he whispered. "If only we had some idea where the attack was coming. And when. And how."

"But we don't."

"We've got to flush them out."

Aubry turned to Jeffry. "I hate asking this. Marina mentioned that you have an emergency path into DeLacourte's network."

"But if I use it, they'll be able to trace it back. They'll find me."

"They'll find your home in Bismarck. They won't find

you. A promise. We need to bypass the police. We need to get right into the convention center, and fast. How long will it take you?''

Jeffry looked around. "All I really have to do is patch into the telephone lines to get to my system in Bismarck. From there I can activate the satellite patch, and . . . about fifteen minutes. I won't be able to keep it going for more than about fifteen seconds.''

"Do it.''

Marina walked the floor of the convention center, feeling her stomach knot as DeLacourte's limousine disgorged its passengers. DeLacourte, his wife, and their security personnel were moving toward the massive concrete podium, moving toward President Harris, who stood addressing the people below him. They hung onto his every word, waving their flags, singing their songs of support.

Oh, God. God. Where was it? Where were the killers?

DeLacourte, and his wife and child, took the podium, and he and the President of the United States shook hands, hard. DeLacourte took the podium and began to speak.

"My fellow Americans—''

There was a sudden burst of static from the hundred television sets mirroring his words around the room as their pictures wavered, and turned to fuzz. DeLacourte smiled indulgently. "My technical people are a little excited today.''

There was a general ripple of laughter.

Then laughter died. *"This is Moonman,"* Jeffry Barathy said. *"I have to warn you. Sterling DeLacourte has planned the assassination of the President of the United States. The attempt will occur at this convention. This is not a joke. He has addicted the following senators to a longevity drug called Androeternalone, extracted from the blood of unborn fetuses. Scofield—''*

The crowd reacted with stunned silence. A dozen hands flew to the television monitors and turned them off, but still, a few sets remained in operation.

Then there was nothing on them.

DeLacourte stood at the podium, his face ashen. "I—''

And above him, an explosion. A section of ceiling gave way, collapsed. DeLacourte screamed, and ducked beneath the cover of the podium, the only cover on the entire stage. But the Secret Service men, primed and alert from the abrupt, incredible message, were already in movement. They hit the President and Mrs. DeLacourte instantly as concrete and steel rained down from thirty feet above, a ghastly avalanche of wires and chunks of glass and steel and plaster.

Death.

CHAPTER THIRTY-FOUR

Madness

Gretchen DeLacourte knelt in the rubble, crouched over her son, holding him, moaning softly, kissing his brow, as the entire room dissolved into confusion.

Marina came in more closely, feeling as if she were watching the entire scene through a holo viewer. She found herself mentally calling camera shots, mentally composing her narration, and hating herself for it. The holotape camera on her shoulder whirred quietly.

Marina bent, almost unconsciously, and looked into Conley DeLacourte's face. The little face was dusted with plaster, red oozing slowly from beneath the tragic mask.

DeLacourte had crawled out from under the podium, and was in shock. His mouth opened and closed and opened again like a fish out of water. "I . . . I . . ."

He cleared his throat, and Marina could almost see the gears in his head begin to turn, churn, and the words begin to come out. Even as the President of the United States watched him. Even as his wife held the torn body of their child in her arms. The news cameras gathered closer. Marina listened and watched, and couldn't rid herself of the impression that this speech had been carefully rehearsed.

"I . . . I consider this action a direct assault on the Constitution of the United States by its sworn enemies, the forces . . . of, uh . . . the NewMen swore that would never . . ." He shook his head. His eyes met the eyes of the President, and he seemed confused. ". . . this great man who died . . ."

Marina moved in closer to DeLacourte, closer to the

man who had dominated her life for so long, and saw through his eyes, to something broken, whirring out of control in the precious machinery behind them.

Gretchen DeLacourte stood, shaking as the ambulance took her child's body away. "You knew," Gretchen whispered, walking up to her husband. Her voice was gravel. "You *knew*. What happened, Sterling? Did the bomb go off a little early? Who'd you make the deal with, Sterling?" She advanced at him, her hands drawn into claws. "What did you promise them? Twenty minutes in prime time, you bastard?"

"No . . . I . . ." DeLacourte turned and looked at the cameras around him, surrounding him, and he was as white as a sheet.

"I—"

Jack Hands of the security guards moved in next to him, and started pushing the reporters back. "Excuse me. We need to clear a space here—"

"You *KNEW!!*" She screamed, and her hand flashed out, faster than anyone could stop her, and pulled the pistol from the holster of the security guard. DeLacourte reared back, his silver hair seeming suddenly white, his whipcord body suddenly skeletal, lurching back from his wife as if she were the yawning gate of hell.

Hands snatched at her hands, but not before she fired three times, directly into DeLacourte's face.

Aubry and the others sat in stunned silence, the news camera lurching around the room, the wreckage of the ceiling, the crushed bodies sprawled like awful shattered dolls.

"I . . ." Bloodeagle started to speak, to lay his hand on Aubry's shoulder, but Aubry was deadly quiet, deadly silent, and unmoving. Bloodeagle pulled his hand away. Despite Aubry's injuries, there was something about him that seemed to swarm up from the depths of his soul, something larger than pain or hurt, something that was terrifying in its quiet.

Promise whispered, "My baby." Her face dropped down into her hands.

Aubry moved to comfort her, and her arm snaked like

smoke around his waist. She buried herself against him.

"They're going to die for this," he said, his voice barely audible. "I swear to you. Ibumi and Quint are going to die."

"I don't want death, Aubry." Promise's voice was heavy. "I wanted life. Life for us. Together. Life for our child. It isn't about death, Aubry. It's about life."

Aubry looked at her numbly, and slowly his arm fell away.

Bloodeagle brooded. "I don't know where Ibumi is, but we have to find him, and take him. Alive if we can. But *we* have to bring him in, not the police. Not the Secret Service. It has to be Gorgon."

"Why?"

"Don't you understand? This whole thing is insane. No matter how many cut-offs they have, someone is going *down* for this. The public is going to want a patsy. Even though we made the warning, that won't save us. Not in a hundred years. Our only chance is Quint."

"And where is he?"

Darkness. The Stealth ship's engines vibrated through the metal. Leslie shifted his position, and peered out through the grille. At the controls, Ibumi and Quint handled the delicate maneuvers as the radar-invisible vehicle headed out of the city, out to the northeast.

He had been lied to. Used. The only beings that he had ever trusted had tried to kill him. Unbidden, tears streamed down his face. There was nowhere to go! No one to trust.

There was nothing. No one.

Except . . .

For a short time, there had been two people who risked everything. Who dared. Who had been lied about, too. And perhaps, just perhaps, were Leslie's only link to life.

He could barely form the concepts. They were emotional concepts, shadowy things, and incomplete. But they were there.

Leslie turned in the storage compartment where he had crawled after turning, fleeing from the auditorium after placing the bomb. He wasn't sure why he hadn't gone to the rendezvous, but it had saved his life.

From hiding, he had watched six of Medusa's Children slaughtered in cold blood by Quint and Ibumi. Ibumi had counted them, frowning, then turned and returned to the Stealth ship. Leslie had followed, silently, hiding before the cabin was sealed.

His fingers, incredibly strong, ripped at the wiring, until he pulled the right wire free of its moorings. Leslie searched the frayed lines until he found one of the ship's radio cables. The next step was to splice a connection with the terminal implant in his skull. He opened the line, plugged his cranial leads in.

No! No filter! This was direct induction, unfiltered, unpaced, and his brain was overwhelmed instantly. Lost, inundated in a world of fluid movement and air pressure, electron flux and photon rerouting.

It was never meant for a direct linkage, and the overload was almost more than Leslie could take. Without a buffer he was suddenly exposed to the elements. He felt strapped to the outer hull of the ship, wind flensing the flesh from his bones. His mental barriers were crumbling, and awful, raw awareness hammered at his control.

He calmed himself, forced himself to imagine an alpha-theta synchronizer strapped above his eyes, forced closed the door which led to madness.

The streams of lightning slowed, became pulses of information. He flowed among them, matched their speed until they were a flood of facts, an infinite stream of images and sensations coursing through the ship's guidance and communications system.

He sorted through the computer for information, and found what he was looking for. The construction specs on the BioTech building.

Scavengers. The communication codes.

One part of his mind held back the fear. Even as everything in Leslie's world tumbled around him, he reached into the bowels of the ship, and sneaked past the filters, and tentatively, desperately, he sent his message . . .

CHAPTER THIRTY-FIVE

The Belly of the Beast

No one in the room said anything, but the single unanswered, unasked question hung in the air like smoke: Where did this leave them? What would, what could happen now?

Promise's face was buried in her hands, and she sobbed inconsolably. Jenna approached her and held her face in her strong, blunt fingers. "Promise. My sister. You did everything that you could. More than that not you or any other human being can do."

"I had her," Promise said through her tears. "I had Leslie. The child I thought that I had lost. And then I lost her again. Aubry almost killed himself to try to save Leslie—"

And here she flashed a look at Aubry, the warmth and love shining even through the tears. "—but it didn't matter. It was for nothing, because in the end it was a lie, everything was a lie."

She sank her head down into her hands again, and this time she didn't look up again.

Jeffry looked up from the panel in front of him. "The information was there. Everything was there. It was right in front of us all of the time. If only we had known better."

Aubry just glared at him. It was at that moment that the radio chimed.

Jeffry looked at the console. "We've got a message coming out here. I can't read it. Some kind of scrambler circuit."

The flatscreen was filled with unintelligible symbols, many of them simply geometric patterns, some of them lines juxtaposed in seemingly random order, and alphanumeric symbols floating in between, in various depths of field.

Bloodeagle moved closer to the projection field. "Gorgon cipher. That is Quint!"

"Can you crack it?"

Jeffry shook his head. "Hell. I can't break a cipher with a sample that small, Aubry."

Bloodeagle detached his personal communicator from his belt. "I have a cipher circuit in my communicator, but I can't get that frequency."

"Give it to me," Jeffry said eagerly.

The big Indian wedged his hand communicator open, and fished around inside, pulling out a tiny sliver of plastic and ceramic.

"This is it." Jeffry took the communicator, attached wires, fiddled for a few minutes, and turned the power on again. The display cleared. Symbols and letters floated in bunches, still unreadable, but now recognizable as transformed language. The screen cleared again, and this time there was language.

To Scavengers. Please route to Aubry Knight. Quint to following coordinates—

A string of numbers followed.

"What? Where's that?" Jeffry's fingers flew over the keys.

A world map appeared on the holostage, swiftly zoning in on the American Southwest.

"Let's see—Death Valley—"

Aubry became very still.

"That's Death Valley Maximum Security Penitentiary."

"That has to be it," Bloodeagle said excitedly. "Ibumi must be using the abandoned prison as his staging ground."

Aubry leaned back against the wall, and his eyes unfocused. "I can't go . . . I can't . . ." He swallowed hard, and fought to find his center. "How could they be based there?"

"It's been deserted for two years," Jeffry said. "Harris

must have made it available to them as a secret training ground.''

Jenna came closer, gripped Jeffry's shoulder. "Who's sending the message?"

To Scavengers. Please route to Aubry Knight. Tell him. Leslie.

And Aubry closed his eyes, hearing nothing but the thunder of his heartbeat. Seeing nothing but the light filtered through the red of his eyelids. The ground seemed to open under him, swallowing him. He was back in that terrible place, that soul-stealing space, where the red fingers clawed at his body.

But Aubry was above his body now, slightly apart from it. He felt the fear, felt his body's responses to the awful stress, and yet was somehow apart from it.

"All right," he said. "We have to get in there. Bloodeagle—what is he likely to have?"

"Thirty Gorgons. Weapons and food for same. They're probably on their way to South America, or . . ."

"Or what?"

"Africa. The Swarna connection, again."

"How much time do we have?"

"Twelve hours maximum."

Jeffry had been peeking in federal archives, and placed a new outline up on the stage. Seven levels deep and covering fifty acres, a great dome blossoming at the surface. The skeletal outline rotated in the air before them.

"Death Valley Maximum Security Penitentiary," Aubry whispered. Promise took his shoulder.

"We can't get in there," Bloodeagle said slowly.

"I wish that was the truth," Aubry replied. "But I got out, and I know the route. Bloodeagle. How many Gorgons do you have?"

"Ten."

"I can get twenty Scavengers who are up to something like this. Promise, what are our weapon stores?"

"Good. And Jenna brought down more from Ephesus."

"We don't have anything to match the equipment Quint will have."

"Get it straight," Aubry said. "Quint isn't in control,

and hasn't been for over a year. Ibumi doesn't care about Gorgon—although he just may care about Quint. They won't be properly organized.''

"And you can get us in?"

"Or die trying.''

The dome. The great, faceted hothouse dome loomed hugely, even a thousand meters away.

Aubry lay spread-eagled on the sand, watching through a pair of digitizing binoculars.

"We've got one chance," Bloodeagle whispered. "They won't be expecting anything sneaky. They'll figure that either the road is clear, or the Feds will come down on them like an avalanche.''

"Then we have to take that chance," Aubry said.

He wormed his way into his sand-colored camouflage bag, and slowly began to wiggle forward.

The automatic rifle slung over his shoulder itched him, but he shut it away, and continued on.

The ten Gorgons who had joined Bloodeagle and twelve Scavengers wiggled across the dunes, leaving worm tracks on the sand.

As he crawled, approaching the place of his nightmare, he thought.

The dome. And the landing pad. He remembered that. Being taken, shackled hand and foot, out of the skimmer, in for his appointment with total human degradation.

And the utter corruption and human misery of that hell-hole had finally caused a more enlightened administration to close it down?

There was a savage satisfaction in that. But the hole that yawned before him still contained the essence of his dreams, and something within him recoiled and begged Aubry not to go forward.

This was not the place. This was not the time.

No. There was no other time, and no other place. It would be done now, or never. And on some level he knew that better than anyone else could possibly have known, better than anyone could have expected. It was as if he had

created this situation to force him to face something that he
didn't want to face, ever. Something . . .

He remembered the lessons of Warrick. . . .

But Warrick's face faded. There was no strength there.
There was only blackness, and sickness, and the depths of
the cold caverns ahead.

Jeffry and his computer had identified the escape route
to be used by the prison guards in case of a prison take-
over, and the door. Bloodeagle and his Gorgons found it,
buried within the sand. It swiftly yielded to their digging.

It was metal, never used, and the surface was etched
with the words: PROPERTY OF FEDERAL GOVERNMENT. DAN-
GER! WARNING! NO TRESPASSING!

Torches were burning at the metal as Aubry scanned the
dome, his infrared goggles clicking in to the ranges. There
was no movement, no light, no sign of the escape vehicle.
But that was to be expected. Quint was a Gorgon. There
would be no sign if that was what Quint wanted.

The door popped free, and the Gorgons began to wiggle
down.

"You've got a half hour, Aubry," Bloodeagle whispered. "Good luck."

They shook hands, hard, and there was a moment when
Bloodeagle wavered, and then gripped Aubry hard, hug-
ging him, and whispered, "I love you. As a man, and as a
brother. Go with God."

Then Bloodeagle was gone.

Aubry and the Scavengers moved on, wiggling in toward
the dome.

It rose in the sand like an enormous, half-buried egg, its
dirty green walls still emblazoned on his memory.

"Quarry," Aubry whispered.

Aubry's chief executive moved up, and motioned two of
his men into place. A silent, efficient drill cut through the
dome's shatterproof plastic panels in a few moments. They
attached suction cups, and silently lifted it out.

A rush of stale air told Aubry that the hothouse hadn't
been used in years. It was totally dark, and totally silent
within.

He had to don a gas mask, moved in quickly and rolled,

scanning the hundred aisles of dead plants, seeing and hearing nothing.

It was dark, and dry. They wore infrared goggles, which parted the gloom like mist driven before the wind.

Quarry touched his throat mike. "Aubry. What's the layout here?"

"This is the top level," he croaked. His throat was tight, and he desperately craved a drink of water. "There is a central ventilation tunnel ahead. It's how I got out." He loped down the central core until he reached that long-ago path to freedom, a wall grille that had been repaired. He dropped to one knee and listened at the grille.

They anchored lines and tested them while the silent saw cut through the grille, once again pulling it out silently.

Aubry peered at his watch. "We've got twelve minutes," he said into his throat mike.

Aubry was the first into the hole.

Despite the fact that there were others above him, waiting for their turn, Aubry felt alone. He remembered crawling up this tunnel, wedging his hands against the sides, climbing with a man named Stitch, who had shown him the way out.

He hung now at a branching tunnel. Which way? Which way?

Memory returned, and he turned to the left.

Now he was back in the belly of the beast, and his skin crawled with fear. When he finally pulled out of the grid, he was shivering.

He couldn't stand still. He knew he was supposed to wait here for Quarry, but he couldn't. The only salvation lay in continuing to move.

He slid out into the hall, looking up one barred corridor and down the other.

Nothing. Distantly, he heard voices, and the sounds of machinery. He peered at his watch. Four minutes remained.

Promise and Jenna would move in in five minutes, after the first shocks. Bloodeagle and his men would have planted the gas charges by then, and the attack would be on. It had taken a miracle to keep Promise behind in the

skimmer. He remembered the last thing that she had said
to him:

"Do you think that Leslie is still alive?"

"If he lived long enough to get that message out, I don't
see a real problem with him surviving a little longer. After
all—whose kid is he?"

"She."

They had laughed, and she touched his lips with hers.

He reached one of the cell corridors. Aubry touched one
of the transparent plates that sealed the cell doors, and in
the touching, a river of memories flooded.

This was where he had lost his soul. Here. He ran,
quietly now. Over that rail and down the corridor had been
the recreation room.

and . . .

He flattened himself against the wall as heels turned,
and Quint appeared, Ibumi at his side.

"We need to be out of here by twenty-two hundred
hours. Is the relay ready?"

"Totally." Quint seemed to be in charge of himself.
Almost as though whatever drug he had been given worked
only when he was quiet. When action was called for, he
functioned perfectly.

Aubry slipped into the room they had just left.

They had reconverted it—the walls were covered with
maps of the convention center, and the single chair which
had stood in the center of the floor had been removed to
make room for a planning table.

But he would have recognized it no matter what the
changes.

Every movement, every action of the past months, seemed
to have conspired to bring him here.

Outside, the hallway thundered as the first of the explosions detonated. Men and metal screamed, but Aubry
Knight, lost in his past, sank slowly to the ground. The evil
within him, the thing that had withstood all attempts at
exorcism, had triumphed at last.

As plastic explosive punched the plate metal door from
its hinges, Jenna and Promise reacted almost as if they

were different parts of the same body. Promise flattened against the wall, clumsily trying to force her mind to remember the instructions regarding the pulse rifle she carried. Was the safety on? Off? Fear and panic froze her mind. Her breath rasped in her throat.

Jenna hit the ground and rolled. She peered into the gloom. Where was Bloodeagle?

On the other side of the barrier, she heard an explosion, and the muffled sound of shots. Behind them, one of the doors began to rise.

Promise froze. "We can't go that way!"

"Why the hell not? They can kill us just as easily right here, if they're watching. And they are."

She took a moment to blow out one of the cameras, and Promise winced. Metal and glass shards spattered to the ground.

"Come on."

The sound of the firefight on the other side of the wall grew louder. They were running now.

Jenna made it to the central guard corridor, pulling Promise along with her. From where they were, she could see what was happening. Bloodeagle's men were trapped in a crossfire. Quint and Ibumi had men posted on a catwalk across the yawning pit, and they were taking their time. One of Bloodeagle's men threw his hands to his head, and an instant later there was no head, just a flopping corpse.

But where was Bloodeagle himself? The Gorgon was nowhere to be seen, gone like the wind. For an instant, Promise thought she saw something moving against the wall, moving like smoke, but it had to be an illusion. *No one* could move up a sheer wall like that. Could they?

Then something clattered onto the catwalk from above. An instant later explosions rocked the corridor, metal peeled screaming from the wall, and two flaming bodies fell, twisting mindlessly, into the depths of the pit.

Promise backed away from the edge. "There's a door behind us, over here."

She wandered down through the corridor. This place, this awful pit, was where Aubry had been incarcerated? It explained so much. This was no fit place for a human being. And men, violent men, had been jammed together here, and forced to attempt to deal with each other and with their own demons at the same time? It—

And there, ahead of her, was a bundle. Something hanging from the ceiling like a spider's meal awaiting the feast.

It moved, twitched ever so slightly.

Promise moved forward. Jenna tried to pull her back, but her heart screamed at her, and she moved. Nervously, Jenna moved forward also.

The door behind them slammed shut.

A light, a distinct, bright light flared on. In its beam was Leslie. He was bound hand and foot, and swung from the ceiling.

A voice sounded clearly. "Stand away from the walls and drop your weapons, or the child dies."

Jenna pivoted as the voice came into hearing range, but there was nothing to be seen.

"You have ten seconds to comply, and then the child dies. Ten nine eight seven . . ."

Promise spun. "Jenna, please."

Jenna's eyes were hot, and her hands were tight on the weapon. Her breathing was rapid, and her eyes, her eyes. Promise was terrified. "Jenna. I beg you . . ."

Jenna looked at her as if she were a stranger, and in that moment, Promise thought Jenna was about to shoot her. Then she sighed and the tension went out of her body. She relaxed utterly, and laid the gun down.

She stood up straight, her hands out to the side in a clearly scornful position.

"Now you, lady."

Promise bent, and laid it down. As she did, she heard Jenna whisper, "Whatever happens, don't say a word."

Numbly, Promise answered, "Yes."

Three Gorgons emerged from the shadows, weapons at the ready.

They peered into the shadows, and were satisfied. One of them spoke briefly into his microphone, and then they moved forward.

"All right. Against the wall. More bargaining chips. You were fools to come here."

"I'm not moving," Jenna said.

One of their barrels flickered toward Leslie, and Promise screamed to herself. "The child dies."

"I'm not saying that you can't bind me. I'm saying that I won't stand still for it. If you want me, come and get me."

"We have our orders."

"Three NewMen. Two unarmed women. Is this Gorgon?" Jenna's voice was sharp with scorn. "If this is the best that Gorgon has to offer, you really are a pitiful flock of faggots."

One of them, the Oriental, took a step and Promise realized she had seen him before. He was Sawa, and had fought Aubry. His right knee was damaged. She wanted to call out to Jenna!

But he stepped back, and said, "This is not the time for honor. Bind her."

The first man stepped forward, and Jenna extended her wrist. He reached for it, and she slid back a step, her eyes holding his insolently.

Puzzled, he took another step, and her hand was still just out of reach. Angry now, he leapt forward, and this time caught her wrist.

But at the instant that his hands made contact, Jenna was moving, a whiplash of relaxed torque flowing through her entire body. She wore an expression of such ethereal concentration that Promise barely recognized her.

The off-balance Gorgon's own grip and the sudden drop of her body to the kneeling position put him in a precarious balance. She was a mouse guiding the movements of an elephant.

She was beneath him, and his feet ran into her body and she reared up, exhaling harshly. He went over her head, rolling in a breakfall, except that her own hand had gripped his wrist, and she sprang upright with astonishing fluidity. She dug in her heel and jerked hard: his breakfall went bad, and he landed on his shoulder. Jenna was on him as he landed, her thumbs digging up under his ears, into the nerve plexus between the base of the ear and the hinge of the jaw, burrowing with all of her strength. His entire body splayed out in shock, heaved once, and collapsed.

But the second Gorgon was on her, and she barely ducked as the butt of his rifle grazed her head. She dove forward, palms flat against the ground, then forearms folded to take the shock, and she drove her heels back into his body. The butt of the rifle slammed down into her leg. Promise heard the crack as the tibia shattered.

But the kick had been deliberately wide, drawing his stroke, as Jenna had made her move. The other leg slammed home into a perfect heel-thrust to the groin, drove the Gorgon's feet a half inch from the ground with the shock. A perfectly placed blow, perfectly delivered, without an ounce of wasted strength, every erg of energy centered on the most vulnerable portion of his body.

He stood for a moment, aiming his rifle at her, then his face went gray with shock, and he collapsed.

The Oriental's eyes were hooded, staring at Jenna as she lay on the ground, her hands at last moving to her shattered leg.

"Fools," he spat. His eyes were hot. "It is too bad that you are injured. I could have taken you without a hesitation."

Jenna was fighting shock, and the compound fracture of her lower leg was oozing blood. But still she managed to spit her words out through a smile. "Then . . . fight my . . . sister. She is better than me."

He looked at Promise with interest. "Is that true?"

Promise met Jenna's eyes. *Are you insane?*

Jenna spoke quickly. "Durga is related to our dance art. Promise is the greatest dancer our culture has ever produced. She is our greatest fighter."

Utter panic flooded Promise. But Jenna's eyes held her, commanding, then flickered over to the other corner of the room.

Urgently. Meaningfully. And Promise, overcome with terror, looked at the child hanging in the center of the room, and her heart melted. Leslie was unconscious, and utterly helpless. Not the deadly war child, the monster trained and conditioned to kill the President of the United States, but merely a helpless creature who needed her, needed her as no human being had ever needed her before, or would again. The child she had never nursed, the infant she had never cradled in her arms.

She turned to the Oriental and nodded her head. "It's the truth."

"Good. You watched me beaten. I will like killing you." He took the battery cartridge out of his rifle, and set it against the wall.

He pulled a knife from his belt. "Come. Instruct me."

Promise moved away from him, fighting not to show her fear, and walked to Jenna. Jenna's face was ashen, and her fingers fumbled as she pulled the ceremonial Durga blade from her belt sheath, and handed it to Promise.

"Jenna—"

"Shut up!" she said fiercely. "This isn't a fight, Promise! It is a dance." Again, her eyes flickered urgently to the corner, where the pulse rifle stood. "All your life, you've said that you were the strong one, and I the weak. You were strong enough to leave the womb! You went out and tasted the world! I never did. I never dared. You are the stronger." Her eyes held Promise, and Promise felt herself lost, drowning in them. "This isn't a fight. It is a dance!" Jenna's face was ashen. She fought to keep pressure on her leg wound. Blood squirted between her fingers.

Promise nodded, and took the knife. As she turned to face the enormous Oriental she almost fainted. She felt vomit splash against the back of her throat.

But behind Sawa, hanging limply in a sack, was her child.

Promise found her calm. She might die now. She would probably die. But she would die dancing.

Sawa tested her space carefully, not committing anything. *The injured leg!*

Promise clicked her jaw twice, triggering the Plastiskin. It flared like sunlight split through a prism, rippled and coursed with color. She circled, made him put weight on the right leg. He adjusted with surprising ease, but there was no doubt that he was clumsier on that side.

Then Promise began to move. She wound her body, found the rhythms of Durga, but only the dance movements, the movements that the women taught one another in that ancient time. Movements hidden in the ebb and weave of the dance, taught beneath the very noses of unsuspecting men.

Sawa grinned, fascinated with the colors, and slid in. Promise, on the balls of her feet, slid away and away, always just out of distance, cutting off the corners, circling and circling, keeping Sawa's weight on the bad leg. Her movement was hypnotic, and Sawa smiled, enjoying the flow.

He lunged. It wasn't Aubry's quality of speed. It was a frog-jump, a leap forward that penetrated the periphery of her defense. There was no time to move backward or sideways. It was just *there*, and his blade bit into her arm as she spun away.

Sawa laughed, and Promise moved. Somewhere, something in the dance . . .

There was the circular footwork. Sawa lunged, and she let the lunge graze the periphery of the circle, because the circle was moving.

Spinning, the very emotional energy of his thrust impelling her movement, as a partner's movement caused her to respond in dance. It was there! Jenna had spoken true—it had been there within the dance from the very beginning. And the women who had developed it, who had so carefully hidden the truth of their art from their men, had known that the truth could be resurrected. But to learn so late! So late! There was no time to learn now. There was only time to die.

Sawa, new respect on his face, stood still, inviting her to do the same. Promise continued to move around him, turned circling toward his bad leg, weaving as he made his lunges.

But the movement was soothing, almost hypnotically so. And because she faded back, and never made a threatening forward movement, Sawa began to enjoy himself, to mock her movements, to dance with her as she became tired.

The tension was killing her. She couldn't relax! The stress was literally burning her up inside, and Sawa knew it. She was heaving for breath, her movements less fluid, more jerky and desperate by the moment.

Aubry! My darling! I need you—

Jenna! You are the strong one. Help me!

Leslie . . .

For the first time in the engagement, Promise stopped dead. Sawa froze in surprise. Promise lunged forward, screaming, but stopped herself a half step in as Sawa made his defense. Promise flared her Plastiskin up as brightly as she could, a sunflare in a darkened room, and hurled the knife directly into his face.

Shocked and blinded, Sawa was taken completely unaware. The knife, balanced to make one complete rotation in four and a half feet, turned one and a half times, and hit Sawa between the eyes.

Hilt first.

Promise turned and ran. Sawa cursed, slapped his palm to the bruise, then darted after her.

Her back burned. Would he throw the knife? Would he? His every movement seemed to be designed to weaken or tire. *He wanted her alive!*

She heard the first, cat-quick step coming after her. Promise dropped to the ground, and rolled herself into a ball. Sawa, coming too quickly to stop, hit her body and hurtled over her.

The breath was slammed from her lungs by the impact, and she knew her ribs were bruised. She wanted to die, the pain racing up her body, but she sprang to her feet and ran to the opposite corner of the room.

For her rifle.

Sawa realized it the instant before her hands made contact, and jumped at her, screaming.

She pivoted, rifle in hand, bringing the barrel up—

Sawa's body loomed up like a balloon. So swiftly and directly did he come at her, his eyes chillingly black, and—

Her finger pressed the trigger. Sawa spun, his side torn away. His knife flew from his hands but momentum carried him onto her. His hands went to her face, and throat, squeezing with killing strength. She couldn't breathe, couldn't move, found herself falling into a red-rimmed void—

Then his hands relaxed, and released. Sawa tumbled to the ground, dead.

She was too weak to move. Promise pulled herself out from under Sawa's body, staggering toward Leslie, holding the knife that had smashed against her spine.

One more step. Just one.

And then another.

The room was spinning. She sawed through the cords. Leslie fell into her arms. He was curled onto his side, and quite unconscious, and she put her ear to his chest, trying to hear a heartbeat. There it was. There it was. . . .

She held her child, kissed her child, and then plunged facefirst into the ground.

For a few moments there was no movement in the chamber.

And then . . .

CHAPTER THIRTY-SIX

And Death Smiled . . .

The room stretched out in all directions, dark and empty and soundless, save for the distant thrumming of explosions.

Aubry could barely breathe.

He had difficulty catching his emotional balance. He was cut off, sealed off, and trapped back in the bowels of his very worst nightmares.

He squatted back on his heels and tried to breathe deeply.

Suddenly the room wasn't empty anymore. It was filled with the limping, sore-ridden bodies of the damned, and Aubry was just another convict, everything that he had been and done in the past years gone, gone instantly, the only truth the fact that he was back, where he had sworn he would never return.

The thrumming becoming distant, and then silence, save for his own breathing.

And he was drawn deeper and deeper into trance. He had walked these halls how many times?

There were Sugar and Jo Jo. And there was Mother, pushing his book cart, slight, slender, pretty Mother, who had befriended Aubry Knight. It had only cost him his life.

And Aubry his soul.

And he was back in the last place on God's earth that Aubry ever wanted to visit again.

In his mind, the wallscreen was still in place. That was still there, still clearly displayed where they had shown him films of Nullboxing—

(Remember that, Aubry? Remember your dreams, dead

dreams of escaping from Earth, from care, and sharing something of yourself with one of those few men in the world who can understand, who can feel what you feel. Who see the world as a grid of movement options, who look at another human being as a glass object with target points stenciled into place?

God, you FREAK!—)

There was no movement of air in the room, and it was muggy. There was only the glare of his flash lamp, and the ancient play of images behind his closed eyes.

How long does pain last? How long does hatred endure?

But here, in this room, they had stolen his anger, taken the best part of him. The strongest part.

Here, they had played their damned films, and they had pumped him full of drugs, until every time he thought of anger, every time the adrenaline boiled within his body, his stomach spasmed, and the sour fluid would rise to his lips and arc out, and he . . . and he . . .

He bent over, and pounded on the ground.

It was all so wrong, so wrong! If he was wicked, then let him die. If good, then let him live! Or even kill him! But to go on like this, endlessly lost in the caverns of his own regret, tumbling through the well of years . . .

He stretched out phantasmal hands, reaching for the shattered pieces of his identity, slipping away from him too quickly now, just too quickly for him to catch.

Every day, falling, falling, and the weeks, and now the months, and the years, and he was younger, and younger, all of the things that had grasped at him, and pulled at him, all of the illusions, all of the hurts, flowing from him, and flowing. He sat, raw emotion flowing from him in a torrent. His stomach spasmed and vented, and he didn't realize it. Tears flowed from burning eyes, and he didn't think of it. Aubry Knight curled over onto his side, lost in the years. It was more than he could take, more than he could handle, and he was just gone.

A child again, in a cold city.

There was once someone who loved him, wasn't there? Or was everything truly the blur it seemed. Once, wasn't there anyone who accepted him, who just loved him for who he was, and not for what he did, or didn't do.

And he searched back, and back through his mind, and he found, at last, an image. An image of a man, dying in the back alley where he lived, and the child who would one day become a man running to him, and the hands smeared with blood.

Aubry . . . Aubry . . .

And even through the pain, the twisted grimace that fought to become a smile. Even through the final weakness that flooded the man's limbs, the strength of a last hug, a last embrace, and the whispered words, *Be strong . . . for me. Be . . . shhhh . . . no tears. No more tears . . . ever.*

And then the hand had relaxed its grip, and the body had been suddenly totally still.

And Aubry remembered the child who would become a man, and the child held the body of its father, and kissed it, tried to kiss it into wakefulness, to motion. And when nothing, no action or prayer, had had any effect, how that child had cried.

And had gone from there to the home of a sister . . . or had it been an aunt? . . . and been an unwelcome burden. And after that other homes, and finally finding the only home where he really fit. The streets.

And oh, the streets. There, he had found that the rules didn't exist. All that mattered was the quality of fluid violence that came so easily to him as his body began to mature, and finally exploded in an orgy of revenge against a world that had done nothing save turn its head to the death of his father.

Those streets, those sidewalks, were a battleground, and to survive, young Aubry became a child of war, with the skills and attitudes of one who knows death on the most intimate terms.

And Aubry cried.

Light. Sudden, blinding, piercing into this most private of places, the place where Aubry had not been for so many years. Decades. The place sealed up with the rest of his regrets, with the pain that was too much for a child to bear, too much for a man to admit.

"What do we have here?"

Ibumi. And Quint.

The two giants stood in the doorway, their arms lightly around each other's waists. Quint wore a bare touch of rouge on his cheeks. There was nothing feminine about the way he moved, nothing in the least bit humorous about the 20-40 pulse rifle he carried at his side, its bore pointed directly at Aubry.

Aubry looked up. "Where's Leslie?"

"Leslie?"

"My kid, damn you. Where is he?"

"Leslie. Clever. He's safe, unless that fool Bloodeagle has killed him by accident."

"We should really have killed him before we left Arizona."

Ibumi grinned. "A pleasure to rectify *that* mistake."

They moved in closer to Aubry. "We don't have any wish to kill you, Aubry, but we can't take any chances, either. For a nonenhanced human being, you're the greatest fighter that I have ever seen."

Aubry glared up at them. "I'm tired of this. I'm tired of all of it. What fucking difference does it make if I can kill you? If I can kill you both? Or if you kill me? I don't think any of us really cares. But Leslie deserves a chance at life. And if my skills can save my child's life, then they exist for a reason. You idiots. You let McMartin and his stooge use you. You almost helped DeLacourte steal the entire nation. You've doomed the NewMan Nation unless Bloodeagle can bring you back, or bring in your bodies. You bought my child, had him stolen from his mother's womb. You betrayed everything that you're supposed to believe in, and you broke the sanctity of your own goddamned sacred ritual."

Aubry rose, ignoring the rifle that Quint leveled at him.

"The two of you, for your own vengeance, helped

support an operation that killed hundreds of people. That left a trail of death up and down California. You destroyed hundreds of acres of timberland, hundreds of unborn children.

"And the ones you got! What did you do to them? What did you care about, except making your goddamned supersoldiers. Would you like to turn them into me? Would you like a thousand of them like you? Creatures who have no purpose in life except to destroy? Really?

"Then you're not only evil, you're stupid."

Ibumi glared at him. "I'm giving you a chance to stay alive, Knight."

Aubry grinned at them, and his lips pulled back from his teeth in a rictus of pure, unalloyed evil delight. "You don't understand. You can't pull that trigger. Everything that you are, and everything that you've built in yourself, won't let you. And that's the difference between you and me. That's the weakness in Gorgon, Ibumi. You don't really believe that you're a man. And so you go on proving it over and over and over, and in every way that you can."

"I see. And you are sure?"

"I don't care anymore." Aubry screamed the next words. "I see what the hell it has cost me all my life to hold on to something I'm going to lose in the end, and I'm sick of it. I'm sick of this. I'm sick of you. And if you walk out of here, more people are going to die. So you're not walking out. There's only one winner in this game."

"And who is that?" Quint's face was stretched tautly.

"Death," Aubry said. "That's where we are. That's what this is all about. I don't care about holding onto my life anymore. Not now. Not while an evil like you lives in the world."

Aubry took another step, and now he was within personal range, and all three knew it. From the fire in their eyes they knew it.

"You've been looking for death for years, Ibumi. Everything you do is a denial of life. Well, if you've been looking for death, here I am."

Ibumi's rifle dropped first. He stepped back and shut the door behind him, and then deactivated the weapon. Quint, without taking his eyes from Aubry, deactivated his with a *snick*.

Aubry touched a button on his weapon, and the magazine dropped out.

"It could have been so good," Ibumi said quietly.

"It's going to be," Aubry said.

He laid his weapon down.

The child.

The man.

The streets.

Ibumi and Quint separated, flanking Aubry smoothly, as if this was something that they had done a hundred times.

Each of them was larger than Aubry, and they moved like rhinos on roller skates. But Aubry already knew that he would die here, here where, in a very real way, it all began.

It was appropriate. And what was truly important was that neither of these men left the room alive. Aubry Knight wasn't important. Had never been important.

Quint moved first, and his movement was faster than Aubry had prepared for. But still, he spun out of the way, remembering Durga.

There was no Yang response to this energy. There was no Yin response. But there was nothingness. Nothingness might be a response. But that would only be true if Aubry Knight was no more. And Aubry Knight was already dead.

Quint's punch cleaved the air like a whipstroke. His recovery made the punch a feint: with the business technique was the low, crossing kick that came in behind it.

Aubry moved back, creating distance, using the room, using the space as his friend.

Ibumi circled to the side, moving so quickly and smoothly that it was difficult for Aubry to believe his senses. Aubry couldn't afford to allow them to bracket him, and that was exactly what they were going to try to do. He had to run, and keep running for the next few seconds, while keeping his concentration.

Quint and Ibumi were two human bodies with a single

mind. When Aubry stopped his backward race and sprang
forward at Ibumi, Quint was there in an instant.

Aubry's speed caught the two NewMen by surprise.
Aubry was within grappling range, and he smothered Ibumi's
striking techniques and maintained the momentum, hurling
Ibumi through the air over him, and catching the body in
the air with a leaping side kick an instant later.

Ibumi's breakfall was beautiful, but the timing had been
thrown off by the impact of the kick. Quint was there an
instant after the kick, hurling himself at Aubry's back.
With the first moment of pressure, Aubry dropped to his
knees and Quint virtually flew over his shoulder as Aubry's
body offered no resistance.

Ibumi and Quint regained their feet. Both of them smiled
at him, and then at each other, nodding as if confirming a
private suspicion.

And then it began.

The next minute was a hell of retreat. Aubry circled
constantly to avoid the walls, and interrupted his own
patterns to avoid being bracketed by the NewMen. At
running speed. Sprinting speed. Never engaged, or initiated strikes until he had already broken the balance, working on the periphery of his own endurance.

Time and again they scored on him, tore flesh and
bruised bone. But he rode their techniques as if he were a
top, twisted and turned, and went over, under, between,
utilizing his astonishing acrobatic skill, pushing himself
further and further.

What was the end of endurance? He had discovered that
during the Run. There was no end. There was only death,
and Death wanted the three of them. Why settle for just
Aubry Knight?

And as his heart thundered in his chest, as the blood
rose in his mouth, Aubry renewed his deal with Death.
Take us all. Let me live long enough to take us all.

And Death smiled.

The moment came when the two of them trapped Aubry
against the wall, and now he exploded. They expected
Aubry to attempt to float away, and he didn't.

Instead, for the first time, he turned all of his energies to one of them for just a moment. He head-butted forward, and Quint's face snapped back. The two Gorgons sank their hands into Aubry's flesh, and their fingers were like grapnels.

He was too near the limit, but this was his time, this was his moment.

He might have become boneless, so limp was he, sagging in their grip, so that Ibumi's lethal throat strike tore open the skin on his forehead instead. He tore free from Ibumi's grip, went under Quint's arm, and as Quint spun around, Aubry went close. Skill and speed and everything but bare animal ferocity were forgotten, and he bit Quint's throat out.

The man gargled a death cry, hands clasped to the gaping hole. Aubry sensed rather than saw Ibumi's kick. His leg collapsed, but guided by feel alone, his right foot flashed out, the point spearing into Ibumi's solar plexus.

Iron muscle and lightning reflex allowed Ibumi to ride and deflect that lethal strike, but he gasped in shock and pain.

Aubry backed up against the wall. He tried to rise, and couldn't—the leg was broken.

He kicked out with the other leg as Ibumi moved in, sweeping his feeble kick aside, and wrenched him over onto his back, and stomped Aubry's femur.

Pain flared hideously as Aubry's hip dislocated, and he reached out with the last strength in his body, fingers spearing into Ibumi's leg, reaching for the Achilles tendon, pulling and wrenching, damaging the ankle as Ibumi twisted his arm and struck with the edge of his hand, shattering Aubry's arm at the elbow.

Ibumi limped back, surveying his work.

Quint had stopped moving.

Ibumi knelt by his lover, lifted his limp head, and kissed him tenderly. When he looked up, there was nothing but hatred in his eyes.

"Whatever else happens here, Knight, you die slowly.

Nothing fast for you." He stepped closer, limping badly. If only Aubry had been able to move, he could have finished Ibumi off in a dozen ways, with strength, or technique, or sheer speed. But there was nothing to be done now.

Ibumi pulled back a booted foot, and drove it into Aubry's ribs. He felt the thud, felt the ribs beginning to go, and stifled the scream of pain that rose to his lips.

Death. Death was not the ultimate indignity. He had to die, as so many good men had died, had gone into the muck so that Aubry Knight might live. It was merely what was right, what was appropriate. And it felt good to be dying now, in this place, in this way. And if Ibumi took enough time, he would be trapped, so that Aubry's death might mean something, as his life had come to . . .

Ibumi buckled backward, pivoting, swinging one great bladed hand like a scythe.

It should have cut his assailant in half, so swift was the response. But the assailant was too short.

Aubry's breath hissed in his throat, and the pain and the grief broke through to the surface.

"Leslie—"

The child was there, stark naked, scratched from his crawl through the air conduits, his eyes hot as the core of the sun. His body was starvation thin, and bleeding, and there was barely anything human in the face.

"Get out of here!" Aubry screamed, or thought that he screamed, but couldn't be sure, because the world of dream and the world of reality had drifted entirely too close together.

With the fastest human movement that Aubry had ever witnessed, Leslie's foot lanced out and into Ibumi's groin cleanly, and then Leslie danced backward as the giant staggered in pain and confusion, his arms thrashing like a gorilla's. Leslie arced into a picture-perfect side kick, but Ibumi slid out of range. Leslie moved again, as agile as a lizard, gone and gone and gone, and never there, able to make a hundred and eighty degree turn as if turning inside out, as if flowing through himself, and Aubry's heart sang.

My child!

But Ibumi was enraged, and still strong enough to kill Leslie with a single blow, and even Leslie's direct attack on Ibumi's groin had brought nothing but pain.

In Ephesus Aubry had been hampered by near-blindness. Ibumi had no such handicap. Where Aubry had been hampered by ignorance of his adversary, Ibumi knew Leslie better than Leslie knew himself.

And Leslie could not hurt the enormous Ibumi.

And the big man stalked him. Leslie hurled himself, striking into Ibumi's kneecap, with every ounce of stretch, a perfectly executed movement, ripping the patella up so that Ibumi's leg buckled. The blow landed only partially, and Ibumi swatted. Leslie scrambled backward, trying to ride the blow, and was hurled back across the room, smashing into the wall.

Ibumi took a step—

And Aubry had him by the ankles, broken arm and hip trailing. Ibumi raised a leg to stomp, and Aubry punched into the exposed groin, felt the plastic groin protector buckle and splinter, felt the shards of plastic drive into the testicles. Ibumi toppled to his knees atop Aubry, and Aubry felt his ribs go, felt them drive into his lungs.

But Leslie was moving, and in the air, and the side of his foot, bladed, angled with incredible precision, drove into Ibumi's throat.

The giant fell, last breath caught forever in his throat, but not yet dead.

He crawled to Leslie, and the single arm that Aubry locked around Ibumi's legs seemed not to slow him.

It was impossible. The man couldn't breathe. Couldn't walk. His system had to be seething with shock, but still he lived. Still he—

Leslie was backed into the corner, his broken arm dangling at his side, his eyes wide with fear as Ibumi's terrible hand closed on his leg. He opened his mouth and *screamed*—

And Ibumi's giant hand relaxed. The body relaxed.

Aubry and Leslie lay silent for a moment. Then Leslie pulled his leg free from Ibumi's grip, and he crawled to Aubry.

Aubry's face hurt as he strove to smile, to nod. Everything was numb. Nothing hurt. His own blood was everywhere. He had never seen so much of it. . . .

Leslie stood back from him, eyes wide, trembling now, and the pouting mouth finally opened, but said nothing.

"So . . . proud of you . . ." Aubry whispered.

Leslie came to him, squeezing him with the desperate strength of a child, crying over and over again, "Father . . . Father . . . please don't die . . ."

And Aubry smiled as darkness opened its arms for him.

CHAPTER THIRTY-SEVEN

A Beginning

Consciousness returned slowly, just a few lines of light in the darkness, a few scrambled memories, and at last a voice or two piercing the veil of fog.

Aubry tried to move his left arm, and couldn't. He tried to move his hips, and couldn't.

I'm paralyzed. I'll never walk again. . . .

"I think he's awake," someone said. Who was it? Where was he? What had happened . . . ?

At last he remembered what death was like. That was what it was like to put everything you had, everything you were, on the line. It had never happened before, and it was enough to last a lifetime.

What was left of a lifetime.

The bed beneath him sagged slightly, and he felt warm lips touch his.

Promise . . . ?

He reached out, felt the short hair, and knew he was wrong. "Marina." He tried to turn his lips up, into a smile, and didn't entirely succeed.

"Yes, Aubry."

"Where . . . where am I? My eyes . . ."

"Your corneas were scratched. Your right arm is sheared at the elbow, and your left leg is broken in two places. You were unconscious for five days." There was a catch in her voice. "What did you do, wrestle a truck?"

Aubry was floating on a cloud of medication, and somehow the idea seemed hilarious.

"Not exactly, but close enough. Where am I?"

"The NewMan Nation."

"Help me up."

He felt an arm under his shoulders, and then another arm from the other side, and he was sitting upright. His left arm felt fat and sausagy, but he moved it around, and peeled off his patch.

Marina seemed beautiful, and tired. "Aubry." She shook her head. "You're a celebrity, did you know that?"

"What are you talking about?"

"Everything about you—from your role in foiling the assassination to the leadership of the Scavengers, and your escape from Death Valley—all of it came out. There's an extradition battle going on for you right now."

"If they want me, why don't they just come and get me?" He was too damned tired to care.

"Three things," she said. "One, President Harris has commissioned a special investigation of the entire affair, and has given very specific orders that you be allowed to heal. Second, the NewMan Nation has special jurisdiction. Bloodeagle is in Washington now as liaison with Harris. It's a mess. And there's a third, but someone else wants to tell you that. I have to go."

He squinted through the bandages. "Go? You sure you don't want to stick around awhile? I might still manage to die."

She smiled sadly. "Oh, Aubry. I don't know what I am any more than you do. But I'm willing to live in the question. You have a family now. Whoever it was who raped me, he isn't here anymore. And whoever it was who was raped . . . she's not here anymore. I'm not sure who is, but I think I like her. A lot."

"Where does that leave you?"

"With the greatest news story in history, and some damned good lessons. Aubry . . . if hate, or love, was all that mattered . . ."

"But it isn't," he whispered. "It never is."

Marina bent over the bed and kissed his forehead, then stood. "See you around, mister."

She walked to the door and opened it, and Promise was standing there. The two women looked at each other for a long moment, and then Marina leaned forward and hugged her. Promise hugged back, fiercely. "You take care of him," Marina said, the words at the bare edge of Aubry's perception. "That is a very special man."

Promise kissed Marina, and then the newswoman left the room.

Promise entered, her fingertips guiding Jenna's motorized wheelchair.

Without framing the question, Aubry's good eye darted back and forth until the small, slender figure appeared in the doorway.

Leslie walked slowly into the room, uncertainly balancing a plastic-sheathed arm. He came to the edge of Aubry's bed, taking his hand.

The small, dark heart-shaped face was streaked with tears, and Leslie buried his face against Aubry's arm. Aubry felt that he'd never be able to get the words out. "Hello . . ." His throat hurt.

Promise could barely look at him. "The doctors said . . . that you should be dead, but you're not. They said that the Cryo clinics have been closed down, but some of the neural material was scavenged. . . ."

"Scavenged?"

She shrugged. "You never know what will turn up on the black market."

"I see. So I get to walk again, because someone's baby was killed. Died for my sins."

Leslie looked up at him. "Father. Project Medusa is dead. It died for nothing. Nothing can bring them back. Let a few of them, just a few, live on through you. Don't hate yourself for needing. Please, Father."

"I . . ."

"If you hate yourself for what you've been, what can I think of myself?"

Aubry's mouth opened, and then closed. He blinked. "How old did you say you were?"

Leslie buried his head against Aubry's arm again.

Jenna watched them, and shook her head. "Aubry, Aubry. Haven't we all been through enough? Let it go, huh? Let's start over again?"

"That's easy for you to say," Aubry said. "Even if I heal. I'm an escaped convict, Jenna."

Jenna looked at Promise. "Give it to him."

Promise handed him a small box. "According to the note, four copies of this went out. One to the President, one to the Attorney General of the United States, one to Marina, and this one to us."

"What is it?"

"We brought in a projector." Promise's hands were trembling as she slid the cartridge into the holo projector, and the lights dimmed.

Eight years before. Aubry Knight, on a deserted beach, with Maxine Black. Laughing, holding hands. Kissing. And then Walker, with his chain-knife humming. And Walker attacked them. And Aubry killed him—

Aubry's fingers gripped at the sheets. "Holy mother of God. It's Luis's tape! It's the tape from the beach. They said it was destroyed with the rest of his records."

He looked up at them, the first touch of hope filtering into his voice. "Where did it come from?"

"There's no name on the package. But there is a note. It reads, 'Silence is golden.' It's signed 'W.' "

"Wu?"

"He seems to have left the country. I believe this is a peace offering, in exchange for leaving his name out of any discussions we have on this matter."

Jenna smiled and backed her wheelchair up. "We'll have time to talk. I just wanted to tell you that you didn't let me down, Aubry. I knew it was in there." She grinned, although the effort was obviously painful. "Welcome to the family."

She hummed out of the door.

Aubry watched her as the door closed. "Everyone seems so damned sure."

"If you don't want us, Dad, just say so . . ."

Leslie looked up at him, a touch, just a hint of defiance entering those eyes. For a moment, Aubry saw himself, kneeling in his father's blood, and saw the life that yawned to receive him. Leslie's fine-boned features implored him without asking. There was so much strength, so much intelligence.

"Jesus. Whoever had a kid like you?"

"No one." Leslie grinned.

"What the hell. I can't just turn you loose on the world."

Aubry closed his eyes. And the image that came to his mind was the succession of people he had been in his life, and the thread of possibility that stretched forward to his future. He could be free. He could have his life back.

Perhaps it was too late for his dream of Nullboxing, but there were other dreams, and other hopes. And in all of them that were worth living, he saw his family. He saw his child, and he saw his child's mother. They were family, and it seemed more natural and normal than any alternative he could imagine.

"I can't start over again," he said to Promise. "Nobody would put up with my bullshit like you have. . . ."

"You don't have to say it, Aubry. I know."

He reached out, and pulled her down to him, and kissed her with lips that were numb and bruised.

A great sigh went out of her, and something left Aubry at that same instant, something dark and terrible, something that had been vital and utterly irreplaceable for so many long, lonely years.

Something that, somehow, would never seem so important again.

EPILOGUE

Dateline November 23, 2028. Ephesus, Oregon.
Item:

Aubry Knight, 34, married Promise Cotonou, 32, in a ceremony witnessed by several hundred members of the Ephesus Feminist nation, the surviving forces of the counterterrorist force Gorgon, and the California-based Scavenger Coalition.

Knight was instrumental in the foiling of the recent assassination attempt on President Roland Harris.

Cotonou, with Knight, helped to build the Scavengers into the nationwide assistance and educational organization it is today. It is the first marriage for both.

Their child Leslie, 3, at his own insistence, was both ringbearer and flower "girl."

Although this made for a somewhat unorthodox ceremony, the guests didn't seem to mind at all.

—UPI. Marina Batiste.

Acknowledgments

In some ways, *Gorgon Child* marks the end of one phase of my career, and the beginning of another. Its completion represents a personal odyssey almost as arduous as that of its protagonists. I could not have survived alone.

In recognition of this, thanks are humbly offered:

To Lauren Nicole Barnes and my beloved wife Toni, who together performed the hardest day's work I have ever been honored to witness.

My friends and teachers Ray Doss, Rod Kobayashi, Jim and Beth Shibata. To Richard Dobson and Natasha Frazier of the Transformative Arts Institute, Dawn Callan, and Harley Reagan, who together gave me seven truly fascinating days in the high desert. To Ed Parker the nonpareil. These, and others, have widened my knowledge of the warrior arts I love so deeply. No words of thanks could be sufficient.

Larry Niven: mentor, collaborator, friend, and Godfather to my child. You have given me more than you know, and more than I ever hoped for.

Mickey Spillane, whose *One Lonely Night* asked the right questions.

Tim Piering, Paul and Diana Von Welanetz, Mary Charles, Conley Falk, and Robert Stadd, members in good standing of the Samurai Sandwich Club. Meghan Lancaster, Marty Clark, Janet Gluckstern, and Karen Willson, for innumerable infusions of faith, love, and understanding.

To my sister Joyce, who taught me to read. To Mrs.

Elaine Otterness, formerly of Mt. Vernon Jr. High School, who convinced me that I wanted to write.

To my Oregon family: Becky and Joshua Bryant, Jonna Goad-Wingren, Ariel Shattan, and Lori White. Slightly farther north, love to Kathleen and Bob Greco, and their radiant child Jessica.

Dr. Richard Landers and Dr. Michael Goerss, for invaluable technical support. And in the same vein, to Mary Mason, of *Merry Badger* Enterprises.

To Leslie Fish, P.O. Box 429, El Cerrito, Calif., 94530 for permission to quote from "Susan B.," the battle hymn of a new republic.

And finally, to the hundreds of readers who asked me: "Whatever happened to Aubry and Promise . . . ?"

Now you know.

—Steven Barnes
Los Angeles, May 18, 1988

KEITH LAUMER

Buy them at your local bookstore or use this handy coupon:
Clip and mail this page with your order.

Publishers Book and Audio Mailing Service
P.O. Box 120159, Staten Island, NY 10312-0004

Please send me the book(s) I have checked above. I am enclosing $_____
(please add $1.25 for the first book, and $.25 for each additional book to
cover postage and handling. Send check or money order only — no CODs.)

Name _____

Address _____

City _____ State/Zip _____

Please allow six weeks for delivery. Prices subject to change without notice.